1543
The Disfiguration

Robert William Jones

Copyright © 2020 Robert William Jones

All rights reserved.

ISBN: 9798669287726

To my dear wife Joanne for her love and patience.

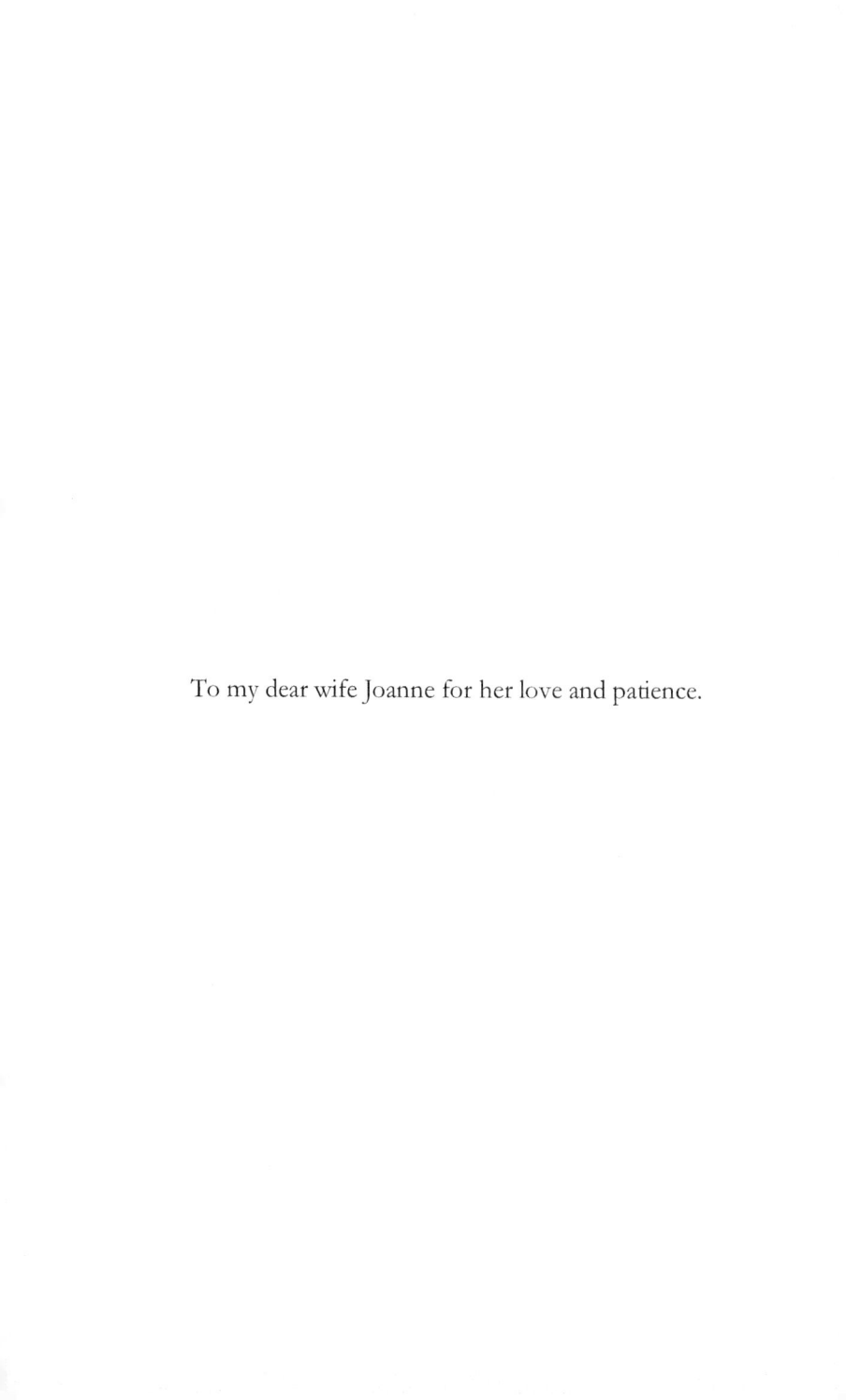

TABLE OF CONTENTS

1 the aftermath 1

2 scarborough fair *11*

3 the device *43*

4 the wedding *59*

5 the future *80*

6 micklegate bar *93*

7 the mary rose *109*

8 the adventurers *133*

9 an old friend *146*

10 my return *161*

11 cloth of gold *170*

12 the rally *181*

13 reggie pole *198*

14 the seduction *203*

15 lady bask *209*

16 a sailor's death *216*

17 york ransacked *227*

18 agents assemble *239*

19 food and weapons	*258*
20 hampton court	*261*
21 The argument	*268*
22 we attack	*284*
23 after the storm	*310*
24 the holy relic	*320*
25 healing wounds	*326*
26 robin hood	*338*
27 the inescapable error	*352*
28 the Keel	*358*
29 home again	*363*

1 the aftermath

Peter stared into the distance. He stared, not even understanding fully what he had just been subject to. The snow was now, very slightly, melting but his eyes were fixed on the road south over the river toward Micklegate and he suddenly became unaware of the climate or even that he was now standing, inadequately dressed, outside the front of Barley Hall. He could still hear muted, quiet conversation, the pathetic fallout from the day's revelations. He had boldly traversed the north of England, just months earlier, intending to seek adventure, avenging Brother Bernard's death and becoming a member of the Agents of the Word. He scoffed to himself as he thought this, deeply hurt at how some of those supposed heroes had let him down and yet, it was hard for him to put his finger on who was to blame. Yes, they had found Elspeth's murderer but it came at the cost of peeking into the sordid lives of many adults. Is this what he could expect as he grew older? He asked himself, still craving that role of adventurer, of a hero and a man of integrity. Truth be told, the whole day was a complete shock to almost everyone involved but now he was left feeling alone and completely adrift. He certainly wasn't alone in this assessment and consideration but, at that very moment, he thought only of himself and what would become of him. His attachment to Edward, to me and to Silas had bestowed fulfilment, purpose and friendship upon him but it was as if all he knew had been shattered in one day. Following her stoic response to the day's dark, unravelling events, Wynnfrith had broken down and Peter could hear her sobs from within. He knew that, quite rightly, Silas would be comforting her but this also weighed heavily on his heart. The mouse had gone, Edward had gone, Godwin very definitely had gone and, in a sense, he would now lose Silas to Wynnfrith. You could suppose that Peter just hadn't a clue as to what to do next and, for the first time in over a month, he thought of home and his family and then felt ashamed at how little regard he had given them previously.

Ahead of him, he could detect plenty of activity as some of the day's trading was coming to a close. He could see someone winding their way through the carts, horses and stalls and shouting as he neared. It was Edward and, to Peter, this was probably as welcome a sight as he could imagine.

'Ho friend!' shouted Edward looking completely drenched.

Peter just waved, delighted that his fellow Agent seemed to be heading toward him.

'What have you there?' asked Peter as Edward arrived.

'A bit of cloth. That's all. Just a bit of old cloth' and then he wept.

'Why young Ed, my good friend what troubles you?'

Edward looked at Peter, then the cloth, turned to look back just one more time toward Micklegate and, pulling himself together, said

'At the end of each day, Godwin would use this humble scrap to dust off all his tools. It was always a happy sign that the day's work was done. When the mouse arrived last year, old Godwin placed it down as a bed for him.'

'You are allowed to be upset at what is happening to Godwin' said Peter 'I'm sure he held you in the highest esteem. Something dark got a hold of him and he will, deservedly, meet his maker today.'

'I know' said Peter 'all those tales. The secrets. Those people...' Trembling, he pointed toward the now almost empty Barley Hall 'those people have ruined everything. I have just stood looking at the workshop. The last time I will ever set eyes upon it and, right before my eyes, Micklegate mouse just disappeared. Disappeared Peter! I fear I will never see him again. I am left wondering who to trust and what to do next.'

Peter, quite impressively, became, in an instant, like an older brother as this was exactly what Edward needed at this moment.

'Why Ed, you just go and enjoy school. You are to be a gentleman! This life of running around trying to apprehend one fiend when, seemingly, we are surrounded by others, was never the intended one for you. Worry not! Good times are ahead.'

Edward smiled, sure in the knowledge that, for the time being, he had one reliable friend. Then, they were temporarily distracted. A stray animal had found itself trapped within a small cupboard that was in the hallway.

'If only...' said Edward.

'Do you think we'll ever see him again?' asked Peter.

'He said not. I do miss him already. I also worry that one or two months past, no one on earth will believe the tale of the talking mouse.'

They both afforded themselves a little chuckle but were then interrupted as Wynnfrith began making her way out. She turned and then approached the boys putting an arm around each of them.

'Now, you two take care. You have nothing to fear. Nothing. You still have friends and, although every fibre in me wishes that everything was now behind us, I can't help thinking that the Agents, although depleted, may be needed again. And, you can both depend on me and Silas.'

Her words were now almost being drowned out by the pet within the cupboard although, strangely, it now started to

1543 The Disfiguration

talk in muffled tones.

'Mullo mulloo!'

'Why is Silas in the cupboard?' Asked Peter.

'Why is he ever anywhere he shouldn't be?' added the somewhat exasperated Wynn.

She opened the door and put the question to him.

'Aha! Ladies and…err…gents…err…you see only yesterday this was…err…the way out of Barley Hall!'

Silas was content with this explanation and that was that. Wynnfrith paused, hand on the door handle, wondering whether it was best to leave him in there a while longer but thought better of it, so let him out.

'I have to face the wash house. Do you think you could help me without setting the place on fire?' she said to him.

Silas sputtered, and then muttered some more but, ignoring him completely, she walked away through the slush wishing the boys farewell.

'We will meet very soon!' she shouted as she trudged forward, trying to keep her pet upright.

Peter was feeling better already and decided he too would wander off, without any clues as to where he would go. However, he was soon stopped by a firm grip on his shoulder.

'I'll not see you a waif, lad.'

It was the Mayor, Robert Hall who, despite having the second-worst day of his life, thought it was about time he gave some consideration to others. Peter didn't know how to react but, whichever way you looked at it, Robert was by some considerable furlongs, his superior and, despite the afternoon's revelations, Peter still held a healthy respect for him.

'What are your plans young man?' asked Robert.

'Well Sir, err…everything has changed so suddenly. The truth is…I don't have any.'

'Would you like to go home now?' said Robert.

'I wanted to be here, to stay here Sir, but I suppose all is lost now?'

'Nonsense!' said Robert reclaiming some of the confidence that had been whittled away throughout the day 'I have an idea…'

Kindly, the Mayor took the two boys into the living room where the fire was still blazing. He shut the door and sat them down. Already, this had some semblance of normality. He made an offer to them both, on the basis that Eirik sat with Peter, at some point, and drafted a letter to Peter's kin in Bamburgh.

'They'll be missing you terribly lad. Letting them know what you're about is the least you can do.'

Somewhat ashamed, he agreed, now hanging onto the Mayor's every word. This was an early sign that Robert wasn't going to ditch his altruistic nature just because he'd had a public humiliation and he was very quickly regaining the admiration of the two boys. He suggested that rather than leave the carpenter's workshop to fall to pieces, that Peter could make use of it. Robert would pay a local carpenter to fast track the boy in woodwork. Ambitious as this was, it was a lifeline to Peter and also meant that Edward wouldn't be losing his friend. Robert then left the room without any explanation although the boys could hear hushed tones without. Shortly, he returned having spoken to William Fawkes and informed Edward that, allowing that all his school work and obligations were fulfilled, in addition to his family duties, he could spend a few hours a week at the workshop.

Robert now had before him the like of two toddlers on Christmas Eve. Delighted, they thanked him and asked when they could start. The Mayor insisted that nothing would happen until Peter's step-father had been informed of his welfare and whereabouts.

Robert knew what he had just done and, in the process, had given himself a little dignity. As he opened the door he caught the eye of Mrs Hall who still could not look back at him. The boys ran off to share their good news, well, with themselves.

One can only imagine what Wynnfrith must have felt as she struggled to open the neglected door to the washhouse. It was damp, dark and left exactly as it was when Elspeth had been rushed to Barley Hall as life began to leave her. Silas affectionately placed his hand on one of the multi-purpose barrels and mused at the number of times he had fallen of it and then looked at the blanket that must have so recently fallen from Elspeth's lap and onto the straw floor. Everything was still as it was, and to see it so, was chilling. Silas wanted to weep and who could blame him for it was a melancholy scene resembling a painting where the subject had suddenly been removed. However, as he drew in his first snorting breath, he noticed that Wynnfrith had leapt into action as if she had secretly been employed to tidy up a completely alien property.

'Soon have it right! Just a question of rearranging a few things. Oh, that old shawl, must be ancient, that can go out…'

Silas realised that this incredibly animated narration was a guise for the enduring hurt and so he decided to throw himself into the activity too, although he was doing little to make things better. The more he tried, the more untidy it became and the faster Wynnfrith seemed to move after him. Then, responsibly, he walked right into her path and put his arm out to both stop, and then embrace her. Now she wept.

'The very seed of my love for you was planted right here, the very first time I laid eyes on you.' He said softly.

'You mean' she replied sobbing 'you mean when she kicked you out?'

'Yes..' and they both laughed.

'She's here isn't she?' asked Wynn seeking reassurance.

'Oh yes! And she's got her eye on me too, my love'

Again they laughed and, somehow, the task seemed that much easier. As their laughter died down, they could hear someone approaching the door and both of them were surprised to see Mrs Hall. She first thought to reference some of the many confessions raised that day at Barley Hall but then thought better of it.

'Now then, you two are going to be married?'

'Yes' said Wynnfrith 'but not for a while…you know, with all that has happened.'

'Hush' she said 'I think it is possibly a priority for us all now and I'm sure it's what…your…erm sister would want. So, to the point!'

This was said in such a way that it immediately took Wynnfrith back to that day when she had lost her parents and, Mrs Hall, in a very matter of fact manner, delivered the bad news leaving Wynn a little nervous about what was coming next.

'Whilst Mr Hall is still Mayor we will still be residing at Barley Hall and whilst we are, you two can take a room each until we decide where you are going to live.'

Although a little dumbfounded, Wynnfrith accepted this sudden generosity immediately and with gratitude. Silas, however, insisted that he wanted to tend to his home which had been somewhat neglected. So, within the hour, the three of them had transformed the wash house and, although they didn't know it, they would never set eyes on it again. That is if you ignore the sudden impulse that Wynnfrith had to return. She shared this with Mrs Hall and Silas but also insisted that she returned alone. She opened the door and immediately reprimanded herself for that sudden folly. What am I doing here? What on earth am I doing at all? she asked herself. And then, she believed supernaturally, she saw a rugged piece of sackcloth hiding beneath the very same barrel that Silas had mused about only minutes earlier. She turned again, continuing to chastise herself and, as she placed her hand on the door handle to leave, she looked back once more at those ragged threads.

Who knows what drives us in such situations but there

are times when we cannot explain our actions and it was one such mystery that led to Wynnfrith investigating further. Checking to see that the other two were now some distance from the washhouse, she knelt and placed her palms at the bottom of the barrel and gave it a firm shove. As it moved, the sackcloth jammed and moved with it. Impatient, she then decided to tilt the barrel and, it was at this point, that she determined that this was not a sack but a small parcel and, unquestionably, it had not been there long as it was clean and dust-free. She peeped inside. More documents. What more could her sister have had to say that wasn't contained in the volumes of letters that she had already left? She thought. Pausing only for a moment, Wynnfrith decided to conceal the parcel in her gown and, for the time being, say nothing to the others. As far as she was concerned, this was none of Mrs Hall's business and, if anything, this decision was intended to save her beloved from any further anxiety as they had both had such a horrendous day. As they walked, however, she glowed, ecstatic that she had found another piece of her sister and excited to find out what it could be.

As they reached Swinegate, Silas parted company with the other two and ventured toward his home via that well used, but bizarre, route through All Saints Pavement churchyard. His pace quickened, anxious to put distance between the noise, smells and pigs and himself. Suddenly, there was a hum inside his head, an orchestra of voices. Familiar voices of those that had been at the meeting that morning. Not for the first time, he began to chastise himself, particularly for his mother's death. By the time he had caught a glimpse of Dead alley, he had decided that he should have killed his father whilst still a small boy, not even considering that he had seen him but a handful of times. Subsequently, Silas was to blame for all the deaths and for Roberts's infidelity. Oh, and yes, the Purge and the Cataclysm too. If only Silas had had someone by his side to explain the luxury of hindsight.

He pushed through the ever-expanding bracken and

roots that were signposts to his home and entered. He slumped onto the one, and only, stool and looked at the naïve pictures of his mother and himself that he had drawn growing up and tears gently oozed from his eyelids. He didn't sob or even sniffle but his body desperately needed this catharsis. He then mulled over his future. Both Silas and Wynnfrith had been so excited about their plans but there had been an unwelcome pall drawn over it and then, he thought about what it meant. I can't have her live here, he told himself but also conjectured that he could never live anywhere else either. With no solution to hand, he decided to eat. His entire domestic provision comprised of one piece of bread that was at least a week old. Nevertheless, he had eaten worse and this was to be his meal for the day. Where he did find solace was in tending to Annie who, patiently waited and grazed on her patch of grass which, no matter how small it seemed, was still twice the size of Silas's accommodation. Silas sat again, put his head in his hands and, before he was aware of it, had fallen into a deep sleep in which the whole world was his enemy with only one exception. In this surreal tale, there was a fat King who had no friends but he had ridden all the way from his castle to ward off Silas's enemies and tell him that he would always be there to protect him. At least when he awoke, he was reminded of the great works carried out in the Agents' name, not least when wrestling with the mischief prevalent at Hampton Court Palace. However, downhearted again, he decided that he wasn't the right man for Wynnfrith, exercising his God-given right to denigrate himself continuously and completely. She could have someone much better and much richer. Why would she live here? This is no place for a lady. And on it went. He then rehearsed how he would tell her this, certain that it would be welcome news to Wynnfrith. Annie was the ideal foil. Once the devastating news had been bestowed on this ageing horse, she glared at him with contempt to which Silas added,

'It is better for you dear! I want you to have the best of lives.'

As much as a horse could look disgusted, she did, leaving Silas wondering, yet again, what he had done wrong. He decided to mull over this conundrum a while longer whilst clearing out leaves, snails and debris from his domicile floor.

Across town, Robert was in conversation with Eirik. The Mayor apologised for the uncomfortable revelations of the morning, still embarrassed and wondering how best to negotiate relations with, well, almost everyone. Eirik told him that he was happy that the secret was out, tired of suspicions about whether he was in fact related to Elspeth and Wynnfrith. It would be fair to say that the conversation was light and they managed to reflect on many of the issues and events that had transpired that day. However, Robert was to astonish his son by referring, yet again, to his unusual birthmark. Eirik, confident that everything had already been said on this subject, untied his doublet and pulled his shirt open to display the notorious scar. So confident was he that he decided to tell Robert for the first time about how it had faded and, as a goodwill gesture, Thomas Farrier had branded a new one. They both laughed. That was until Robert asked,

'Uncanny how it is in exactly the same place.'

To which his son replied,

'Yes, father! Astonishing, an incredible coincidence.'

Suddenly, the conversation became much cooler, although Eirik wasn't sure why. Nothing else was said and talk then turned to business and political matters imminent. Robert tasked Eirik with finding the mouse as he wished to have further conference and suggested that he started at the carpenter's workshop along Micklegate. However, Eirik left taking an entirely different route. He was intent, on this day, to watch Godwin hang and nothing would get in the way of it.

2 scarborough fair
1525

The baby cried and cried, although everyone's attention was diverted as there was so much going on. He cried and cried but then suddenly stopped. He had heard the voices of his sisters, Wynnfrith and Elspeth and this was enough to, momentarily, soothe him. The servant who cradled him was kind and, she herself hadn't got a clue what was going on. At first light, and also as they had eaten breakfast, all was well but now, the house seemed full of people and there was a great deal of fuss. Jenny, the servant was particularly nervous as the sheriff was dominating the hallway, voices were raised and, before she knew it, the sisters were bundled into the living quarters with Mrs Hall leaving her literally holding the baby and watching Robert Hall break down in tears. Coming to his senses for a moment, he advised her to take the baby upstairs and see to his needs. Years later, when she would retell this story, Jenny remembered that she had been upstairs so long that, before she knew it, the sisters were moving their belongings in. The whole experience was heart-breaking, she recalled, but the worst of it was that the baby wasn't to stay there alongside his sisters. As best she could, knowing her

1543 The Disfiguration

place within this hierarchy, Jenny protested, telling the Halls that the baby would be best brought up with his sisters but, of course, she wasn't to know the unpleasant mitigating circumstances that had led to Mrs Hall's decision.

Neither was Jenny told where the baby had gone but, for some time, and in vain, she tried to find out. Robert and Mrs Hall had concocted a water-tight scheme and a story to go with it which would leave this child untraceable. Well, that was their hope at least. A very close friend of Mrs Hall, called Mrs Baker, was seemingly the answer to their problem. This wasn't a glib or joke name. She was called Mrs Baker because she was married to Mr Baker, a baker. Her first name was Ryia. This had nothing to do with rye bread either, it was just her name. Together, Mrs Hall and Mrs Baker were the lieutenants of the church busybodies, the church being Holy Trinity in Goodramgate. To be fair they were, now and again, a blessing to the priest particularly when it came to keeping the place tidy and welcoming but, for some strange reason, this gave them the idea that they owned the place. A trait amongst Christian women that would last for centuries. If nothing else, it gave them a sense of purpose, power and a forum in which gossip could ferment. Ryia knew something of Robert Hall's straying nature but Mrs Hall was circumspect enough not to share every detail of their marital woes. And, Mrs Hall had been the best friend possible when Ryia Baker went through her own trials and tribulations. Ryia had had four children. Three boys and a girl. Not one survived beyond the age of ten. Mrs Hall had suffered two miscarriages after which point, particularly as they were incredibly secure financially, she and her husband decided that they should endure life childless.

Ryia felt differently. Daily, she bemoaned the loss of her children and, at twenty-six years of age yearned for more. However, there was an overarching problem that got in the way of her prospects. Her husband, Mr Baker, had buggered off. Now, it's up to you to judge. You can either decide that his overwhelming bereavement pushed him over the edge, or that he was a complete and utter selfish bastard. However, it doesn't much matter as he was gone. Neither was she missing him much anymore, but the humiliation for Ryia was practically unbearable. And, she so wanted children and Mrs Hall knew it. In different circumstances, Mrs Hall may well have delighted at the arrival of a baby. However, as this was Robert's illegitimate child, it was understandable that she wanted nothing to do with it.

As soon as things had settled after the murder of Elspeth and Wynnfrith's parents, the Halls knew that they had to make a decision about baby James as soon as possible. Robert agreed that Ryia would be told that this child was an orphan and had come to them in tragic circumstances and there were to be no additional questions asked. In response, Mrs Hall told her husband that he was never to seek out this child, ever, and neither should he talk about him. Seemingly, in the heat of what had taken place, there were no other options.

Ryia Baker sat in church next to her friend, worn out but delighted at how attractive everywhere appeared after applying their artistic touch.

'Ryia, my good friend' said Mrs Hall, already sounding quite nervous.

Ryia immediately knew that Mrs Hall was out of sorts.

'Why Jane whatever is the matter?'

Besides the fact that Mrs Hall had already been uncovered, she unconsciously acknowledged how close they had become as this woman was possibly the only person, ever, to use her first name.

'There has come into my husband's knowledge...a child that has been orphaned. Completely without a home...'

Not yet putting two and two together, Ryia clumsily asked,

'Has it anything to do with those awful deaths?'

Mrs Hall took in a sharp breath. This was unexpected and

she immediately panicked wondering what Ryia knew of the murders.

'Sorry, Jane. Silly thing to say. I just heard that a craftsman had been killed although no one wants to talk of it'

'Oh, that!' Said Mrs Hall feigning ignorance 'on no...oh no no no...oh no. Oh no no no...'

Ryia stared at her friend concerned for her sanity.

'Put simply' said Mrs Hall returning to her usual business-like mode 'he needs a mother and he needs a mother soon.'

This unsettled Ryia. Every fibre of her being told her that she should have a child in her home but she had hoped for a new husband, her own children but, as she contemplated this, she realised that it may now be very unlikely especially as, legally and in the eyes of God, she was still married. She paused, and wisely, so did Mrs Hall. There seemed to be an endless silence. Ryia then looked up from her lap and directly into her friend's eyes.

'Are you sure there will be no consequences? No-one knocking on my door whether it be some other woman or the constable?'

Mrs Hall took her hand.

'Absolutely, the sheriff already knows of our intent.'

'May I think about it?'

'Why of course' said Mrs Hall 'but the sooner we can find a home for little James, the better.'

The cunning Mrs Hall had sealed the deal by giving this infant stray an identity and for the next twenty-four hours, Mrs Baker thought of nothing else but baby James. However, she had one more question. A serious one that really would affect whether this would work out best for all parties. So, the next morning when they met again, Ryia said,

'When he left, he had at least the decency to leave me the ownership of our home in addition to five pounds but, it won't last forever. Please, it's not that I'm asking you for...'

'Nonsense!' interrupted Mrs Hall 'you will receive a monthly stipend for the child's care and it will be generous.'

Slightly embarrassed at raising the issue, Ryia could see no further obstacles and within the week her world was complete. It was also beneficial to both parties that she lived south-east of the castle which, at that time, may as well have been Portugal. When Ryia and Mrs Hall met, they would talk about James's progress but always as if he had been her own. And, adoption wasn't to be mentioned. As far as her close neighbours were concerned, this was her sister's child who wasn't well enough to bring him up.

The bigger problem was Robert. This was his child and, more importantly, the child of a woman who he had adored, so he remained conflicted. He felt overwhelmingly guilty. Guilt that he couldn't save James's mother, guilt that he was letting the child go but also guilt that he had hurt his wife so much. Drained of any courage, he acceded to this plan with every intention of following each one of the agreements that Mrs Hall had made with Mrs Baker. However, as the weeks and months passed, he found himself straying in the direction of the castle and then chastising himself for his folly. He hurt deeply but, as he was considered the culprit and the guilty part in all this, he knew he could confide in no one. Particularly as the sisters had now given the Halls renewed responsibilities, he eventually gave up on any notion that he would either bring this boy up or ever see him again. For her part, Mrs Hall never mentioned him even once.

James was a bright and happy child who confidently played with children in the nearby snickleways and benefited from his mother's business-like nature. On the very first day that she took him home, swaddled and welcoming the incessant affection bestowed upon him by Ryia, she stood resolute weighing up the small oven in which Mr Baker had spent most of his days. She knew the trade. He very rarely involved her but she could bake and she could bake well. This is our family trade, she told herself, and it would be James's trade too. And so it was, by the time he was seven years old, he could bake bread. More than that, he was suggesting ideas for varied ingredients and encouraging his mother to make cakes. Mainly because there was a male involved again, their produce started to sell well and, without question, by 1535, this was the best bakery in York. Robert knew of it and tried to console himself with the knowledge that James was enjoying a good life,

However, James soon got itchy feet. Moreover, he got ambition. The success had gone to his head. By and large, this didn't bother his mother except that she did not want him leaving York. In fact, she didn't want him to leave home. But, as the months and the next couple of years went by, he persisted, each day concocting a greater case for, what he called, expanding. If this had meant setting up another bakery a mile or two away, Ryia may have conceded but that wasn't his intent. One day, whilst taking their products to the local market, he got talking to a man called John. John had been permanently established on a pedestal the very first time that James had met him. The boy hung onto every word as he explained the encounters he had had when travelling to market. The people, the clothes, spices, beer, wine and mead, jewels, ornaments, leathers and on it went. The sun always shone and people parted with their money as easily as they would sweat. Oh and the women. The stories John could tell about women.

Inside James's head, this was paradise but only translated as nonsense and danger to his mother. As with all teen obsessions, this became a war of attrition and Ryia's love for her son meant that very soon her defences were down. She agreed to let him set forth on this entrepreneurial quest with certain stipulations. She didn't like John or how he had bewitched her son but insisted that if James was to go, he would go with John. Neither was he to be away for more than four weeks. Then, completely bemused, she told him that all the bread would be mouldy by the time he got there. He laughed. Not at her, but amused that she would think him so stupid. No, where he was going, he could rent a small kiln and work all hours to make their fortune.

So where was this Valhalla, this oasis beyond the limitations of the city? Scarborough Fair. That was what John had planted very firmly inside James's noggin. In some ways he was right. At Scarborough, where the months-long fair was held, there would be more people than James had ever dreamed of. People of all races and all colours he was told. There were to be games, dancing, jollity, entertainment. People selling things that you couldn't even imagine. Pageants, parades, tents, pennants, flags, jousting, archery. Colour. Colour and excitement. That's what filled James's head. That and selling cakes by the bucket load.

Four weeks. She could manage a month, Ryia told herself and what good would chaining him to the bakery in York do? She knew this would make him happy, so conceded. However, this came at a price. Regardless of what Robert Hall and his wife thought, Ryia loved this child with all her heart and wanted him to know the truth of his origins because, of course, by this time, she knew herself. This was not an easy decision as she had wrestled with it for years considering that he might bolt and end up knocking on the front door of the Halls. This obsession with Scarborough, however, had helped her to make her mind up. There was nothing the least bit sinister or eerie about the thought that she may never see him again, many males left home for all sorts of reasons, including war, and never returned and that included her husband, the rotten bastard. However, she pondered endlessly as to how she would approach the subject. He will be devastated, she told herself and then, almost within the same thought, chose not to tell him at all. In the weeks before he set off for Scarborough, he could tell that she was both agitated and hadn't slept. Concerned, he insisted that she tell him what was going on.

'You'll need to sit down. You know how I love you, my dear James? More than my life, more than anything?'

'Why yes mother…' he said smiling.

'And I'd never lie to you?'

'Of course…'

And this went on for at least another five minutes before she got to what she wanted to say at which point James thought it wise to take the reins.

'Is this about the Halls and the MacManus family?' He said.

Dumbfounded, she said nothing. Ryia Baker leant back and gave forth an almost terminal puff of breath.

'What? Well…how?…'

Before she completely walked backwards into the wall, he interrupted.

'Known about that for ages..' and almost as if they were talking about the size of the cakes, he picked one up and started examining it.

'You know?!' said Ryia now completely breathless.

'Oh yeah. All the other kids knew when I was little. Rather be with you, I thank God every day you saved me from that lot.' He added nonchalantly.

'Why is there something wrong?' he then asked innocently.

'No…erm…not at all my love. Have you seen to the fire?'

'Yes Mater, all as it should be! Just nipping out for a while.'

'Ok, my love.'

And, as he left, she found herself weeping and, if at that time, you were to ask her why, she probably wouldn't have been able to tell you but most of it was pride. She had worried for years that her child may have been taken back to where he had come from and here he was, happy and with her of his own free will. What more could a woman want? she asked herself.

As July ended he put together a few provisions, only to find out that Ryia had packed four times as much, and headed toward the local market to meet John.

'What in God's good name you got there young 'un?'

asked John.

'Oh, this?' He replied looking quite embarrassed 'think mother may have over-compensated!'

John laughed.

'So you're off then?' said John.

'Err, yes' said James quite confused.

'Well, I wish you all the luck in the world lad. You'll see some things, that you will…'

James stumbled onto his words a little but then forced out,

'I was sure we were…err…well…going together?'

John laughed.

'Got the wrong end of the stick there, young James. I'm going but won't be free for a week or more yet. You don't need me to hold your hand do you?' he added, laughing again.

'No, no of course not. But…the journey?'

'See' he said bending down and now, seemingly trying to help 'that way is Heworth. The church? You know it?'

'Yes' said James.

'That's your way, keep on that road north-east toward the coast. By the time you're out of Heworth you'll see travellers, lots of them. Some in groups, some alone. Find someone you like the looks of and ask if you can travel to the fair with them. It really is that easy.'

James looked at him suspiciously and then John reassured him once more.

There was no doubt that he was feeling better about things at this point and he certainly did still trust John. Added to this, was the certainty that there was no way that he was turning around and going home. The weather was fine and so he ambled in the direction of Heworth, content that he was doing the right thing. Within the hour he was by the church in Heworth and, exactly as John had said, there was already a stream of people heading toward the coast. Feeling much more confident, he travelled alone for a while intending to make company when it suited him. However, he needn't have dwelled long on this as, before the sun was failing, he was approached by a young man, possibly only two or three years older than himself. Assured that he was no threat, James congratulated himself that he had found a cordial companion so soon. His newly acquired friend talked. In fact, he probably talked too much and by the time that they had reached Kirkham Abbey, James knew everything about this young man's family and business and even some local gossip. However, he never mentioned his name and James didn't think to ask. They rested around the outskirts of the Abbey. Without doubt, they could have made many more miles before dark but they chose to set up a small camp there and spend the night. They were in awe of the Abbey buildings as the sun began to set behind it. The Priory was huge, every architectural detail a work of art worth lingering upon. It was, for a while, their sole topic of conversation which was only interrupted by compline, the final prayer and obligation of the day for the monks. Their singing was both haunting and beautiful and it was to this backdrop that James and his companion shared prayers for their safe passage and successful trade. Little did they know that within a few years all that they surveyed would be gone. The windows, the buttresses, the roof, the cloisters, everything and that included the monks themselves. If you would have said this to anyone camping within the environs of the Abbey that evening, they would have thought you mad. In that sense, if no other, they had no idea how lucky they were.

When prayers had finished, James wanted to know even more about his friend's trade.

'It's is so much more exciting than mine!' said James meaning every word of it.

'Oh, not at all friend. It can become quite repetitive and you rarely know what becomes of them when sold.'

Nevertheless, making arrows seemed much more interesting than baking, thought James.

The next morning the baker and the fletcher found the

road that would take them nearer to their destination and, for a while, they hardly spoke. It was then that James chose to address his new friend as "fletcher." If he was a baker and his name was Baker then, sensibly, if he is a fletcher, his name must be Fletcher, he deduced. Once this name was employed, Fletcher never flinched so this was now his accepted name, solving yet another conundrum.

James learned at an early age that he functioned better when he was with an elder, someone to guide and advise him, which also told him that he was still a long way off being independent. Yet again, he had put his faith in someone older, albeit only a few years. It was a blessing that James was able to trust so easily but it also meant that he could be managed by others too. Not that Fletcher had any ill-intent, but he knew that the boy was inexperienced, to say the least. Before they had even got to the coast they had shared absolutely everything about their lives. Generally speaking, Fletcher only lied about one thing. He gave James the impression that he came from a similar, loving home and that the business belonged to his only relative, his father. What did give him away was that, at times, he was surviving on scraps. Truth be told, he was simply ashamed to share his real story with his newly-found travelling companion. In return, James told him everything which, as you can imagine, was quite enthralling for Fletcher.

'So you say he's rich?'

'Yeah, rich and getting fat I believe.'

'Your life would be so easy. Think of the clothes, the food!'

'Don't want or need any of it, I have the happiest of lives and the most wonderful mother.'

'And you never wish to see your sisters?'

'I'm just not bothered. I wish them well but I wouldn't know them if I saw them now. Truthfully I wish none of them any ill will but I'd like, eventually, to be as far from York as possible.'

1543 The Disfiguration

Fletcher was incredibly impressed by this. Someone so young who already knew the difference between happiness and pleasure. Those transient pleasures that can be bought by those with the means but are short-lived. Yes, I'd take love any day too, deduced Fletcher somewhat envious of James.

Fletcher was a kind and responsible young man and made it his business to look after his friend simply because he liked him and, he became the perfect companion for someone so vulnerable. There was never anything but true friendship between these two and it would have given Ryia much comfort.

Having spoken about his past, James then found himself in deep thought about it. Whilst in York, the one person that James felt that he had had a brief connection with was Wynnfrith. Almost every Tuesday in York, a young lady, who would walk with some difficulty, would buy his bread. Some fussed over her, others mocked, but he had always liked her and looked forward to her visits. It was, of course, his sister and he knew this because his childhood friends had told him. How he longed to say hello to her and, once, as her companion used her lifelong and affectionate nickname he simply wanted to use it himself and tell her who he was. Although he didn't show it, Fletcher was deeply touched by the affection displayed by James as he talked of her and, slowly, a healthy but unbreakable bond developed between these two travellers.

James didn't know what expectations to have of Scarborough Fair but it was ultimately, as sold: paradise. When they arrived, they stood at one of the entrances stupefied. It was too much to take in. Colour as they had never experienced before. Stages, tents, arenas, stalls, workshops and people of all shapes and sizes and, girls. There was food he had never seen before including cooked meats of all types that could be bought, and girls. There were heavenly smells everywhere and girls. Lots of girls. James turned to Fletcher.

'What do I do?'

'Haha! Where to start! Well, you won't make much money staring at maidens and, I'll tell you for free, if you're caught looking at one that's married or one with her father, you'll end up on a rope!'

James immediately looked at his feet.

'See that man over there?'

He looked up again trying to avoid all the pretty dresses and hats in his view.'

'He's one of the officials and you'll have to arrange with him the rental of a tent or workshop and then you can set up.'

'Ah, wonderful' said James 'I have money' and as James enthusiastically disappeared, Fletcher was left alone laughing at his friend's enthusiasm.

Although somewhere on the outskirts of the field, James had managed to rent a small outdoor kiln and a covered stall. Of course, there were dozens of bakers but he believed he could compete with anyone. It was also relatively easy for him to purchase flour and other raw materials and, although every fibre of his being was telling him to party, he wanted this business up and running more than anything. By the end of that day he had produced three types of loaf and a variety of, what he called "Ryia cakes from York City." At first, there was nothing, the general human traffic that much quieter in his spot. But then, a particularly well-dressed man, a merchant he presumed, came to his stall with three ladies in tow, all of which pleaded with him to buy the cakes.

'I'll tell you what boy, if my good lady here takes a liking to these I'll buy the lot.'

Hesitatingly he said,

'Please my lady, take any one for free' and, as he did, he realised that his voice was trembling.

Giggling, the young lady in question stuffed a warm currant cake into her noisy gob but then went quiet.

'Mmm...mmmphh...um...vewy narce....'

1543 The Disfiguration

'Pardon my dear?' said the gentleman.

'Very narce! Nice! It's really good. Well done boy!'

James held his breath waiting to see if this man was as good as his word and before he knew it, the man had thrown several coins onto his bench.

'Thank you Sir…thank you so much…bless you…ladies! Thank you!'

This was an auspicious start and it was to get better. This was as good as an endorsement. A proverbial royal flag above his stall for, this was observed by others who now formed a modest queue. For the rest of the day, James wore himself out trying to bake, present and sell almost at the same time whilst reassuring potential buyers when his stock became low. As evening came, he was exhausted but happy and elated to hear the sound of his friend's voice.

'Well well, you've cleaned up, young James!'

'I'm worn out! But what a day Fletcher! I couldn't have imagined…how did you fare?'

'Oh good. Not like this mind! But good. Biggest problem with my trade is that everyone wants to try first! Endlessly playing with my masterpieces!' he laughed 'and often give them back broken! It's hard to believe that every male above sixteen in this land is supposed to have some archery skills! However, I have sold well and met some interesting maidens if you get my drift?'

James thought he did but didn't. He was at an age where he knew he liked to look at members of the opposite sex and also found that he wasn't too fussy about the almost inexhaustible variations in age, shape and size. But, he just liked looking . Beyond that, he was quite green. Fletcher wasn't. Now, to put this into perspective, this was the sixteenth century. Young ladies weren't normally given to rolling in the east-coast hay with any traveller that they met. But glances were often exchanged and flirting was seen almost as a social skill, sometimes a sign of good breeding. Suffice it to say, these two had altogether different ambitions

1543 The Disfiguration

and, for the time being, James was very happy just to have a glance returned.

Bearing all of this in mind, these two were, unquestionably, having the time of their lives. The sun shone, the fair had its own energy, a life of its own and trade was good. James was as good as his word and headed home at the end of four weeks, filled with an excitement that he could barely contain. Fletcher didn't travel with him but neither was he short of companionship on the journey. As he arrived home, his mother collapsed. Certain that the temptations of Scarborough and beyond would mean that she would never set eyes on her son again, she wept and almost crushed him as she embraced her son. He talked endlessly and she listened, marvelling at how he had matured in a month. What a practical and independent child, she thought and acknowledged that he had probably inherited some of his business skills from both his natural parents.

'So what now?' Asked Ryia.

'I will work to make this the best bakery in York!' He asserted and she was in no doubt that he would 'but' he added hesitatingly 'I would like to go again next year?'

'Why, of course, James as long as you return safe and happy again!' she said.

They both worked so hard that year and rightfully gained a reputation for their integrity, diligence and good cakes and bread and, they were happy. James was blossoming into a handsome teenager and the young ladies noticed and he noticed that they noticed. Moreover, Ryia, noticed that they were noticing her son and the maidens were noticing that Ryia was noticing them noticing him. Just the ways of things, she told herself.

The following year, there was a period of over two months during which he couldn't contain himself and, as summer came, he was off again having prearranged the previous year to meet Fletcher. This gave Ryia some confidence that her son was being looked after and, although she had never met Fletcher, she had, quite rightly, put all her faith in the arrow maker.

Overjoyed to see one another, and for celebratory reasons, they once again camped at Kirkham Abbey which was still intact with the general populace yet to grasp what the "dissolution of the monasteries" would mean. Little did they know that the monastic population beyond the walls were already feeling very nervous. Their experiences at Scarborough Fair were similar to the year before except each of them kidded themselves that they were now so much older. James, having previously been introduced to copious amounts of ale, made straight to the makeshift inn on the first evening with Fletcher, laughing, only steps behind him. This, of course, became a nightly ritual, not just because of the beer but because of Meg. Meg was possibly as old as eighteen but certainly not much more than sixteen and, apart from being particularly good at her job and sharing her gregarious and humorous personality, she was unquestionably good to look at. James was smitten. From the very first night, he was under her spell. Unfortunately, over forty others were too. But, for him, he saw his immature banter with Meg as a burgeoning relationship. Being so young, he was content with a glance or a greeting as she poured him another, and yet another, drink but what did not escape his attention was Fletcher's natural flair with Meg and, he observed, most other women. Fletcher was bold enough to touch her, put his arm around her waist and she also laughed at his witty remarks. James's head was filled with this festering competition. In his mind, he envisioned either himself or his friend settling for life with this remarkable barmaid. What escaped him was that Fletcher's desires and intentions were very different. A few years older and James would have understood what he was up against but the back street baker from York just hadn't had that much life experience. So naïve was he, that each night as they stumbled home, he was certain that Fletcher had turned back again but never once questioned it.

It was, again, a warm and successful summer and they left, still close friends, proud of themselves. They made a point of bidding farewell to Meg and she embraced James which had his little Yorkshire heart bouncing into his head and then to his feet and then back again. Just as he was about to declare his undying love for her, she lunged forward and kissed Fletcher on the lips. They wandered away and this was never spoken off but, needless to say, James was left overwhelmingly confused and heartbroken.

Almost totally relying on his older companion, James found himself on a different route and, in what seemed no time at all, they arrived in Staxton. Here, Fletcher amazed his friend with stories of Viking invasions, telling of how his ancestors had settled in that part of the world and James announced that, he too, was descended from Vikings.

'Ah, you remember that I told you about my natural mother?' said James.

'Yes. Didn't she die?'

'Yes, I believe so. She was of Viking stock and my father and…well…I suppose part of me must be too?'

'Why of course!' shouted Fletcher as he stood 'you and I can take that town yonder as Viking brothers!'

They both laughed and then thought it wise to head toward the road that would, ultimately, take them back to York. However, for the first time, they came across a crowd. At least they understood it to be a crowd and presumed that they may have been revellers from the fair. As they got closer they could see that these were all men and that some were armed.

'We're not going through there' said Fletcher and pulled at James's jerkin as they backed away. For a few steps, they found themselves cautiously stepping backwards only to come to a complete standstill.

'In a hurry maidens?' Boomed a voice behind them.

They both tried to turn but the owner of this rather coarse

voice had hold of them both by the scruff of the neck. Next to him were two other huge, armed men. Fletcher struggled and nobly attempted to swing a punch at this brute but this just made things worse. They acknowledged that they had become the focus of the men's insults but had no clue as to why they had been stopped. The money! Thought James. All the earnings that he was to take home to his mother were concealed in the lining of his jerkin. It wasn't a great stretch of the imagination to presume that these men were thieves but that assumption would soon be put to bed. Fletcher was in no doubt whatsoever about what was going on, especially when he saw all the armed men group together and make camp, as there were several other young men now in exactly the same position as them.

As night fell, the two boys sat, tied back to back, watching those thugs drink and make complete arseholes of themselves.

'What is happening?' whispered James nervously.

'In a word my friend, impressment.'

'What?'

'And it couldn't be worse. These aren't even official soldiers, they are mercenaries.'

James didn't understand this term either so Fletcher explained that they were people who fought or made arrests for money only and, usually, they didn't mind who was paying. Fletcher also guessed that they were probably in the employ of the King because of all the talk about how people, particularly in the north, were generally against the Reformation. The King knew that there was bound to be a backlash, possibly even a revolution because he was now head of the church and was to take back all the wealth from the monasteries. All this was news to James who still didn't understand why they had been arrested if they were not monks or rebels. Fletcher then explained that impressment meant adding to your ranks by stealing people, often slave labour. Both of them would now be mercenaries and may, or may not, get some pay.

'But I don't want to be a soldier!' Protested James to which Fletcher, once again, explained that he would have no choice. Neither of them knew that, eventually, this would become common practice, particularly by the navy, where pressgangs would be seen in, almost all, coastal towns in England. Although Fletcher constantly reprimanded him, James kept crying, his dreams now completely shattered and leaving him wondering whether he would ever see his mother again. Fletcher was dismayed too but didn't have a life to go back to. That didn't mean that Fletcher was complacent, he simply understood that they were unlikely to get out of the sudden predicament in which they had found themselves.

As dawn broke, the gaffer confirmed what they had feared and they were now to head north. They were both told that, if they behaved themselves, they would be fed and may, eventually, get some wages. Also, they were told that they had to give any worldly possessions that they had, over to them. Fletcher, now completely disheartened, gave up the few arrows he had left and his purse. As he did so, the ropes binding them were loosened but, as much as Fletcher knew that he had no choice but to comply, James instantly turned into a wildcat. Screaming, he ran and, to his credit, he made some distance very quickly but was, almost instantly, apprehended. The guards made it very clear what would happen to him if he continued to resist but something inside him had now completely snapped. Out of the dark came one of the crew that neither of them had seen before. He was different. Tall, scrawny, incredibly unkempt and menacing, his smell preceded him by over thirty yards. He had in his hand a cudgel and walked toward James who was now partly restrained again. At first, he made no sound except for a course grunt which was the unfortunate natural sound of his breathing. His face was, almost completely, covered with hair and his eyes practically shut. You would have thought that he was going to shake the boy's hand by the way he approached him. That was, unless you knew him. There was something unnervingly sinister about this man and the others smiled as he approached James. Clearly, no one was going to intervene. He grabbed James's jerkin and found the purse inside which delighted all present except, of course, the new arrivals.

'You can't have it!' shouted James.

This invited sudden laughter and, as the thug emptied this purse onto the ground, there was an intake of breath from everyone, including Fletcher.

'Nice!' Said the man who had taken the purse. He had finally spoken but still, James tried to grab at the coins with his free hand.

'This belongs to my mother!'

Syllable by syllable, he was making things worse and Fletcher did his utmost to advise James to the contrary. Soon, the laughter stopped. James had crossed the line. The gaffer approached him again and warned him. He made it clear that it would be the end of him if he didn't comply but it seemed to have no effect on James. The scrawny, creepy mercenary with cudgel, yet again moved nearer to James, who was now like a spinning top, unable to get away but also, seemingly, unable to give way to their demands. Fletcher was watching every move that James made, willing him to stop but, as Fletcher opened his mouth for the last time to convince him, he heard a sound that would stay with him forever.

The cudgel, with some force, had met James's still-developing cranium and he instantly collapsed as a bag of beans would when dropped from a cart.

Nothing. All was now completely silent. Even Fletcher thought it wise not to comment but, as blood pooled around the boy's head it was clear that he was dead. Moreover, no one besides his friend seemed bothered. They told themselves that he would have been more trouble than he was worth and revelled in the bounty he had brought.

'So do you want to go the same way?'

Fletcher, still coming to terms with the loss of his friend, as well as lamenting the fact that he would never see Scarborough again, assured them that he would be no trouble and that they could untie him.

'So is that your name then?' asked the gaffer 'Fletcher?'

'No, no. Just what the lad called me. It's what I do, I make arrows.'

'Might come in handy then' said the gaffer bizarrely trying to lighten the situation somewhat.

'Well out with it. What you called then?'

'Eirik. I'm of Viking stock.'

Eirik adjusted to this lifestyle quickly mostly because he knew that he had no choice. But, he was resourceful. There was no way he was going to do this all his life, particularly as it wasn't in his nature to be cruel to others. Even when he tried, he couldn't understand why the mercenaries were so brutal and why they took pleasure in the suffering of their prisoners. As the youngest, he was vulnerable but kept his head down as best he could, determined to make life as easy as he could for any of the prisoners and himself. Although he would be with these people for years, he started planning his escape from day one. He hadn't had much of a life, he had been orphaned and was taken into the employment of a local Fletcher. He had lied to James. He had no father, he never had anyone that he could call family, James had almost become family but for whatever reason, he felt he couldn't tell him about his past.

After the first year, Eirik became aware that his predicament was not going to change for some time. Monasteries, Abbeys, Priories, Nunneries and Convents began to close one after the other. Many of the occupants took pensions or sought-out long lost relatives. But those devoted to their faith were not to give up so easily. At one point, when travelling south from Yorkshire, they found themselves in Lincolnshire and the movement that became known as the Pilgrimage of Grace was rapidly gaining momentum. So much so, that the gang of mercenaries went into hiding for over a month. This must be it, thought Eirik. When the northern army eventually rebels against the King, they will demolish this band of thugs, he told himself. This thought, at least, gave him some hope for a while but it was not to be. By the end of 1536, they were receiving orders directly from Thomas Cromwell and all rebels were to be apprehended and taken either to local jails and castles or to the Tower itself. However, this crew were also a bunch of cowards as they had no intention of doing any real fighting, but instead, picking off the odd stray monk, nun, noble or cleric that had been peeled off from the movement. So, their work continued which, largely meant apprehending monks, fettering them and making their lives an utter misery until they reached their assigned destination.

Eirik had twice made a run for it but was apprehended both times, once, sadly because he lost his footing and fell. On that occasion, in particular, he was certain that he would endure the same fate as his good friend James. However, it did strengthen his resolve. As the years passed, he promised God that he would do his best to make life bearable for the prisoners, escape when possible and find his way to York to personally deliver the sad news of James's death to his mother. At times, he was sure that it was this reason alone that drove him on.

Eventually, his name went too. The gaffer thought it clever to refer to him as "Dung" and, of course, everyone else did too. He covertly worked on his strength, volunteering to take on any tasks that involved manual work. He had a plan and knew that one day his fortunes would change. Now and again, he would think about Scarborough. At first, this only served to break his heart but as the years went by, he found that it gave him strength. Yes, he told himself, one day I will return there. However, there were

1543 The Disfiguration

times when he was sure that this was his lot. Life would not change and he would be doing the same thing forever. He took some solace in the fact that some of the older mercenaries died from time to time but, as the whole enterprise was driven by money rather than any loyalty to one cause or another, it seemed like it would go on ad infinitum. By the end of the 1530s, he realised that he was, generally, feeling more fulfilled as many a monk had told him that he had made their ordeal that much easier and there was no doubt that he had saved a life or two.

In March 1541, he was no more aware of his manifest than he had been previously although two monks, with completely different and bizarre accents, took time to care for one other and went out of their way to thank Eirik and also prayed for him. By the time they had reached the Thames and the gaffer thought it wise to wash his prisoners by having them thrown in, chaos gave way to Eirik's eventual escape. He swam like he never had before and, besides being preoccupied with the floundering monks, none of the other mercenaries were fit enough to give chase. He swam for his life and, once completely out of sight, he clambered onto the bank on the south side of the river. The weather was dry and he was determined, over the next few days, to improve his appearance. A small, discarded, shard of rusty metal became scissors, razor and comb and, except for a few minor scratches, he was already becoming unrecognisable. He planned to find work as soon as possible. He had learned long ago that the route to survival and general contentment was by accruing funds no matter how little. However, people naturally asked questions and he was, more than once, looked upon as a vagrant being asked by almost everyone if he was a beggar. He sustained this strategy for almost two weeks until he started to be concerned that word was getting around about him. In the evenings, he sheltered under an old, upturned boat which, for the greater part was useless as it was full of holes. Crestfallen, he sat awake one night listening to the boatmen call to one another. This told him that, with the right licence, you could practically work all hours on the river. If only I had a boat, he kept repeating to himself and eventually fell asleep. As the sun peeped through one of the rotting boards that was now the roof to his home, he thought for the very first time that he did, indeed, own a boat. Two weeks. That is what he said to himself. Two weeks and I'll have it fixed. Driftwood and waste timber was everywhere but he knew it would be impossible to get hold of any tools. And then, he had another useful idea. Every day, approximately two miles along the south bank, he would pass a yard where Scots pine trees were unloaded and, nearby, pitch was being extracted from them. I could die if I am caught stealing, he told himself but his common sense also informed him that he had few options as he was now losing weight and weakening rapidly. He had learned stealth, he was sharp, strong and quick and didn't want to lose any of those attributes. Although there was a very strict curfew in place, he decided that he would make the journey in the dark staying as close as he could to the bank. That night, he muddied himself from head to toe and, in manageable distances, almost crawled toward the dock in question.

It was so very dark and, even if he could have lit one, there was no way that he could use a torch. Added to that, was the realisation that there was no available bucket of tar that he could just pick up and run away with so he looked around. To be truthful, he was hardly looking at all, he could barely see but, he could make out the shape of, what seemed to be, downed tools, planks and barrels. By feeling around he realised that there was sufficient residue on all of these items to help him repair his boat and then, almost miraculously, he walked into a bucket and even better, some ragged ropes that he could use for caulking. His mission complete, and the bucket half full he made his way back, sleeping better than he had done in weeks. The next morning, he started a small fire and, piece by piece, sealed the smaller holes with rope and the tar. That very same piece of metal that he had been shaving with every day was used to hone stray pieces of wood and these would fill the gaps. Within days, he beheld the most ridiculous aquatic vessel ever known to man but it was his, and it was also his ticket back to normality.

That evening as the light was lost, he dragged it to the water's edge where the bank was most shallow and then threw it in. Delighted, he marvelled at his creation. Proud, he saw it rock back and forth. Panicking, he saw it start to sink! He jumped in to rescue it, only just managing to get it back onto the bank. This was a mild setback and there was absolutely no way that he was going to give up, so this became a game of trial and error until, within a week, his ship was afloat. He watched it at twilight hoping no one else could see. So proud was he that he even managed a laugh when realising that he had never thought about oars. This then would be his next project. Filled with positivity and enthusiasm, four days later he owned what reasonably passed as a passenger boat. Now he had to think through the next set of obstacles. Boatmen on the Thames belonged to a proud profession where rates were set by the crown and they had to hold and be able to show, a licence. He decided there and then that he would only work during the evening where, often, officials (including members of the Court) would travel between the city and Hampton Court Palace on business and, more often, pleasure. He knew this would be risky and thought to try his idea out the following evening. His first customer may well have been a lawyer who appeared cold and impatient at the lack of traffic. Eirik ably rowed over to him announcing that rates were "half price. No questions asked." He was amazed at how attractive this offer seemed to be. For the whole of the journey, the gentlemen said nothing and happily parted with his ha'penny. More astonishing was that he did not once mention the, very obvious leak or how inappropriate Eirik's general appearance was.

When Eirik wasn't rowing, he was spending his time fixing up the boat and ensuring that he was better fed. He told himself that he would spend two years or so in London and then would travel, ensuring that he gave Ryia Baker the traumatic news regarding her son. At least she would know what had happened to him and why he had never returned from Scarborough Fair. Content in his business and his greater plan he found himself most nights, illegally, navigating the Thames.

Bizarrely, one evening whilst waiting for custom, he heard a slight commotion at the other side of the river where the Tower was and thought to row nearer to see what was going on. There was practically no light at all but he could see two old men fumbling about at the top of the cradle tower. They were no more than shadows but he did not doubt that, from their silhouettes, they were monks. Perhaps some of those that I had travelled with, he presumed. Before he knew it, one of the daft buggers had hurled himself off the Tower and along a rope but disappeared somewhere around the vicinity of the Tower moat. Guards were now moving, shouting, and as they got closer, a second geriatric, hardly in control of his mobility, lunged off as well, only to find himself in dire straits. Eirik was sure that the monk had either hit the wall or was downed by some other fashion and he heard the splash as he met with the moat. Then, for a few moments, quiet. Had they both died? He asked himself. What on earth were they thinking of and how did they get away? Then, scrambling toward him was the first escapee and it was then that Eirik recognised him. It was Brother Bernard.

'Monk. Monk!' whispered Eirik and again, 'Monk, here.' He could see this shadowy face, eyes as if on stalks trying to see, so Eirik continued, 'it's me!' and again, 'it's me, Eirik.'

Bernard felt his facial features and was in no doubt that it was his saviour from the prison gang.

Eirik was incredibly happy to see this man and to help him escape but wasn't prepared for what Bernard was to impart. That very day, in the Tower, he had overheard a plan so diabolical that it would change completely the world in which they lived. Moreover, Bernard decided, in part, to share this with Eirik, enlisting his help. Eirik did not hesitate. This would now be his path, an opportunity to fight for a cause, have real purpose again and, ultimately, get to York.

Bernard's plan was, to say the least, complex. Nevertheless, Eirik was up for it and diligently followed his instructions to the letter. When, finally, in May 1541 he arrived in Lindisfarne to meet up with Bernard, and his newly-formed moral army, he was, instead, to witness Bernard's death. Now a very much changed Eirik, tall handsome and sporting the most fashionable attire, he set forth for York to speak with James's mother and to seek out Bernard's ally, Elspeth.

Arriving in York gave him a renewed sense of purpose and a determined start to a new chapter in his life. His only hope of finding the bakery was by looking for the stall on the market but this was completely fruitless, no one had heard of Ryia or, if they had, they weren't saying. Eventually, an older man selling basket-ware engaged with him.

'What you asking about her for?'

'I have a message for her sir, but it is private.'

'What message?' He said almost as if he didn't understand the word, private.

'It is for her ears only' he asserted and wondering why he was being so obstructive.

'She's at the church' he said bluntly and pointing in the direction of Holy Trinity.

Grateful, he walked into the church as the door was ajar only to find a priest there. He wasn't to know it, but this was Father Matthew

'Please forgive my intrusion Father, I was told that I would find Ryia Baker here.'

Father Matthew gave him a very suspicious look.

'Is this some kind of joke?' Said Father Matthew.

Eirik assured him that he was not joking and that he was at a loss as to why everyone was so secretive about this woman.

'Fine' said the priest 'come this way.'

Eirik immediately found himself outside again.

'There lad.' And he pointed to a humble gravestone. Been there almost two years. Died of a broken heart, I'd say.'

This is the one thing that he hadn't planned for. He never for one moment thought that she would be dead as well. The hundreds of times he had rehearsed that conversation, even in the darkest of his days. He simply just wanted to return a part of James to his mother. He wept which immediately made Father Matthew curious although no further questions were asked by either party.

He still had a mission and did not want to let Brother Bernard down. He, unwisely, asked after Elspeth and, in doing so, considered that this may have been the one and the same Elspeth that James had mentioned. However, once he had seen the scale of population in York he told himself that this was unlikely. However, his investigation put him near to the washhouse along Bootham bar and, on seeing a woman that fitted the description, he almost made a move but his nerves got the better of him. After all, he had lived for years where he hardly seen a woman let alone spoken to one. He then thought to eat and rest before going any further. A kind gentlemen suggested respectable lodgings nearby and Eirik thanked him. He did, however, find himself in the darkest of alleys, that the gentleman had referred to as the Shambles, and as described, found an even smaller ginnel that led to an ill-fitting door. Surely this can't be it? He asked himself and, as he turned to leave, the door was opened by a rotund, middle-aged woman bearing a candle.

'What can I do for you lad? Bun? Beer? Lodgings? Extra comforts? 'Ave them all of you want. All the same to me.'

She had grabbed his cuff and dragged him in at the same time as aggressively selling her wares. He could hardly get a word out nor escape. He then witnessed the smallest, dimly lit room and presumed that if he ate in there, he would be ill for months.

'Oh dear, I think I may…'

'Oh tush tush laddie. This way!'

And he was dragged as if a snared animal up a small flight of stairs which left him wondering how possibly this woman could manage to negotiate it. Before him was a cot with straw and little else. In an attempt at seeming alluring, she grinned but to poor Eirik, this translated into a deathly and terrifying, toothless grimace. However, all was not lost as years of hardship and conflict came to the fore to save this noble warrior.

'Ah, madam! A bed! Yes…yes. I'll just take the bed for the night? So tired. Yes…yes…long journey! Goodnight.'

And, as she opened her overactive gob in an effort to persuade him otherwise, he pushed the door shut jamming her tight in the stairwell. For almost ten minutes he could hear, from his side of the door, her grunts and groans as she attempted to free herself. What on God's name have I let myself in for? He asked himself. He then pictured the man that had recommended the lodgings presuming that he must still be laughing. Unortunately for Eirik, this wouldn't be the last that he would hear of Mrs Grindem.

Unsurprisingly, he didn't sleep and so decided to think through his plan, reminding himself of how important Brother Bernard's discovery was. His mind wandered to the priory at Lindisfarne then back to Staxton where he had been captured alongside James but in this version, James was embracing him as a brother would and repeating a singular phrase,

'Take mine as yours. Take mine as yours.'

He jumped up. He had been asleep. What did this mean? Yes, yes, he told himself, we made a pact there and then to share whatever we had, always. Why the devil has that come into my head? he thought and then realised that he still missed his lively, baker friend. Realising that it was not yet dawn, he creaked open a window that looked like it hadn't moved for decades. Whether he did this speedily or slowly, it made no difference, it still made a noise. So, he just went for it. He pushed as hard as he could only to find the little quarter light still in his hand, not attached to anything else so flung himself and what was left of the window out into the street. He walked back a few yards to the door and left more than enough money for the window repair as well as the bed bugs, strange smells and the cot that had fallen to pieces.

It was then that he decided to return to Holy Trinity Church. Father Matthew looked as if he was expecting him, greeting him like a long lost friend. They sat while he confided in him all that Bernard had said and Father Matthew reassured him that he had found the right people. That very morning, they were to have a meeting but he told Eirik that he could only introduce him at the right time. The priest left him with some food and beer promising to return. When he did, he asked Eirik to conceal himself, promising him that he would allow him to tell his tale once other matters were settled.

During the meeting, Father Matthew mentioned to Elspeth that a young man was seeking her out and she acknowledged that she had seen him hovering but questioned his intent. The priest assured everyone present that Eirik could be trusted and brought him into the group. Astonished, Elspeth approached him, pointing to his chest and, it was when she told him that he had an oak leaf birthmark there, that he had an out of body experience. For a second, he thought her mad and in the following second, he understood that she thought him to be James and, before he could think on it any more, she actually told him that his name was James. In a gush of honesty, he told her that it wasn't. He was not prepared for this. This girl was having an epiphany, her brother had returned. In all innocence he looked around but, almost immediately, everyone was convinced as the whole tale of the loss of their parents and James's adoption was unfurled. It would be almost impossible to say whether or not his deceit had clear intent or he simply went with the flow or even that it was connected to his prophetic dream but, at this juncture, he decided, inexorably, to fall into the role.

He looked over at Wynnfrith and started to feign 'W' sounds which led to him shouting out,

"Wi…Wil…Wynn. Wobbly Wynn. Wobbly Wynn!!"

This, of course, sealed the deal. He had no shortage whatsoever of information about James so became instantly very confident that he could maintain this guise. He looked over at the ostentatious, lardy man that was overseeing everything going on and deduced that this was Robert Hall the birth father of James. Robert was suppressing a child-like glee and it was only when Eirik thought on it that he realised that Robert was the only other person in the room that had all the information about James. Eirik, wisely, didn't even respond to inaccuracies like James being two years old when he was adopted, he mostly played dumb. Realising already that this was going to be a convoluted path, he chose to cascade all he knew about the Cataclysm which completely diverted the attention of all present. Although it was but a grunt, Bede was able to identify Eirik but, of course, he had only ever known him as Eirik.

Although Eirik's ill-intent was minimal he had, unwittingly, placed a mountain before him which he would be climbing daily for some months to come. Silas was, of course, right to be suspicious of this young man particularly when, at the battle of Shakespeare's farm, he was found to have no birthmark. And then, the bizarre gift from Thames Farrier as he almost died, branding a new oak leaf on his chest.

Added to that, of course, was that Elspeth soon knew. Seemingly, she knew everything and that included all the affairs and mistakes of the heart. As she lay dying she forgave him, not as people thought because he was Robert's secret son, but because he was a stranger who stood in her brother's shoes. Eirik wasn't to know it but the branded birthmark, gifted by Farrier, was in the wrong place and, eventually, Robert would trap him by suggesting it hadn't moved at all.

It would be fair to say that the Agents of the Word had in their midst for some time, an unknown element and this meant that his actions and intentions would be forever beyond their understanding.

3 the device

So disheartened was Robert that he decided to seek the counsel of Viscera. This had the distinct odour of desperation after all, who in their right mind would regard the local barber-surgeon as the York's new sage? However, he found himself in a mental state resembling a typhoon, where images from long past and present loomed to the fore and then recede again as they changed priority amongst his anxieties. However, prevailing overall, was the issue of his only son, Eirik. That day, one year earlier, when Elspeth, completely out of character, had identified her lost brother, meant more to him than Saul's Damascus vacation. The same evening, so giddy was he that his wife caught him dancing the length of Barley Hall which told her that something was afoot. Very much out of character, he told her what had happened and asked, bearing in mind that Ryia had passed away, that they not cast him out. Mrs Hall could have been forgiven for not giving Robert an immediate answer when he asked if bygones could now be bygones regarding his illegitimate son. After a week or so, Mrs Hall mellowed and conceded that none of the sins could be placed at the feet of this boy, curtly implying that they all belonged to Robert.

Admirably, after a month had passed, she prayed for the fortitude to be like a mother to him and she was as good as her word in this matter.

Of course, the fact that Robert was his father was a secret to everyone else until the revelations that followed Elspeth's death. Behind the scenes, Robert was constantly fussing and praising the boy. Bestowing manly hugs and gifting him with expensive clothes. Eirik, of course, felt very awkward. In this he did, indeed, have something in common with the Mayor as he was learning how a small lie birthed, just grew and grew until it almost had a will of its own. However, Eirik had made his bed and was content to fill James's shoes, acknowledging that it benefited others as well as himself. He also had to acknowledge that he had aroused suspicion, particularly in Silas. It was almost as if Silas knew that there was something disingenuous about Eirik, ironically, and finally, putting his doubts to one side once it was revealed that he was Robert's son.

So, at a time when everyone was hoping for a return to an even playing field, the perimeter was still constantly shifting. He never flinched when I said that the oak leaf brand was in the same place as his birthmark was, Robert said to himself. How would he not know that it was originally much higher up? Ah! It faded before he was old enough to notice, came an incredible but reassuring thought. But why, then, would he say that it was in the same place? Robert's head was starting to hurt and he needed to find someone who could reassure him that this boy, Eirik, was unquestionably his baby boy, James. As he arrived, Robert beckoned Viscera to come outside as he had no intention of experiencing the horrors of his inner sanctum.

'Why Lord Mayor! What can I do for you this fine day?'
Robert immediately blurted out what he wanted to say.
'Can a birthmark disappear?'
'Pardon?..' certain that he hadn't heard correctly.
'Birthmarks? You know? Can they disappear as you grow

older. C'mon man! You know what a bloody birthmark is! You're meant to be a man of medicine!'

Although this was possibly a great stretch of the imagination, it was reasonable to expect that Viscera might know something.

'Well…yes…yes they can just go away.'

'Good. Good and…well…err…do they ever move?'

'What?!' Exclaimed Viscera so loudly that he may well have said, are you stupid!

'You know. Move from one place to another as human flesh grows.'

Viscera laughed. He laughed so much, his head was right back leaving Robert staring at his Adam's apple. When Viscera recovered and became aware of the Mayor's expression, he was surprised to discover that he wasn't joking at all. Slightly embarrassed, Viscera wanted desperately to know why he would ask such a silly thing but Robert chose not to reply.

'No, Sir, that's not possible or, at least, I've never seen it happen' he concluded.

Robert wanted so much to keep asking over and over again until he received the correct answer but, crestfallen, thanked Viscera and wandered away completely unaware of Viscera venting forth thanks and compliments to the Mayor as he had had, so recently and frequently, been so kind to him.

You would have thought that, by now, the matter would have been at an end. Not so. The argument resumed in his head. It's something and nothing, he told himself. A minor detail which can be easily explained. I shall not think on it any more but, as much as he tried to think of happier things, the doubt came back and nested like mould in a neglected loaf of bread. Whether he liked it or not, he was now suspicious and there were to be times ahead when Eirik would be aware of it. The worst of it was that having so recently been uncovered as Eirik's real father, he could now

1543 The Disfiguration

tell no one of his dilemma. He stopped to ask God why one burden had been replaced with another. God told him that if he kept in contact with him more regularly, he would be happy to help him with absolutely anything.

Even though we had saved the King from almost certain assassination and found Elspeth's murderer, it was hard to find joy anywhere in York. Those events had taken a heavy toll on everyone and Wynnfrith, despite her best efforts, was feeling the loss of her sister as well as the loss of innocence thanks to the indiscretions of those around her. Her church, of course, was Holy Trinity, Goodramgate but since the thwarting of the Cataclysm, she was given the right to pass freely through the liberty gates that normally confined York Minster. Happily, she would sneak into the smallest of recesses to pray, ponder and reflect but, on this day, completely alone, she privately unfurled the documents that she had discovered in the washhouse. The Minster interior on this day was like a kaleidoscope. Shades and hues cast in a painterly manner upon the limestone pillars and the wooden carvings. It was a sanctuary where, apart from the cold, the weather never changed and where angels could be heard almost constantly in song. Silas would often comment that it was the most beautiful building in the world.

However, on this day, much of this bypassed Wynnfrith's sensibilities. She thought only of her sister and the documents she carried.

They were quite bulky and obviously quite new. She diligently separated the contents so that she could not be heard and moved them around until she found something that looked like an introduction and there, scratched out in Elspeth's hand, was a letter.

"To my most beloved and blessed sister. I leave you my heart and devoted spirit which speaks directly from the Lord."

Wynnfrith was already in tears and speaking back quietly to her sister taking care not to obscure the ink with her warm, sincere tears.

"I apologise, for I have interrupted your quest to clean our wonderful washhouse."

Wynn stifled a giggle, Elspeth knew that she would find the letters.

"I am you and you are I. Take my spirit and carry on my earthly life, dearest, for there always was much to do and there is still much to do."

At this point, Wynnfrith found herself muttering, mostly agreeing that more cleaning needed to be done, and as such, clearly misunderstanding Elspeth's intent. However, as she read on, she found Elspeth's message deep, incredibly personal and spiritual. She taught Wynn about Julian of Norwich and her claim to have been as one with God. As Elspeth had written, aware of her imminent death, she would stall and reprimand herself for waxing intellectual for she knew that to succeed, she would have to write in such a way that made sense to her sister. Wynnfrith was no dullard but she hadn't had the education that her sister had enjoyed. Already rambling about Julian, she had stopped and corrected herself in order to make her message straightforward.

"I too believe that we all have a direct relationship with God, dear sister. Julian stopped short of criticising the established church and, believe me, we still need it during these dark times but I am now persuaded of the ills of the old ways."

'What?!' Wynn said out loud, stifling herself instantly and coiling back into her cocoon. Surely she cannot have turned her back on the Catholic Faith? Wynn asked herself. Is this what she is saying? And so, she read on.

"I believe, that above all else we must try to find a peace, a middle way in this argument but those of the old persuasion need to move on."

Wynnfrith was taken aback and conflicted, not least as she could no longer reason this through with her sister.

1543 The Disfiguration

Wynnfrith realised that she was becoming agitated, even a little annoyed. Of all the things Elspeth could be saying, she is now rambling on about bloody nuns and religion? I need some advice about my wedding night, lady! she thought. Realising that frustration would gain her nought, she persisted. Whether Wynn liked it or not, Elspeth was accentuating her renewed beliefs. God is good. She knew this, was certain of it and she needed her sister to know it too.

"My dearest sister, I am so sorry but you must know that, still, all is not at an end. I pray as I write this, that you and the other Agents have managed to keep the King safe and free from harm."

'What?!' she inadvertently shouted, alarmed that Elspeth was now insinuating that there may be more danger ahead. A young priest hurried over.

'Maiden, is all well? Do you require prayer?'

'No Father, I am so sorry. I was stupidly reading aloud, it is time for me to go…'

The kind and concerned priest tried to engage with her but very quickly, and apologetically, she left the Minster bundling up this strange bunch of disparate documents. He stood watching her scarper, fascinated that a woman was reading what may have been Biblical text. Perhaps even in English, he mused. As she left the Minster, Wynnfrith realised that there was a weighty package amongst the documents, but she simply hadn't had the chance to examine it yet. As she limped, stumbled, dropped things and then scraped around in the wet earth to pick them up again, she grumbled.

'The thing I want more than anything is peace for you, Elspeth. I pray that you sit with the angels and you are happy basking in all that is good. But no! What do you give me? More bloody documents and secrets and hiding places and politics. Why! I've a mind to ditch them all in the river!'

As she said this she was only yards from the Ouse but

knew she would rather forget her sister's memory completely than ignore her wishes. Wynnfrith then turned and headed for the ruins of Saint Mary's Abbey. Here she would be secluded for, within the ruins, were neglected cloisters that kept out the rain. She was alone and spread out the bundle on the floor in front of her. Another single sheet had the word "Marcus" amongst the script and this, of course, piqued her curiosity. Wynnfrith had already come to terms with Marcus and had chastised herself for believing that he was responsible for the poisoning of Elspeth. And, she had been rude to him, often. Amongst the letters left behind immediately after her death, there was an instruction to everyone to "give that respect unto Marcus as if he had been my betrothed." Wynnfrith had no quarrel with this and found that the first part of this parchment said much the same. However, as she scanned it again, she saw the word "device" and it was written more than once.

"You must uncover the device given to me by Marcus. It is of the utmost importance at the highest level."

'Oh, Elspeth. Can you not just rest in peace? Please?' She muttered.

Wynnfrith felt that she had no choice. Even if she had decided to throw the bundle into the river, none of the ideas contained within it would have sunk with it, as they echoed around her innocent head repeatedly.

"You can speak plainly, but in private, to Marcus but only after you have constructed the device."

'Device? Device! What on earth does this all mean?!' She asked of the parchment in front of her. At the bottom of this declaration, it said,

"Keep everything, but ignore all for now except the package tied with a red ribbon."

Ah the package, she thought. That bloody thing that drops to the floor every time that I move. She carefully untied it, making sure that there was no one around. Layer upon layer was removed and, upon each layer, were directions. These too, had been tied together so that there was an order to them but it was what was at the centre that intrigued Wynnfrith. It was, to her, just a lump of metal about an inch square with no two sides being of the same shape. It was, irregular, to say the least. She perused the object, turned it around between her finger and thumb, yet again grumbling at how tasked her brain was already. She looked at the first sheet that had previously enveloped this piece of junk.

"There are three parts, this is the first. Do not look at the second sheet until you have the second part. Here is your clue to where it is: giggled and confined, the best days but also the last days."

'What?!! You bloody kidding!' Wynnfrith was now upright and shouting and all that she had so carefully carried around York was, yet again, on the floor. '

'Puzzles! God's teeth, Elspeth I can barely remember the Lord's Prayer! I can't…why have you?..' and, feeling quite alone and inadequate, she became increasingly upset.

She scrambled once again amongst the documents praying that somewhere it granted her permission to show them to someone else but, no, this was now her cross to bear. Wynnfrith then decided to make her way to the washhouse and hid, as best she could, the documents taking care to conceal that lump of incredibly uninteresting metal in her garments.

Every day, she wore around her waist a braided cord on which she hung her purse. This normally sat delicately on her left hip but, as she chose to put the annoying metal anomaly in it, it swung around to her front which further hampered her gait. As yet, she had still not come to terms with what she had read and, put simply, was now feeling sorry for herself having been bequeathed this, literal and metaphorical, heavy burden. She also realised that remembering conundrums did not come easily to her so she would have to keep referencing the documents frequently. Wynnfrith secured the bundle of letters between two beams in the washhouse and kept the notes that accompanied the so-called device about her person and, chose for the time being to completely forget about it all.

Later that day, she arrived unkempt and flustered at Barley Hall only to find Mrs Hall asking her husband, Robert, why he looked so depressed and he, in turn, was declining to answer. Silas was looking particularly gormless and could easily have been mistaken for one of the upright beams in the hallway except that he wobbled slightly now and again.

'What you doing?' asked Wynnfrith, uncharacteristically sharp.

'Nothing' he replied, taken aback at her attitude, then thought on it again and said 'well, I'm standing here and…well…yes…standing.'

'Give me strength!' muttered Wynnfrith. In contrast to Silas's catatonic state, she had now become incredibly animated.

'Why Wynn, whatever is the matter?' Asked Mrs Hall.

'Nothing…except…well…nothing. Just had a busy morning. Sorry!' and then she inadvertently spun around walking straight into a post, the one that wasn't her fiancé.

Clang! The metal object struck the wood, slicing a small slither off as it did.

'What on earth was that?' asked the Mayor and Wynnfrith blushed. What a crap job of pursuing this intrigue I'm doing, she thought. And then, all of a sudden, Mrs Hall's expression changed.

'Oh Wynnfrith, I am surprised!'

Both Silas and Wynnfrith's faces twisted with confusion, almost in unison.

'What's a good girl like you going to those lengths for?'

And, as she said it, it was clear that this also meant something to Robert. He raised one eyebrow, winked and gave Silas a knowing look, except Silas hadn't got a bloody clue what it was that Robert knew. This was now rapidly declining into a gurning competition.

1543 The Disfiguration

'Silas! Shame on you!' said Mrs Hall doing that thing where she would change from one person to another in a nanosecond.

'Poor girl, she can hardly walk as it is!'

Having completed numerous missions over the last couple of years, conversed with the King of the land and mixed with nobles, Silas sadly, still had the intellectual reflexes of a plank on the hull of the Mary Rose. So, instead of asking what they were on about, as anyone else would, he said,

'Oh, dear...I am so sorry to offend...why...'

Wynnfrith was now getting the gist of what was going on, so decided to save him.

'No. No Mrs Hall, entirely my own idea, now I don't have Elspeth to look after me and all...'

'None of my business' said Mrs Hall returning to her "there, there" voice.

'Anyway must hurry' said Wynn 'have to see Father Matthew today about the wedding.'

Before anyone knew it, Silas and Wynnfrith were out of the door and down the path heading for the church.

'What was?...' started Silas... 'was that my fault dear?'

Once around the corner, she stopped him.

'No, no, not at all my love, and I'm so sorry for being moody.'

'Then...what...'

'Mr and Mrs Hall thought I was wearing a chastity belt!' and then she giggled.

He bent forward to examine her braided belt.

'It's the same one you always wear, my dove.'

'Bless you, so it is' said Wynnfrith 'Silas...'

'Yes, dearest?'

'You won't ever change will you?'

He nodded not knowing whether, this too, was a trick question.

They then hurried to church and Wynnfrith couldn't stop

giggling to herself leaving Silas further bemused. Such a thing as chastity belts would never be a part of Silas's world and it was probably just as well. Wynn did her best to negotiate her movement with this weight constantly swinging around her waist, reprimanding Elspeth for her decision and looking upwards awaiting an apology.

Father Matthew was possibly the one priest in the world that would have been able to settle these two down and get them to focus on the wedding. After the events of the day, Wynnfrith was pleased to see him but, as soon as she set eyes on him, she saw him as a keeper of the old faith rather than her old ally, and recent friend, Father Matthew. Although she was undeniably fond of the ageing priest and, she knew him to be kind, he would be forever a Catholic. What would he think if he could see those letters? thought Wynnfrith. Again, she managed a little grumble at her sister as she wanted none of those inner conflicts.

The rehearsal was also stressful. Trying to get Silas to learn anything was a stretch but on this day he was so nervous that he was trembling. Wynnfrith put all her efforts into supporting him, both spiritually and physically, through this trauma. However, just as they were getting the hang of it, Robert walked into the church, stood and waited patiently until he could get their attention. Eventually, he said,

'All well Father?'

'Yes, Lord Mayor, I believe that we are at an end for today.'

'There's something I must ask and I think it only right to do it in the presence of the good priest here' he said looking as uncomfortable as he never had done.

Wynnfrith looked suspicious as both Silas and Father Matthew nodded their approval.

'I beg your patience as this is such a difficult subject.'

Robert was even more nervous than Silas, so they thought it best to just let him talk.

'Very recently. Well…you know…when the

mouse…very recently…. so many of my indiscretions and sins have been revealed for which I am ashamed and…wholeheartedly repent. Wynnfrith, you have been dear to me. Very dear to me…if I may say…as a…well…er…as a daughter. It only seems right, if you will give your blessing…of course…that I err…am as a father at the wedding.'

This wasn't a completely unexpected request but, especially as Wynn had had such a difficult day already, it could have been better timed and received. At first, there was silence. Silas didn't know what to make of it but was sure that it was none of his business. All three of them looked at Wynnfrith as she considered this and eventually, she looked up and asked,

'Well cousin, I have a question for you first. Do you ask because you believe it is your duty to ask, because of love for me, or is it guilt?'

Harsh as this was, it was incredibly important to Wynnfrith to see how he would respond to such scrutiny. Robert, having promised himself that every word he would utter for the rest of his days would be true, answered immediately.

'My dear. I ask because of my unquestionable love for you. The love a man can only have for a daughter but, yes it is also my duty and, yes, I am a guilty man too.'

Presuming that she would want some time to think this through, he turned to leave thanking all present.

'Of course. It is what I want, it is what Silas wants and it would please my sister too.'

It took a couple of minutes for Robert to digest this and, as he tried to inconspicuously wipe away a tear, he said,

'Then, you have made me a very happy man. I have one further request. Would the couple oblige me in taking a short walk?'

Wynnfrith's thoughts immediately warned her that there was to be more intrigue afoot but then she calmed herself

1543 The Disfiguration

and agreed that they would accompany Robert even though it was now getting late in the day. They walked south along Goodramgate and then toward Coppergate until they were at the end of an alley.

'You confuse me cousin. Why have you brought us to such a dark place?' said Wynnfrith.

As she said this and in wait of a response from Robert, she caught the expression on Silas's face. It was one of shock but then she also detected tears.

'What's going on?' she asked both Robert and Silas for the first time and sounding anxious.

'This is it' said Silas.

She knew what he meant immediately.

'This is Dead alley? Where you lived as a child with…Mary?

'Yes' he replied almost as a whisper.

This wasn't having the desired effect that Robert had envisioned. He stepped in front of them both so that he could catch their attention and break the confusion.

'Silas. My good Silas. You too, at times, have been as a son to me although…how I wish I had treated you better…Look…there at the end. That was your house?'

'Yes' said Silas 'the same as it was. The whole alley looks the same but I never, ever come here. I have a little shack that I access through the churchyard. You see?' He pointed toward the trees that confined the churchyard. 'All Saints beyond the overgrowth?'

'Yes, yes!' Said Robert now excited. 'Your shack is actually a lean-to, adjacent to your mother's old house.'

'Well…yes. I suppose, but there is no doorway between the two.'

'Look again' said Robert excitedly 'what do you see?'

'Oh' said Wynn 'it appears empty.'

'And why is it empty?!' blustered Robert who was now grinning and bursting with pride.

Nothing. Wynn and Silas looked at each other presuming

that the Mayor had gone mad, but they were becoming increasingly anxious as to why they were being quizzed.

'It's yours!' He bellowed.

Silas looked at him and before he could say, no it's not, Wynnfrith intervened,

'You mean you've bought it for us?'

'That I have and, before you get all upset about your current abode, Silas, we will have them both made into one, ideal home. A door through from one to the other! An ideal nest for you, your new wife and countless children!'

The conversation, yet again, stalled as the couple could not look at one other. The idea of children, and all that would come before that, frightened the bloody life out of them both.

Then, Silas wept. He said nothing but wept silently. Robert and Wynn comforted him.

'I will be forever in your debt, Lord Mayor. My mother would be so pleased and she thanks you too. I promise you that rent will never be late and I will deliver it personally every Thursday.'

'Silas' said Robert putting his arm so far round Silas's skinny frame that his hand almost ended up meeting his other shoulder 'it's yours, for all time. So it will be your children's too and their children's. You own it.'

Silas then, slowly, started to flap his arms, simply because he didn't know what else to do. And then he began slowly spinning around leaving the other two completely confused.

Whilst all this was going on, Wynnfrith kissed Robert on the cheek for his love and kindness. He would never have said that the house was hers and she would never have expected that. This was a society where property was property and property was owned by men. Remarkably, women were also owned by men and, although Silas would never subscribe to that model, he acknowledged that that was the way things were, and the establishment's interpretation of the faith did little to help, incredibly ironic when you think how important women were in the life of Jesus Christ.

Silas slowed down as a merry-go-round would and then, excitedly said,

'Can I see it?'

'Of course lad. You sure you are ready?'

'I think so…yes.'

Even that short amble from the end of Dead alley to the house, inspired so many thoughts within Silas that his brain was now a soup of memories and he was desperately trying to sieve out the horrors and keep the happy times to digest whenever he fancied. It was during this short journey that he realised, having spent most of his life alone, that now, he could not manage without the support of this amazing woman so he turned and smiled at her. So close to him was she now that she understood every syllable of that smile.

As they neared, Silas realised that Robert had gone to great lengths to smarten it up, he was mightily impressed and his heart glowed. Such a property, especially considering the extension that was currently Silas's home, was beyond any expectations that Wynnfrith could have ever had. She fell in love with it immediately but thought it wise not to say so. Silas said very little. He stared at every corner, every crevice, every beam. He could see Mary and little Silas everywhere and he took comfort in it. He was certain, then and there, that this would bring him closer to his mother. Uncannily, the three of them had entered, looked around, and left without saying a single word.

Once outside, Silas thanked Robert again who insisted that he wasn't to mention it, ever. Robert had also gained a little more respect from Wynnfrith as he had asked about walking her up the aisle before showing them the house and she was now content that he would have given it to them whatever her answer had been.

As the three of them turned to go their separate ways, Wynnfrith was left thinking that it had been one of the most bizarre days of her life and spent the whole night awake reflecting on it.

Conversations with her sister became confused with clandestine meetings and artefacts that took place in the house down Dead alley. She found herself sitting up trying as best she could to put it all into perspective not realising how difficult the next few months were going to be.

4 the wedding

As the weeks went by, the Halls and practically anyone who had been associated with the Agents of the Word, saw the wedding as a cure-all. The last twelve months or more had been difficult and, without question, everyone needed some healing. The cold weather was passing and they were all enjoying a pleasant April. The birds could again be heard in chorus and York itself looked as though God himself had smiled upon it once more and there was a joyous attitude as Easter came. Easter Sunday fell on 12th April in 1542 and almost everyone that had either been involved in the events surrounding the Cataclysm, the York murders, the threats to the King or all three, chose to celebrate in the Minster. As Father Matthew bathed in the aesthetic and spiritual glory of this architectural masterpiece, he was reminded of that day when all were congregated to witness the cold and wicked deception that became known as the Cataclysm. On this Easter day, he was happy, sure that all was as it should be and that included the natural sunlight that cascaded rainbows through the stained-glass east window. Even he considered the simplicity of the message of Christ on this Holy day. As warmth, light, music and prayer wrapped themselves around his very soul, he was in no doubt of the beauty and love that consolidated his faith. However, it was then that, he too, contemplated so much of the nonsense that was pedalled in the name of his Lord and wondered if it would ever go away.

He glanced at the early marigolds that festooned the Minster and then at the congregation. On this day, the liberty gates were open and everyone could worship. How many of these people are forgivably and understandably simple? he thought. He wasn't being unkind, he was considering how easy it was to scare and confuse them. What must the Reformation be like for those people who barely understand the Gospel? He pondered. It was only just being read in English for the first time. And, the greater flock would normally have conceded to anything as long as they were left in peace and did not have to constantly fear what followed death. In thinking such thoughts he pitied them, perpetually at the mercy of those in power. Surely it will all change for the better one day, he naïvely told himself, and then questioned whether some of the new ideas that accompanied Protestantism were seeping into his psyche.

Father Matthew then glanced to his left and saw Wynnfrith. Kneeling was both awkward and painful for her but dutifully she gave herself unto prayer. Silas, with half an eye, was looking at her, admiring this angel and then closed it again as he muttered thanks to God. More than anything, Father Matthew was absorbed by the peace that had descended on this astonishing space. He looked at the figure of Christ on the Cross and thought about his sacrifice. Nothing for himself thought Matthew. Everything for others, even his death. Oh how I wish I could be like him, he mulled and then realised that this also became a petition, a prayer. However, he conceded, that was the whole point. There was no one like Christ, no one like God. And it was unreasonable to expect any living being to match that perfection. Despite our failings and our sins, he told himself, we are all saved, all forgiven. Thoughtful and fulfilled, he stood to leave, very happy with both the Mass and his personal experience and pondered again as he left. If ever, he mused, ever, all of mankind could put others first, the world may well be perfect.

'Father. Father!'

'He turned to see Eirik, dressed in his finest, running after him.'

'My boy! What a morning! How are you?'

'Well Father could I…I need to ask you about a quite delicate matter…' said Eirik.

'Of course. Would you like to speak in private?'

'No, no, if I may walk with you?'

They walked side by side away from the Minster heading east toward Goodramgate.

'It is about the wedding.' Added Eirik sounding decidedly cautious.

'Ah! The wedding. A tonic for us all I believe.'

'Yes, yes Father. Well…you see…I was hoping…err…I thought I may have been asked to be Silas's man at the wedding and…'

'Mm…I see' interrupted the priest 'well, of course, it is entirely up to the groom and, I suppose the Mayor as well whilst he is so involved, but I would imagine that you would be the obvious choice. Has nothing been said?'

'Well no Father, that's the problem. I find myself hinting, but to no avail.'

'As I say, it should be their choice but I am happy to ask for you. Would that help?'

'Oh Father Matthew, I am very much indebted to you..'

'Not at all, young man. Give me a few days.'

Was Eirik now pushing his luck? Possibly, but it was more likely that, by this time, he did feel like he was a member of this family and his feelings for the couple were certainly real.

They parted company and, for a day or two, Father

Matthew thought nothing of it until he saw Robert again. Quite nonchalantly, the priest mentioned this burning matter and instantly realised that all was not well. He asked Robert what was troubling him but he just grunted no matter was said to him.

'It's about this birth-mark nonsense, isn't it? About time that was put to bed!' said Father Matthew.

Robert, not wanting to raise suspicion about Eirik, played it down as best he could.

'You see, Father, it's other people. Still have doubts. You understand, don't you?'

'Well' started Father Matthew 'I may have something that will put everyone's mind at rest.'

'Really?' said Robert, so excitedly that he startled the priest.

'On the very first day of his return, he was searching. He was searching for Ryia Baker!' He said as if he had just discovered fire and invented the wheel on the same day.

Robert grabbed the priest's shoulder and thanked him profusely. Then, he ran for the door but turned to do the same again. Later, when Father Matthew was to recount this tale, he swore that Robert had danced out of the churchyard. So, all was well. As far as everyone was concerned, Eirik was, once again, Robert's son although, in reality, he was a complete imposter. You could imagine that this may have stayed this way for good, except for one tiny detail. Elspeth knew. But, had she conveyed this information in any of her letters? No one would know until Wynnfrith had got to the bottom of her sister's weighty memoirs. It was just as well. After all the Agents had been through, they needed a wedding with no interruptions, issues or suspicions.

Silas happily accepted Eirik as his man at the wedding and they, along with the Halls, decided to encourage a large congregation. This was to be as much a celebration of the Agent's success as it was holy matrimony.

At six o clock in the morning on the day of the wedding,

Robert was tending to Silas's needs, meaning that, mostly, he was trying to calm him down. Silas was so highly animated that, at one point, Robert was practically chasing him around the room. And, all the while, he was venting forth his greatest anxieties. These were often disconnected, senseless and mostly incomprehensible.

'Oh…what if she?…have I got the?…oh, err…is it time? Shall we send someone to see if all is well with Wynnfrith?! Where is my?...perhaps we shouldn't…' and on it went. It was out of character for Robert to be so patient but every hope he had was resting on this union so he persisted in as calm a manner as he was able, realising that Silas was now managing to wind him up as well. Several times, Robert reminded him that Wynnfrith was alive and well in the upstairs room with Mrs Hall. In fact, you could hear them through the floorboards. At one point, Robert sat Silas down and tied his hands together, so desperate was he. This only resulted in every part of Silas moving except for his hands but at least it gave the Mayor some time to ready himself. Eventually, standing face to face with the strict instruction that he was not to move, Robert tightened every piece of the groom's clothing. Nothing, Robert had decided, was going to slip up, down, left or right or fall off completely on this day. He even tasked one of the maids with pinning Silas's shirt to his doublet, his doublet to his hose and so forth which was a commendable strategy until Silas announced that he needed the privy.

'I'm not going with you! Absolutely not and, if you return dishevelled, I will disown you! You hear?!' Robert, unsurprisingly, had lost it and this led to Silas reverting to his manic and broken state.

'Just go before you wet yourself!' shouted Robert.

Silas ran off.

'God help me!' screamed Robert.

'Everything alright down there?' said Mrs Hall sounding quite concerned.

1543 The Disfiguration

'Yes, dear. Everything as it should be.' He lied.

Robert then had almost ten minutes to compose himself, see the bigger picture, remind himself of the magnitude of the day's events and put all into perspective. He gave forth a long, slow breath which helped to relax him but before it was out, he stopped and held it again, his eyes now so big they nearly left their orbits for, before him, was a sight so worrying that even he could not have predicted it.

In the doorway stood Silas with a dozen pins in his hand, two others having already found their way to the floor, garments dishevelled, contorted, misplaced and looking as though they would have been happier on the floor alongside the pins.

'Sorry' he said as if he had just sneezed. Robert was speechless. Truly without words.

As luck would have it, Eirik walked in. Initially, he looked confused, trying to work out if Silas had done this as a last-minute jape on purpose and then, he remembered that this was Silas.

Eirik rushed over to Robert first and took him by the arm. As he led him out, he patted Robert as one would a small child, reassuring him that all was well.

'This is a job for the groom and his man! No need to bother you further Sir. Get yourself prepared for this great day!' and, before he knew it, Robert was in a chair in the Great Hall, in a trance.

In the meantime, Silas had done nothing, he stood, arms in the air, like a child who expected his mother to wash his armpits.

'There my good friend' said Eirik cheerily and then leaned in close to whisper 'and York's finest groom! We'll soon have you in tip-top shape!'

Silas, probably at his most useless, succumbed to his friend's offer of help and the next hour saw Eirik, more or less, dress him all over again. When he had finished he stood back to admire his handiwork.

'Every bit the gentleman! Why, thank God you are betrothed, for every woman in the city would want to claim you on this day!' he added laughing. As the laughter stopped he became aware that Silas was not laughing and neither was he at ease. Eirik noticed a slight tremble that very quickly turned into an uncontrollable shake.

'Oh Eirubble…Whatubble ab I gggoin..to doobble?'

Eirik put his arms around his friend and gripped him tight.

'I have you, Silas. I will keep you this way until you are at the altar. Put your faith in me.'

Surprisingly, this did help except that one of the maids then entered and it did all looked very odd. It looked even more strange as Eirik attempted to negotiate the walk from Barley Hall to Holy Trinity Church embracing a trembling beanpole. Nevertheless, that's what he did.

Affairs upstairs were only slightly better. Wynnfrith dithered, was certain that Silas must have made a mistake, was convinced that she would stumble and that people would make fun of her as she spoke.

'It's all a really silly idea!' she said almost shouting at Mrs Hall 'how do I get out of this?!'

It's a wonder that Mr and Mrs Hall were in any state to attend a wedding at all after so much fuss. Mrs Hall was so short of ideas that she told Wynn that Catherine Howard made less fuss going to the scaffold only for Wynnfrith to remind her that the Queen didn't have to remember any lines! So, she put all her efforts into trying to calm the girl. As Mrs Hall stood back to admire the bride she cried into her apron.

'Whatever is the matter?' said Wynnfrith looking horrified.

'It's just…oh…oooo….oh my…you look so beautiful…oooerrlub' and gave forth a terrifying howl.

The dress was, indeed, a spectacle. Mrs Hall, along with her maids had modified an older dress so that it was every bit the fashion. It was tightly fitted around the upper body with a wide, square neck and sleeves that became wider and billowed as they neared the wrist. It was in bright emerald green with matching headwear. Wynnfrith, calming somewhat, said that she felt like a Queen. However, it was very different from her daily attire and, particularly considering the problems she had walking, she decided to practice walking up and down the length of the upper hallway. Very soon, Mrs Hall called her back in.

'This may be a little difficult for you dear, but it is essential. She bent down and opened a large box and, within it, were the most beautiful pearls that were to be used to decorate her French hood and her neck, now naked to the public for the very first time.

'Oh, Mrs Hall. Thank you so much for your kindness but I could not wear your jewels, it just wouldn't be right.'

'Not mine, my dear. They are yours.'

In a second attempt, presuming that they were to be a gift, she again refused them but was abruptly stopped as Mrs Hall interrupted her.

'They were your mother's. Robert decided that the appropriate time for you to have them would be when one of you was married.'

Wynnfrith was dumbfounded. Not least that her mother had owned any jewels at all. Then her mind raced. Did Robert give them to her mother? Is Mrs Hall lying anyway?'

She stopped, realising how suspicious both recent and current events had made her, and then, she wept.

'Oh can't do that dear, spoil all our good work!' said Mrs Hall fussing over her.

She left Wynnfrith, briefly, upstairs for a while and as Mr and Mrs Hall confronted each other in the Great Hall, they agreed that they now looked as if they had just returned from battle. They allowed each other an embrace, perhaps the first one in years and then got themselves ready.

There had, for many reasons, been a considerable fuss

about this wedding. It represented so much to their circle of acquaintances and friends. It was certainly not essential that the couple rehearsed but, considering the totality of their issues with social anxiety and, many other anxieties as well, it seemed to have made sense. Three times, the priest had asked about the banns during Mass. Normally, as it would be for hundreds of years to come, this was no more than a formality. That was until someone did genuinely have an issue. Particularly when people, usually men, decided to travel a lot, it wasn't uncommon for them to have two wives living hundreds of miles apart. Added to that were objections raised solely on the unsuitability of a match. However, a marriage in 1542 was a contract made with God. As yet there wasn't any legal certification, a couple were married if they both declared it before their maker. It didn't always have to be in a church either, although it was usually wise to have a priest witness the agreement as well as some family members. This then would be a union for life and that included the obligation to procreate. The latter had already been mentioned more than once and always led to both Silas and his beloved metaphorically running for the hills. On one occasion, a very slowly spoken peasant, unknown to Father Matthew, took him to one side following the Mass.

'Father, I thought it ill-mannered to shout out, but I do have concerns about this union.'

The priest, a little taken off balance, made sure that they were out of earshot before any more was said.

'Then you must just state it, my child, before it is too late.'

'Well, everyone knows…' he said winking.

'Knows what?' quizzed Father Matthew.

'The man's a complete idiot. Thinks he's a duke or summat. Definitely too dim to have children.'

'You think that one needs to be clever to have offspring?'

'Oh yes!' he said assertively, 'everyone knows it. Look at me. Got eight!'

Father Matthew wanted to inform him that his argument

had fallen down already as there wasn't much going on between this man's ears either.

'I'm sorry, my son, being stupid does not prohibit a man from getting married. It may get in the way of him getting himself a woman but, in this case, that couldn't be further from the truth. The betrothal stands' and the priest sent him away with a flea in his ear.

On the day of the wedding, Bayard was the first to enter the church. Holy Trinity Church had, and still has, a large wooden door that doesn't look along the length of the aisle. As you walk in, you have to turn right to proceed to the altar. Bayard politely approached the priest as he was making preparations.

'Anything I can do to help Father?'

'Ah, Bayard! Good man! Looking smart today as well…'

'Happiest day of all Father, love these two as my own.'

'Well, why not usher people in and show them to their seats?' said Father Matthew proudly.

It was only recently that common churches had started to have benches which was something, ironically, Father Matthew could thank the Reformation for. They both looked at this magnificent concession which, although very basic and simple backless wooden seats, were certainly an attractive upgrade. Father Matthew would never know it in his lifetime but, eventually, the most elaborate box pews would be installed and remain unaltered for hundreds of years.

'These people wouldn't want old Bayard showing them in, Father..' he protested.

'Nonsense. Today is a time for bonds, reconciliation and love. The couple were quite concerned when they thought you may be leaving the city during May, so you need to be seen, my good fellow.'

Bayard was so touched by this that he employed his skills immediately. There was nothing to do, he just decided to buzz about as though there was. However, before he knew it, familiar faces were streaming in and Bayard was in his element showing deference to members of the congregation and directing them to a designated bench to ease any confusion. Mrs Fawkes and Edward walked in first as William Fawkes was duty-bound that day. Edward was beaming and had brought Peter along with him looking every bit as though they were brothers. As they sat, Mrs Fawkes kept hushing the boys who, seemingly, had some important, pending business.

'Why does no one talk of it?' said Edward.

'I really don't know. At first I thought it was just an adult thing but, now, it's almost as if nothing happened!'

'Hush' said Edward's mother.

'It seems so unfair. Unkind. We could all be dead if it wasn't for him. We may not even be sitting in this church today if it wasn't for him' added Edward.

'I think we all are meant to pretend it was made up. When I last mentioned it to the Mayor he told me I was not to speak of it or else people would think me mad.' said Peter.

'Hush' said Mrs Fawkes.

'I asked about' said Ed, now whispering 'Micklegate to my father, he said that I must forget the whole incident.'

'I have an idea' whispered Peter 'can you, meet me at the workshop tomorrow?'

Edward saw his mother's neck wind up one more time and so just winked an acknowledgement at his friend. Then, they all turned as a whole party arrived together having only landed from a long journey from Stratford upon Avon a few hours before. The whole Shakespeare family were there, John looking very weak after his ordeal and Abigail dressed in her finest. What a grand sight and, to top that, was the appearance of Maud, practically healed after being subjected to torture a year earlier. At this point, Father Matthew was unable to control his inquisitiveness. His neck stretched so much that it seemed to be at the rear of the church peering around the door. He needn't have concerned himself for

1543 The Disfiguration

there, looking magnificent, was Thomas Farrier who made sure to smile at the priest before acknowledging anyone else. The whole Stratford contingent, however, looked quite comical as they all tried to squeeze together onto one bench. Bayard, now an expert in crowd management, directed all the children to the bench behind, as the adults breathed out again and relaxed. Marcus walked in alone, now considered a friend and ally by all and many made an effort to stand and embrace him. He was, and certainly looked, taken aback and almost moved to tears. How powerful Elspeth's letters are, he told himself, like the woman herself. I am treated almost as her widower. What more could I ask for? he mused. Mrs Fawkes beckoned him to sit with the boys which slightly undermined the now seasoned usher but Bayard told himself that this is what he would have done anyway. Emotions were already delicate, especially once they had received all the guests from Stratford but tears would be shed properly for the first time when Scorge walked in, with a man on his arm that was limping. It was Bede. Who in their right mind would ask a man almost out of his mind to a wedding? The Agents, that's who. It was hard to tell whether he was aware of where he was or what he was experiencing but the very fact that he was included on this precious day, spoke volumes. A few more people who regularly worshipped at Holy Trinity joined and then the wedding party arrived all together. No nonsense about not seeing the bride or a groom, they had arrived and they were to be married. Eirik looked every bit the modern gentleman and, so dapper was he, that he could have passed unnoticed at Court on this day. Well, unnoticed by the men, that is. And, as much as it was possible, Silas had on a fitted outfit that included an amazing ruby red leather doublet and matching hat. Robert wore his chain of office which, soon, he would have to relinquish as all Mayors held office for just two years.

The ceremony was a religious one. This ritual was still a Mass and even the couple were expected to read or recite psalms. Mr and Mrs Hall volunteered to take this onerous task away from the couple as there was no doubt that it was going to be incredibly daunting for both Silas and Wynnfrith. After forty minutes or so, it was time for the ceremony which was, often, all too brief.

All was quiet, completely quiet, as the priest asked Wynnfrith to declare her intent. However, all that Wynnfrith could hear was her heart. Not only could she hear it she could feel it pumping out of her chest and presumed that everyone else could too. Her mouth was dry and nothing came out. Oh Lord, please help me through this. I so much want to just run out of the church, she prayed. But then she looked up at Silas. Any previous thoughts that she was falling to pieces did not compare to this pale, gibbering wreck that she beheld. So bad was he that his lips were wobbling and he was, unintentionally, mumbling and drooling a little. Wynnfrith told herself that she had to do something, rapidly, to save this wedding.

'I take thee, Silas Smith to be my husband and with this, I plight my troth' she confidently stated.

A sigh of relief could be heard throughout this little church although it was not, as yet, over. Wynnfrith detected amidst the dribble, a smile although, to everyone else, this seemed like constipation or worse. They waited. Wynnfrith waited. The priest waited. They waited even more and then, his mouth started to open. Silas sucked in the drool and began to speak.

'I'm your wife…and I will bite your froth'

Wynnfrith would recount, years later, that she was sure that all the blood drained from her body at this point. The congregation reacted in several ways. Those more astute remained silent, others gasped in horror but the two boys giggled. And they thought it was going to be boring.

As discreetly as he could, Father Matthew whispered to Silas.

'You have to say it. You won't be married otherwise.'

His second attempt was a complete false start. He just made a few bubbles in his dribble and then drew it back in again. The two boys laughed out loud at this, despite the reprimand of Mrs Fawkes. Again, the priest reminded him that there was no getting out of it. Eirik leaned in as close as he could to stabilise his friend and shielded his mouth from the congregation.

'I am Silas…your husband…it is my desire..'

Now, everyone's heads went down. Even Peter and Edward were embarrassed for him. Eirik whispered the words in Silas's ear. Both Wynnfrith and Eirik were very concerned that now, he may have bailed out completely

'Your husband and…my tight cloth!' he managed confidently and loudly. He smiled at his perceived success.

Edward Fawkes howled with laughter only to receive a sharp prod from his mother.

'Ouch!' shouted Edward.

'Again!' Said Eirik assertively and, as he opened his mouth one more, Eirik turned away from the congregation and said the words with him, more or less drowning out any noise that Silas would make.

'Will that do Father?' asked Eirik.

'Oh thank you, my child! I believe you have saved the day!' said a grateful Father Matthew.

Everyone cheered and Silas and Wynnfrith then made an awkward hash of trying to kiss one another but it didn't matter, it was over. Well, except for the important part that was to come later.

However, Silas and his bride had barely relaxed when the wedding was disrupted. A horse could be heard entering the churchyard. This did, of course, raise alarm bells and Robert was first to confront this stranger only to discover that this was a messenger sent by the King himself, all the way from Hampton Court Palace. Once sure of his credentials, the equerry marched to the altar sharing his intent with the priest and then held the whole congregation's attention as he read out a proclamation. With less than five minutes to relax, Silas was now on the verge of publicly shitting himself. Nothing short of a miracle had seen this wedding to its natural conclusion and now it was to be stopped. For both Silas and Wynnfrith, their natural response was to presume that they were both to be told that they were, after all, not worthy of matrimony. Too weak to protest, he stood frozen waiting for this next hammer to fall. However, as the citation burst forth from the messenger they were all to be left in a state of complete disbelief.

He read,

"You are this day, from the very moment of this proclamation a Knight of the realm and although, not of noble birth, you are to be known, henceforth as Lord Silas."

A few cheers and a trickle of applause came from the congregation but, for the greater part, people were dumbfounded. Robert thanked the equerry on behalf of Silas as he wasn't able to react in any meaningful way whatsoever. However, it was when he offered him, what he presumed to be a gift, that he again became animated. As he examined it he fought back tears for this was one of the fine quills manufactured by his dear mother that he had so recently gifted to the King. The King had awarded his Knighthood using the very same pen. Now completely oblivious to all around him, Silas's thoughts turned only to Henry who had thought to return Silas's kindness which said so much about the soul now hidden deep within the ailing and unpopular monarch. Then, as the equerry departed, loud cheers could be heard from all in attendance and, as the couple left the church, everyone followed them on the walk to Barley Hall. Without question, the next two hours were to be the finest times that these people had enjoyed in years. The feast was fit for, well, a Lord and Lady and, on this day, Robert had employed his musicians and, yes, there was dancing. Silas, half pissed, happy and now relaxed, decided to interpret a galliard as simply leaping up and down as a child would the very first time they attempted to dance. So merry was everyone else that they took no notice, with those most merry, making complete arseholes of themselves. These people deserved a celebration and at least a few hours where they weren't contemplating something sinister. And, just as they thought it couldn't get better, the musicians left signalling the time when the couple were to go to their new home, accompanied by all who attended the ceremony. They laughed, danced and skipped as they teased Silas and Wynnfrith along the short route, joined by citizens of York cheering them on. As they reached the front door, Father Matthew went up to the bed to bless it. Mrs Hall witnessed the blessing and then, it was all over. Silas and his bride stood in the living quarters of their house staring at each other without a clue as to what to do next. This sudden seclusion, as they could hear the cheering and singing slowly disappear, had them sobering very quickly.

'Well, what a day!' said Wynnfrith bravely breaking the silence.

'Oh yes…' said her husband.

And that was it. Well, for at least another fifty minutes. Fortunately, they had a chair each to sit on but, even that activity only lasted another half hour. Silas jumped up, frightening the bloody life out of Wynn.

'Must see Annie is alright!' he said, not even looking at her and proceeded to open the brand new door which connected the two properties, the old and the new. Content that he was happy, she tried to turn to domestic matters only to discover that he didn't return at all. After some time, she opened the adjoining door and peered around it. Silas was not only talking to Annie but asking for her help. This faithful horse that had negotiated marshes, mountains, streams, all weathers and had been with him on mission after mission, triumphed at the battle of Snitterton, was now was enlisted to tell her master what to do on his wedding night.

'I think we should retire soon, dear.' said Wynnfrith.

Silas jumped as if he had just been caught burgling.

'Oh…yes…why, of course…dear' and then he turned to her, smiled, and said 'well, my dove, I will bid you a good night' and pointed to his bed, the one he had slept in all his life.

Wynnfrith told herself that she would have to be patient, knowing that he meant no harm.

'We have a bed upstairs, Silas. It is intended for both of us.'

Immediately his breathing increased,

'Oh…I…err…I see. Mmm…a bed…yes..'

She took his arm, looking him in the eye to calm him.

'Wynnfrith …my dear…you know….I mean you no offence.'

He was now terrified that he would upset her. He was so very happy with how the day had turned out but there was nothing, nothing at all, within his skill set that would inform him of how to proceed on this evening. Wynn patiently guided him upstairs and instructed him to get undressed, promising to wait outside the room until he was ready. As you may imagine, the attire worn to bed was almost as far-reaching as day clothes. Silas had been gifted a new white nightgown and hat that covered practically everything apart from his nose. Wynnfrith had, almost exactly, the same attire except it fitted better and, whether it was intentional or not, when both were put together there wasn't much to tell between them except he was much taller and she had long raven black hair. Wisely, she had decided to disrobe in the lower room and then knocked to enter the bedroom. As the door opened he stood staring back at her looking as though someone had stuck a broom up his arse and painted an inane smile in his face. This, presumably, was Silas attempting to be enticing.

'To prayer?' said Wynn and this instantly put him at ease. They knelt, one at each side of the bed and Wynnfrith led them in prayer. This again was almost a first for Silas as he had prayed alone since his mother had died. When this was complete, Wynnfrith arranged herbs around the bed, and also within it, to help them sleep peacefully. They then found themselves sitting on their own side of the bed looking outward so that they, more or less, had their backs to one another. The silence. Poor Wynnfrith, completely short of ideas, just waited but, within ten minutes, she heard a soft thud and, as she turned around, she could see that Silas had keeled over, fortunately landing on the pillow. She covered him then tucked-in herself, placed her hand on his cheek and said.

'God bless you, husband' as he snored contentedly.

They both slept like fully fed babies, not even aware of the first bird song of the morning. But, this was not to last as, shortly before six o clock, there came a banging on their door, the like of which neither had heard before. Silas became like a spinning top, mumbling that he knew not where he was and tripping over everything in the bedroom. By the time he had come around, he saw that Wynnfrith had already opened the door only to find Father Matthew standing there.

'Well!!' he bellowed.

'Yes, Father?' responded Wynnfrith timidly.

He then looked directly at Silas who was rapidly depleting his restored calm and energy.

'Is all well?!' the priest said rather aggressively.

'Oh…yes Father slept really well!'

If this had been anyone else. Absolutely anyone else, you would have thought that they were winding him up. Thankfully, Father Matthew knew that this was going to be an uphill struggle so, again, he addressed Wynnfrith,

'You haven't, have you?'

Her head went down as she replied,

'No Father, not yet' and she wept quietly.

'Now, now child' he said still quite flustered 'no need to get so upset.' Then he stood back so he had both of them in his sight,

'You know you're still not married! We can't be having this! You offend the Lord!'

He slammed the door and marched off. Silas had never seen Father Matthew so agitated and, it wasn't that he hadn't got a clue as to what he was referring to, he just desperately needed help.

'Not to worry for now my love, not your fault' she said very calmly 'I will seek the advice of Mrs Hall this afternoon.'

This was very difficult for Wynnfrith. She knew what she was taking on, she would have to be friend, wife, mother, advisor and therapist for Silas as long as they were together but, at the same time, she was already wondering if his lack of interest was because of her. Less than a quarter of an hour later this seed had planted itself in her head, she was certain that she would be unattractive to any man and couldn't blame Silas for not wanting her. For both of them, this was not the happy first day that they imagined. Wynnfrith being Wynnfrith, in order to put his mind at rest, got dressed downstairs and went off to Barley Hall.

'Come in my dear' said Mrs Hall 'what on earth is all this then? Never heard the like!'

Although probably unintentional, Mrs Hall was also sounding very disappointed in her.

'You know you're not yet ma…'

'Yes, yes!' answered Wynn now losing patience.

'I'm sorry dear, you'll just have to take him in hand! There's nothing else for it.'

'I know, I know' said Wynnfrith 'I have spoken to him this morning.'

'No, no, dear. You'll have to take him in hand!' she said very slowly accentuating all the wrong words as far as Wynn was concerned.

Wynn froze. She thought she knew what Mrs Hall meant but it sounded so vulgar.

'Like leading a horse to water! You need to grab his reins

1543 The Disfiguration

first girl!'

Then, as Wynnfrith was checking every available exit, Mrs Hall asked one of the maids to bring a sausage from the kitchen. Both Mrs Hall's and Wynnfrith's eyes watered when they saw what she brought back so Mrs Hall sent her back into the kitchen with a flea in her ear,

'You must be joking, go back! One of those little ones will be fine…'

Sometime later, Silas would recount to Wynnfrith that horrendous day when he had had to be locked in with Viscera and witness an embalming. She told him, in return, that it was very similar to the experience of the sausage and Mrs Hall.

So, fortunately, the second night was different. Little was said but when Wynnfrith did speak she was much more assertive. Well, she tried to be anyway.

As the knock came the following morning, Silas rushed to the door.

'Well, have y…' started the priest.

'Yes!!…oh yes…yes Father…oh yes!…yes…oh yes…oh yes…yes' said Silas.

Father Matthew was almost back at the entrance to Dead alley before he had stopped saying it.

Things would continue to be uncomfortable for this couple for some time, as they both believed the other deserving of so much more. Wynnfrith, in particular, knew that she loved him partly because she could see herself, her frailties and her suffering, in him. As for the new title, Silas was now grown up enough to know that it didn't matter anymore whether he was a Knight or not but felt happy for his mother. As he didn't own land, he had the added problem of being a Lord of nowhere and nothing. He couldn't say he was Lord Silas of York because he wasn't so, he understood along with others, very quickly, that it didn't have a lot of use except that, if he ever did want to call himself Lord and call Wynnfrith Lady, he could do. And, he would be very content supporting the King in battle, as Knight's do. Well, that's what he said but didn't know at the time that he would have to one day soon.

Simply because it represented so much more than a couple coming together, people would talk of that wedding for years to come and it was, in many ways, a milestone in the fortunes of the Agents of the Word.

5 the future

I had absolutely no idea how long I had been convalescing for. Despite uncountable issues with our techniques, public pressure, opinion and also my general health, I was looked after and, mostly, was left to my own devices at home. Physically, I was now much stronger, had returned to writing and had almost completed the report on my most recent mission. I cannot lie, for every hour I spent excited, certain that I had accessed the sixteenth century as well as people and incidents that had never been recorded or known of, I spent another three hours questioning the science, my sanity and even why I had got involved in all of this in the first place. However, I was, unquestionably, again Dr Nick Douglas. My voice was my voice and, thankfully, some of my manners had returned too. My wife, April, regularly indulged me as I recounted my tales of Hampton Court, of Elspeth and all my other friends but, every night as my head hit the pillow, I wondered whether she was just humouring me and whether it was all part of my recovery plan. If I were to trust my colleagues, there were now two certainties about what I had written in my report. Firstly, a document that, for the first time, mentioned some of those people whom I had held so dear and, amazingly, the discovery of a Micklegate mouse figure carved atop Micklegate Bar. But then again, I questioned this. I needed to authenticate those discoveries myself and I had to consider, as suggested by one of my colleagues that, unknowingly, I may have been aware of these before I had even started my mission. Although a respected historian, I was also meant to be a scientist. My record of events did not fare well during reading back and intense scrutiny. It was like a second rate quirky fiction written in the twenty-first century. A talking mouse? Details of the King on his stool? A Knight who wasn't a Knight? A bizarre travelling entertainer who was a complete stranger to the truth? And, yet, there was something very real about all those people and, I missed them. Yes, that was the one detail that I could not share with anyone. I was walking around with a large hole in my gut. I so wanted to see them again but, at the same time, had no desire to get back into that forsaken machine. Now, there was mounting pressure for me to present my findings. The general public, particularly the nerds, were very excited to hear details of the Cataclysm. Or, were they again, throwing me a fish? Perhaps there wasn't any public interest. Paranoia, a known symptom of our missions was now also a regular companion.

In less than a week's time, I would have to attend a professional meeting at the institute, my first since returning. I was terrified. I could say with certainty that the cocky historian of a year ago was gone. Whether imagined or not, my experience had changed me for good. Added to this was the strain of my previous mission, the one we never talk about. The one that I do not wish to talk about now despite the pressure. It was, to the say the least, far too ambitious for where we were in terms of our progress. My biggest concern was this: I was certain of many things that, when recounted, seemed ridiculous. Having said that, I would have to discuss

1543 The Disfiguration

those topics at the meeting and I was dreading it.

One week later, April accompanied me via shuttle to the institute, everything now seeming so unfamiliar. The institute itself was daunting, reminding me that I was, at that time, but a shadow of my former self. By my request, I did not want any celebrations or fuss as I still needed space, time to think. To put this in perspective, I was on the brink of becoming the Neil Armstrong of our age and looking back, it seemed to me that he never had a moment's peace since he set foot back on earth. Like him, I craved the research and the missions but nothing else. Having said that, I was sure I would not return again to the 'past' under any circumstances.

I was even aware of the impending insecurity as April left me. Constance had been told to greet me in reception which eased the blow somewhat and her cheery, positive, character did help to get me through the door. Over twenty people! What were they thinking of? This was meant to be a low-level, initial debriefing. However, meekly, I sat down and tried my best to adopt the usual social graces. There was a lot of preamble about what the mission was, why it was attempted, where we were up to with the technology, and so forth. As the monotonous drone became unbearable, my mind drifted back to the humble origins of our institute. Technologically, in a nutshell, all this had started with the developments made by the Brunestein brothers over eighty years ago who, although obsessed by quantum mechanics and technology for most of their lives, also came up with the almost ridiculous notion that, coupled with virtual reality technology, mankind may be able to access events long past. This, of course, was met with a great degree of suspicion as, quite sensibly, even experts believed that the past had already been and gone for good. However, Einstein, Hawking and Carpentier would have, and did, disagree. After seven years or so, the brothers offered the world a brief image of Victorian society using their contraption which, of course, was laughed at. Why? Well, everyone presumed this simply to be bogus, just old film footage as the quality was that poor. And, even if they were telling the truth, what use would it have been as we already had old footage, the cynics would say. The scepticism was understandable as it was seemingly a ridiculous idea and the streaming they offered was sometimes so poor that, truthfully, you could have been looking at anything. As they were not historians, however, their thinking at the outset was too ambitious and too commercial. It seemed that, particularly as the results were so dismal, that the general public would very quickly lose interest.

In the first decade of the twenty second century, the study of history became as scientific as it ever had been, professionals striving to offer the public a version of events past that was as accurate as possible. As an institution, The Society of Historical Analytics was well respected and, by this time, it was also an international organisation. It had no interest whatsoever in the ramblings of the Brunestein brothers. That was, however, as long as the brothers were keeping their developments secret. It was during this relatively quiet time, however, that their ambitions changed. Rather than trying to produce streamed and channelled images of the past, they tasked themselves with the consideration that one person may, for a period, be submerged in times and events thought gone forever. To say the least, it was considered dangerous and reckless and it was very likely that it was. In a time when animal testing was long gone and neither was anyone going to get excited about being a test pilot, we were still unsure as to how they evolved their initiatives. We were very much in the dark as to how the first versions of this came about although there is little doubt that human guinea pigs must have been involved. It's hard to imagine what they must have gone through in those early days, forty years ago, bearing in mind that I, a seasoned pilot, was still suffering from the effects of the process years later. Added to that, was the uncertainty of what those people were actually experiencing. If you accept that they really were,

1543 The Disfiguration

virtually, part of past era, they had no knowledge of how to interpret what they saw and heard. The reality is, for example, that fourteenth-century language would be completely alien to anyone living in my time unless they had prior knowledge. Reports of a whole array of mental health problems ensued and ethically and legally the Brunesteins were soon in a lot of trouble. Nevertheless, there was no doubt that they were onto something and, give them their due, like us, they always maintained that there is no such thing as time travel.

'Are you ok to start Nick?'

I was miles away, or years away depending on how you wanted to interpret what I was feeling.

'Mmm, yes, of course.'

There was a lot of ramble about why the mission was set up in the first place. Much of it was a repetition to me but then I realised that something being said, suddenly made sense.

'Hang on, hang on. At the start of the mission, I had nothing to work with but one word. Cataclysm, and, if my experiences are genuine, this was a real and imminent threat in 1541. So what prompted the mission?'

At least six or seven of those present turned their heads as if to look for some affirmation of how to proceed.

'It was based on two documents that had been discovered within five years of one another, Nick. One is a, sort of, memoir from, we think, around 1560 and the word, Cataclysm, also appears in one of the later letters of Henry around 1556. You weren't told because, as you know, we are still testing the complete efficiency of Magna Carta. Didn't want to put ideas in your head.'

Of course, Magna Carta. Ultimately, this would be what the Brunestein brothers would be remembered for. I drifted again, momentarily. I believed Magna Carta still to be quite crude technology but designed to keep its host sustained whilst all normal senses are removed. Initially, the idea around it was to ensure that the 'pilot' concentrated fully on the stream. By the time Magna Carta was first tested, the limits of human endurance had almost been completely covered. People in isolation for months preparing for the first Mars missions as well as long induced sleep practise to better understand the dream state and human psychology. So, there was nothing particularly sinister about the one-person pod that became known as Magna Carta. Within months, the licensed test pilots reported wandering Roman streets but without any self-awareness and, sadly, no evidence to prove it.

'You ok Nick?' asked Constance.

'Yes yes,' I said turning to her 'my apologies everyone, not sure that I have yet acclimatised to being back.'

One or two members of the board seemed to wince at my turn of phrase. Technically, I hadn't been anywhere.

'Your report is extensive, detailed and, dare I say, entertaining, so you can see the problem we have Dr Douglas?'

'No.'

'We are in danger if we release this to the public. For instance, take that Silese?...

'Silas.'

'Yes, Silas, your village idiot would become more famous than Queen Victoria!'

There were a few sniggers around the room.

'But surely that's the point?!...and he's not an idiot!' I was now out of my chair 'if Silas Smith helped to save the King's life then he is absolutely a significant person historically and, have we forgotten?!' I realised I was now angry 'have we forgotten that we wanted to learn about those who normally do not get a mention in popular histories!... You conceited bastards! Can't you remember anything?!'

What? Had I just said that? Constance was in stitches but this was not received well by the others. I did, of course, apologise immediately.

'Seems as though the mouse is still with us Doctor? And

that, I suppose, in itself gives some credence to your account. Also Nick...' he said softening a little 'the animal avatar thing is not uncommon. We are just concerned about how we now present this.'

'I assure you that every detail that I have written was, as far as my judgement informs me, exactly as it happened. I either experienced it or, it was told to me by one of the other people involved. The only question that remains is whether my experiences were real or not and, surely, that has to be down to the technology.'

That was and had always been, the problem. The litmus test for the efficacy of Magna Carta was to see if people's 'past' experiences matched known facts. This soon went out of the window when, seemingly, it was clear that we knew very little anyway. Contradictions and alternate histories seemed to be common which further questioned the work of the Brunestein brothers. My view? It is possibly the greatest technological invention to date and, yes, it works. However, as only the pilot experiences anything, the rest of the world has to rely completely on his or her account. And, yes, the avatar doesn't, as yet, work properly (hence the mouse) but I was certain that this would improve given time.

'There is so much more detail in your report than anything we have heard before Nick' said another member of the board 'and I'm personally not sure that you had recovered fully from your previous mission.'

There was suddenly an atmosphere as my previous mission was rarely mentioned and the findings never published. He was also right. Unless you had lived it, the mix was powerful. For a time, well, virtual time, I was completely absorbed in that other world. So much so, I was entirely sentient as that other character. This was where my fear of returning to a virtual sixteenth century came from. I was convinced that, if I was to go back again, I would never return and, in reality, that surely meant death for Nick Douglas.

1543 The Disfiguration

'Listen' I said 'if it helps, I'm not entirely sure of my own mind. Once I am fully immersed, there is absolutely no doubt that I am as much there as I am, here, now. But, that could be said of a dream, couldn't it? However, we have some corroborating evidence, perhaps we just need to find more. What about the mouse? The mouse statue on top of Micklegate Bar?'

'I believe that we will find much to support your findings and…' he looked around for approval 'we are quite satisfied that this is the most successful mission to date. However, we are left wondering why you believed that you were interacting with these characters, why they could see and talk to you.

'So, is that the problem?' I asked, now tired.

'There's more.'

'What do you mean…more?'

'Ok. Well, there's little surprise that the likes of Seymour and Wriothesley and others wanted to secure a Protestant throne once Henry died and…there's little doubt that there were many who wished to expedite the King's death but, we believe, there was a greater, extensive, plot of which we currently have only a few details.

'Fine. But I'm not returning.'

'Please be patient Nick. Of course, of course, and, we aren't short of pilots but, as yet, we have no way of ascertaining the significance of each avatar. Why a mouse? Someone clearly thought there was, at least a fable of an aproned mouse in York but was this you? If so, what were you doing in the recorded past?!'

'I don't have the answers and…I feel so tired' I looked up and remembered something, 'ok, how did you know that, by putting April in the system, that she would appear as a mouse?'

'We didn't. We didn't know what would happen. She recalls seeing you exactly as you are now and imparting a brief message. Following medical advice, she was in there no longer than fifteen minutes.'

1543 The Disfiguration

Now I was really confused. I was paranoid, tired, socially anxious and was losing interest, I wanted no part in this.

'I'm not going back. You can either use the report, or not, but I'm not returning.'

Constance took my arm and whispered.

'Truth be told Nick, this has now got to be mankind's greatest development to date. There's no doubt it is working, everyone is just confused by the extent of the virtual reality.'

She glanced to the chairman and the desk screen illuminated simultaneously, on it appeared an antique document.

'Can you read that Nick?' He asked.

I stood up and then spent some time perusing the document and, eventually, slumped back into my chair. I did feel some sense of relief but I also felt like a trapped animal with no way out. And, in an instant, it had changed my mind.

'Ok' I sighed 'Ok I will consider this. However, this has to be done, not only on my terms but all my previous records of 1541 and 1542 are not to be published until it is all over.'

'There's no hurry for that, Nick. The fanatics can wait for your story. You have my word that people are working night and day on the technology and they have your report to hand. We all know that last time, for want of better words, you got stuck in there but we also need to ascertain whether part of that was your will. It is so important that you cooperate with all the medical staff and the science team. We envision no more than an hour or two in MC this time and then you can retire if that is your wish.'

'I will need some reassurances about that too. I am not to become a celebrity, I intend to write and nothing else.'

'Agreed' he replied, looking away and I was sure that, out of view, he had crossed his fingers.

What followed was a short, but unwelcome, interrogation by the Brunestein team. I acquiesced only so that I could get away. After this, I met with April again, her smile a welcome tonic for all this nonsense. I daydreamed on the journey back.

1543 The Disfiguration

I was questioning myself and, in doing so, everything became so clear once again. I could see York as it was in the sixteenth century. Even allowing for my imagination, everything was perfect. My version even allowed for the fact that the Barbicans and walls were hardly worn, being just a few hundred years old and each had a gatehouse and portcullis, long since collapsed and removed. I knew of buildings that once existed, now lost, but since my mission, have been confirmed to have once been there. I decided there and then that I was completely sane and everything happened as I remembered. Micklegate mouse, I muttered quietly to myself and then chuckled.

'You ok dear?' asked April 'must have been some ordeal?'

'Yes, thanks my love. Feel much better now.'

'As best you can, try to put all that behind you for now. We're going to have a day out!'

'Dear...thank you...but..'

'I won't have you becoming a recluse Nick and, I'm convinced you'll enjoy it. Nothing too taxing I promise.'

I was past arguing and, truth be told, in the frame of mind I was in, I didn't have a clue what was good for me. It wasn't a secret for long either. Within the hour I was relaxing on a steam train, truthfully a real treat after my isolation. It was a beautiful day and we enjoyed lunch as we travelled west. Whether April thought this a secret or not, I don't know, but I was sure of our destination. Modern synthetic replacements for coal and oil were amazing. I had the window open and could smell the bogus smoke as we gathered speed. The Royal Scot, still maintained and in service gracefully guided us into York station. As we arrived, we walked in through the now, very extensive, railway museum but once outside we were on foot. All vehicles had been banned from towns and cities during the first half of the twenty-first century. Everyone was now mobile to one degree or another, thanks to advancements in medicine, science and prosthetics so, regarding traffic, York was much as it was in the sixteenth century but without the horses and carts. I was happy to be there or at least, I thought I was. We meandered through Bootham Bar and before we knew it we were, once again, admiring the beauty of the Minster but that was when I could feel things becoming somewhat uncomfortable. I found myself pointing at the square between St Michael le Belfrey and the Minster.

'There' I said calmly 'that's where the travelling entertainer was when I first saw him.'

'Bayard?'

'Yes, yes. And there, the church which was as home to the Fawkes family and…and the Minster.' Unwittingly, I was becoming excited 'I was here. Absolutely was! I did not imagine this. He stuck a pin in me and I felt the pain! Pain! How could I feel pain, April? It doesn't make sense!'

She comforted me, although I had already made a fool of myself, people were staring. Social behaviour was, comparatively, quite restrained in my time so I stood out almost as much as Bayard himself.

'Truth is, dear' said April 'no one knows. I don't doubt what you say at all, but you must stop. Try to relax.'

Strangely, it was cathartic. I needed simply to be in York as it helped to ground me. As we ambled further and across the river, I knew that, naturally, we would be bound for Micklegate. This is when I became increasingly sensitive to the changes. Despite quite ingenious efforts, the magnesium limestone that was the foundation of medieval York was in a state of ill repair. The archway through Micklegate had eroded and expanded making it difficult to see where the original gate would have been, the extended barbican and portcullis long gone during the nineteenth century. All the same, I could still see familiar features that, so very recently, I had touched. Well, virtually at least. We were still inside the wall when April walked away from me. She went straight up to it and stuck her fingers in the mortar or, I should say, where the mortar should have been.

1543 The Disfiguration

'See the anomaly here Doc?' she asked teasing me.

I approached and could see that there was, clearly, a recess than ran along between the stones for about sixteen feet.

'Follow this all the way around and you very probably have a lean-to, outhouse or workshop.'

'Yes,' I said 'there's even some correlation between the dimensions you suggest and the discolouration on the limestone!' This was the exact spot where Godwin's workshop had stood.

I looked up. She was doing her best to support my mental state and, no, she wasn't humouring me, this was a reasonable archaeological presumption.

'Shall we?' she said, as we walked through the bar to the other side.

Once a good twenty to thirty feet beyond, April just nodded toward the castellation at the top of Micklegate Bar. Famously, three carved soldiers were atop the tower that were replaced in the twentieth century but there was also reliable evidence that the originals had been there since 1603.

'Well?' she said quite incisively.

'Oh yes!' I replied enthusiastically 'they were there. Looked slightly different but yes, they were probably there since the Middle Ages.'

She then prompted me to access my binocular app. Just to the right of the nearest statue was, unquestionably, the head of a stone mouse. I was guessing he was upright as, from where we stood, you could not see any more. A student at the institute had already confirmed this but, to see it myself, meant the world to me. There were now only two possibilities, either I did influence events past or, I have been unconsciously writing a story around events that had already happened. One thing was for sure, few people would be happy with either version. All investigations and missions would stop completely if it was thought that the 'past' could be tampered with (and there was no one on the planet, including me, who would think that possible) and neither would anybody be happy with billions being spent so that well-qualified individuals could enjoy psychotic episodes in a hi-tech coffin.

As we travelled home, I thanked April for her thoughtfulness as I had truthfully really enjoyed seeing York but it left me with a heavy heart still. Would a return convince me for good that I really am travelling to a different time or would it drive me insane? I asked myself. April quipped that, if all else failed, there may be plenty of people who may enjoy reading my stories which did, at least, leave me determined to yet again record every detail. As I closed my eyes, intending to put away this conundrum for which I had no answer, I became worried for Wynnfrith. Realising again, that this was both unreasonable and unhealthy, I chose to sleep only to dream of being, yet again, in the King's presence.

6 micklegate bar
May 1542

Wynnfrith found that she had developed a habit of muttering to herself when she was alone. It was Thursday and she was heading toward the market for some basic provisions. She looked at the bread stall, correcting herself for thinking, after all these years, that Ryia would be there when in fact she had been long dead.

'Can't imagine what you would want to bother yourself…bother me in fact!...with more nonsense after all we've been through. I've a good mind to let sleeping dogs lie. Bury your lump of metal where no one can find it! I'm a married woman now! Don't want to be keeping secrets from my husband!'

Wynnfrith had now spent over a month chastising her sister only to regret it immediately afterwards. Quite naturally, at a time when she had settled down and all danger and intrigue seemed far away, she was the only one left worrying. She kept wishing and praying that it would go away but found it incredibly difficult to disobey her sister. That first, unwelcome lump of metal was now concealed beneath a squeaky board in her bedroom. Their bedroom. The marital bedroom. And, this meant that she felt continuously guilty. She had no wish whatsoever to keep anything from Silas and neither did she want to burden him with this nonsense after all he had been through.

'Can I help you?'

'Mmm....oh yes!' said Wynn snapping out of her daydreams and then bought some bread but then wandered away from the market forgetting almost everything else. She was trying to remember Elspeth's riddle attracting all sorts of responses as she wandered back,

'Best of our days....refined and...worst of....oh bugger! What nonsense!'

She knew that the only way that she could tackle this was conundrum was to read it again. Once home, she checked that she was alone and went upstairs to remove the squeaky floorboard, again grumbling about the unacceptable scale of documents left by her sister. These now included everything that had been left at the washhouse by Elspeth. Scrambling through this, seemingly disorderly, collection of letters she read out loud,

'...giggled and confined, the best days but also the last days..' but she was immediately interrupted,

'Oh...hello my dear! Didn't know you had returned!' came a dopey voice from downstairs.

Hurriedly, she threw them all back into the chasm beneath their bedroom floor and stealthily replaced the board or, at least, that's what she thought she had done but had instead, created a racket which had Silas running up the stairs. Silas didn't do running upstairs. In fact, it would be reasonable to credit him with inventing falling upstairs, an almost improbable feat but something that he was somewhat accomplished at it. However, he seemed to manage it on almost every occasion and, this time, succeeded in missing out almost half a flight. Not for the first time, he landed, face down on the landing only to feel Wynnfrith fall on top of him as she was mid-escape. Her desperate attempt to secretly replace the papers overwrote her common-sense that told her that she could never, with the greatest will in the world, project herself upright and start running.

'Are you ok my dear?' they said simultaneously and then struggled to help one another up. The silver lining in this accidental cloud was that, for once, neither had an audience which also meant no ridicule so, within a minute, they were together, downstairs, benignly ignoring each other as if nothing had happened. However, Wynnfrith was not happy. She had been put in a very difficult situation and it made her uncomfortable. She also found it very hard not to keep reciting Elspeth's stupid rhyme aloud so, for the first time in her life, she decided to take up singing. That is, at least, what she told her husband who, as always, was completely away with the fairies and took no notice whatsoever.

She slowly returned upstairs to tidy the room when the words "giggled and confined" sang once again in her head. Of course, she thought, when Elspeth was confined to bed in that room at Barley Hall! How we laughed at Mr and Mrs Hall. She giggled at the very thought. The best of days but Elspeth's last days. Yes, she told herself, I must go to Barley Hall. Without any thought of construing some cunning, clandestine plan she just went, then returned to tell Silas that she was going out and limped out again as fast as she ever had to Barley Hall.

Her plan was utterly and completely crap. Elspeth might well have given her some pointers as to how to approach this posthumous puzzle but didn't. It was so bad that Wynnfrith knocked on the door and, as Mrs Hall answered, she just stared at her, not having thought of a reason, no matter how absurd, of why she was there.

'Oh, how lovely to see you, dear' said Mrs Hall 'come on in.'

Wynn was, at least, smart enough to make idle chatter and she was truly keen to see Mrs Hall so, eventually, mid-conversation, Wynnfrith said,

1543 The Disfiguration

'Oh Mrs Hall, I have just remembered. Do you remember that bonnet of Elspeth's that sat near the window…'

'Of course dear, I was wondering when you would come for it. Didn't want to mention it in case it was too soon, you know?'

'Oh yes, I understand' said Wynnfrith.

'I'll just go and collect it for you' offered the kind Mrs Hall.

'Oh…no…err…no don't trouble…' and, for the first time in a while, Wynnfrith had an idea. A quite good one to be fair.

'It would comfort me to see the room one last time…if that is alright?'

For a moment, Wynnfrith was worried that the glare she was receiving from Mrs Hall was one of disapproval.

'Well, there's a brave girl. Yes, best thing to do. Deal with things straight on. Get on with life!'

And, before she had finished, Wynnfrith was already halfway up the stairs, this time without falling. It took her another five minutes to work out that this curious object would be concealed so she then scrambled about like a madwoman. Although the cot was very low and almost touching the floor, she managed to get a hand underneath and there, atop the lateral beam was a lump of metal like the one she already had. She pulled it away realising that, yet again, there was a small piece of cloth attached to it and, yes, there was more writing on there. Wynnfrith then construed that the quickest way out of Barley Hall was to re-run the chastity belt scenario but then decided that this would raise eyebrows even further now that she was married. So, she put it on her head with the bonnet on top. Every step that she took downwards rocked the metal to one side and, of course, it eventually fell down the stairs along with the hat. Clung! It rested on the wooden boards, the hat uncannily falling on top of it in the hallway with Mrs Hall staring at it.

'Never knew it was so heavy my love' she said scratching

her head.

Wynnfrith scooped up the hat with the offending item inside and scarpered shouting,

'Thanks for everything. I'll see you soon!'

Mrs Hall watched, spellbound, as this loveable wobbly, woman, hand on head, wobbled even more than she normally did, certain that she was cursing as well.

The performance at the other end wasn't much better. In her mind, Wynnfrith was sure that she now had the hang of it. I'm not wobbling at all, she told herself. As she entered their marital home she greeted her husband with the rather formal but habitual kiss on the cheek whilst holding the bonnet tight to her head.

'Oh that must mean so much to you' said Silas looking at the bonnet 'I'm err...so pleased...pleased you have it, my love.'

She said or did nothing, she just stared at him but now, for some odd reason, she was holding her breath. She turned to negotiate the stairs but, as Silas watched his dear wife navigate those stairs, he was sure that she was drunk. As her left hip would swing out to negotiate each step, the hat would tilt dramatically to the right. This meant that she had to compensate by swinging her right leg to the left. If it wasn't for the certainty that he had seen Wynnfrith battle almost daily with difficult routes and objects, he was now worried that she might fall all the way down. Her efforts to keep the object secret at the same time as combating the stairs eventually became too much.

'Oh damn it!' she said 'damn it!! Oh, my dear Silas, I am so sorry!'

She slumped onto the fifth step and wept, resting the lump of metal and bonnet down. His natural inclination was to comfort her and he would have done so if it wasn't for the fact that he had already deduced what was wrong. He instantly ascertained that he could never make her happy, she simply couldn't cope another day living with an idiot like me, he told himself, and it has driven her to drink. My wife is so inebriated that she can no longer navigate the stairs or look me in the eye. Accepting of his fate, he went up to assist her only to find that she was looking straight at him with a lump of metal in her hand. Fortunately, Wynnfrith spoke before he ran, he presuming that this weapon was the means by which she would dispatch and replace him.

'It's all her fault!' She started 'I can't tell you how angry I am at her!'

Silas looked around. Nobody there. Thankfully she continued, for he had no thought to ask her who she was talking about.

'Elspeth! She still writes to me from beyond…and…and…I would never deceive you for the world…she made me…the barrel…keys…oh! I don't even understand myself…'

Although Silas could not make head nor tail of this, he was mightily relieved that his wife wasn't running away with the pub landlord after all. Gentlemanly, he guided her back into their living quarters and they talked. Wynnfrith was at ease in minutes and she relayed the whole tale.

'I know why you are so upset dear' said the new sage of York 'I've had to do so many things alone. It's a burden and this…is too big a burden for you. You must come to terms with what your sister has done as it must be important. Remember! We are Agents of the Word!.. so we will follow this trail wherever it leads.'

Silas had said this with such conviction that Wynn had to pinch herself but, all of a sudden, everything seemed to be alright again. They ate and then sat down together to look at the latest strange lump of iron and read the message attached to it. Well, at least Wynn did.

'Mayor's letterbox'

'Is that it?' said Silas.

'Yes, just says, Mayor's letterbox'.

'It will be where you used to exchange secret messages

with Robert at Holy Trinity Church.' Silas said in a very matter of fact way.

'Of course, it is!' she leapt up and kissed him 'the last piece will be there.'

Now that Silas was the wisest person in the kingdom, he suggested that they looked for it the following morning and his dutiful wife obeyed.

This part was easy. They went to visit Father Matthew to give thanks for their wedding. Silas would distract the priest whilst Wynnfrith moved the stone, took the offending object away, and then they would leave. On the way home, as much as they could, they danced, as this was the first scheme, for either of them, that had gone to plan except, perhaps, the part where they didn't realise that Father Matthew had a wry smile on his face as they left.

At home, Wynn showed her husband her under-the-floorboards stash. Now they had three very similar looking lumps of nothingness, except that they were all heavy. The final one, however, did have a ring on it, the type that you would find at one end of a key. This, if nothing else, gave them hope. Silas laid them out on the floorboards and simply glared at them. Presuming that, quite rightly, they would get no further by just looking, Wynn started to pick them up one at a time but neither did this reap any illuminating knowledge. She then tried putting two pieces in the palm of one hand. Clank! They were instantly adjoined. Magnets! They were magnetic and now, there was no pulling those two apart again. Silas took the, now extended, object off her and put them in his hand whilst picking up the third piece. Clung! Schernapp!! This, too, instantly found its place. Both of them were thinking that, yes, they now had one big lump of iron with a ring on the end of it, instead of three, but could not determine its use. They both played with it as a child might, pulling, tugging and turning it. However, it was only when Silas held it by the ring itself that pieces began to fall away. He almost dropped it as he was now panicking, presuming

1543 The Disfiguration

that it was broken.

'No…Silas, keep hold of the ring' instructed Wynnfrith and, as they watched and listened, pieces, ever decreasing in size, dropped away. It chinked and clunked and even whirred, frightening the bloody life out of them. Finally, it all stopped. Silas stood holding a key. It was beautifully crafted, engraved and gold in colour. Although they could not be sure what it was, it was intricately decorated.

'Aelfraed!' shouted Silas.

'Aelfraed? The man from Knapton?'

'Yes. These are similar to the pictures on his leg. Well…when he still had a leg…when..'

'Yes, I know, before he died.'

'Yes…cannons, ships. It was something like this.'

'It's quite beautiful' she said 'but I have no idea as to what we to do next, not without reading more of Elspeth's letters.'

'Then, until we know more, we will do just that my dear. And, we must keep this to ourselves.'

Silas had no idea how prophetic that statement was to become as, within hours, Robert had called a meeting of the Agents of the Word. This sent chills down the spines of everyone who received the invitation, partly because they presumed that there would be even more danger ahead but also because most of them weren't sure any more as to who was and who wasn't an Agent. At least two-thirds of them felt that the mouse should be mentioned once again as it was their understanding that his had been the greatest contribution but, alas, Micklegate mouse was not spoken of at all pushing him further back into people's memories and also sowing the seeds of doubt regarding his very existence.

Father Matthew thought the meeting premature. The previous meeting, at which Elspeth's murderer had been exposed, shook everyone to the core and the dark revelations left a nasty taste that had still travelled no further than most people's throats.

Robert had called everyone to Barley Hall and sat in

exactly the same seat as he had during the recent deliberations. He had put signs in front of two seats, one that read "Richard Shakespeare" and the other "Thomas Farrier" although they would not be in attendance. Eirik was sat to Robert's right and Father Matthew and Brother Bede to his left. William Fawkes sat opposite with Peter to his left and his son, Edward, to his right. Marcus was next to Edward and Bayard next to him. They sat patiently and, as all the doors were open, they immediately knew of the impending arrival of Silas and Wynnfrith by their slow and shuffling gait and constant chatter. Silas stopped and stood in the doorway of the Great Hall looking for his seat. As he did, everyone in the room stood and then knelt, almost simultaneously declaring, 'My Lord.'

Silas wasn't given to giggling but on this occasion, that is what he did.

'Oh…Ha Ha…a jest! "My Lord!" Thank you my servants!' he said attempting to join in with the joke but then Wynnfrith thought to prompt him.

'They aren't making fun of you.'

'What?'

'They're serious. You need to bid them rise.'

'Oh!...oh yes…rise…mm…yes…Haha…' and they did.

This left Silas shocked, mortified and compelled to say something immediately.

'My friends. My very dear friends. Please…I am just Silas, more humble than you could imagine.'

'I don't think he wants you to do that again' said Wynnfrith quite sheepishly 'ever!'

And they all laughed, possibly relieved that Silas was still, their Silas.

Robert made a quite formal speech where he summed up the events of the last couple of years, the part the Agents had played, the successes, the highs and the lows and eventually, he got to the point.

'I thought it prudent to call all those that are still with us to put an end to any confusion about our role. As I understand it, we are still duty-bound to our King. However, I think it highly unlikely that he will call on our support again and, even if he does, it will be some while from now. Therefore, as all other issues have been finalised, it is my suggestion that not only do we disband but that neither do we mention any of the aforesaid events.'

He paused for a moment and then looked at Silas.

'If that is acceptable to you?'

There was no doubt that, in deciding to favour Silas, Henry had changed all his friends' perception of him. As you'd expect, he looked around to see who Robert was talking to and eventually just agreed, not understanding at all why he had asked him. There was, unquestionably, a looming, dark atmosphere in Barley Hall. A sense of things valued coming to an end, good times lost, loved ones passed and even one, who was never to be mentioned, that had disappeared.

'However' continued Robert, attempting to once more raise spirits. 'We will still see each other regularly. There will be significant work…missions…for both my son and Silas. We are now, in many ways, a family!'

Even though it would have been a stretch to state that Marcus had been betrothed to Elspeth, he was, you could suppose, almost family which left only Bede, Bayard and Peter in the room that were not related to anyone. The Agents of the Word had, unwittingly, almost created a family of its own. No one quibbled, it made sense to everyone. Everyone except Silas and his wife, that is. How were they to tell Robert about the consequences of Elspeth's passion for writing? After all, the key, and all the other nonsense, may have had nothing to do with the King. Only Marcus knew something. Wynnfrith glanced over at him and he returned her look. Yes, she thought, he does know about this intrigue but she felt that this was not the forum in which to mention it. Boys being boys, Edward and Peter wanted assurances

1543 The Disfiguration

that they could carry on accessing the workshop and they weren't disappointed. If nothing else, this final gesture by the Mayor did seem to clear the air somewhat and most people left feeling as though they were still part of something bigger.

'Father, would it be permissible...?' asked Edward

'Yes, of course' said William Fawkes 'but be home by six, no later.'

So Edward and Peter rushed along Micklegate, not wasting one second and leaving the slowly rambling Agents behind them as, one by one, they left that meeting.

Once inside the workshop, Edward started to apologise about the limitations of his stone masonry. At first confused, all that Peter knew was that Edward had a surprise waiting for him and realised immediately that it must have been the lump covered in sackcloth on the bench.

'Well, go on then, I'm dying to see it!'

Edward whisked the cloth away and there, about one foot tall was an excellent carving of a mouse wearing an apron.

'Oh...that is just spectacular my friend. Are we allowed...?'

'Not bothered whether we are or not. You know don't you Peter? You know that, within weeks, they'll all say he never existed. So, I don't care. He's going up tonight!'

'What...what do you mean? Going up?'

'See this?'

'Yes' said Peter bewildered.

'This will make a cement. Help me with it.'

'Going up where?'

'Micklegate mouse will be placed where he belongs, atop Micklegate Bar!'

'Are you mad?! What about the heads? Why would you choose...there?!'

Edward took his friend by the arms. 'This is, was, his home. My dear friend has gone. I know not where, but he has gone and I want something permanent that says he was here.'

'But the heads?!'

'I'll do it' said Edward sure of himself 'up to you if you want to watch but I do need help with the cement, it hardens very quickly.'

'Of course' said Peter completely blown away by his friend's gall, sure that he wanted to be part of this but not sure which part.

They had one hour to complete their mission before Edward had to be home so they grabbed a knotted rope, a trowel, a baton of about eighteen inches long, the statuette and a small basin containing the cement. Before Peter could ask any questions, Edward was already scrambling onto the workshop roof so he followed. Peter was quite sensible in thinking that, not only were there dead people's heads on top of the Bar but also guards. However, seemingly, his friend had already thought of everything or, at least, that is the impression he gave. Once steady on the workshop roof, Edward tied the stick to the knotted rope and slung it upward to lasso one of the broad castellations along the perimeter wall. However, he was unpractised and practically hopeless at it. Realising that already he was making too much noise, Peter took it off him and succeeded at the first attempt. Edward looked at him incredulously.

'Years of casting nets and ropes my friend!' he whispered.

In seconds they were on the walkway that ran along the whole perimeter wall of York. Peter turned to his friend with a puzzled expression. In truth, neither of them knew where guards would be posted so they were now ridiculously exposed.

York was no longer the fortified town of the Middle Ages, built to keep those inside safe, and anyone else, out. The great wall that encircled the city had, at regular intervals, barbicans, each with its distinctive name. Generally speaking, each consisted of a tower that intersected the wall and an extended tunnel at the end of which, would have had a portcullis with another, secure gate below the tower itself. Many hundreds of years after its erection, visitors to the city would unknowingly wander in and out through the strange-sounding Monk Bar, Walmgate Bar, Bootham Bar, amongst others, without realising that they had breached a fortress. As weapons technology advanced, medieval cities were no longer impenetrable and the Tudors, when designing, building and constructing, chose to move well away from that tired castle mentality. However, in York, 1542, the structures were reliably still in place and the entrances were guarded but not with the same degree of paranoia as when they had first been built. Nevertheless, the two boys were taking a considerable risk on this late May evening. But, it is what boys do and have always done. They looked south over the wall and along the length of the tunnel that led to the portcullis with the tower to their left. As far as they could see, there was only one porky guard at the entrance with the portcullis up, sensibly presuming that there would be little traffic coming in or out as evening fell. Peter glanced to his left and squealed in horror which made Edward giggle and then they shushed one another. He would have done better not to even look at the heads on spikes, as from where they stood, they could now smell them as well. At this point, Peter in particular, was getting cold feet. There was no way that they could accomplish this without going up onto the tower wall itself and he certainly didn't fancy the company up there.

'Follow me' said Edward and they both skulked up the steps. Atop the tower they could see the miniature stone statues of soldiers but, crammed between them were heads.

'Where are we meant to put it?!' asked Peter now sounding angry and stressed.

'Don't worry I'll make space' answered Edward, not having a clue what to do next.

Edward, mouse statue in hand, pushed his arms upward to feel where there was a space between the rotting faces and tried to jam the mouse into it.

'Can't reach. You try and I'll give you a peg up' said

1543 The Disfiguration

Edward dropping down.

Unfortunately, as Peter zoomed skyward and Edward not knowing his own strength, he felt something move and, almost as if in slow motion, he watched as one of the heads cracked, lifted and then tumbled downward bouncing on its way. He ducked down, just as the guard looked up to see what the fuss was about. Luckily, it had landed on the roof of the tunnel beyond sight of the guard who now stood, hat off, scratching his head and telling himself that he was sure that there had been five heads up there earlier in the day.

'What's happening?!' asked Edward now straining under the weight of his heavier friend.

'Lost a head!'

'What?'

'One of the heads has gone' he grumbled, now losing patience.

'Stick the mouse in the space…no, no get your face down here.'

In years to come, Peter, especially as he was the elder of the two, would wonder why he followed such instruction without question but put it down to the stress of the situation.

As Peter tried as hard as he could to crane his neck back down toward his friend he was horrified to see that Edward was now smearing some of the smelly cement onto his face.

'Take the stick and hold it under your chin and then just put your head above the parapet. The guard won't know the difference.'

Mortified, Peter complied and, as he lined his head up against the others, he could see the guard jump backwards as if he had seen a ghost. To be sure, that expensive grammar school education hadn't been wasted on Edward Fawkes. The cement had been made from the same local limestone that had built the walls and the Minster of York and, as such, was yellow. By now Peter could not move any of his features and gawped, tongue out and cross-eyed, glowing in the dark, at the guard who was now on the verge of shitting himself whilst on duty. The guard ran in to alert his colleague but, no matter how much Peter wanted to pass on this information to his friend, he found that nothing around his mouth would move. He felt Edward pass him the bowl containing the remaining cement and, with his left hand, splurged it on the wall just about where he was holding the stick. He jammed the mouse statue on top and let himself fall the full distance down to the walkway.

'Well done brother!' said Edward patting his friend.

'Mmm…frrkg…bast…..!!' said Peter, which Edward presumed to be a Northumbrian celebratory chant.

As they fled, they could hear the guards arguing which gradually faded as they returned to the workshop. Little did they know at that point, but the mouse would remain there for thousands of years, although few would see it.

Using everything he had at his disposal and swinging his arms and feet frantically, Peter protested. This was to no avail as his friend was already running back toward the city shouting,

'Late! Thank you, Peter! See you on the morn…'

Peter spent two hours with his face soaked in water only coming up every so often for air worrying that his face may well be permanently disfigured. By the morning, some feeling in his face was returning but, as he walked across the river, he knew that all was not well by the glances and comments he was attracting. Two weeks later, he still looked somewhat jaundiced but had, at least, started speaking to Edward again.

The day after their church adventure, Silas thought it wise to bring up the issue of the keys again.

'You say Marcus has the other one?'

'Yes, dear' said Wynnfrith 'that's what Elspeth has said in her letters. He will understand what all this is about.'

'Then we must confide in him. Put an end to all this so that we may enjoy our peace at last.'

They wisely decided to wait until midday, knowing that Marcus would have been available as he always took a short break at that time.

'We mustn't sound suspicious. I fear I have already worried Marcus enough. Let's just see what's he knows.' said Wynnfrith

'Agreed.' And, hand in hand they made for the undercroft.

On arrival, they waited respectfully and patiently for someone to speak to.

'Scorge!' shouted Wynnfrith, happy to see a familiar face.

He rushed over, telling the couple that he was delighted to see them but then he knelt.

'Please, please' said Silas ' we're not doing any of that but, thank you.'

'If possible, we would like to talk with Marcus, just for a few moments, if that is possible.'

'Why, my lady, haven't you heard?'

'Heard what?'

'Marcus left the city yesterday with no word of whether he would ever return or not.'

7 the mary rose
1512

When Silas had first met Aelfraed on that cold day in Knapton, he was immediately impressed by the old veteran sporting an elaborately carved wooden leg. Happily, he would have spent the day listening to his stories as a child would for, although most people had heard of Henry's navy and knew all the names of his ships, it was almost impossible to access first-hand accounts of battle. However, the little information that he was able to cull from Aelfraed was all true.

To understand Aelfraed's memories and, indeed, the birth of the English navy as it was to become, one needs to grasp the astonishing leap in technology and ambition that took place in the sixteenth century. The basic principle behind a sea-faring vessel, historically the most dependable and popular form of transport, was that you had a hollowed-out piece (or pieces) of wood that would float and, ultimately, carry people and some other stuff. It is, therefore, easy to imagine a time, not that long before, that people would have laughed at the idea of populating it with ridiculously heavy cannons and shot. However, once the benefits of explosive technology were fully appreciated and desired, there followed a race to see how best it could be employed in all modes of warfare but the balance between speed, safety, and firepower were ill-balanced at sea. Nevertheless, by 1512, Henry had a sizeable fleet and he was determined that it would become the envy of the world. His wish came true, but not necessarily in his lifetime. Glorious in design and scale, those ships must have been a breath-taking sight when first put to sea and they were very soon to be put to the test. Boasting over six hundred tons and sporting a brand new addition, the gunport, the Mary Rose put its sister ship, The Peter Pomegranate in the shade. Unsurprisingly, Henry's pride was dependant completely on the wind and its very inconsiderate habit of being inconsistent. So, in addition to the swashbuckling, combatant heroic events of folklore, considerations of how to navigate foul weather and water were paramount. At an early age, Aelfraed could tell you exactly what a call of 'on a wind,' a 'bowline inboard' and 'sheets let fly' would mean. And, although expert at manipulating both rigging and sail, he was also adept with an anchor, the anchor being one of the ship's greatest assets. Where the wind was not favourable, the Mary Rose would regularly anchor down until circumstances changed.

By the 19th August 1512, St Matthews day, the crew of the Mary Rose had already successfully captured forty French ships and sacked some of their coastal towns. Aelfraed, barely fourteen years old, had gone from a regular ship's skivvy to supporting gunners engaged in cannon fire, in less than a month. Regarding the battle, he would tell you, honestly, many years later that he was completely terrified but assured of some safety as his role had been minimal, although he was worked almost around the clock. However, the 19th August brought with it possibly one of the crew's most intimate encounters to date. Successfully destroying the mainmast of their enemy, the Grand Louise, they were also close enough to receive close-range fire. A French cannonball ripped through the hull of the Mary Rose just to the left of one of the gun ports, not low enough to sink the ship but powerful enough to almost clear the gun deck and injure dozens. Such a shot on striking wood created a thousand splinters and shards. Some would kill instantly whilst others would permanently maim crew members and the noise and voluminous smoke from just one such incident could leave even a professional crew off balance for minutes. Although above deck, discipline and order remained, all Aelfraed would remember was mayhem. He would later recall that he felt the sheer chaos in both his blood and his bones as, at this point, he had no hearing, sight or feeling. That was until he became suddenly aware that he was being dragged by the leg along the length of what remained of the gun deck. Still numb, he was now suffering endless additional cuts, bruises and injuries from splintered decking as he was forcibly removed from it. The first person recognisable to him was the barber-surgeon, already bloodied and awaiting his next patient. Aelfraed was bewildered, completely confused as to why he was being thrown onto the table but, as he glanced down, he saw how reddened his leg was from the grip that had pulled him away from the melee and then into the cabin. Almost simultaneously, his hearing and sight returned. The blast of cannons, the creaking of the ship's timbers, voices, some shouting orders and others crying for help drowned out only by the overbearing and incessant screaming. However, the howling that overwhelmed his senses was an unpleasant mix of almost unbearable tinnitus and his own cries as he looked down at his other leg for the first time. From just below the knee, a bloodied stump of broken bone replaced what was so recently a fit and healthy boy's leg. Blood pumped from the gaping wound at such a rate that Aelfraed, amongst others, was astonished that he still lived. There was no discussion or preparation. It would even be fair to say that the barber-surgeon didn't even take time to look at the face of his patient. Those who assisted knew what to do and the boy's heart-breaking screams and protests did not affect them whatsoever. Not one of them even took the time to speak to him. At least, thought the surgeon, this would be speedier than the complete removal of the limb although he knew it was essential that the bone was removed before he could do anything else. A bloody belt applied almost without notice, served as a tourniquet and, in later years, Aelfraed would show this off as he proudly relayed this story. The saw was through that bone in fifteen strenuous strokes and, almost before it had struck the deck, what was left of his living leg was plunged into boiling tar. Aelfraed trembled, vomited, squealed and then passed out. He was thrown, ungraciously out of the way, into a corner alongside two other injured sailors. Tar, if available, was more useful than gold aboard a fighting ship. It was most reliable for repairs and, although unspeakably painful, was also a useful way of sealing a wound and reducing the risk of infection.

Soon after, the ship was setting sail for England again and many repairs took place whilst still on the journey. Prior to any voyage, the commanders had been given strict instructions not to return any ship looking as though the enemy had got the better of it so the work being carried out had a dual purpose, to repair and also to give the impression of not being seriously damaged or harmed.

As Aelfraed returned to his senses, he was wishing that he had died. Nothing in life was worth bearing that amount of pain, he told himself and seriously considered throwing himself overboard. Jack, one of the gunners, gave as much time as he was allowed to care for the boy, benevolently passing up on his full ration of brandy to help Aelfraed with the pain. Aelfraed would once comment that he thought God himself distilled brandy for it was the only respite he had found during the weeks following the battle. Jack also kindly fashioned a two-wheel trolley with the good intention of allowing the boy some mobility although it often led to involuntary excursions back and forth along the gun deck much to the chagrin of the other soldiers. Now, if you're thinking wheels as in round wheels, then you would be mistaken for one was almost square but it did, of sorts, move albeit offering a very bumpy ride. And, it's worth adding, the poor little bugger had no control over it whatsoever.

You may well call the crew sailors but it was a term that few were using as yet and each member of the crew saw themselves as essential to the voyage and everyone a proud man. Mariner was an oft used term but those aboard tended to refer to themselves, and each other, by what their function was. Gunners, soldiers, carpenters, cooks and the pilots were proud of their position as was the surgeon. As repairs took place and a warmer atmosphere settled on this swaying hulk, Aelfraed now almost certain to survive, became a plaything for the crew as he was pushed from one end of the deck to the other and, truth be told, between the bouts of agony, it offered him some light relief. Relying solely on brandy and, at times, losing all sense of reality, he told Jack that he would never wish to do anything else but sail on the Mary Rose. Knowing that this was practically impossible and deciding to spare the boy any further indignity, he kept to himself the reality that Aelfraed would never walk or work ever again. In total, two men had died and six were injured which, in terms of expected collateral was deemed to be reasonable. However, everyone on board knew that there were still challenging times ahead. Admiral Edward Howard, the well-respected commander of the ship, gathered his men to remind them of the dangers. Although they weren't to know it at the time, some of the waters around Britain were amongst the most dangerous in the world. A fact that kept Britain as a well-protected island but one that also threatened its own navy on every excursion. Although Howard was well practised in negotiating the difficult last lap to Dover, he knew that his return would also meet with interruptions. He withheld any detail that he may have been aware of from the crew but insisted that they would have a difficult journey ahead still and that they must all prepare for it.

As expected, with the cliffs of England barely in sight and the Mary Rose now separated from the rest of the fleet, a small ship ploughed its way slowly toward the Mary Rose. Once alongside, Edward took the message himself, completely unsurprised as to what was being asked of him. The course on which they were set would reveal the damage to the ship and the King's instructions were that "no Englishman should behold any weakness in our superior fleet." All well and good, except that the Admiral's orders were now to sail north, turn around 360 degrees and bypass Dover close enough for crowds to cheer but then to dock further along the coast. This meant it almost impossible to avoid the dreaded Goodwin sands that were to become known as England's underwater graveyard.

It was rumoured that, although the commander was always a good servant of the King, on this occasion, he quipped that 'His Grace must have suffered from temporary madness.' As the weather worsened and the ship's manifest was tossed from larboard to starboard, the recent repairs were speedily becoming undone. Then, Edward was seen praying on the forecastle, for providence was the only thing at this point that would stop them floundering on rocks or the banks. A gaping hole reappeared where the sheer force of the waves had overpowered the makeshift mended boards. Water started to flood in. In the retelling of this tale, Aelfraed would forever claim that he found himself hurtling toward the breach, involuntarily, and was certain that he would be projected through it, that being the end of him. The fifteen-yard journey from the cannon to this hole in the side seemed to take forever and, in that time, he, for whatever reason, decided to stick out his good leg which ended up protruding through the hole in the ship. His trolley then jammed up against the hull and his little body became a make-do plug, his chin on his chest shouting for help,

'Mmm…schtuck! Erlp!'

Jack later recalled that he didn't know whether to laugh or get down on his knees and give thanks for Aelfraed's squashed and deformed little body that was now adequately sealing the hole and possibly saving all their lives. The commander cursed as the limping ship with starboard (its pretty side) on show, was now used to entertain the waiting crowds.

Further south and in calmer and more dependable waters, the crew gathered to laugh. Yes, they laughed heartily at the boy jammed into the armature of their moving home. The more he squealed and begged them to get him out, and the more his face gradually disappeared up his own arse, the more they laughed. Finally, Jack himself took the weight of the lad and gently removed him from his new residence. Now above the waterline, there was no risk of a flood but his backside was as wet as a shark's lunch. Jack took hold of his trolley to still him and quietly reminded Aelfraed of God's wonders. Two legs and he would certainly have gone straight through, to which Aelfraed replied that if he had two legs, he wouldn't have bloody travelled at breakneck speed along the deck in the first place! For the very first time, Admiral Edward addressed the boy personally,

'In our maritime world, we have order. We have discipline and we observe hierarchy but, in the midst of danger, we are as one. Every man equally useful in defeating both enemy and sea. Be proud lad to be part of the King's service and to have kept the ship afloat with thy skinny arse.'

The laughter eventually died down and Aelfraed, dumbfounded, said nothing but Jack requested permission to speak.

'Sadly, sir, sailing is all he wishes to do with his life but I've told him that it's now at an end…'

'Ah!' said Edward almost before he finished speaking 'well, I'll tell you what lad. I'll make a deal with you, witnessed by all here. You get back on two legs and we'll find work for you. But no bloody silly trollies! Two legs.'

Aelfraed didn't understand this. Unsure as to how to grow a new one, he sought the advice of Jack who put his mind at rest. This was an age where, generally speaking, and barring a miracle, cripples remained cripples. That didn't mean that they could not or did not contribute to society but usually, it did mean that a limb lost was just that. Few people resorted to utilising artificial limbs but it wasn't unheard of. Jack promised to hew a crude stump for him but also told him that this route would be a very painful one.

Once home, the Mary Rose had a refit befitting its grandeur and, to show England's good people that all was well, the following March, a race was organised along the Kent coast in which she beat the Sovereign by a good half mile. However, Aelfraed was feeling a little left out in the cold. Still barely standing, he watched his beloved ship from a distance wondering if he would ever board her again. He would never forget the afternoon of that very day when he sat and made a bold choice. On the verge of accepting his lot and wallowing in pity, something told him that he had to fight for his dream and henceforth refused to unstrap his leg for any reason, bar having a wash.

In April of 1513, the fleet was once again set to challenge the French, with Admiral Howard's fiercest challenge being the men that were deserting at Southampton. However, eventually, he wrote to Wolsey saying that he believed them to 'be strong enough to take on the whole French fleet' but the wind, initially, was not favourable.

Aelfraed, eventually seeing his beloved Mary Rose sail away and particularly dismayed that anyone would want to desert, pondered the fate of himself and the ship. Self-assured that she would return covered in glory and that the commander, puffed up following the victory, would then seek him out and give him not only a position but a promotion. Excited, he exercised regularly and even took a job on a farm a few miles inland where he could adequately display his renewed if somewhat awkward mobility. It was on that very farm that news was delivered of the dramatic conflict in which the Mary Rose had found herself. Innocently, young Aelfraed listened excitedly as the tale developed, saying nothing until the visiting farmer said,

'The sunken ship!'

'What sunken ship?' asked the boy tentatively.

'Well...one of our own I believe. Don't think we came away too well lad and the worst is...the commander was killed, heroically boarding a French boat.!'

'Commander...are you sure they said, commander?'

'Oh yes, Lord Ted Howard. No more. But...they say he died a hero.'

Aelfraed, now numb, took a moment to examine his feelings. Was he upset that this kind and inspirational man had died or was it because his hopes of a life at sea had just disappeared?

The rest of the day was a blur. He worked as ten men would wondering if he would ever see beyond that farm ever again.

Every hour that he had ,when he wasn't working, had him inquiring about the whereabouts of the fleet which, even with the best will and the latest knowledge, was very hard to keep track off. The Mary Rose, still in one piece, along with fourteen other ships, had been used to carry troops as far as Newcastle to be utilised in the battle of Flodden field but, by and large, the Great War with France slowly fizzled out. The marriage of King Henry's sister to Louise X11 in 1514 calmed things for a while and, despite Aelfraed's anxious enquiries, few people had any facts about the Mary Rose except that she was static and enjoying long-overdue repairs and an upgrade. The reality was that, at this time, the ship was being stripped down with its future in question. He wasn't to know, but his beloved ship had been mothballed along the Thames. The Mary Rose, whilst not in use, was taken to pieces. All the cables, mast, fittings and her two boats were delivered to John Hopkins who, at that time, was controller of the King's ships. Guns, shot, cooking utensils and flags were looked after by John Bryarley who was the master and purser and, bows, arrows, gunpowder and pikes were taken by John Millet and Thomas Elderton. So, it was probably as well that Aelfraed knew nothing of this. As shocking and aggressive a policy this may have been, it was certainly preferable to her having been looted or left to rot.

As the years disappeared and Aelfraed's dream disappeared with them, he acclimatised to his agrarian position and mastered his stump. This was now his third. The sudden realisation that, as his leg grew, his stump would not, meant that he would have to find a suitable furniture cast-off or log to keep him mobile and upright. However, eventually, you would never know that he was hampered if you saw him walking from a distance. As a man of twenty-two years of age, he had forgotten about the ship except when he had a few drinks and told his tales of watery adventure. Nobody believed him but it passed the time and was certainly therapeutic for Aelfraed. He drank in an inn just one and a half miles from the farm, called "The Bull." The farming community was notoriously one in which outsiders were not welcome. They presumed that, as they were feeding the local population, they were therefore somewhat superior. It was just as well, as outsiders didn't tend to go anywhere near The Bull unless they were pilgrims or they were lost.

Now an adult and far from the drama of conflict, Aelfraed's head was the first to turn when, in late May 1520, a stranger confidently wandered in. And, it wasn't that the clientele were necessarily antagonistic, they just glared, and then completely ignored, any new face that appeared. Aelfraed turned back to his friends asking them where he was up to in the delivery of his old and repetitious maritime saga when he realised that the stranger was talking to the innkeeper. Unusually, the innkeeper laughed and then pointed. He was pointing directly at Aelfraed. Aelfraed stretched himself, as a beast would in preparation to devour its prey. Then, he stood. Thud, his stump made contact with the wooden boards and the rest of his body turned to join it. Aware of the man grinning, his hackles were up. His mouth was just about in motion, deciding to deliver his opinions on strangers, grinning and anything else that, on that day he may have taken some offence at. However, Aelfraed was stopped in his tracks as there, before him, was a face he had not seen in years and believed he would never see again. His bravado turned to uncertainty and then anxiety and he was sure that even his wooden leg started to wobble.

'Alfie!' shouted the man.

'Jack? Is that you Sir?'

'Well haven't you done a bloody good job of hiding yourself? You any idea how long I've been on your trail?!' and then he laughed.

Bewildered, the rest of the pub looked on, entertained, but unsure as to what this all meant.

'I've…err…I've been working on a farm' said Aelfraed almost apologetically. Jack thought to deliver some cunning quip about farmers but thought better of it as he looked around.

'If it's all the same to you, it might be as well if you and I talked in private. If that is agreeable to you?'

'Yes' answered Aelfraed, still nervous

They moved to a small table that seemed to be half in and half out of the inn. The sun shone on Jack's oval face transfixing his old friends glare as they talked.

'Well, I can barely recognise you, what happened to the lad?!' said Jack laughing.

'You saved my life. I'll never forget it. You were the only, one…'

'Now, now Alfie, lad. I've not come to have praises sung to me! Why the Heavens themselves would close for good. Haha!'

By this point, Aelfraed was almost speechless. The whole

1543 The Disfiguration

situation was completely surreal to him. Even he had started to believe that his stories were made up, but there, before him, was one of the main players in his tales, Jack hardly looking a day older.

'Why do you think I've spent so long seeking you out my young friend?'

'I really do not know. I hear that the navy is out of use…' he leant forward almost as if to check that this was really his Jack 'I never thought I would set eyes on you again. Years ago, when the Admiral died, I gave up hope of his promise. Truth be told, Jack, I was devastated.'

'You know the bulldog, his brother, took his place?' whispered Jack

'Yes. Thomas Howard.'

Now, this was the twenties. That name could be expressed in the same tones that any other name would. In later years it would send chills down the spine of almost every Englishman as he was to become Henry's dependable terrier and also uncle to two of his wives, each benefitting from the guaranteed Henry the eighth diet, losing ten pounds in a single stroke of the axe. Nevertheless, he was the right man to manage the fleet if, and when, needed. Moreover, he was respectful of his brother's successes and strategies as well as his wishes.

'You still have a place' said Jack nonchalantly, as if he was simply remarking on the weather.

'What?'

'Still have a place if you want it. The late Admiral, God rest his watery bones, wrote down his arrangement, not only with you but many others, including all debts. A true man of honour he was too.'

'You mean all this time…'

'Yes! Well…not all this time, but I have been trying to bloody track you down this past three years. What the hell you hiding from anyway?!'

This was issued with such passion that heads turned.

1543 The Disfiguration

Aelfraed gave him a look that informed him that upsetting locals would be ill-advised.

'I wasn't…err wasn't hiding…just..'

'Bollocks! You'd given up hadn't you?! Well, …what do you say?'

Truth be told he didn't know what to say. For years he had dreamt of such a thing but now? Was it too late? Am I too much of a farmer? He asked himself. Am I settled?

'Look, Alfie, I'm staying here tonight, but will be gone in the morning but this is how it is. Next month, the King is making a grand visit to France. A show of union but also an opportunity for he and Francis to impress one another. We are told that it will be a spectacle never to be repeated and the Mary Rose will be in the thick of it. You think it ove….'

'Yes! Yes! Absolutely' said Aelfraed with hand outstretched to seal the agreement.

Jack smiled, took his hand and gave the local clientele a friendly nod to let them know that all was well.

'Then,' said Jack 'if it is as well with you, we will leave today.'

'Yes, yes.' Answered Aelfraed still enthusiastic.

'Then just two more things before we leave' and Jack handed him a small purse.

'I'm guessing that you are a farm labourer?' Aelfraed nodded 'Right then, pass this on to your gaffer. It's not a fortune but it will compensate him for your sudden disappearance.'

'Thank you, yes…that would do it. Yes, thank you.'

'How do you travel then?'

Aelfraed immediately understood the question. Jack was asking about his possessions. Somewhat embarrassed, Aelfraed told him that, bar a few trinkets that were back on the farm, he was worth nothing.

'Good. Good. Then we will away within the hour.'

Aelfraed jumped up, turned to find his employer but then, as quickly, turned back again.

1543 The Disfiguration

'What's the second thing?'

'Ah, yes. Come outside with me.'

Just seven or eight yards beyond the front entrance of the inn stood a boy possibly as old as ten years of age except he looked like no other boy Aelfraed had ever seen. Aelfraed glared, now certain as to why Jack hadn't brought him into the pub. Aelfraed took time to walk all around the boy examining him and looking for exceptions or anomalies to his condition. Jaw dropped, he looked to Jack for answers.

'The Africas!'

'Quite right Alfie' said Jack.

'Well I never…' said Aelfraed jaw still open 'he's that colour everywhere?'

'Well, I can't testify to his bollocks if that's what you're asking!'

'The boy laughed. Aelfraed laughed and so did Jack.

'Well, I never…' repeated Aelfraed.

'This here is Marcus and he is an amazing ship's hand. When you come aboard again, Alfie, you'll see that Henry employs the best from around the world and this boy is strong, dependable and hard-working.'

Aelfraed looked at Jack with admiration.

'You're the patron saint of lads at sea, Jack.'

This was said with such sincerity that it left Jack dumb and embarrassed.

'Yes' said the boy using perfect English 'I would be dead if it were not for him.'

'Right…ahem…best be on our way. No…err…time…idle chat…mm.'

That afternoon, belongings gathered and flanked by his two greatest admirers on the planet, Jack led the way out of the village leaving a chapter in Aelfraed's life firmly closed.

'Tell us the story of the trolley' said Marcus enthusiastically.

'Oh you don't want to hear…' started Aelfraed with feigned modesty, secretly hoping that the boy would push the issue.

It was a very silly story, very silly indeed, of Aelfraed uncontrollably spinning from one end of a deck to another and, finally, plugging the hole that would save ship and crew, that now bonded this new friendship. Aelfraed became quite obsessed with the boy's skin and awkwardly asked questions, almost incessantly. After only just one mile, he asked if he could look, again, but more closely. Not only did Marcus take no offence, this gave him an opportunity to have some fun with Aelfraed as he had done with so many French and Englishmen.

'Are your feet like your hands?' asked Aelfraed innocently.

'Look!' answered Marcus showing him the bare sole of his foot.

'Well, I never…'

Marcus came to learn that Aelfraed said, well I never, to almost everything and found it somewhat endearing.

'Why do they look like that then?' Persisted the one-legged sailor.

'God saves this colour for those most righteous' he said pointing to his face 'and these parts' he said showing his palms again 'are to remind us of sinners.'

Jack had to back away and cover his mouth as Aelfraed's ignorance was overwhelming. As best he could, he stifled a laugh.

'Well I never…' said Aelfraed shaking his head and, then again 'well I ne….'

Jack could not hold it in any longer and burst forth with a deep guffaw with the child's giggles harmonising.

'Oh, you're too smart for Aelfraed…..sinners! Haha!'

To say that the three of them bonded instantly would be an understatement as they practically laughed all the way to their destination. Only a mile beyond the village, Jack turned into a field and took his companions toward a horse. "Horse" would be a very general description as, before them was the scruffiest old nag imaginable. Nevertheless, it belonged to Jack and he had come to pick her up. Jack signalled to Aelfraed.

'Oh no, Sir. Not me, if anyone rides it should be you. I can walk fine I can. Seen me you have...'

'Get on the bloody horse! The boy here can practically run the distance and, in case you haven't noticed, I've got twice as many legs as you.'

Aelfraed was perplexed. He felt that he should do the right thing, that being that Jack was, and would remain, his superior. Ultimately, he conceded only to declare within the hour that his arse now hurt twice as much as his leg. He wanted so much to ask Jack if he couldn't have run to buying a used saddle but then thought better of it.

On the journey, it was Aelfraed who became, mostly, the butt of the jokes but, besides the real butt pain, he was happier than he had been in years. Nevertheless, he wanted to know Marcus's story, presuming that he had been stolen from some exotic port, mid-battle.

His companions were happy to comply.

Marcus was the baby of African slaves, used and abused by the Portuguese and Spanish for some time. As Marcus and Jack began to relay this tale, Aelfraed had asked what a slave was, such was his ignorance and subsequently ranted at the idea of a man labouring without remuneration. It was, in the late fifteenth century why many, including the English, hated the Portuguese and the Spanish. They were viewed as a race that was violently enforcing their own bastardised version of God's law at the same time as making many of their own and others miserable. In the telling of Marcus's tale, Aelfraed was not to be disappointed.

Whilst barely old enough to speak and walk, he was thrown overboard a Spanish ship that was in port at Santander, as a way of punishing his mother. As Spanish sailors peered overboard for any signs of survival, little

Marcus clung to the hull whilst still submerged, vowing not to surface until he had reached a count of a hundred at least. Unfortunately, he still did not know how to get to a hundred so just held his breath as long as he could. As he surfaced, he saw no sign of a search so, freezing, he clung to the ship until nightfall. Realising that he could easily float on his back, he would later recall using his arms as oars which eventually took him to the wall that ran along Santander port. Again, he hid with no further plan or hope of surviving. Cold, tired, hungry and terrified, he decided to move inland and away from the bustle of Santander and kept on going for countless miles. Eventually, as dawn came, he found himself asleep in a field, comfortable but jammed between corn stalks. With no new ideas, he remained there, resting until he could hear movement. Chatter, he could hear two distinct voices of people wading through the corn stalks. He stood and ran, now having the advantage of being small enough to negotiate the stalks but then, he hit something hard and fell backwards with a squeal. He realised that he had run in the wrong direction and right into a man and a woman, presumably the same ones who had been talking. The man picked him up by his neck as if he were a puppy and irreverently examined him. They spoke in concerned tones but Marcus had no clue at all as to what they were saying. He was so young that his Spanish vocabulary was limited but, apart from a few sounds, he could not make out anything that was said by the couple. He was then carried to a distant farmhouse where they sat him down and started to question him. After what seemed like forever, the woman said,

'Can you understand me now, boy?'

To which Marcus nodded.

'You speak Spanish?'

He nodded again.

'Ah!' said the lady 'you've been in the navy?'

Marcus was not sure this time. He knew what the navy was but neither he, or his mother had been in it.

'Bad men threw me in water. I was hiding.'

The man turned to address the woman.

'Slave. Absolutely. Rarely seen one as black.'

'What are we to do?' she said sounding increasingly anxious.

'Do?! Well…he's property. Someone will be after him and we can't keep him. Would be too dangerous' said her husband.

'I don't behold with children being owned wherever they are from but, you are right, he cannot remain here.'

Marcus looked at them with puppy eyes seeking any solace that there may have been in their conversation. She turned to address him.

'You were with Spanish sailors…Do you understand? The way we speak is partly French and partly Spanish as we are so near the border…'

Marcus didn't know what a French was, or a border. He knew what bread and cheese was so he stared at it in the hope that it might gradually make its way in his direction.

'You can stay with us for now' said the man.

He understood that.

'We will think of a way of getting you to France but you must not steal from us.'

Marcus knew what stealing meant and as he, yet again nodded, the man passed him some bread.

This was the shortest meal in the history of mankind. The couple would one day remark that they had never seen a child consume so much in one go. As he finished he stood up and said,

'Thank you, I will always be grateful.'

And, as they turned to each other with some astonishment, he threw himself at the lady and hugged her. She puffed and almost fell over, her arms outstretched. She looked to her husband who simply gave an affirmative nod and she hugged the child back. He lapped this up, the only affection he could remember. Not surprisingly, as the next month or so passed, she didn't want to give the boy up at all.

'Goodness, how that boy would work' was her mantra for years to come as she shared her story and, during his days there, they had taught him French and Spanish and all the shades in between.

They also prepared him for his departure. They were consistent and insistent that he could not stay and they were right. Stealing a slave boy could cost them their lives and they were adamant that they wanted to spare him a life in chains. Young as he was, he grasped this although he yearned to adopt the ageing farmer and his affectionate wife. When, eventually, they had a plan, they talked to him about it over and over again. They were sure that he would get better treatment in France although this was somewhat optimistic on their part. Where they were right, was in thinking that if he could avoid those with slave mentality and intentions, he would find work and a decent living. Little did they know that his adventure would become erratic and almost without plan or purpose.

Their design for getting him across the border was one that he was happy to take part in but they, for their part, were terrified. With the cooperation of a friend who owned a modest wine distribution, they decided that it would be wise to have the boy sealed in a cask. Wine was imported from the southern regions of France into Spain and it came in barrels. Once used, the barrels were returned. The couple intended to get him as far north as possible and so set him on a route that would deliver him in Bordeaux. Marcus hadn't got a clue who or what Bordeaux was, but by now fully trusted his temporary, adoptive parents.

'Gérard will let you out of the cask once a day but no more. Otherwise, you will have to pee and shit on yourself. Do you understand this Marcus?' said the man.

Bravely, he said that he understood.

'Once there, you are to seek work. It's very unlikely people there will want to work you for nothing but you do realise that you look different from most other people?'

Marcus laughed. Although he never understood why, he had been constantly reminded of this in his short existence and, to some degree, he was sure that it would never go away.

Long ago, England had, very much, been a slave nation. However, thanks to William the Conqueror, slavery was abolished so, as little as two hundred years before Marcus had been born, the very idea of slavery would have confused most Europeans as the social and economic structure was only just fully emerging from the feudal system, a strict hierarchy within society which graded people according to their class and wealth. Those at the very bottom, although poor, and also those most likely to suffer the ravages of famine and plague, did have a sense of purpose and fed themselves from their own smallholding or from payment. Dignity had been and still was, a virtue during the Renaissance with only beggars being vilified within society as they were seen as not contributing. And, although the age of discovery wasn't solely the reason for one man systematically exploiting another, it very much was a trigger. Early Portuguese and Spanish ambition to explore and conquer, had them believing that whatever they found they could keep. Why not people as well? Then, they deduced, if you can convince your own kind that these are not as other people, even throw in a few suggestions that slaves enjoy labouring for free, then, society, eventually, accepts it as the norm. There were always those in opposition and, at the time when Marcus was making his escape, France and Britain were relatively slave free. So, his makeshift parents were right, his chance of a better life lay north and they were certain that, to keep him, would lead to his death and perhaps theirs too.

They rehearsed the first part of this venture so many times that all three of them were left certain that it would be straightforward. However, come the day and, as the lid was pushed firmly down on the barrel, he howled and as soon as his howling started, she started too. Marcus embraced them both once again, believing that they would now keep him. But suddenly, she straightened herself, dried her eyes and said,

'You must go child. You will be killed if you remain and that's the end of it.'

Already aware of responsibility at this tender age, he quietly complied and off the cart went.

As he was relaying the tale to Jack and Aelfraed, he told them that he thought he had been in the cask for months although it had only been days. The man driving was kind. When he could, he let Marcus out to relive himself and would thrust bread into his small mouth. He hurt all over. He recalled how the roads weren't roads at all and he was certain that the wheels had kept coming off. However, one day stirring from his slumber, he heard voices and one was angry. He had been taught French well and it was evident that the man in Bordeaux wasn't happy about the arrangement. The voices became louder and louder only quietening when they heard a crash as the kid was propelled out of the cask. As they looked on, silenced, out rolled a little black ball.

'Goodness, he's no age' said the man at the vineyard, now quietening.

'If you please, sir, I can work. I can work as a man and expect noth...I would want food and somewhere to sleep if that is agreeable' he paused to reflect 'and, yes...I will work for nothing this week and if you don't want me I promise I'll be on my way.'

Gérard, the driver of the cart, looked the man in the eye and shrugged his shoulders.

'You can't say fairer than that.'

'Well, ...you'll need a damn good wash lad! But I dare say you will be perfect for the grapes.'

Marcus looked back and forth at their faces for a clue.

'You tread on grapes to squash them and that makes wine' said Gérard.

'Oh yes, I can do that. Do that all day and night!'

This made both gents laugh.

Marcus, temporally breaking from his tale, looked up to Aelfraed on the horse and said,

'My feet were black then!'

'So how the bloody hell did you end up here lad. Didn't you just want to tread grapes with the frogs?' said Aelfraed.

'Ah, well' said Marcus 'that was when I knew I didn't fit..' and he continued his tale.

Marcus told Aelfraed of how he was well looked after, the work being easy, but he could not settle. Every day he would ask about the coast to the point where it became an irritation to others. Constantly wanting to know which way the sea was and where the ships were. Marcus, in his ignorance, had decided he was a sailor.

'I was never a sailor, I was just a slave but, for some reason, it was in my blood.'

As he chose to travel northwards through rural France, he found similar work and, apart from being an oddity, he was treated well. Every time he believed himself to be settled, it would take one word, idea or notion and he would be off again. Paris was the big one. Whilst working with other children just eight miles south of Lyon, they started to talk of, and describe, Paris. Moreover, they obsessed about Notre Dame Cathedral. So exciting were these depictions that he told himself that he would go and see it.

'Hang on a minute' interrupted Aelfraed 'you're telling me that you journeyed almost the whole length of filthy France and people let you be?'

'By and large, yes. Of course, I was stared at, poked and bullied, but I had and seen, so much worse. I prayed three times daily and I knew, and still know, that the Lord would keep me safe and that I would one day reach my destination. I just didn't know where that was!'

They laughed together again and Aelfraed said, 'well I never…'

Lucky he may have been, but Marcus was a one-trick

1543 The Disfiguration

pony. Wherever he found himself he had offered the same deal knowing that no one worked as hard as he did, moreover, revelled in this style of business which also led him to show off when often it wasn't necessary to do so. Aelfraed's jaw nearly touched the floor when Marcus told him that he found work at Norte Dame. Offering to do absolutely anything, he found himself at the top of the bell towers cleaning, replacing rope, assisting builders. He refused nothing. This was to be his training for becoming a ship's hand.

'That's where I found him' said Jack in a very matter of fact way.

Now, Aelfraed was totally confused and wondering if he was being sent up. Truth be told, Aelfraed was clueless as to where Paris or Bordeaux or anywhere else was but it sounded like a grand adventure. He pushed for every detail but was told by Jack that he may have to wait for another day. They stopped, sat by a riverbank and Aelfraed opened a cloth containing fruit, berries and a little cheese which they shared.

'You can't have been in Paris!' He said directly to Jack. You would have surely been killed!'

Jack explained that the unlikely events of this protracted tale were made so by Mary Tudor herself, Henry's sister. At long last, a marriage between her and the French King calmed things. At least for the time being. Jack had sailed with the, no expense spared, entourage, their destination being in Abbeville in the north. For the first time in memory, those in Henry's service were allowed to tread French soil. Moreover, permission was granted, not only for shore leave but for travel. Were Jack and his companion allowed to wander as far as Paris in the days allocated? Well, probably not, but that is just what they did and had few regrets as they marvelled at the Cathedral.

'So, I'm guessing...' said Aelfraed 'you saw him working his bits off up and down the Cathedral and decided to take him back with you?'

'Almost right' said Jack 'except, once he had found out that we were with the English fleet he promised this and that endlessly until we conceded. But, I did confess I was astonished at how hard working this little boy was and presumed that we may have use for him.'

'Damn sight better than a lad with one leg and two square wheels..' offered Aelfraed and they all laughed, spitting seeds all over one another.

'The time I had explaining to the pilot, surgeon and cook what it was I had brought aboard! Before we had set sail, he had proven his worth and I have never known men to be more accepting of a stranger. Before Calais had faded from sight he was one of us.'

Aelfraed realised that joking apart, he was now feeling some envy. He was meant to be that boy, the one the crew couldn't do without, agile and respected. He shook it off, telling himself that he was lucky to be found again.

He did, however, constantly probe, wanting to know more about Marcus's journey, the people and his obsession with the sea but as soon as he had started, Jack stopped him as they had almost completed their journey. There, between trees was a view of the coast. The sea! The cliffs! They were all three, breathlessly excited.

'There!!' Shouted Jack 'can you see her?'

And, there, partly visible beneath the cliff was the Mary Rose taking stock for Henry's ostentatious meeting with his French counterpart.

At that very moment, this unlikely and motley crew saw great things ahead, the Mary Rose without battle, the King and his entourage. The gifts, grand clothes, tents, horses. A manifest beyond their imagining and beyond that, a life at sea. But, alas, the greatest gift that God gives us all is that which keeps the future veiled as their union would eventually see the dismantling of their beloved ship and an encounter that would lead them to York and change their lives forever.

8 the adventurers
September 1542

Wynnfrith was finding herself increasingly irritable to the point where Silas started to notice the difference. He did, of course, put it down to the fact, once again, that she had tired of him, their marriage, his horse and so on and so on. Frustrated, she sat him down in their home and vented forth.

'I've tried so hard to forget about Elspeth's letters, and the key. What am I meant do now?…Marcus gone. Gone forever for all I know…'

'Well, dear..'

'And then there's all these papers and…and clues and God himself watching my every move as well as Elspeth. What happened to our happy ever after!..'

'I think…'

'I can't help wondering if Robert knows more…probably whispering his secrets to fat Mrs Grinditt every other evening!'

'I think it might be Grindem…'

'I'll bloody grindem, sort all of them out!' she screamed and then ran outside and threw up violently.

'My dear!' said Silas now increasingly concerned for his

wife who was slowly going off her rocker 'you are sickly my dove, please calm down....'

She sat, unmoved that she was now soaked. Her dress was marked by soil and puke and she then quietly wept as the storm passed. She looked at her husband and placed her hand upon his cheek.

'Oh my dear Silas, I know not what to do but I love you so. I'm not angry at you. Do you think I'm sickly because of my anger?'

'Why? What else dear?'

She took his right hand and placed it underneath her belt and softly smiled at his simple but benevolent face.

'Ah! You are eating too much. Too much of the good life methinks?! Plenty of weak ale, no food and you'll be right as the sky in days'

Deflated, and up to her eyeballs in shit, she slightly shook her head and stood.

'We are to have a baby, husband'

For a moment, nothing happened but, as Wynn thought to repeat it, Silas's head started to wobble. Only slightly at first but then it became somewhat uncontrollable. Now in tandem with his bony knees, a stranger may have interpreted this as a celebratory, ritual dance.

'Well, how on…where did…what did you do?'

'Really husband? You really don't know where it came from?'

Then the tears started. He withdrew, sobbing and turning away from his wife, overwhelmed by what he had been told.

'Everyone, every…one, every person, everywhere, since I was a child told me that I would never be man enough to sire a child. I did not think this possible. You may be mistaken, my dear. Are you sure?'

Softly she said,

'I'm sure.'

For the remainder of the day, Wynnfrith was kept busy tending to the man who had had an almighty shock. He stayed in his chair whilst she massaged his feet and hands, coddled him and took him wine and cheese. As the sun fell, he sat there covered in a blanket very much the patient and so she asked after his welfare.

'I do think I might get through this' he said 'will it get much more difficult?'

Trying her best not to laugh, she assured him that all would be well and then it became quiet.

That was until he leapt up and said.

'But who is it? What is he called? What if he doesn't like me?'

'Well…for a start, I can't promise you that it will be a boy but, we won't know who they are or what they will be like until they are born and then start to develop but, hopefully, he'll be a mix of me and you.'

And, for the first time in a while, they laughed, they really loudly belly-laughed for they knew that the world saw them as a couple of misfits and Silas and his wife possibly imagined birthing the most clumsy child the world had ever known.

With no intention of doing so alone, Wynnfrith fell asleep on the bed only to jump out in the morning, and go down to find Silas still in his chair. He was crying.

'Oh Silas, why did you not come to bed?'

'I am truly overwhelmed, what…' he sniffled and splattered 'abundance. How great is the Lord that I could be granted a child with you? How very blessed I am.'

'Silas, dear. My Lord Silas, you deserve all of this and more. Your pure heart has been rewarded.'

'I am so sorry I haven't been more helpful, well…you know…the keys…'

'Oh, it's not you…I do need to calm down' said Wynnfrith 'and I also have an idea of how we may move forward.'

They broke their fast and Wynnfrith shared an intelligent, but dangerous notion, that Silas agreed, would be their next step.

'But where would we start?' he asked.

'We will start by being patient, baby will come first and, between my duties and your missions we will keep watch daily until our endeavour bears fruit.'

At the very least, this stopped Wynn's mind from trying to find a solution every minute of every day. She had decided to play the long game and, in doing so, would prioritise her marriage once again.

Her plan involved lurking around the worst tended corners of the exterior of Barley Hall. Mrs and Mr Hall were to move out, within the month, as a new Mayor took residence there, so Wynnfrith knew that their clever design would have to be successful during the coming few weeks.

One morning, Robert looked out of his bedroom window to find Silas crouching in the bushes. He watched him for a while but, as his patience was leaving him none the wiser, he shouted down to him.

'What in God's name are you doing, man?'

Wynnfrith had rehearsed Silas dozens of times as to what to do in such an event but, of course, this plan was left at home with the rest of his common sense.

'Woodworm!' he shouted in his defence.

'Woodworm? What the bloody hell has got into you Silas?'

'I thought I would come and check on you and check on your woodworm.'

'What woodworm?!'

'Ah…there…see…yes…def…'

'You don't get flaming woodworm in flowers.'

'Oh…that's a because I have rid you of them. I may return tomorrow…' and mumbling complete crap, he wandered off leaving the Mayor in his night attire scratching his head and checking the window sill for infestations.

'Silas was in our garden' he said approaching his wife as he descended the stairs.

'Oh yes dear…be nice to see him, is he coming in?'

1543 The Disfiguration

'Err, no…no…I don't think so.'

And, for the time being, that was the end of the matter. Little did he know that both Silas and his wife were spending a lot of time creeping around his house and, what had seemed at first to be a remarkable idea was now leaving them feeling deflated.

However, at dusk, one Saturday evening, Wynn, for the first time thought that she detected a shadow about Barley Hall. She was certain of it. Immediately she returned home and within a matter of minutes, she was back flanked by her husband and his horse, Annie.

'There!' she said in her loudest whisper 'see?'

That very infrequently used rear door, that would jam on bracken and roots, was being slowly pushed open. A figure, barely a dark outline, rushed out and leapt onto his saddle and in an instant, was away.

'Give him a few furlongs' said Wynnfrith and before he had disappeared completely, both Silas and Wynnfrith were aboard Annie and giving pursuit.

'Remember, he is expert at this' she puffed 'and will easily know if he is being followed.'

Silas held back a little and Annie, fully cognizant and obeying Silas's every whim, eased into a gentle, but paced trot. Within the hour they were way beyond the walls of York, astonished that they had not been stopped at the Barbican. For the first time ever, Silas would use his title and the freedom of the city to his advantage and exit York without harassment. Now, there was hardly any light at all but Annie was now galloping with the stranger still in sight but, barely a black-blue dot. As he entered the woods, the path thinned and he slowed down. Silas may well have been ridiculed relentlessly for years and all sorts of reasons but his many missions and his solitary status left him accomplished and well-skilled, particularly when in pursuit. Finally, the stranger dismounted and started to proceed on foot.

'Just as I remember, except his attire is new. Quite a fancy fellow now I think, but it's him. Of that, I am in no doubt' said Wynnfrith.

Annie was left tied to a tree whilst our unlikely adventurers continued afoot. This, to be fair, was not their strong point. Unquestionably, Wynnfrith and Silas would come fourth and fifth in a walking in a straight line competition, even if there were only three in it. However, their nervousness and their awareness of their limitations only added to their combined bravado as they were determined to snare their prey.

Finally, a door. A door that to all intents and purposes looked like a church door but flanked by two trees and therefore, barely visible.

'Let him go in first' said Wynn.

The door cracked open and the light from a single candle flame burst forth from within.

'Are you sure this is safe dear? I wouldn't want any harm to become of your person, for anything?' asked Silas chivalrously.

'We must go on. For ourselves, for Elspeth, and even the King' she whispered.

This was fighting talk. Silas, knees knocking, grasped his dagger and crept, as best he could, toward the ancient door.

'Do it' demanded Wynnfrith 'throw it open.'

They both lunged at the door and almost fell in, and onto, the straw laden, stone floor. Before them he stood, visibly shocked and reaching for his sword. For an instant, they all just looked at one another, Silas somewhat unsure as to whether he would engage with this very able looking man and the stranger himself deciding to do nought.

Truly, he was a sight to behold. Most of his outfit was a shade of midnight blue offset by claret gloves and crimson waistcoat. He looked strong and confident, the mask affording him an air of mystery and power. Wynnfrith remembered that, on previous encounters, he had been dressed in black, everything was black. However, Moonlight was now adorned in a fashion that would fully represent his moniker.

As this stand-off continued, Wynn lost hope. Finding Moonlight was going to be the answer to her puzzle. And, it wasn't that she, or Silas for that matter, were not impressed by the man in front of them, it was what was behind him that left them both completely dumbfounded with no idea whatsoever as to what it meant.

In the centre of this reclaimed chapel was a single candle that now flickered violently as the breeze blew through the open door. Around the candle were people. Many people, possibly over twenty, reckoned Silas. And, that in itself, may have been daunting if it wasn't for the fact that they all looked exactly the same. Moonlight slowly sighed and then invited them to sit.

'You are in no danger, please sit.'

Overwhelmed, they made their way to the table, all the time unwittingly counting how many 'Moonlights' were in the room but all they did was look at one another, unmoving and silent.

'What do you think it is that you have discovered?' he said.

'I'm so confused' said Wynn 'I've seen you coming and going all my life at Barley Hall, you've been seen in Stratford, Hampton Court and…'

'So what is it you think you see here?'

Silas was busy getting his breath back and looking, jaw-dropped, at this astonishing spectacle.

'I don't know…I thought…I once thought you were a ghost, a guardian angel…I…I don't know what.'

'Did you follow me for mischief or do you need help, Wynnfrith?'

A little surprised that he knew her name, she tentatively said,

'Help. We mean no harm, we just need your help.'

She hesitated, unsure as to whom she should be directing

this appeal.

'Do you understand what you see?'

Silas, as it turned out, in a very successful attempt to intellectualise the situation said,

'There's lots of you. Like an army. That's why it seems like you can get from one place to another so quickly.'

'Yes my friend, but more like a guardian angel than an army.'

'But why us? Why Robert? I seem to have seen you coming and going all my life' asked Wynnfrith now a little more relaxed.

'I have been there to assist Kings and Queens, the persecuted, the overlooked and the innocent for hundreds of years. If you wish to know my connection with the Mayor, then I will grant you that.'

One of the group huddled around the candle took up the story in a most bizarre manner. It was a completely unbroken continuation of the tale with each of them speaking in the first person. It became instantly clear to Silas And Wynnfrith that there was no 'them,' just Moonlight. Together, they created an awesome spectacle, the cobalt blues and crimsons graduating to shadows as the flickering candle provided an artistic chiaroscuro in the centre of the table.

'Your father, Silas.'

He jumped. He had heard enough about his father recently to last him a lifetime. He had no desire to have the story elaborated.

'Do not fear' said a third 'I am simply informing you that I was on his trail for some time but, sadly, too late to save Wynnfrith's parents. However, I could hardly have turned away as I watched the courageous actions of the young Robert Hall as he slew that brutal killer. By choice, I consoled him that very night and, in doing so, did at least save his life.'

Silas now had a dozen questions brewing in his tiny noggin. Shocked at the very thought that Robert may have taken his own life, he understood how Moonlight remained on call for him but had no idea whatsoever how on earth this apparently, young and athletic adventurer could possibly have been around in the 1520s.

Wynnfrith started to stretch herself, craning her neck to get a closer look at the figure at the foot of the table. There was no mistaking it, his face was black,

'Marcus?'

'I am not Marcus. I am Moonlight. I do not know where Marcus is.'

'That's why we came!' shouted Silas. 'Is he here?'

'He is not here but I am willing to help you.'

Wynnfrith and Silas turned to one another and gurned as if they were in the national gormless expression finals 1542. This, Moonlight would once reflect, was one of the greatest tests they had ever faced as this improvised village idiot convention would have had anyone else in stitches. Eventually, Silas decided to verbalise his contorted thoughts,

'It's a woman!' he whispered.

'I am not a woman, I am Moonlight' she answered.

This was now starting to become a little monotonous and Wynn decided that, as Moonlight or, Moonlights, or Moonlight and associates, or silly sods in fancy dress had been of such service to the Agents of the Word, she would now be very direct with them but before she did, she found her mind drifting. She had once had a dream similar to this and Elspeth was in it. They still lived in York but it was populated with people, all of whom were given equal regard. The cripples, oddities, beggars, small, large, rich, poor, stupid, clever, men, women and all kinds of people in between. Yes, she thought, this dream probably did come from Elspeth and, no, it was not Thomas More's Utopia for no one would be burned to death in this place. For a moment, she fantasised that this secret society was completely inclusive, a social group where she would never be mocked again. Unwittingly, she then found herself looking around the room trying to find the one that was most like her, willing them to move so she could study their gait. And, there is no question that she would have persisted in this activity if it wasn't for Silas giving her a sharp dig in the ribs to snap her out of it.

'Oh!...yes...so, you are like us? The Royal Secret Agents of the Word!'

Silas was very impressed, as he had given up trying to get that phrase out successfully, months ago.

'No I am Moonlight.'

'God's teeth! What is wrong with you? Are you going to say that to everything? Have you any idea…'

Silas, realising that, once again the ghost of sister Elspeth was well and truly in control of his beloved, gently touched her arm in an attempt to draw her back in again.

'I mean you no harm' started one of the group that hadn't spoken before. 'I am not appointed by the King or influenced by any political or religious rivalry. I do good where I think it is needed, for the welfare of all.'

Wynnfrith started to mutter into her dress almost incoherently.

'Well, …that's what I bloody said. I don't know what the difference is…awkward bug….'

'You are with child' said the first, devoid of any emotion.

'Yes! I'm having a baby!' blustered Silas, smiling inanely.

'You must take care. I know that you have the key. You must not ask me what the key is for, that is your destiny. You must contact Marcus. This is where I will help. I only know that he is not in Yorkshire but I will find him. You will give me two months to execute this task at which point you will gather the Agents, for you will be mightily put to the test. Even more so than during the Purge or the Cataclysm.'

Seamlessly, another picked up the instruction.

'You two are now amongst the very few that have exposed me…'

Silas then made to ask what had happened to the others but a large, occupied, crimson leather glove was raised to stop him.

'You will make an oath on this Bible..'

They looked toward the candle which rested on a large, dark blue, leather-bound Bible.

'…to swear that what you have seen this night, you will never speak of. When Marcus is discovered you may tell your fellow Agents that Moonlight assisted, no more. You must never seek out this location again.'

As they all backed away, Wynnfrith realised that the table was much larger than they had, at first, thought. As Silas moved toward the grand oaken bench, he found himself standing side by side with Moonlight. Well, one of them at least. Whilst the soft light shone and glimmered on the satins and leather of his garb, they both looked down to examine, in contrast, Silas's legs. He had rushed out of the house wearing only an old woollen jerkin and even older wool hose. His knees seemed to extend an unnatural extra two inches further as the wool had been stretched to its limit during the ride. One knee, rather seductively, was exposed through a broken repair making a large hole and revealing a grazed and muddied knee. Moreover, he had forgotten to adorn himself with a codpiece. Truth be told, few men wore one in the home but, on this night, it would have been wise for Silas to have thought twice before racing out. There, where that most audacious of Tudor male attire should have been, was a soggy leaf. His reaction to this? He looked Moonlight straight in the eye, shrugged and smiled, in his head presumably thinking: 'well, what can you do?' Moonlight, wisely, averted his eyes and then, they all sat, providing places for the two dopey newcomers.

Now, quite comfortable within this environment, the pair happily swore an oath as they sipped wine. Silas had already worked out that those around them could not be the entire secret society. He deduced, and to be honest Silas didn't do a lot of deducing, that for Moonlight to disappear in York and, within a day or so, appear in Stratford upon Avon, there had to be a network of them working in a relay. He pondered for a moment whether they all did believe they were as one or if they had just spent too long going in and out of the dressing-up wardrobe.

Calm and pleased with their brave outing, Wynnfrith reached for Silas's hand and he held it. She then turned to face him realising that they were in their own bed and that it was morning. Without even a hangover to evidence their escapade, they questioned each other as they rose to face the day. When they fully came around, they were buzzing, constantly congratulating each other for what they had achieved. After all, they had risked their lives.

Silas thought it particularly funny to answer every question of the day with 'no, I am Moonlight' or 'yes, I am Moonlight' which had them both constantly giggling.

Unusually, they went to market together to celebrate their renewed freedom. As they stepped over their very own threshold, they both tripped. This wasn't the first time but it did leave Silas on his skinny derrière awaiting support from his forlorn missus. As he stood, he saw a damp bundle and on opening it, he discovered two gold coins. On the bundle was an expertly drawn baby. Bewildered, he held them up to show Wynnfrith.

'Marcus' she said without hesitation.

'What…how could…'

'I just know. He is a master at draughtsmanship. It's a gift from him and Elspeth and it's for the baby. I would swear both to be clairvoyant.'

Accepting this explanation, and the gift, they secreted the coins under the now, somewhat tired, boards upstairs and finally set off. Happily, they neared the market place and waved as they saw Mrs Hall in the distance.

'How lovely to see you both. All well my dears?'

'Oh yes' said Wynn 'yes, very much Mrs Hall. Look!' and she placed Mrs Hall's hand on her belly.

Mrs Hall squealed. So much so that half the marketplace

turned around.

'Oh my! Oh my, oh my!' and then she cried blubbering endlessly about what it would mean to Robert and how Eirik would now have a nephew or niece.

'Oh my!' she said once again for good luck.

'And are you two all well?'

'Oh yes, Mrs Hall' said Wynnfrith. Things have never been better.

At that very moment, a noticeably attractive woman sidled past but was obviously trying to catch Mrs Hall's eye and, as she eventually made contact, Mrs Hall became doubly excited as she wanted to introduce her new friend.

'This, my dears, is someone who will be helping out in the kitchen at our new house. She's just come over from Scarborough. Silas, Wynnfrith, please meet Meg.'

9 an old friend
3 weeks earlier

Marcus drew the table near to the window and removed his belt to put under one of its legs that was making his task that much more difficult. It also constantly reminded him, not so much of Wynnfrith herself, but of the affectionate names given to her by her sister and Silas. The way she still giggled when they called her 'Wobbly Wynn' as if she revelled in it. His heart became heavy, his love for a woman recently passed, was far from diminishing. He thought of Elspeth every minute and when, if ever, there was respite, he thought of her family with as much affection but, now and again, his mind would turn to his renewed purpose. Riddled with guilt, he almost wished that he hadn't shared his burden with Elspeth. Discovering that she, in turn, and posthumously, had revealed all to her sister left him startled, confused and feeling somewhat betrayed. It was only when pondering on her intentions that he became certain that her wish was to ensure that he would get some support. However, he had fled York, absolute in his decision that he would endanger no one else, especially those now dear to him at home.

At last, the table was level and there was just about enough space for him to lay out his documents, only for him to realise that the chair was now rocking as well. He allowed himself a smile acknowledging that both Wynnfrith and Elspeth would be on his shoulder throughout, whether he liked it or not. He sat back, momentarily defeated, and took in the view. He had rented an upstairs room along Friar street which, like most upper floors of half-timbered buildings, overhung the one beneath. Walking right up to the window he found himself peering directly downward on passing hats of varying quality and style. As his head came up again, he beheld the magnificent Cathedral ahead and acknowledged the parallels with York. It towered benignly over everything it surveyed and informed all from miles around that God was manifest in all things. However, in York, people knew him. Well, that it is to say, not everyone knew him personally, but there was nothing outrageous about a well-spoken African wandering around the streets and snickleways. And, he was well respected, by the sick and dying, the young and old, by citizens and Agents alike. It had been so long since he had ventured out of York that he had also put to the back of his mind that life-long and perpetual experience of being stared at, questioned and sometimes assaulted. He had attracted the most curious responses as he had arrived at this destination but kept his head down and only spoke when it was absolutely necessary. The lodgings had been recommended to him by someone he had sailed with long ago and, apart from the landlady gawping incessantly as they agreed to business terms, Marcus had no complaints so far. Soon, he would seek employment, work by day and use his evenings to make plans. He did, of course, have the other key, whatever that meant and Wynnfrith had already been informed of this in those copious documents left to her by her sister. Marcus knew that by absconding, he would leave that young woman stressed and confused but was certain that she would settle down to married life and forget about the

1543 The Disfiguration

keys and the, surreptitiously bequeathed, papers. Marcus didn't need to work. Few people knew this in York but Marcus had long ago become a wealthy man, although it did not sit comfortably with him. However, one thing was clear, he would always work. He hadn't been idle since the day of his birth and he understood that he simply wouldn't cope in a world where he wasn't useful. Hence his role at the undercroft in York. This had started with a few hours helping out but, within days, he had come to realise how overwhelmed the place was and, he had never had more than a day's break from it since. So, it was with some trepidation, that he suddenly left the undercroft and York, promising himself that, one day he would return. It would be difficult to measure the sincerity of that promise as it was unquestionably well meant at the same time as being impossible. To take on this mission alone would surely lead to his death but, for the moment, he chose not to dwell on that certainty.

He gathered his cloak and hat, looking every bit the gentleman and headed out, unsure as to whether to keep his head proudly held high or, to hide his face, just to make life easier.

He then found himself looking left, and then right, to see if anyone was abroad that morning but then, in an instant, realised how ridiculous this was and looked up and ahead at the thriving city of Worcester, in all its glory and beauty. Like York, a city of remarkable contrasts, the rich almost existing side by side with people struggling from one meal to the next. The Cathedral, an astonishing tribute to what mankind could achieve with the dedication of generations, had streets leading away from it that were covered with filth. All the same, Marcus had been there just once before and he was not disappointed by his return. He noticed a man who was situated in the very same spot where he had first encountered him the previous evening. To passers-by, he may well have seemed a beggar but he laboured, making little stick soldiers that he then tried to sell to passers-by for their children. One day earlier, Marcus had asked him about his trade and kindly gave him a farthing for a few troops. He too had been in the navy, injured and laid off, during a period when the ships had been dry-docked for repair. Thaddeus, the carver of those stick figures, was also almost blind but swore to Marcus that he would refuse to beg even if he were dying in the street and delivering his final breath. He was thin, frail and could barely stand. He told Marcus that his last abode had been on a ship and that he now spent day and night trying to trade, although there was nothing at all on his broken plate apart from the new farthing that Marcus had bequeathed him. Seeing him again, the following morning, brought home the plight of this man. Marcus, yet again, engaged him in conversation.

'I cannot thank thee enough for thy kindness, sir and for choosing to give of your time to such a lowly man as myself. May God bless you and your children for all time.'

Realising that the conversation alone was bringing a little life into this unfortunate man's day, Marcus stayed another five minutes before addressing his, somewhat urgent, business. What Thaddeus didn't know was that, whilst they were chatting, Marcus was surveying the man's clothes. Scant as they were, he had a tired and dirty cloak that was full of holes, but it did have one pocket with a good degree of integrity. Marcus then apologised, explaining that he had to make business within the hour and Thaddeus, yet again, showered him with thanks and Marcus was never to set eyes on him again. That day, Thaddeus unsuccessfully traded without a break until it was dark. He slumped down to take rest and grunted in disappointment and disbelief as he was sure that he had just crushed what was left of his stock. He stood again, and felt around, discovering immediately that all the little figures were still intact. He then explored his pocket. Never usually the first place to look for anything, he now discovered that it was heavy and making a noise. He stuck his emaciated hand into it and felt the sheer weight of the coins. He took his hand out and then tried again, presuming that this was some deception. The weight alone told him that he would be able to eat that day and, possibly, for a few more days after that. He wept. He wept so much that he howled, praising God and the stranger who had been sent to him. He then sat down and slept with a renewed peace of mind. However, it would be some time before it dawned on him that he had enough stored in there to buy himself a home. It would be when the sun came up that, even his limited vision, would inform him that this was gold and strangers gathered around as this mad tinker danced manically in the sunshine.

When Marcus had left Thaddeus, he ambled and eventually approached a fine building just south-east of the Cathedral, standing exactly where he had remembered it to be. Sure of his plan, he threw the door open but then stopped, looked back again to see if he was, in fact, in the correct destination, and then in again, only to see two astonished faces, one standing and one behind a desk.

Confused, Marcus was a little unsure as to how he should proceed and then noticed that the upright gentleman drew a dagger.

'Please, gentleman. I mean no harm, I may be in error.'

In truth, the man looked terrified. Marcus was an imposing figure. Enough, perhaps, to make one think that he may be a threat but, added to that, was his face. Will the world ever get used to this? he asked himself.

'Please, good sirs' he said holding up his palms to reassure them 'for a short while I was employed here. Or, at least I thought it was here. The infirmary? I helped the sick.'

The portly man, behind the desk, stood.

'If it wasn't for your abrupt entrance, young man, I would be certain that you jest. Have you been living in a box these last five years?'

Marcus stood, eyes glancing around the room for clues, trying to work out what the man meant.

'Did they never have monks where you come from?'

He was struggling somewhat with this rhetoric, particularly as he presumed that he meant Africa in an attempt at being facetious but then, the groat hit the cobbles and Marcus heard it.

'Ah! Gentlemen. I see. As the monastery went so did the provision to the poor at this establishment?'

'I think what you are trying to say is that those goat buggering, purse picking, useless bastards have been quite properly discovered and put out to graze. I warn you, your kind of talk will only cause trouble for you around here. Now begone before I take your hide as a tapestry!'

The other man laughed.

Marcus, most familiar with this rough treatment, which had been put temporarily to the back of his mind, turned to exit. He was shocked to the core. At least in York, there had been some provision for those most in need but elsewhere, clearly, the removal of monastic bodies and buildings was having a profound effect on those suffering. Disappointed at what he had seen, it was at least as well that he could not see ahead and worse things to come as the very same building would later be used during the English civil war once it was requisitioned by Royalists as a command post.

Already feeling both humiliated and defeated, he turned but then stumbled. Even worse, he fell back into someone else, expecting a further reprimand. This man was even bigger than Marcus and grabbed the collar of his gown, not to apprehend him but to stop him falling. Once upright, the two men stared at one another, unable to speak.

'Marcus? That's your name? You're Elspeth's husband?'

As best he could, Marcus was trying to adjust to these two extremes. Inside, someone with offal for brains was threatening his life and, here, was a man gracing him with all he had ever wished for. This was the first time he had heard someone fully acknowledge what had been pledged between Elspeth and himself before she passed.

'Thomas Farrier! Sir! What brings you…'

'Well, young man! I'm thinking the very same. My, you are a long way from home! Is he...is he, with you?' asked Thomas who was really in the mood for a good laugh.

'Silas? Ah, alas no, sir. I am alone on this quest...err...journey. I am...err' and then he ran completely out of steam.

Thomas Farrier, acknowledging instantly that something was awry, suggested that they took themselves to a nearby inn. Marcus explained that, beyond the walls of York, he found it more comfortable to keep a low profile. Realising that one of the aggressors seemed to be in pursuit, Farrier turned around to let him know that he been seen. Sensibly, seeing the full and upright physique of Thomas Farrier, he fled. Marcus told Thomas that he had wished to keep hidden but had fallen at the first jump.

'Nonsense! I'll bloody low profile anyone who even as much as looks in our direction. We are fellow Agents after all.'

Marcus wasn't sure whether he was or wasn't an Agent. Elspeth, in her last days, had told him all. He had been welcomed into the family and invited to, what turned out to be, a domestic trial that uncovered the murderer of both Sir Anthony Bask and Elspeth. He broke from his thoughts. This had been a very difficult start. Only half an hour ago he was confident that he was starting to get to grips with his grand plan, only to be kicked out of the first building he went into and now he was going to be questioned by this hulk of a man. At his very core (somewhat like master Farrier himself) Marcus was incurably honest but he now found himself in a situation where he would have to lie. Once shared with Farrier, this information would then be shared with all the Agents back in York. Thomas Farrier even noted, and mentioned, how slowly Marcus walked to the inn.

Generously, Thomas Farrier bought food and ale for the pair of them and, for a while, asked of the welfare of those in York even though it hadn't been that long since he, and

1543 The Disfiguration

the Shakespeares, had been at the wedding of Silas and Wynnfrith.

'They are happy in the knowledge that they are now probably the most dangerous couple in the land!' Said Marcus in response to his enquiry, Thomas laughed knowing exactly what he meant.

'Bless them both and may God watch over them always' said Thomas Farrier.

'And, erm the priest? Father err..?'

'Oh, you mean Father Matthew. He is well. A good man.'

Marcus knew that here was no chance of avoiding Farrier's enquiries as he was so far from home, so thought to avoid a defence by querying the blacksmith first.

'What brings you so far out?' asked Marcus attempting to delay the inevitable as long as possible.

'Not so far, my friend. I come here about once a month. I pray in the Cathedral yonder and then to the market. The market here is second to none!'

Temporarily he had managed to derail Farrier so continued to take advantage.

'How fairs the lady? The one who owned an inn and was tortured at Warwick castle?' Asked Marcus.

'Ah! Maud. Maud, dear Maud. She recovers week by week, my friend. Salt of the very earth.'

'She lived with you for a while?'

'Yes, yes' said Thomas Farrier. 'She was left without a seed to her name, least I could do. She has reopened the inn now that all has calmed down. Left completely, and stood rotting so I bloody well opened it up again! Haha! With a little help from the Shakespeares and some locals, it was looking like its old self again. No, no. That's not right.' He closed in on Marcus 'truth be told it was forever a shithole but much improved once we had finished. And, I asked her to ditch the 'dirtye' part.'

Marcus, unsure as to what this meant quizzed him.

'It was called "ye dirtye pesant" but now just "the

1543 The Disfiguration

peasant."

Marcus now believed that the remainder of the conversation would be both pleasant and cordial, Farrier insisting on doing much of the talking.

'And how is young Eirik? Who is, I believe, more or less, your brother by law now.'

'Yes, I would say that is the case. He was out of York when I left but seemed well when I last saw him. 'You saved his life?'

'Nonsense' announced Farrier a little too loudly and then apologised, also promising that the drink in his right hand would be his last one 'just fixed up a scratch. Fine young fellow. Was once a mercenary like me you know?'

Marcus acknowledged this with a smile.

'You knew Brother Bede well I believe?' asked Marcus.

'Does he still ail? Can he walk? Talk? Oh…how I miss him.'

'The monk has surprised all, master Farrier, he has started to make sounds again, Father Matthew hopes daily for something intelligible.'

'That's wonderful news…I suppose Wynnfrith has the same hopes for her husband!'

They both laughed so loudly at this affectionate quip that the innkeeper put his head around the door to see that all was well. Farrier, still the gentleman despite being pissed as a pond, gave the proprietor two coins, apologised and made him a promise that he would keep the noise down.

'Ah, Bede. My friend the monk. The tales I could tell you about our past.'

Marcus, realising that time was passing, thought to encourage more rambling as he thought, surely, that Farrier would want to be making his way soon.

'Everyone alludes to the adventures of Bede but I know nothing. I'm sure nobody in York knows the full story.'

This was the greatest lie that Marcus would tell in some time as he had, in his past, known Bede well and was keeping his own secrets about the man, close to his chest.

'Well...' started Farrier, the newly appointed bard of Worcester. Marcus knew he was in for the long haul so duly took advantage of it. He sat back and relaxed into the bench as story-time began.

The epic began with a caveat,

'I do not know how Bede got from London to York. I do not think any of the Agents do either. How wonderful it would be if he could tell us, hey?'

Marcus nodded.

'I had fought against the Scottish and the French since being a young man. Always on the King's side but in employment if you understand. I was never one to give total allegiance, if anyone wanted my skills they had to pay well for it.'

Surprisingly, Marcus was already intrigued and wondering if their paths had ever crossed. He thought to raise the issue but decided to let him continue.

'You see, young Marcus, my grandparents and their parents lived in an age where the crown was still unsteady. Why, even the great battle at Bosworth that put the King's father on the throne enlisted all sorts on both sides. They would have you think that it was a tale of Yorkists against Lancastrians and...it was, but not necessarily on the battlefield. Many men lay awake for days deciding which horse to back if you get my meaning. And, it could happen again. If fat Harry loses his young prince, well...God only knows who will take the crown and how. Have you any idea the strength of support behind Mary, Princess Mary, the bastard...oh! call her what you will? The crown isn't, and never will be, secure in our lifetimes.'

Far from relaxed, Marcus was becoming uneasy. If Farrier only knew how close to the truth he was. He rambled for some time on this topic which he clearly felt strongly about but, following a polite prompt from his companion, got back to his tale.

1543 The Disfiguration

He told him that he had suffered an almost fatal leg wound that left him completely useless as a mercenary, in constant pain and danger of infection. He then stood and wandered outside for a moment leaving Marcus bewildered but soon returned sans hose, his cloak delicately wrapped around his whole body. Then, he revealed his left leg. Marcus was shocked. Of course, he had seen all kinds of mutilation in naval service but never would have dreamt that any man could walk or hide so well a serious injury. Farrier's whole calf was missing leaving the lower part of his leg looking completely withered. Farrier, now laughing, revealed the inside of his cast-off hose which had within it, padding that resembled the lost calf muscle. Besides reminding him instantly of Aelfraed, Thomas Farrier was promoted even higher in Marcus's esteem as, mentally, he recalled the many recent adventures of the blacksmith that had been shared with him by the Agents. Then, quite suddenly, his mood changed. Sombre, Thomas made sure to cover himself again and started to apologise.

'I am so sorry my friend. You do understand, I was illustrating my story for you. No more. I hope there is no offence.'

Marcus was clueless as to what this meant but if Silas had been there he would have put Thomas Farrier in his place once again. For whatever reason, Farrier was absolutely determined that his sexuality would never again surface, as one could only presume that he had been discovered sometime in the past and made to pay for it. The tone in his voice would have Silas in no doubt that he needed his counsel once again.

Uncannily, he then disappeared once again only to return fully dressed and continued his story as if nothing had happened. He then explained how his town of origin had been Stratford upon Avon but, having been cut down in the north, found himself resurrected in Oxford. Despite the influence of the alcohol, Farrier noticed that Oxford struck a chord with his young companion as soon as he mentioned it so paused to see if he would take the bait. As Marcus managed to hold his tongue, Farrier then went on to explain that he was in a Monastery at Abingdon.

'You should have seen it my friend. Magnificent! The size of Westminster. That was until Cromwell took their goods and had the building destroyed.'

'Some of it still stands' said Marcus, realising immediately that he had given something away.

'I believed I was in Heaven, Marcus. I do not jest with you, it was beautiful to behold. I was treated with herbs, poultices, massages. Bandaged daily with the infection inspected regularly. And…would you believe, they had maggots in my wound. Maggots! I watched them eat away the disease. The food! And mead! But more than anything, it was such a beautiful, peaceful place. How I enjoyed the gardens as I recovered and, eventually, I was able to help with repairs around the Abbey and tend to their horses. The architect of all this benevolence? Why none neither than the Godly and gregarious Brother Bede. How he would revel in my stories and how we would debate theology. As much as a blacksmith can…Haha!

But, as you know, there had been stirrings in Europe for some time about religion. Having said that, no one could have foretold the timing and extent of the Reformation. I saw the fire in Bede's eyes as we talked about it, he wasn't one for giving in. I vowed that when I left, I would do anything, give my life for him if necessary. He flatly refused to acknowledge that King's marriage to Boleyn and laughed at the very idea of him being Supreme Head of the Church of England.'

'So what became of him?' Marcus said now genuinely engaged with this tale.

'He fled in order to join the Pilgrimage of Grace, the northern rebellion. When things started to go sour for them, he returned south and sought me out whence I hid and took care of him. Using a code name, 'nails' he knew that he could find me anytime but I awoke one morning to find a note. Need to reconnoitre, it said. Reconnoitre! As if he was a soldier himself. Gone to join, God knows how many other waif and stray monks, hoping to change Harry's mind. Last I saw of him until he turned up in York!'

Marcus thanked him for his magnanimous hospitality and for sharing his life stories, now being the proud owner of a throbbing cranium and genuinely tired. They sat for a while, silent, either reviewing the highlights of the conversation or simply nodding off.

Ironically, there were incredible similarities between those two. Thomas an ex-mercenary and Marcus an ex-mariner and, although neither of them knew it, they both had enough funds never to work again, but they did. And then, following ten minutes of silent stupor, it came.

'Am I detecting that your visit to this good city is a secret?'

This was a tougher question than Marcus had expected. Already having prepared some nonsense about visiting a relative, it was now clear that Thomas Farrier had detected his guest's clandestine mood. Added to this was the fact that they were now several drinks in. Marcus hadn't had a drink since he had kept company with Aelfraed and Jack and so he was now ready to confess the sins of a lifetime which, actually, weren't that many. He tried telling Farrier some tales of the sea which did push his 'back in my day' button even more and then they shared even more adventures for almost another half hour. Nevertheless, they still ended up in the same place. Not that Thomas Farrier was being pushy, it was a perfectly reasonable question to ask when you take into account the, adventure, danger and intrigue that Farrier had seen those previous two years and the huge distance between York and Worcester.

Eventually, Marcus put down his drink, sighed and said.

'My good sir. I cannot lie to you in the face. My beloved and angelic Elspeth would not condone it but what I may impart is neither easy in the telling or the hearing.'

Thomas was genuinely surprised. He had thought that Robert may have sent Marcus on some ridiculous errand for a particular bow, piece of cloth or small pane of glass, as he was prone to do. He took Marcus's arm and led him down a short and dark, panelled corridor. At the end was a snug where the two of them could talk in private. Marcus was wondering why the hell he hadn't done this before deciding to undress in public.

'You can speak freely here but I need you to know that I will not pressure you lad. You must speak of your own free will but…I am at your service. I will help and, as sure as God has ears, so will the Agents.'

That was the problem, explained Marcus. He saw this as his mission only. However, he felt some obligation to share as much as he could, not least, because he trusted this man. Marcus told him the tale of how he had escaped Spain, worked in France, Notre Dame, joined the English Navy and so forth but then stopped.

'What is it, Marcus?'

'I will tell you more, sir, but I cannot tell all. I just cannot.'

'May I ask why' queried Farrier, puzzled as to why he now hesitated.

'Everyone…the Agents…the King. They think it is all over. The attempts on the King's life, the design that would have perverted the faith for all time…there is more. It so pains me to say this but there are people who will not be happy until the King and his son are dead and a there is a Catholic sitting on the throne.

'Well, that's not a surprise Marcus and, really, I do think , as Agents, we have served the King well.'

'Oh, God. I am so confounded !' said Marcus almost wailing.

'It must be stopped' he added.

'Then' said Farrier 'we will, as we have before, stop it.'

'You can't. I must do it alone.'

'In God's name, why man?!'

1543 The Disfiguration

'Because, my good Thomas Farrier, I am the sole cause of it.'

10 my return

You may well ask, amid all this confusion, where was I? Having prevaricated, planned, recanted and almost secluded myself at home, I was left realising that I had no option to spend some, otherwise valuable, time once again encased in Magna Carta. Of course, there were other, adequately trained, pilots but the knowledge I had gained of that brief window in time was unique. That is if you accept that I was accessing anything at all. Clearly, my superiors thought so and also thought it was worth me, yet again, becoming a lab rat, or mouse if you like, and worth the added information and revelations that I would acquire. Once my mind was made up, I was fine and, I had hoped to see again many of those characters whom I had regarded as friends but, realistically, knew not what I would now encounter. I remembered little of the process excepting that I must have gone through with it as, there I was, feeling completely devoid of all my normal earthly and human senses. The overriding mantra of my service is, repeatedly, that time travel doesn't exist. Not, by the way, that they are telling anyone exactly what is going on, but I have always understood our missions to be ones in which we use virtual reality to replicate singularities. And, although I am considered primarily a historian, it isn't that I don't understand the science, it is just that it is now, not quite adding up.

I was soon overwhelmed by the speed in which all that pondering and contemplation fell away. I thought only of food and, almost simultaneously, became aware of my form. A mouse. Not necessarily unexpected I supposed. Then the shadows moved away, I was secure and, as I looked down, saw that I was on a common wooden beam. Following that, there were voices and within seconds I could also see. My very first reaction was, on reflection, troubling as I felt well. Not well. Happier, I should say, more complete, if that makes sense. For a moment, I made an effort to stop thinking and chose to look around. I knew exactly where I was and even 'when' I was but it left me disappointed and hurt. I was in the upstairs room of Barley Hall and there, before me, was Elspeth on her deathbed. Leaning over her, holding her hand close to his chest, was Marcus. To be dropped in on such a moving scene was not what I wanted, neither did it make sense. Did this mean there was another Micklegate Mouse in London at the same time? Again, reminding myself to intellectualise less, I told myself that, here, was information that I had not been party to previously. Perhaps something may be said here that would assist me in this, my new mission, I considered.

I made sure to hide inside a break in the daub but peeked out as best I could. The scene was heart-breaking. To find love at a time when you are compelled to leave this world seemed so cruel and ironic. However, there was no question that there was something powerful taking place between these two although, as yet, they were not speaking.

He put his head close to her and started to whisper.

'In so many ways, I feel selfish my love but I have never been able to unburden myself to any man or woman, just the

1543 The Disfiguration

Lord.' He said.

'Shhh...' she breathed 'all things come to good. God makes all good. Finish your confession to me.'

I was also already passionately thanking the Lord for my new ears as those two were talking very quietly. He rambled for some time about the navy but then started to talk specifically about the Mary Rose. Then, without any interim detail, he spoke of documents and keys, clearly arranging with her that he would keep one of the keys.

'You take mine' she whispered.

I was on the verge of shouting out, wanting so much more from them. Why was one of the keys Elspeth's? What did this mean? What bloody keys?!

However, she didn't give him anything. Then, he started to list locations in which parts of the other key had been hidden and, despite her poor state, it became clear that Elspeth was taking a careful, mental note of all he said. He beseeched her to tell no one and, knowing her so well, I detected that she was avoiding making that promise. Otherwise, it was all complete nonsense to me. Keys? More documents? None of this was mentioned whilst I was previously here. Was this an alternate reality? I pondered. Immediately, I knew that my mouse personality had returned. Cursing and muttering to myself, I almost gave myself away. Every fibre of my being was wishing to ignore this latest information that I was struggling to compute but knew that it would be wise to retain it as, at some point, it may have been important. However, I kidded myself that it did fit the profile of the discovery revealed to me at the institute.

She became incredibly tired and fell asleep. Marcus kissed her tenderly on her cheek and went downstairs. I then noticed that she had been left paper and also pen and ink. At first, I presumed that it had been left there before she had even arrived to convalesce, but it clearly had been used and I also recognised her hand. Nothing made sense as I chewed this over but, before I could even consider any reasonable conclusions, I heard fresh footsteps.

Almost immediately, Robert came into the room, his face distorted with worry as he looked upon her. He went to open the window but his gut got between him and the casing so he huffed until he got a little closer.

'Might try losing a few pounds, you chunky bastard!'

It was me. Mouse had said this, practically without my permission. The poor bugger's head was whipping around so fast and in so many directions that it was a wonder he ended up facing forward when he eventually stilled. And then, the fool looked to the sky. A voice in my head said: what fun you could have if you were God for just a few minutes.

'Gluttony is a sin!' bellowed a voice from inside the bedroom wall.

For some bizarre reason, I wanted to laugh whilst trying to control this ridiculous change in persona.

I took a deep breath and looked up. He'd gone, in a flash, down those stairs and Heaven knows where.

I then looked upon dear Elspeth. I had lost her once and now, here I was, experiencing her demise once again.

Eventually, I found myself not knowing what to do. Intellectually, I considered that if I lived through these few weeks again, I may find some anomalies. Perhaps Elspeth would live? As I went around in circles, both physically and metaphorically, I grounded myself in the findings and ethics of the institute. Our best research told us that we were, undoubtedly, getting genuine glimpses of the past or there would be little advantage to me being where I was. That did, of course, leave me wondering what to do about it. The devil inside the mouse played with these ideas as well. I had so much fun with Robert's head, think of what else I could have gotten away with.

I had an idea. Barely scientific, but was, at least, based on my previous experiences. I remember, on more than one occasion, disappearing from one place, and time, to another suspecting that I may have had some control over it. I shook my head, it made no sense. However, after another three hours of being stuffed into the wattle and daub of Barley Hall, I needed to do something. Every time I had been swept up and moved from one plane to another I had, at the same time, been falling. I deduced that the last time I had appeared in Hampton Court Palace, I could make changes by thought alone. It made some sense. After all, I was locked in stasis within a cocoon, projections existing only in my mind. I looked down. Perhaps not. There was absolutely no doubt that, if I threw myself out of the wall, and nothing happened, I would be cat fodder.

Two hours later, having watched Mrs Hall and the servants repeatedly attend to Elspeth, I changed my mind yet again. As the door shut, I hurled myself off the wooden beam thinking as hard as I could of Godwin's workshop, which is where I had very first arrived and also the last place I saw before returning to my home. As the floor, very quickly, neared, I was squealing. So much so, I detected Elspeth's head raise a little and then, inevitably, I hit the deck. Cursing and trying to evaluate what did and didn't hurt, I had managed to get upright and onto my hind legs. Grumpily, I dusted myself off but then stopped, frozen, as I realised that I had done it. Not only was I within the workshop but I was right by my makeshift bed, in the hidden part of the building.

It was only as I relaxed that I realised I wasn't alone. At bottom of the bench was a covered body, clearly breathing as the blanket moved up and down again. Godwin sometimes slept at the workshop, had I slipped even further back? I asked myself but then, possibly the first time since my arrival, told myself to calm and take one step at a time. Drawing conclusions without considering properly what was before me would have been a waste of time. I scurried away from the body to get a proper look. This wasn't Godwin. I managed to work this out simply because there was a huge swelling missing from the centre of the figure, namely his gut.

1543 The Disfiguration

I considered that it could possibly be Edward Fawkes, my friend, companion and fellow Agent since the very start of my, somewhat uncanny, experience. I moved back toward him and stopped about six inches away from the nose that peeped out from the covering.

'Bloody rats! Begone!' A hand swiftly brushed me away and I collided with the bench.

'You arsehole! Could have killed me!! What on…'

The sleepy head suddenly thrust itself upward and upon it, emerged a broad smile.

'Why Micklegate! Micklegate. You're back!'

It was Peter and his warm demeanour calmed me instantly. If any lesson had been learned it was that I really should have made an effort to stand out from other rodents. No matter how much I deplored being dressed up for everyone's amusement, it did help to maintain my individuality and I could see myself requesting it this time.

'Where you been all this time? Have you been here?! Here whilst we worked?'

'No, Peter, no. Am I to assume that you and Edward now own the workshop?'

'Yes!' he said excitedly, now upright and cradling me in his palms 'well…when Ed is able to… He still has school. How good to see you Mouse, no one talks of you, ever. Well, that is, except for Ed and me…'

'I'm guessing that is because no one would believe you? It makes sense and probably for the best...'

Excitedly, he insisted on immediately taking me on an excursion. Very reluctantly, I agreed as it seemed to mean so much to him. Within minutes, we had scrambled onto the workshop roof and then onto the city wall at Micklegate.

He held me high above his head.

'Can you see it Mouse?'

There it was, the same mouse statuette I had seen in the old photograph and later when I had visited York. I implored him, for safety reasons, to take us both back to the workshop.

1543 The Disfiguration

'No one will ever forget what you have done, dear and good Micklegate.'

I was moved by this expression of gratitude and love from these two growing lads and told Peter how much it meant to me.

Once back in the workshop, we chatted calmly, possibly the first time I had been still since my arrival.

'Do you not miss the fishing, Peter? The coast, the sea?'

He paused before answering and then went to the small, singular window that looked upon the Minster in the distance.

'Yes, I do at times. And, truth be told, I miss my family and, I will return. But, Micklegate, this has become my home now. Wait a minute…'

He scrambled amongst some scraps of paper and there, amid them, was a letter from his stepfather, scribed by the able and perhaps not-so-trustworthy Gilly. In it, he thanked him for sending a letter but also gave a severe reprimand for running away, troubling them so and highlighting how he had damaged the family business. The more I read, however, the more respect I had for this man as there was love in there too and he asked only for one concession.

"Before we celebrate the Christ birth next, you are to return for a period of no less than five days to pay due respect to your family" it read.

'That sounds like a fair arrangement' I said to Peter and he agreed, clearly relieved that Robert had put pressure on him to make amends with his kin. There was, however, no question that he was enjoying York and his new employment. I looked around at some of his recent carpentry. There was even some sculpture here and there and, it was good. Some way off what Godwin could have achieved, mind you, but good. In the corner was a piece of work that I reckoned was about two to three feet in height but it was covered with hessian cloth.

'And this?' I asked, now curious as to why it had been

allowed special treatment.

'Oh Mouse. Oh, how I wish that wasn't there. It's a wonder I sleep. Please, just pretend it's not there.'

I laughed.

'Whatever could be so bad that you won't reveal it. It isn't the bones of an ancient Cistercian monk?!'

'Do not jest. It may as well be, and I would not have it here for anything, except the Mayor ordered it. I spend my days and nights just pretending that it isn't there. I'm even getting the shivers now as we talk of it. Shall we cross the bridge and we can see….'

'Nice try' I said 'I am determined to know what it is that you keep concealed and I will be satisfied!' said I, quite authoritatively but, in truth was just teasing.

He reluctantly wandered over to the corner where this conspicuous object lay and, looking over his right shoulder in the opposite direction, whipped off the hessian.

'Good God!' I said 'why in the Lord's good name is that there, in the workshop?!'

'The Mayor wouldn't say. There have been times when I have wanted to burn it but he says it must be perservered.'

'You mean preserved?' I asked.

'Yes. That. Oh dear Mouse, if you can change his mind, will you do so?'

'That I will Peter although I do not doubt that Robert has a reason, no matter how devious. It is quite beautiful though, do you not think?'

'Ugghh…' he said 'I know what you mean, but so recently it was…well…you know…'

'I know' I said showing him that I understood his revulsion. However, there it was. Aelfraed's leg in all its glory. That's the one that he had at the end of his life. The one that Silas had admired on his visit to Knapton. The carving was exquisite and this piece alone would have possibly confirmed Godwin as the finest woodman in York. Three-dimensional galleons mid-battle. Cannons roaring and seamen either fighting hand-to-hand or being thrown overboard. Neatly, as you walked around this sculpture, you could only marvel at how the design was continuous, no clear start and end to the action. Not that I didn't understand Peter's dilemma either, the story of Aelfraed's hanging was the stuff of nightmares. At first, he refused to die without his carved leg attached but this had resulted in him spiralling in all directions and also protracting his death. So, during his final hour, two constables were pulling at the damn thing unsure as to whether they were doing it to stretch his neck or just to get the bloody thing off. Nevertheless, it would be talked about for years after and, not surprisingly, all sorts of questionable characters made claim to it once he was down from the gallows. That is when, as Mayor, Robert stepped in and took possession of it.

'So are you guarding it?' I asked.

'I bloody hope not! Who would want..'

'Best just to keep it covered then Peter. I thank you for showing me.'

He grunted something offensive which I thought best not to repeat in the retelling of this tale. It was then that I realised I was not on task. Half an hour had passed and I was no wiser as to where I was in terms of events. Clearly, this was after Elspeth's death and both Godwin and Aelfraed's executions. And, there had also been enough time to have the mouse statue placed atop Micklegate Bar. I estimated, then, that Silas's wedding would be due and that would put me around somewhere around May 1542.

I then chose to be direct to save time.

'Ah yes, Mouse' he said now giggling 'that thing where you appear and disappear through a window in the past!'

He was mocking me but I didn't mind. After all, on the few occasions that I had tried to explain my presence, I did make a hash of it.

'It is now the second month of 1543.' He said.

11 cloth of gold
Dover 1520

As Aelfraed, Jack and young Marcus pushed their way through the trees, they were completely silenced by what was before them. Even the few days that Jack had taken out to find Aelfraed had made a difference. There were now so many people, horses, boats and ships and so much cargo that, from that distance, it was not possible to see any space between them. Excited, Marcus ran ahead whilst Aelfraed and Jack, pulling the horse, trailed behind trying to both comprehend and put into words what was ahead.

Henry's meeting with his French counterpart was to be the grandest spectacle in Christendom, ably boosted by the enthusiasm and compliance of King Francis. Although the aim was to present the Kings as equals to all of Europe, it would be used to promote all that was virtuous and opulent about both states. So, everything possible was done to ensure that this performance and exhibition became viral. Although, short, the King and Queen made progress through Kent stopping at Canterbury to entertain none other than the Holy Roman Emperor. This was Henry at his most devout. Catholic to the core and already deserving his title of Defender of the Faith that would not be bestowed on him for another year. Visibility was what promoted an event of this nature, in addition to letters and communications speeding back and forth through counties and continents. King Henry the eighth of England and Queen Catherine of

Aragon would gather such a retinue that it would read like a who's who of Tudor society. The King's sister, Mary, Wolsey, the Archbishop of Canterbury, additional bishops, priests, Lords, Earls and Dukes, including Suffolk, Northumberland and Buckingham. All in all, six thousand and, for many, their horses as well. Every one of these needed appropriate attire for travel and also for the series of events that would take place on arrival. One can only imagine the strains put upon the victualler who had to source supplies for the sea journey and beyond. Voluminous amounts of beer, wine, sheep, porpoises and even swans were checked daily for their quality and sheer numbers. The King was used to grandeur and riches and, since 1520, had developed a habit of eating throughout the day. There was absolutely no expectation that standards would falter, even slightly, just because he was heading overseas. Henry would never expect, even briefly, to rough it.

There was, of course, the expectation that the fleet would be perfectly ready, not only to transport all of this to France, but to do it in comfort and, at the same time, ward off any possible hostility at sea. Thomas Howard had his work cut out. Sadly, often caricatured as an ageing and bad-tempered sidekick to the King, whose only role was to supply him with concubines, Thomas, the current Duke of Surrey, was unquestionably an admirable and accomplished mariner and soldier, being able to adapt to enemies both north and south according to the King's whim. What essentially set him apart from his brother was, simply, that he lived. The very essence of why he was both respected and feared in later life lay in the fact that he had faced so many dangers and had survived. Moreover, in 1520, his men respected him. Faith in a commander took away their personal fear and had men working as a single, cohesive machine.

'There she is!' shouted Marcus enthusiastically.

'Is too!' responded Jack. 'Can you see the boards?'

Marcus and Aelfraed gasped at what they beheld. The

1543 The Disfiguration

Mary Rose and the Great Harry had been adorned with painted boards. They stood beside each other as lions surveying their territory.

'So many ships. So many people' said Aelfraed now a little nervous as to what he had agreed to take on.

'Aye, but, until a week or so ago there was only me, two others and William Mewe aboard.'

'Ah..' said Aelfraed 'I see. Was she in ordinary?'

'Been in ordinary some time, many of her parts distributed elsewhere but she's coming alive again now lads!'

In ordinary, was an unusual term but simply meant that she had been stripped down whilst not in use and many valuable parts of the ship were either restored or looked after inland. A crew of four, the head of which was the trustworthy William Mewe, made sure that she was both looked after and secure. In years to come, the Mary Rose would spend some considerable time in ordinary.

Under Jack's supervision, they reported for duty which, to begin with, was whatever was needed at that moment. They would, as the ship set sail, be given specific duties but, for now, they took part in practically anything from reassembling the ship to taking stock and baggage on board. Aelfraed took some time to adjust, realising that there would be a burden upon him to work as fast any other man. Except for the odd glance, no one said anything, correctly presuming that he had lost his leg in battle and, therefore, deserving of respect. However, just one day into their labours, Aelfraed was aware of an almighty fuss behind him and his training kicked in. If every sailor took time to have nosey every time the wind changed or a seagull landed aboard, not only would he get nothing done, he would deservedly have received a good bollocking.

'That the man there?'

Aelfraed still ignored the conversation, absorbed in his duties.

'Yes sir!' came the reply.

1543 The Disfiguration

'Ah yes...of course! I can see now. Haha!'

The laughter now piqued his curiosity. Patience lost, he whipped around, his new leg clunking hard onto the deck as he shifted.

'It's not your bloody face I've come to see! Haha ha!!'

It was Lord Howard and Aelfraed wanted to kick himself with his own wood leg for his sudden lack of discipline.

'Is it true you have the King's face tattooed on your arse man?'

Now, everyone was laughing and Aelfraed didn't know how to respond. As he looked upon this jovial but ferocious warrior, he decided that crawling into his shell may well have been a bad idea.

'No my Lord' he said looking Howard directly in the eye 'just the commander's'

Howard looked around at the crew, back at Aelfraed and took two steps back, his legs now shoulder-width apart and his hands rested on his hips.

There was a pause that seemed to last forever but then, Howard exploded with laughter.

'Ha Ha!! That I'd like to see! Harry always said I have a face like a kicked arse! So...very fitting!'

Everyone laughed. Only after Howard had, mind you, but on the surface, it now seemed that all was well.

'Most famous seat in the realm! Haha!' and then he landed his huge paw on Aelfraed's shoulder.

'See lad?...see how your commander keeps his word and that of his brother too? We Howards like a hero!' And, with that, he stomped away leaving Aelfraed in a stupor but happy that he seemed to be held in such high esteem.

On the day that they sailed, they were told that the King would also make passage on the Mary Rose. As he arrived, he strode, manfully aboard and straight into his privy quarters with no acknowledgement to either the men or their commander. Few questioned this as they were to be busy from the outset. Jack, Aelfraed and Marcus stood shoulder to shoulder as they were told that the Mary Rose would be employed to scout for 'those that may wish harm upon the King's person' amongst the seas. Her speed meant that she was best suited to both flank the fleet when necessary but also to take to the front and rear if needed. Aelfraed was both amazed and delighted that the ship was battle-ready and he never thought that he would see action again. There was also another issue that befuddled him. So he sought counsel from the boy.

'Marcus…have you noticed that the King comes right out onto the forecastle half-hourly, almost as if to expose himself?'

'It's very strange Aelfraed. He, speaks to no one, head down, and then comes in and out like a mouse.'

Aelfraed laughed and thought no more about it until Jack came along and gave him some work to do on the mizzenmast rigging.

'Jack…the King?…'

'Ha Ha!'

Aelfraed didn't understand but, already, Jack was finding his question very funny. Aelfraed then elaborated, saying that it was not how he expected the King to be. Jack laughed again, looked around to see if they were being watched and leant in toward Aelfraed's ear to whisper.

'Not him'

'What do you mean…?'

'It's not the King. He is a decoy in case we meet with the enemy. It will draw their attention.'

'Well, I never…so….'

'And, yes, Alfie, he's probably as dumb as he looks. You are not to let on and, no, I won't tell you which ship the King is on. That's the whole point.'

Feeling somewhat deflated, Aelfraed spent the rest of the journey trying to impress his seniors, including Jack, which was, apart from the unpredictable weather, somewhat uneventful. Jack, meanwhile was adequately establishing himself as a leader as well as a knowledgeable and efficient seaman. He had become known as the 'bucket man' as he had successfully employed buckets on ropes to haul himself perilously over the side when inspecting the integrity of the vessel. It wasn't long before Aelfraed attempted the same but wished that hadn't as his arse, yet again, became the focus of everyone's attention. On one occasion, dangerously getting the rope length completely wrong, he found himself completely upside down, head trailing in the channel whilst his peg projected vertically skyward and further jamming his backside into the pail. Marcus, in contrast, astonished all on board as he could be seen atop the crow's nest one minute and then perilously hanging over the larboard bow disentangling ropes. On one occasion, the boatswain called Marcus 'the cat' and the name stuck. He beamed with pride every time someone said it thereafter.

On arrival, and once all ships where correctly anchored and notice had been given for egress, boats came in their dozens to transport cargo, crew and nobles to shore. Our three heroes missed most of the ceremony that accompanied this activity and were kept, without any respite, incredibly busy.

The meeting of Kings was to take place on neutral land between the English-owned twin of Guines and the French town of Ardres. If the crew was to think that their labours were done with they were to be left very disappointed. Once on land, there were those of rank who ably organised both the progress and the impressive scheduling but everyone who had been in employ aboard the ships were put to good use. Where Jack, Marcus and Aelfraed counted their blessings over and over was when they arrived and witnessed the amazing makeshift kingdom that would host the festivities and challenges. The prevailing theme was to be one of renewed peace between these two powerful and enlightened Renaissance monarchs who wished, at least during this short window of time, to be seen as equals.

1543 The Disfiguration

Thousands watched on as the two Kings walked to meet one another in a designated vale, immediately embracing one another, to cheers from the growing throng. They separated whist, as some reported, they engaged in brotherly banter and then, embraced once again. Over the next week, there would be jousting, archery, wrestling, hawking and all manner of challenges. Competition of every shade and colour was indulged in, as long as it was deemed to be manly but, they would sometimes concede at archery to the ladies, as gentleman were wont to do. Few, in the 1540s, would consider this either patronising or condescending and, yes, some of the ladies were excellent archers anyway. As Henry would gain an inch or two when wrestling with Francis, he, in turn, would draw blood in the joust. Whether there was some attempt to ensure that the balance remained, it would have been hard to say but whatever your stance, view or opinion, the meet at the field of cloth of gold was an overwhelming success. A flat-pack version of an English palace had been erected which, thanks to Wolsey, was somewhat Hampton Courtesque. Incredibly, it had many rooms including privy quarters for the King and Queen. The French had erected tents that were festooned and decorated in maroon and gold but they were, unfortunately, left crestfallen as their piece de resistance, a 120-foot high tent, floundered in the summer gales.

They remained there for two and half weeks and, as well as making many new friends and acquaintances, our three sailors now had an arsenal of tales that would last them a lifetime with even Marcus dwelling momentarily on his grandchildren and what he would, one day, tell them. One morning, they found themselves resting on a nearby bank watching people that mattered, congratulating themselves. Munching on apples, you would have thought them also to be royalty.

'My, how blessed we are' said Aelfraed.

'Isn't that the case' answered Jack still gawping at the

hunting birds 'and when all this is done lads, I think we may be promised a life aboard our lady.'

Mouths stuffed, they both nodded in response to this affectionate name that had been given to the Mary Rose. Almost as content as two men and a lad could be, they dozed off in the sun only to receive a sharp prod moments later. Neither did this ruffle them. So happy were these three that they would have worked all night and day in the King's service.

Like all good things, this expedition was at an end sooner than expected and the journey home was, again, without exception apart from one event.

Aelfraed, content and pushing rope into the cracks in the ship's timber, heard the commander's voice booming again, although he only stirred when he heard him say,

'Ok lads, pick him up!' realising that he was referring to him.

He was terrified as punishments aboard ship were harsh, although he knew not what he had done. Added to this, was the unnerving truth that, yet again, everyone was laughing.

'Brace yourself, young man, for what we do here, today, has been sanctioned by the King himself!'

He suddenly found himself, ungraciously, hauled onto a platform and then laid out prostrate and face down. His slops (sailors baggy shorts) were removed revealing his bare backside. Everyone cheered as this full moon temporarily lit the ship and, there, although seeming to be upside down to Aelfraed, were his two friends, also laughing and cheering. It would be hard to exaggerate those immediate feelings he had of complete betrayal as he noticed that they were all supping beer. He was both scared and devastated.

He then heard a soft voice break through the frenzy.

'Be still lad, it will only hurt a little and, when I'm done, you'll thank me for the rest of your days.'

It was then that he saw the filthy bottle of ink and, for the first time, had some idea of what was happening. At this juncture in this, somewhat irregular, ritual, Lord Howard deemed to kneel beside Aelfraed which, besides being the most curious circumstance Aelfraed had ever found himself in, would normally be unheard of.

'You are to be honoured young Alfie, the King himself hath granted that the royal standard be marked upon your very common arse!' and then he laughed again.

It did hurt. It bloody hurt but, about fifteen minutes into the procedure, Aelfraed realised that he was in a unique position both figuratively and literally. By the time it was done he leapt up, his wooden leg thudding against the deck. He raised his arms and cheered, still butt naked.

'I give to you: the Royal Arse! Never to be touched without His Grace's permission!' announced their commander.

Everyone, now three quarters pissed, whooped, cheered and admired the somewhat slightly wonky design on his backside. Aelfraed joined in, drink in hand and feeling so much better. No matter how makeshift this may have been, the King's standard, including the cross of St George, a dragon and several Tudor roses were clear enough and Aelfraed, now a celebrity, was delighted. The fact that his shipmates referred to him as "The Royal Arse" thereafter only made him feel more proud.

Now they were nearing England and, following days of unloading and sprucing up the ship, they were allowed one half-days shore leave.

Their partnership and, yes, friendship, was to last. Unsurprisingly, the agreement between Henry and Francis didn't. Commanded by Sir William Fitzwilliam, in 1522, they were at war again and, although the Mary Rose and the three bucketeers were involved, there was little action beyond a few skirmishes. Come 1525, the active life of the ship seemed to be over as she was again in ordinary at Deptford with instructions for caulking over the greater mass of the ship. This involved using rope fibres and sometimes tar being jammed between boards and planks to create a seal and rendering her watertight. By 1526, Henry had ordered the building of new docks at Portsmouth that included a device for winding ships onto dry ground. During this time there seems to have been constant repairs to the Mary Rose.

Throughout this period the trio stayed together. As fortune would have it, they were kept as part of a small team of eight men that were responsible for their beloved ship whilst it was in ordinary and they would stay aboard and make her ready as soon as she was needed for battle again. This was not to come. Well, not, at least, for some considerable time. Content in their new appointment, Aelfraed was now as able as any other a man, only hampered when his leg needed an upgrade. During the rest of the 1520s, all was well, the daily work hardly taxing and, in the company of people they respected and, when not on board, they did, well, what mariners do. Although Cardinal Wolsey seemed to have had a healthy regard for the navy, one of his council members appeared somewhat more sinister and invasive in his regulatory interest. Thomas Cromwell had started to monitor the condition of those ships that were intentionally marooned. Aelfraed, Marcus and Jack, didn't question this. In fact, they had never heard of the man previously but they did get notice, eventually, in 1529, that there would be someone new taking over operations and repairs at the shipyard. As was often the case, the new boss would visit regularly and could be seen at a distance. As they already had many gaffers, it didn't matter a jot if another Lord this or that took over so they took little notice. However, one day, that same summer Marcus, atop the mainmast, soon to be dismantled, could not control his curiosity. As they shared lunch, he felt compelled to say something.

'He has plans…'

'Ooh they all have bloody plans!' said Jack.

'No, I mean drawings. Lots of them. Almost as if they're building a ship.'

'Well, I can tell you now young, un, they won't be building more ships.'

'So what are they doing Jack?' asked Aelfraed.

'I haven't got any idea whatsoever. But, you can be assured it will come our way soon enough my friends.'

People were very astute when it came to their jobs being threatened. Those dark glances and meetings with their superiors. Then the foreboding appearance of more people of note. Yes, change was afoot and that change would be significant. It would be enough to change all three of their lives for good. It would also lead to the end of their naval adventure and their association and, yet, they would not have believed any of that if you told them straight to their faces before those changes had occurred.

One day, William Mewe slowly made his way toward the gangplank that was used to board the Mary Rose except on this day he was accompanied by the stranger that had shadowed them all for so long.

'Good day, lads. May God be with you. There is to be a change in developments and repairs under the supervision of this gentleman here, although, if I am to understand him correctly, he won't be around very much. Can you all work with carpenters if need be?'

Anxiously, they agreed. Mind you, if he had asked if they would work with mermaids they would have said yes. They simply wanted to stay where they were and carry on doing what they were doing. Nodding, breathlessly, they all turned to the businessman bedecked in the finest leathers and silks.

'May I introduce myself, good fellows' he said smiling 'I am Sir Anthony Bask.'

12 the rally
York 1543

'It is now the second month of 1543' said Peter leaving me speechless and wondering why I was being thrown from one place and time to another.

'Alright. Tell me what has taken place since…say….Elspeth's passing.'

Quite coherently, he talked me through the events that followed, including her burial and our return from Hampton Court Palace. I nodded patiently, acknowledging that everything he said, I had, previously, been aware of. As he spoke of the meeting, the trial as some would have called it and where Godwin was exposed, I listened with interest at how Peter had seen it from his point of view. Almost on conclusion, he said,

'And would you believe, Elspeth, the nun, forgave him from beyond? Forgave him from beyond!' The words echoed in my head as if I was victim to some cheap market stall spell. Then came the most unpleasant sensation, not dissimilar to having had too much to drink. Peter and the workshop pulsed in and out. I heard myself moaning and then, just as suddenly, it stopped again. Unbelievably, I was back in that room with Elspeth once more. I so wanted to curse. This was becoming the scientific equivalent of being on a treadmill, perhaps a very appropriate scenario for a mouse although I felt no levity whatsoever at that thought. Then, I thought about the science. At the end of the day, I was an explorer, it would have been ridiculous to assume that everything on this mission would go seamlessly and consecutively so I told myself to be calm and observe. What followed is so very hard to describe, as I became most aware of that young woman's physical presence and I thought that there may have been a reason why I had bounced back again, that reason being that I had some degree of control. This incredibly unscientific thought, at least, calmed me down.

Immediately, a visitor. This will be as a rerun I told myself. I would witness the same conversation between Elspeth and Marcus. But, I was wrong. Here was Eirik, presumably making his peace with her. It is only with hindsight that I realised that in that mouse form I was not just ill-tempered but almost incurably arrogant. Back in my little hole in the wall, I believed that I could pre-empt this conversation between the two of them, verbatim, exactly as Eirik had told me. What I didn't account for was that he had only told me part of his exchange with Elspeth. He broke down in tears at one point and, Elspeth, acknowledging his sins, took his confession, insisted that he repent and forgave him and, as a remarkable sign of her trust in him, she shared much of what Marcus had confided in her.

'I would not betray him for anything, Eirik, for he is now as dear to me as anything ever has been in my life, apart from Our Lord Jesus Christ himself. The task he has set himself will not only, assuredly, lead to his death but will also fail. It is too much for one man.'

'I am entirely at your service and that of your man, sister. You have my word. I pledge my life in this.'

Elspeth then explained to Eirik that she would be leaving messages and clues for her sister, but that Wynnfrith would then also be sworn to secrecy.

'I would have her, God rest her soul, fathom the gravity of events and persuade Marcus to employ the assistance of all the Agents, thereby giving better odds to a successful outcome.'

So, Eirik was to be used merely as a labourer until he was called upon by Marcus to do more. It was to be him that would hide the key parts which had so recently been entrusted to Elspeth. Originally, it had been her idea to have them buried with her for, that one key, in particular, was, potentially and immeasurably dangerous.

'So why would you have Wynnfrith find that key if it is so dangerous?' asked Eirik.

'Because, I believe there are others like it and, if Marcus fails, the Agents will know what to look for.'

She also confided in Eirik that she had kept in her possession another key, completely unrelated to the one that Marcus spoke about and she had then passed it on to him. Uncannily, not only had Marcus and Elspeth swapped secrets but they had also swapped keys. This seemed incredibly convoluted but I was picking up that Marcus, with the noblest of intentions, was to take on some of the most powerful people in the land, single-handedly. If there was one thing that the Agents had learnt, it was that they were more efficient as a team. Had Elspeth done the right thing? Who was I to say? But she was to be applauded for seeing the bigger picture and, yet again, exercising her strategic management skills from both sides of death.

As Eirik eventually left her, he was beside himself, genuinely broken-hearted.

This left me, yet again, staring at this poor dying young woman as she slept, wondering how the hell I would get myself out of there again. But, as I pondered, there on cue was Robert. Although Eirik had taken some documents and key parts with him, there were still some scribblings left around Elspeth's bed. Robert looked at her and started to speak.

'I keep my oath to you dear cousin. My eyes will not set upon your writings but I will keep them in order and dispatch as you have requested once you are with The Lord'. And, he did just that. With not even a glance toward the script, he bundled them up neatly and took them away.

As he reached the door, almost completely out of the room, I drew on the deepest tones I could muster.

'I saw you take that last pie when no one was looking....'

I could hear him vent forth a continuous whining sound as he rapidly descended the stairs.

Having amused myself, I then became increasingly anxious as I really did not want to, literally, take the plunge again. However, as soon as I had contemplated this, the room began to spin. Whether I liked this or not, I was now telling myself that I had to go with the flow when the flow came. Seemingly, I was not in control and, thankfully this time, it was soon over with.

I then struggled to digest what was before me. What I saw was so much like an engraving from an old school history book that I believed, at first, it to be pure hallucination. There were two men drinking ale and I knew who both were instantly, and was desperately wishing that I wasn't there for all sorts of reasons. One of them left me feeling emotionally compromised as, strangely, I had a connection to him. So, there I was in a pub, in London, called the Duck and Drake. The man facing me, but unable to see me was Thomas Wintour and, astonishingly, this was the year of Our Lord, 1604. If it wasn't for that fact that I had a, somewhat distant, relationship with the other man, this would probably have made no sense at all. To his side, sporting every bit the costume of the day, was Edward's son. Yes, the son of Edward Fawkes who, in my consciousness, was still a boy in his teens. However much I didn't want to be there, the irony was not lost on me. Like his father, William, Edward Fawkes would become a well-respected Protestant, a Proctor

Advocate of the Consistory Court.

Edward's son, however, Guido or Guy Fawkes, as he became known, could not have been more Catholic and there he was before me. I had found myself at the first proper meeting of the gunpowder plot conspirators and I was driven, drastically, to dissuade Guido from his intent. Logic had left me. I felt it my duty, on behalf of young Edward to save his son, not only from his own fate but this diabolical pathway. I boldly climbed the table leg until I was peeping over its edge, now close enough to hear them whispering to one another.

I opened my mouth to intervene,

'Guido, please I have been a friend of your father. If for no other reason…'

Impressive. Yes. However, it wasn't me who said it. As I looked beyond his lacy sleeve I encountered what was probably my most bizarre apparition to date. There, tugging on his sleeve, was a mouse. And it talked. And, it wore a similar outfit to his. Surely this was me. What did this mean? Why 1604? I presumed that historians knew everything there was to know about the gunpowder plot. Besides that, I simply did not want to be there but there I was.

Again, falling, spinning and back to where I had been, with Peter in the workshop.

'You're not listening to me are you Micklegate? If I did that, you'd say I was rude!' said Peter with a chuckle.

'No, no. Not at all. I'm so pleased to see you! Is it still 1543?'

'Ha Ha! Not been at the ale have you Mouse? Come on, let's have you, we'll make way to see Father Matthew.'

'Yes! Yes! Father Matthew. Thank you!'

He put me in a box and away we went over the river and I was delighted to see my beloved York again. Already I was feeling more stable but pondered endlessly at what had happened, wondering if my jaunt, sixty-one years hence had any significance. As we reached Coppergate, we were aware of cheers in the distance.

'It can't be!' I shouted.

'Oh it is, just arrived back here again and performing daily. You must see what he has come up with, mouse.'

There was simply no way I was going to miss seeing Bayard one more time, just to set eyes on him would raise my spirits. As we found ourselves in the square, slightly south of the Minster and to the west of St Michael le Belfrey, there was a crowd like York had never seen before. There was no mistaking Bayard's scruffy cart and misspelt sign but, currently, he was not visible.

'Puppets' said Peter pointing toward the stage. Curiously I remembered how I had met Bayard. How he had kidnapped me to use as an oddity and then stuck pins in my backside! I chuckled and asked Peter if we could stay to watch. I needed something normal. That is if you can call one of Bayard's shows normal.

Centre stage was a quite remarkable likeness of the King. A puppet. It was grossly overweight and when he spoke it was with an annoying London accent but there were no words. It sounded a little like 'fwaffaf...Bubub...flafwafaf...' which was hilarious in that it amply characterised the nonsensical way in which he seemed to rule. At first, I wasn't sure whether there was a story but neither was I bothered. Fortunately, we seemed to have caught the production at the very beginning. Another puppet moved to centre stage, the King still blubbering, and a voice, from backstage, announced,

'1534, Elizabeth Barton!'

Of course, this puppet was a nun. The King mumbled and she was then dangled from a rope. The audience loved it and, already I was getting the gist of what this was about. Bayard must have invested some money in this colourful array of marionettes.

Then a cleric,

'John Fisher...who says the King isn't in charge of the

church!' and his head, still connected by thread, popped off and bumped onto the stage. The crowd thought this was hilarious and those that didn't, knew it to be audacious. However, once Thomas More, who was beheaded in the same year, followed on, the mood changed. It was at this juncture that I realised how much Bayard had honed his craft. Apart from lampooning the King, he left the audience to decide what they thought of the narrative, the characters and the, rather silly, puppets. The general sympathy for the Catholic faith in the north was ably expressed as they decided that they didn't wish More to lose his head yet again so, on this cue, the More puppet swung a thump at Henry who fell on his backside. The crowd were loving every second of this and were showing it by opening their purses. The cream on the cake had to be the silly voices that were attributed to the puppets. This, I recognised instantly, accepting that, at last, Bayard had found useful employment for his very strange friend, Dramaticus. He had also set the pace expertly as the audience knew what was coming next. 1536 would see the execution of Anne Boleyn, her brother and a host of alleged lovers. What the Anne Boleyn puppet was meant to be doing with all those men, God only knows but it had the crowd, laughing, shouting and jeering. I enjoyed it so much that I believed that my chubby friend had struck gold. Of course, he also had thousands of characters to choose from as Henry's cull rarely took a month's rest during his whole reign.

I looked to Peter, tears rolling over his cheeks. It was good, at last, to be settled and feeling as though I was where I was meant to be. He turned to me,

'Funny isn't it, Micklegate?'

'Yes. The puppets are hilarious!' I said.

'No, I mean Bayard. Have you noticed that he's only around when you are? He seems to arrive when you do.'

Absorbed in the nonsense before me, I amicably agreed whilst, for some minutes, his odd observation bounced around my tiny skull. Then, I mulled it over. Surely that must be a coincidence? I'm placing conspiracies where there are none. So, then, I chose to ignore it.

'Well, to business young Peter. Might as well let everyone know I am returned.'

I cannot ably express what it meant to me to set eyes again on Holy Trinity Church. It was like rediscovering something lost and my heart was bursting. Father Matthew was at prayer so we waited a while. He strained as he pushed himself up from his knees and, on seeing Peter, seemed surprised.

'Why young fisherman, what can I do for you?'

'I have brought a good friend to see you Father' and he opened the box.

'Micklegate! I thought you gone for good. My...it is good to see you.'

He then screwed his face slightly as if somewhat suspicious.

'I am pleased to see you but...well...where you are, there is often trouble not far behind.'

I laughed at his presumption and chose to correct him only slightly.

'Actually Father, there is trouble already, I'm just here to get to the root of it!'

'Ah wise mouse, but...you missed the wedding!'

'I would not have missed it for the world but simply was not able to attend.'

I could tell from his reaction that he presumed that I had been, all the while, with the King but thankfully he didn't ask.

'I believe we need to gather the Agents Father. I can say no more as yet but it is of great importance.'

Father Matthew knew that, for some, my return would be a shock. In fact, it would have been fair to assume that many had convinced themselves that I had been nothing more than a bottle of dodgy wine.

My heart sang as he agreed to arrange a meeting in the church as soon as possible whilst I resided at the workshop along Micklegate.

Later that day, the priest made his way along Stonegate stopping at the grandest house in the street, Mulberry Hall. This was the new residence of the Halls. Having relinquished his Mayoral office, Robert had decided that he would continue to live in some style. After all, he was, possibly the wealthiest person in the city. Two storeys and the width of four houses it was now over a hundred years old but stood proud and beautiful amidst Stonegate. Father Matthew was welcomed inside by a beautiful young woman called Meg who, quite recently, had been employed by Mrs Hall. He waited in the hallway and Mrs Hall, enthusiastically, beckoned him in. There was Mrs Hall, beaming as she looked upon Wynnfrith who was cradling her new-born baby, now sleeping. Meg could not resist walking over to have another peep at the child and, seemingly, Mrs Hall didn't mind. Meg was introduced to Father Matthew and Wynnfrith explained that, since her arrival, they had become good friends.

'Would it be alright if we all broke fast together…including Meg?' asked Wynnfrith.

Although uneasy at first, Mrs Hall agreed as long as Meg prepared food and served the rest of them first. Of course, all attention was on the smallest object in the room, reducing well-respected adults to cooing imbeciles.

'Let me see' said Mrs Hall and Wynnfrith peeled back a woollen hood to reveal one long strand of red hair. We all laughed, Silas couldn't deny this child even if he had chosen to. Very solemnly, Father Matthew turned to Wynnfrith.

'How is he, my dear?'

This changed the mood immediately for, Meg, eavesdropping, presumed that some unfortunate event must have befallen our good friend, Silas.

'I have left him this morning laid out on the bed, a compress on his forehead but he still moans so.'

'And it's now three days?' asked Mrs Hall.

'Yes' said Wynn 'but we pray that he will recover soon.'

'Tell us, dear Wynnfrith, what exactly has befallen Silas'

1543 The Disfiguration

asked Father Matthew.

'When my…well…waters…you know….broke? I then called him for help. Almost immediately, he started squatting up and down where he stood but I have no earthly explanation for it. Then, he shivered constantly saying 'oooh…oooh err…ooh.'

Try to get hold of yourself, husband, says I, but by now Mrs Leeds had heard the moaning from across the alley. Well, she had actually heard his moaning thinking it was me. She first shouted at him and called him all sorts of names and then told him to sit outside next to his horse. The birth was difficult but, as you know, I thanked God there and then for this gentle gift, particularly as she seems so healthy.

When all was done, I called husband upstairs and, on seeing the child, he wept uncontrollably, his little knees knocking together and the up and down thing starting all over again. Truth be told Mrs Hall, he's been much more trouble than the baby.'

Wynnfrith looked over at Father Matthew who was trying hard not to laugh but Mrs Hall started him off. Wynn joined in and then the baby cried.

'I wouldn't change him for gold, though…'

There was some idle chatter whilst they ate and Meg asked if she could hold the child.

'What's she called?' Meg asked.

'Silas, as always, of good heart, said we should call her Elspeth, after my sister, but I had already decided that she was to be named Mary after his mother. Mary Smith. He collapsed once again when I told him this. No more news for my husband for the time being, methinks.'

'I had a baby once. Died' said Meg.

Wynn was so shocked that she did not know what to say. This was such a hard-hitting statement and yet, Meg had said it in a very matter of fact manner.

'Mrs Hall knows, I was honest with her when I took the job. Shamefully, Father, he was born out of wedlock and I think his death was punishment. I have confessed to my own priest and repented.'

'My child' said Father Matthew 'repentance is, indeed, the better option, always, but be assured that the good Lord does not punish mothers or babies.'

'My sister knew that God was good. All things of God come good.' Added Wynnfrith.

'Amen,' they chorused.

Without prompting she continued.

'Stupid girl I was. Thought it was love sent from on high but it was just a handsome young traveller I had met at Scarborough fair. Still ashamed I am.'

'Oh, my brother went to the fair when he was young…Eirik. Don't suppose you met him?'

'Eirik? No, not as I recall, although there were thousands there my Lady.'

Wynnfrith thought to pursue the matter but realised that they hadn't yet asked Father Matthew why he was visiting. He remained coy until Meg had left the room to tidy up.

'He hath returned!' he shouted, purposely hamming up the news. They all giggled.

'Well…who?' asked Mrs Hall.

'The mouse..' he whispered.

'Oh my!' said Wynnfrith 'Silas will be delighted.'

Robert then made a timely appearance and, between them, they arranged a time when the Agents would meet.

Months had passed and the Agents hadn't met as Agents in some time. Naturally, the meeting was delayed whilst everyone made a fuss of the baby. They sat, as best they could, encircled inside Holy Trinity Church. Father Matthew was solemn, with his back to the altar with Robert, now even heavier, squeezed tightly into his right shoulder. There was a conscious attempt not to repeat any past arrangement as the passing of Elspeth was still, deeply, felt. Bayard was there. Bede had a seat and, although he squirmed somewhat, it was clear that he recognised everyone and that he was happy to see them. Wynnfrith nursed little Mary and, Peter and Edward, either side of her, were letting the baby hold their fingers. Edward, delighted to see me, placed me on his lap. Acknowledging that the Agents were somewhat depleted, Father Matthew politely asked Wynn if her other half would be attending.

'Oh yes, Father. I think he fares a little better today and says he will try to attempt the journey alone.' As hard as he could, the priest tried to divert attention away from Robert whose eyes projected skyward in response and then clucked his tongue quite loudly. Then, the door opened. The wind blew in leaves from the graveyard as a shadowy figure slowly strode in, tripping over the same flagstone that had got him twenty times or more before already.

'Mouse!' he said 'what a delight. We thought you gone forever.'

As I stretched upward to see beyond Edward's shoulder, I was ecstatic, seeing, once again, this skinny outline but I noticed that he hobbled. As he got closer, it was evident that he had gestated a curious and out-of-place looking pot belly. Was this Silas adapting to his new role as a father? Embracing middle age whilst still in his twenties? I asked myself and then realised that I couldn't take my eyes off him as the rest of his body was still so incurably scrawny.

'It's alright' he said looking around 'I can manage, just draw up a stool for me.'

Ever kind, Edward asked him if he was feeling better.

'Oh…I cope. Been a very difficult time' and then he sat, holding his pot as if it were a baby in the womb. It was then, and then only then, that I diagnosed him as having a phantom pregnancy which meant we could be putting up with this same performance for another eight months. Unsurprisingly, Robert looked disgusted but tolerated it for the sake of all present. Bede shifted slightly as Silas approached, presumably ready to dart in case he felt like kissing him again.

'Thank you all' started the priest 'I know I speak for everyone when I say how delightful it is to have our very own Micklegate Mouse here once again to advise and steer us.'

There were smiles and a trickle of applause. Mary burped.

'I must remind you that, as Agents of the Word or, more recently, The Royal Secret Agents of the Word, we may only meet with the King's permission. However, on the advice of the good Mouse here, I have called this informal get-together. Eirik is away on Robert's business and of course, the good Richard Shakespeare and Thomas Farrier are home in Stratford. In line with Elspeth's wishes, Marcus would be welcome here but he has left York leaving no word of where he is. So, for now, that leaves us.'

Then, he stared at me for what seemed like an eternity.

'Yes, Father?'

'Well, dear Mouse, we are here because of you.'

I realised that, if appearances counted for anything, all was well in York but, unless I was hopping between alternate dimensions, I knew that something was definitely afoot. So, I just went for it.

'I know about the keys.'

The atmosphere changed instantly. I could tell that this so-called team were now, individually, keeping their cards close their chests.

'It wasn't my idea!' confessed Silas before he had even been questioned.

'Oh Silas! Must you?!' said an angry Wynnfrith.

He looked around acknowledging that everyone now wanted more. I intervened to save his neck.

'I suspect that you Silas and your wife, and Father Matthew, and Robert all know something about this. You might not all know everything, but that is what the Agents are for, after all. I know there to be another real and imminent threat to the King and nation whilst, seemingly you're all sitting on your hands.'

Bugger, I had said too much. The brief, but alarming,

information that was shared with me at the institution didn't even mention keys but I had a strong suspicion that what Marcus and Elspeth had been dealing with was, almost certainly, related to it.

Nothing. I looked at Wynnfrith again who was cleverly diverting her eyes toward the baby.

'Wynn?' I said softly.

Her head came up, she gulped, handed the baby to Silas, taking care to instruct him on supporting her head.

'What was I meant to do! All that nonsense and…would you believe she had me making oaths between here and the Heavens themselves…had me hither, thither..' and this became an, almost endless, rant. She told the whole story of how she had found documents, then more documents, lumps of metal, everything. Silas looked straight ahead with an expression that bordered on catalepsy. She was becoming very upset so I stopped her.

'Wynnfrith, dearest Wynnfrith, there is no blame laid at your door. You are to be applauded for respecting your sister's wishes. Truthfully, others in this room have some knowledge of this matter' heads suddenly went down 'and Marcus is no doubt trying to resolve this threat single-handedly as we speak.'

She then told everyone of how she had employed Moonlight to find Marcus. Robert was astonished but before he could butt in, I asked her how that had progressed. At this juncture, she said nothing of the multiple identities of Moonlight.

'Moonlight promised that he would find Marcus and take us to him within a few months but I have seen both moon and moonlight but nothing of that dodgy, over-dramatic and overdressed bastard since!'

Shocked, we took a moment to absorb Wynnfrith's frustration. Understandably, she had prioritised their daughter and, since the birth only days ago, she had put it all behind her.

'If I had any inkling why, on God's good earth, a key or two would matter then I might be more invested!'

Then the door opened again. This always made Agents nervous when meeting, especially when meeting without the King's permission. Again, at first, all that could be seen was an outline. However, it was nothing like the previous one which had, sideways-on resembled a small letter b. This was a tall and muscular man, masked and striding in without invitation.

'Where the bloody hell have you been?!' said Wynnfrith in a most unladylike manner.

'Yeah and the rest of y...' Wynn speedily put her hand over Silas's mouth.

Moonlight spoke.

'The Information that I have to impart is only of use now that the beast hath returned. He has information that will help you. The King, the crown and the faith are in danger. Marcus is in hiding in Oxford. Pole is your enemy.'

Before anyone had the opportunity to respond, he was gone, leaving them speechless. Somewhat chagrined at being called a beast, I decided to take advantage of this sudden, and somewhat weird, announcement.

'We must find out what has become of dear Marcus. We will rally our Agents in Stratford upon the Avon and also give them support.'

'What does Pole mean?' asked Edward.

For a while there was silence. For the first time ever we were entering new and difficult territory. Even I found myself looking around and weighing up the stance of everyone in the room. As Agents, we had sworn not to get drawn into conflicts regarding the old and new faith but beliefs, real people's true beliefs were deep and they meant a great deal to them. Peter. Bless him, he was interested only in truth and good deeds and he would talk directly to Jesus daily, something that would not go down well with staunch Catholics. I looked to Edward. His family was part of the

1543 The Disfiguration

Protestant vanguard in York, well established and respected in the Minster. Then I paused. Of course. Was that why I saw Guido? That massive family shift to Catholicism following Peter's death. I shuddered, I didn't want to think upon this child's death even if he was a good age when it happened. What a minefield, I thought to myself. Robert. Well, Robert would change his allegiance more often than his hose if it meant that his coffers were filled. Wynn and Silas were truly so close to God that they probably didn't give a fig about either old or new. I looked at Bayard. I realised that I hadn't got a clue what was going on in his head. In fact, part of me really didn't want to go there. Bede, if he could speak, would bring down the King and his phoney religion tomorrow and, truth be told, Father Matthew wouldn't be far behind him. What a bunch and what a conundrum.

'I will surmise' I said as, at last, I had their attention 'during these last few years, we have had to face the reality that the King has many enemies and much opposition. We, as Agents, have had to deal with the ruthless ambition of Protestants, so hell-bent on cementing it in the English psyche and getting Prince Edward firmly placed as a puppet on the throne, that we have forgotten the opposition. The very foundation of our comradeship was in the trials of Brother Bernard and of Brother Bede, sitting yonder. If you recall, even our beloved Elspeth was part of the infamous Pilgrimage of Grace but, dare I say, seemed to have found some reason in the reformation following her revelations.'

There was a pall about the room as the King had forbidden anyone to speak of the Pilgrimage of Grace again. However, there had been, continuously, a drive both abroad and at home to ensure that England, once again, would be a Catholic state with a Catholic monarch. Everyone in the room knew this, but it was not a topic that was verbalised often, if at all.

'Look, I know there are people in this room that have strong feelings. Powerful beliefs. It is understandable. Our dilemma is whether we believe still, that we are bound by oath to the King?'

Father Matthew, now clearly disgruntled, raised his head from his hands and looked at everyone.

'We did, indeed and…absolutely, pledge allegiance to our King. We either disband as Agents, as we have not been contacted by him or, we organise ourselves this very day!'

There were many reasons why the people in the church that day could have chosen the easy life. Who, with a new-born child, wouldn't? However, I could already see them stirring. Elspeth's integrity and Marcus's safety was at the heart of this matter and so it was Wynnfrith who first reminded us of our duty.

'We must see this through. We have succeeded before with the leadership of the good Mouse here, and we will again.'

Even Bayard was supportive which cannot have been easy as his business was faring better than it had ever done before. I looked around. It seemed hardly likely that this band of misfits and miscreants could make a difference once again but I had faith in them. Complete faith.

'Pole?' said Bayard which invited responses from almost all present. The Pole family was inexorably tied to that drive to bring Catholicism back and that included the Pilgrimage of Grace. They had a strong and powerful lineage going back to the Plantagenets and, given the chance, may even have argued for a place on the throne but more likely, would have favoured Mary, the daughter of Catherine of Aragon. Everyone in the room had their own take on this, between them, covering the whole flaming Pole family and, of course, opinions were now simmering. I stopped them and immediately started to organise them once more, struggling as to how I would now include a baby in our plans. However, by sunset on that day, we had forged a plan that was to be put into action immediately.

13 reggie pole

If you were a member of the Pole family, you would constantly be reminded by your family of how your blood had been derived from that of the greatest Kings. Reginald Pole, himself, was the great nephew of Richard 111 and Edward 1V. So, it is no surprise that Henry V111 tended to keep the Pole family close to him, particularly through difficult times. Whilst still a teenager, Reginald had graduated from Oxford and was offered the position of Dean of Wimborne by Henry. He became a young, rising star and, in the 1520s was tasked with gauging opinion regarding the validity of the King's first marriage.

It is difficult to say when Henry V111 first became obsessed with Anne Boleyn but it is very likely that this may have been as early as 1523 and there was no doubt that he was becoming disillusioned with Queen Catherine by the mid 1520s. Most historians agree that, most probably, Catherine of Aragon would have made an ideal long term Queen for both Henry and England but she was of course, in his eyes, responsible for the absence of a male heir. And, it is

1543 The Disfiguration

reasonable to assume that Henry's wandering eyes (and the wandering of dubious other bits) were not solely responsible for his desire for a divorce as he had free rein of mistresses, if required. The issue of a male heir became his life-long obsession and this, combined with his child-like infatuation with Anne, meant that he was determined to make changes. Added to that catalogue of woes, around 1524 physicians told Henry that it was unlikely that Catherine would ever conceive again.

It was around this time that Pole established his somewhat inflexible stance and was not to shift an inch for the rest of his days. When offered the post of Archbishop of York in 1526, it was with the understanding that he would support Henry in obtaining a divorce. Not only did he turn this, and also subsequent offers down, he completely buggered off, exiling himself abroad in order to avoid the issue, only returning to England in 1532 when, temporarily, he worked as a cleric in Dorset but he would not be in England long. He became widely known as someone who was continuously uncomfortable with the King's plans for divorce and his ambitions for Anne Boleyn. Eventually, so significant was Reginald deemed to be, that Chapuys, the Holy Roman Emperor's ambassador in England, began scheming, ultimately proposing a marriage between the Emperor and Princess Mary. This failed. There was already a brewing undercurrent supporting the idea that if Henry did not come to his senses of his own accord, there would be a push to attribute more power to his Catholic daughter. However, one immovable fact remained, Mary suffered from almost constant ill health and hoped herself, whilst her mother was still living, that her father would experience his own road-to-Damascus restoration.

Unlike many influencers around Henry during the Reformation, his divorce and re marriage, there were no grey areas in Pope-populariser Pole's, permanently polarised position. Whereas Thomas More embraced the law and remained silent, Pole responded to the King by sending his 'Pro ecclesiasticae unitatis defensione.' This was a clear rebuttal of Henry's position regarding his own brother. That being, that Henry had declared that, in marrying Catherine of Aragon his dead brother (Arthur's) wife, he had sinned and this was the reason why the Queen had not given him a son. Pole went further, rallying opposition to Henry. By 1536, the Pope had made Pole a Cardinal and tasked him with seeking support for the Pilgrimage of Grace. By the time Pole had reached Paris, the movement had been overwhelmed and so he returned to Italy.

Not surprisingly, there was now a price on Pole's head. However, frustrated with efforts to bring him to task, Henry V111 turned his grievance toward the family of Reginald Pole in England who were, therefore, much easier to access. The King put pressure on Reggie's mum, Margaret, the Countess of Salisbury, so that she was left with no choice but to write to Reginald in the hope of persuading him to temper his opposition. With no chance of success, Henry then turned to persecuting the whole family, accusing them of treason. This treasonable behaviour was later dubbed the Exeter conspiracy of 1538, the Poles accused of attempting to put Henry Courtney, Marquess of Exeter on the throne. Although undoubtedly Papists, the Poles and their allies were likely victims of Thomas Cromwell's propaganda. The consequences of the supposed Exeter conspiracy were serious and very damaging. Geoffrey Pole, Reginald's brother was arrested and interrogated. He not only admitted to writing to Reginald but also implicated his other brother, Henry. Their mother, now sixty five years of age, along with Exeter, Henry Pole and other family members, were arrested. Even Cromwell eventually admitted that this family were guilty only by association, despite their beliefs.

Reginald was detained in absentia. Which meant, although far away and safe, he was under arrest and lost his lands but stayed clear of the upheaval. Unimpressed, he arrogantly declared that he would be proud to be the son of a martyr.

Geoffrey was the only one pardoned. To start with, all the others lost their lands but were eventually executed. Margaret, Reginald's mother, languished in the Tower in dire conditions until 1541 when she was also put to death. She wasn't even afforded the usual assurances of a privileged execution. A hurried procedure led to a bodged killing, thanks to an under-qualified executioner who only succeeded in dispatching her by hacking away at her frail and aged neck. This did little to appease Catholic sympathisers, particularly as she was old, of poor health and of Royal stock. However, Reginald Pole not only survived throughout, but remained in favour with the Pope and the Catholic Church. Seemingly, for Reg, no price was too high to pay for his continued exile and position within the Catholic hierarchy.

What can be difficult, in retrospect, is to grasp what the average everyday citizen would have made of all of this. For anyone who was over the age of 15 by 1536, there would be only one true faith that had been mapped out in their psyche and souls from the moment that they had been born and, although changes brought about by Henry's divorce itself were, at first, sporadic, there was no doubt that people were now regularly asked to unravel, and confess to, their deepest beliefs. On the other hand, for some, Reformation was long overdue, the power and constraints imposed by the old order seemingly lightyears away from the teachings of Jesus Christ. Nevertheless, those momentous events like the Pilgrimage of Grace and the Exeter uprising would have polarised people. That is, depending on what they heard and from whom. What reasonable citizen would not rally against an attempt to harm the person of Prince Edward? And, would not that same person, having family themselves, feel disgust at the torture and execution of an old lady, possibly guilty of no more than wanting to take Mass in Latin? Common thought was, often, much more straightforward than simply belonging to one camp or another.

What was certain was that the King had accrued numerous enemies for many different reasons. The state of the nation, at times, so confused that people didn't know what they wanted. It was with this in mind that the Agents had to make a choice either to protect the King or not. They had hardly given the Catholic resurgence a moment of thought as they had been consumed with other matters since 1541. But, that force was powerful and for some it would not to go away until Henry's daughter, Mary, was positioned on the throne.

Few commoners knew how serious a threat Reginald Pole was to England but the few that did were left horrified by his plots, plans and long term intentions, particularly those who prided themselves on staying firmly on the fence. It was very likely that, now, the Agents we're facing a new enemy whilst keeping an eye out for the old ones.

14 the seduction
August 1541

Having acquired a post as chamberer in the household of Queen Catherine Howard, Elspeth, as best she could, kept herself to herself ensuring that, daily, she became more adept at her duties. Unfortunately, she rarely saw the Queen which meant that her real role, that of a spy, was likely to fail completely. Lady Rochford, from time to time, could be heard bellowing orders but this was often from a distance and, at times, Elspeth also became aware of the comings and goings of the King and Queen.

Her experience of Thomas Culpeper was somewhat different. On arrival, he had overwhelmed her with his, somewhat nauseating habit of flattering anything that moved. Certain that she was immune to this, she speedily discovered that she wasn't. Some months later, whilst in prayer, she had decided with some certainty that this must be what the devil looked like. Handsome, charming, witty and bedecked in the latest, and most expensive fashions of the day. Delivered in a smooth and engaging tone and accompanied by the most congenial and polite disposition. That was not to say that she didn't like him, just that this was her developing theory on temptation. Even whilst living in the convent, Elspeth would expound her revelation that temptation was the root of all wrongdoing. Well, at least for most people, she would add. Also, what she had discovered in Lincoln was that she had been sheltered from temptation for most of her life and decided that, for a good Christian, that was, ultimately, the best way to live. The reality was, like most monks and nuns, she had been hiding from the realities of life for some time.

Neither did Culpeper force any advances on this new maid but he just couldn't resist employing that tired routine that had worked so well for him, for so long. My own relationship with Culpeper was brief but I liked him and I knew that, despite his dalliances with the Queen, he did love the King.

As daylight arrived on the Monday morn and the Cathedral bells echoed around the lowlands of Lincoln, Elspeth was content but musing as to how she could become a little more successful in her role as a spy. This was the Bishop's Palace and was to be home for the Royal party whilst in Lincoln. However, much of what the Royal couple owned went along with them if that was practically possible. Opening the windows wide, Elspeth took Queen Catherine's embroidered blanket, that had travelled with her, and shook it hard, then grabbed and folded it as she pulled it back into the bedroom. She turned and, seemingly out of nowhere, there he was, before her.

'You startled me, Sir!'

Truth be told, whether she liked it or not, her heart had now instantly developed a mind of its own, and this was, in no small part, due to the appearance of Tom Culpeper, the romancer.

'What a fine morning maiden! Why, a man should be riding out on a day such as this!' he said glancing out of the window and then back at her.

'Yes,' she said, as it was all she could muster. Elspeth was already aware that she was reacting erratically, both physically and mentally to his presence. Having been a nun, she had a default setting for temptation that shouted out, in a very clear and reverential tone, don't look there, no, don't look there at all, don't listen to him, carry on with your work, and so forth, and this was usually adapted to the phantom sounds of Angels that would adequately drain away any sinful thoughts. However, it seemed that this particular default setting needed a long overdue overhaul as, unwittingly, her eyes were covering as much ground as possible in the time that she had been allocated between those two sentences. Shamefully and internally, she then questioned his intentions. She would have been absolutely correct in thinking that they should not have been in a room alone together but it may well have been unfair to presume that he was up to no good. She then asked herself if she wanted him to be up to no good, at which point her brain almost went into meltdown and she started blabbering about gowns, garnets and tapestries. Following that, of course, he again spoke, leaving her feeling like a complete tit.

'I have a task for you maiden that will draw on your skills as a spy and Agent…'

Perhaps he isn't after me, after all, she thought and then wasn't sure what all that nonsense in her head had been about.

'You are bonded to our Lord, are you not?'

Now deflated that she'd been uncovered as a nun and that she was presumably of no interest whatsoever to him, her confusion suddenly turned to depression and, for a short spell, Elspeth lost the plot.

He repeated the question as if he had said it in another language the first time.

'Oh…yes…Sir…yes. That would be correct.'

That would be correct! What am I saying? She told herself to remember the discipline of her order and get her head, body and soul, straight as she was now dithering and curtsying unnecessarily as well.

Culpeper, not completely devoid of sensitivity, asked if they could sit, ensuring her that he was only closing the door as it was essential that they talked in private. The secret that he was about to impart would be both sudden and shocking to Elspeth but he insisted, over and over, that what he was to task her with had to be kept between the two of them. She was to tell no one, ever. Even under pain of torture. This, already, was a million furlongs away from where she had expected to be and wondered if this was now a poor alternative to being wooed.

He put his ungloved hand inside his leather purse and pulled out a small key. It was uniquely beautiful and instantly glistened erratically in the morning sun. She presumed it to be gold and was distracted for some time as she tried to count the tiny jewels. At one point he did take hold of her hand. Reassuring her, he told Elspeth that he would surely die soon. He confessed to her his relationship with the Queen and told her that, although he loved the Queen dearly, he would never want any harm to befall the King. Keeping this key hidden, he said, would be very much in Henry's interests. Again, he insisted that she never share it with anyone and that she had his permission to bury it or lock it away but she could not destroy it. The key must remain whole. As anyone would do, she asked him why. As he explained, she was in no doubt whatsoever that, at the very least, he believed absolutely in the key's origins.

'This has been a key for centuries but it hasn't always had this appearance. When monks first settled on Holy Island in the north, this was used, for good reason, as the key to the sacristy. It had travelled thousands of miles and a lock was forged to fit the key rather than the other way around.'

'So, it is for a church door?' asked Elspeth, seemingly confused.

'No maiden. No. It no longer has that use. It has been melted and redesigned recently but is of the same original metal.'

'Same...?'

'That same metal that was used for nails when Our Lord was crucified.'

He said this so calmly that she stared deep into his eyes to see if he was testing her. Even as a lifelong exponent of Catholicism, Elspeth was aware that so many claims had been made of the crucifixion nails that you could probably armour a hundred knights with them. There had been so many, sometimes ridiculous, objects that made the same claim. She waited. He repeated it. She took hold of the key and then keeled over, overwhelmed. In a gentlemanly move, he gently pulled her back onto her chair.

'Not gold after all?' she said in an attempt to lighten the situation.

'I can't bear to have it with me. I am a sinner, sweet nun and I will go to hell. This...well...this is pure.'

She did not doubt that he believed this and she could think of no reason why it could not be true but took that key as much as a key as a holy relic. There and then, she took confession from this young man smiling to herself as his head went down as this was not what had come to mind when he had first entered the room. She assured him too, that God would not deny him and even advised that, on that very day he should go to the King and confess. This, he told her, he could not do.

Elspeth asked questions about the enigmatic and beautiful key but he would unveil nothing more. Culpeper believed it to have many supernatural properties including the ability to heal. However, if they had talked about it all day and all night, he would not be giving any more information.

Inspired at best and intrigued at worst, that object became very much part of her. And, yes, she had no problem keeping it secret. When she knew that her life was at an end, she thought it best to have it buried with her but knew not how to achieve this without someone seeing it post-mortem. She even considered the ridiculous notion of swallowing it before she expired but, besides the practical obstacles that it would have presented, she acknowledged that, as her sister was likely to still be at Hampton Court Palace at the time of her passing, Robert would most probably have her embalmed. She was right and, yes, it would have been discovered.

It was only when, many tough months later, Marcus had confided in her about his key that she thought about it for the first time in months. Overwrought with confusion and trying to negotiate this uncanny coincidence, she shared Culpeper's bizarre story with him. Marcus, in turn, promising never to destroy it, keep it secret, and so forth, which he gladly agreed to.

So there they were, Wynnfrith with a heap of junk and Marcus with the Holy Grail. Well, the next best thing to it, and neither of them having a bloody clue what to do next. If any of the Agents were to get any further with this matter, they had to track Marcus down and insist that he cooperated.

15 lady bask

He found it. Even he was surprised that he had stumbled upon it so quickly but, thanks to the detailed descriptions provided at the trial by both Eirik and Bayard, he recognised his intended destination immediately. Hesitantly, he drew back the gate, marvelling at the ostentatious front door. This was a grand house fit for nobility and Marcus wasn't in the habit of intruding upon such privilege without invitation. Nevertheless, this was his only hope if he was to have any chance of achieving a successful conclusion to his mission. Even the door knocker was expensive, cast in the form of some unidentifiable mythical fish. Desperate for clues, he stared at it for a while presumably in the hope of it whispering to him some valid secret. He grasped it in his right fist and, somewhat meekly, banged it against the oak. The forty second wait for an answer may as well have been an eternity, for a thousand possible scenarios ran in his head including the notion that he was making an unnecessary mistake. He shuffled, rehearsed and even cursed to himself until someone came. A young girl wearing an over-apron that gave away the severity of her morning's labour (as it was irreparably stained and dusty) welcomed him and asked him what his business was. This alone informed him that many people had been this way already and, even possibly, for the same reason.

'I would like an audience, no matter how brief, with the Lady of the house.'

'Please wait a moment' said the girl.

Another aeon passed whilst he perfected his nervous shuffle, but she did, eventually, return. However, he knew that he would have to work for what he wanted. This time, she wanted to know both his name and his business. Eventually, returning a third time, the girl led him along the hallway to what appeared to be a small office or study. That is, small for the size of the house. The desk alone must have been ten foot by six and the globe, the size of a barrel.

The Lady smiled and beckoned him toward a, well worn, sapphire-coloured leather chair.

'My, look at you. What a fine fellow you have turned out to be.'

'You know me?' said Marcus, genuinely surprised.

'Of course. Mind you, you were just a boy when I last saw you, but I remembered asking about you when I very first set eyes upon you. So, yes, the name and of course…'

'Of course' he said, acknowledging what she meant.

'If he owes you money then I'm afraid you will have to join the line, young man!' she said in a rather flippant manner.

'No, no. I'm not here for money.'

She then stared at him in an attempt to read his intentions. Whatever your opinion of Lady Bask, you would have to acknowledge that she, most likely, hadn't had an easy life. He was surprised, as Bayard had been on his visit to Oxford, as to how young and attractive she was. The stresses of her relationship with Sir Anthony Bask had not, at least, taken its toll on her beauty and figure. In some ways, this made Marcus uncomfortable. He had reckoned on a slanging match with some bitter and twisted old widow. He suddenly felt quite uneasy.

'You can't imagine the burden I've been left with.'

Surprised also that she had chosen to open up to him, a relative stranger, he thought it wise to listen as she may have well have given something away that would have been of use.

'I have this. The house and nothing else. Without offspring, the only way that I will survive is by marrying again and I think that unlikely. Every day, more demands from people I have never met before. He was a complete blaggard. A scoundrel and thief. A blackmailer and liar. A gambler and womaniser. There are few people on God's earth that you could measure to be without any merit whatsoever, but he was, truly, one of them' she said quite dispassionately.

Marcus wasn't in a mood to argue. Sir Anthony Bask had left a trail of destruction wherever he had been. Beyond Marcus's personal experiences of the man, he now knew that he was responsible for blackmailing Robert Hall, the kidnap of Richard Shakespeare's son and swindling Aelfraed right up to the end of his shitty existence. The whole saga was pathetically ironic as only twenty years earlier, he had been one of the most successful glass merchants in England, even securing contracts with the King.

'Whenever he had anything, he'd gamble it away or spend it on diseased women.'

She was now on a roll and Marcus, feeling somewhat uncomfortable asked what Elspeth would have thought of Bask, which, on reflection, he considered to be a waste of time as Elspeth would have forgiven Judas himself.

'Can you imagine, Lady Bask, why I am here?'

'Well, if he doesn't owe you money then I'm guessing he's kept some embarrassing information about you or he's had some dalliance with your wife!'

Before Marcus could respond she reverted to gently ranting again.

'Fancy sending his bloody body here! What would I want with him?'

Marcus paused to recall what had been said about the corpse. Robert had gone to great lengths to have Bask's body embalmed and returned to Oxford. Robert was under the illusion that Lady Bask herself had blackmailed the Mayor following Bask's death. Marcus was about to ask what had happened to the huge sum secreted inside the body when it dawned on him that she had never received it, so he chose to say nothing.

'Lady Bask, you may remember that your husband was appointed to oversee repairs and, well I suppose, upgrades to the King's ships many years ago.'

'Oh, …he'd take on anything! Lie his way to the table and secure this arrangement, that appointment. Nothing, except perhaps his very first business, was honest.'

Marcus knew he would have to take charge of the conversation if he was to get anywhere but at the same time did not wish to give too much away.

'You will forgive me, my Lady, if I don't go into too much detail but I am sure it would not surprise you to know that his involvement with the ships was not entirely above board….no pun intended.'

She started again but, this time, Marcus managed to rein her in.

'If there is anything that remains from that period, from his position at that time, it would be useful to me as I…err…I now find myself in a position to return to a life at sea and may be assuming a similar position myself. And…oh yes!...of course…I can pay.'

That certainly caught her attention.

'Look around you. Can't move for junk. Papers, boxes, letters, memoirs even. Bloody memoirs! Mostly a record of whose wife he happened to be rogering in what month!'

'May I?' he muttered in the hope of being given access to the aforesaid junk.

'I'll get Jane to bring us some cheese and beer. Would that be suitable?' he nodded 'what do you say to sixpence for every piece you take with you.'

'Oh that's very agreeable!' said Marcus realising that he

possibly sounded a little too enthusiastic.

'Help yourself' she said candidly. He stood, looked at her again to ensure that she was alright with this unexpected invasion, and she smiled.

More than that, Lady Bask let him peruse unhindered for some time. He, too, was alarmed at the amount of documentation that this diabolical and bent bastard had left. He found letters from other businessmen, letters from Italy, France and beyond. Messages and affections from lovers but most shockingly were the ransom and blackmail notes which, astonishingly, he had carefully copied. Not seeing any value, even moral, in keeping these now that he was dead, Marcus thought it wise just to keep the letters from abroad. Then, inside a dusty chest, he found diagrams similar to the ones that he, Jack and Aelfraed had seen when they had first met Bask. However, he had hoped for more. He simply could not find what he had come for.

He sat again and shared the cheese and ale with Lady Bask and decided in that moment that he liked her and he gathered from her demeanour that she had been treated like dirt throughout her married life as she trembled slightly when not in role.

'You can carry on if you wish.'

So he did but was now running out of options. Marcus asked if there were other rooms but she insisted that everything was there, he would not find anything worthwhile in any other room.

He slumped into the chair grateful for what he had but at a loss as to what to do next. He noticed a plethora of relics and crucifixes. The Basks were unapologetically old school Catholic, no matter how risky this would have seemed. He looked around one more time and told himself that his work there was done. Then, almost as if it hadn't been there previously, he detected a vertical piece of dowel that looked almost as if it was coming out of Lady Bask's hat. He craned his neck slightly and said,

'A mast! It's a galleon!' it was almost entirely hidden by the large tapestried chair in which she now reclined.

'Yes, in need of a good clean.'

He asked if he could examine it so, happily, she stood up whilst he moved the chair and put the only candle lit, next to it. This was a most meticulous model. Although it was very difficult to identify, as it could have been any one of the ships in Henry's fleet, it had been beautifully constructed with the finest detail. For a moment, child-like, Marcus just marvelled at the object, as it was a delight to see and to hold. However, it was big. He estimated it to be about the size of a greyhound as he was already assessing how he might transport it out of there and out of Oxford. His instant obsession gave him away as he was so engaged with his plan,

'Yours for a price. I don't care what it is or what it means but it's for sale like almost everything else here.'

Her voice echoed somewhat, for he was now immersed in the very construction of this model. On close inspection it was made up of hundreds of pieces, each neatly interlocking with one another. No glue, just expertly crafted joints. As he dared to separate two of them, he noticed that they were numbered and, so too, was every piece. Although Marcus presumed that this represented nothing more than clues to its assembly, he decided there and then that he wanted it.

'And before you ask as everyone does, I haven't seen him in years.'

She mistook Marcus's confused expression as feigned ignorance but as he persisted she added,

'His brother, never been near here, even when Sir Anthony died. Might well be dead himself I suppose but you wouldn't believe the number of strangers breaking my peace in his pursuit.'

Marcus didn't know what to make of this if anything so, temporarily, put it to the back of his mind.

Within the hour he had left, promising to return for the

model, arms weighed down with crumbly documents and fifteen pounds worse off.

As he rode away, he believed that he had connected somehow with this woman. She too had been a victim and this left him also wondering what had happened to the gold that should have been delivered to her, along with her husband's body.

16 a sailor's death

Marcus didn't get far. Tired, he decided to water his horse and rest awhile on a nearby hillock to gather his thoughts. He scanned the skyline of Oxford, admiring the old university buildings, the church towers and the grand, half-timbered buildings. He lay back and thought of the troubled and mistreated Lady Bask and of the kind Thomas Farrier. Marcus thought back to how, months ago, he had scarpered from Worcester without even a word and now he felt guilty. There was no doubt in his mind that, if circumstances had been different, he would have called on the wit and might of all the Agents but had persuaded himself that he alone would undo what he had been guilty of many years ago. It was a warm morning and, as the sun smoothed its way in and out of passing clouds, he lay back in an effort to contemplate what he would do next. It would come as no surprise that, as he drifted away he was, once again, back in that shipyard with William Mewe, Jack and Aelfraed, the events of months, days and years merging into a much smaller number of thoughts, ideas, recollections and regrets.

Everyone that worked in the dry dock became

increasingly mortified at how long the ships had been in ordinary. The good news for King, common man and country was that there was less conflict and death but, to put it simply, the Mary Rose, and the others, were not designed to be ornaments only. The trio rarely saw Bask although they were aware that he visited often. Throughout the first half of the 1530s, Jack, Marcus and Aelfraed were assured that all the work that they were carrying out was essential and would, ultimately, make the ships stronger and faster. Sometimes the ships were completely stripped down and at other times they were reassembled again, a task in which they all delighted. Seemingly, one of the reasons for this was to test how quickly the ships could be made battle-ready. There was much to do. The Mary Rose itself had still not been fully repaired from old battle damage. The greater part of the ship needed caulking and she was constantly being cleaned from head to toe. However, they were all certain that, at some point, further changes would be made. For the three of them and, in fact, all the others employed at Deptford, they had no suspicion whatsoever about these developments but, worrying about losing their positions, it was, with some delight, that when there was talk of upgrading the galleons, they took it in their stride.

Although they were giving the impression of being hard at work, everyone watched with one eye as gun-ports, and their doors, were remeasured and engineers and carpenters were crawling all over the place. Having been quizzed, so long ago, about working with carpenters it now seemed, at last, that it would happen. Out of all this activity, and the one that Bask took the most interest in, was that which involved them crowding into the belly of the ship. One day, as Jack was busy caulking the inner planking and ballast of the hull, he was startled at the number of people that had joined him. At first, they stood, backs to the stern, within a compartment that would normally store ropes and rigging. They then gawped endlessly at the keel and the ballast. The former being the very bottom of the ship and the latter used to keep the ship steady. Although of sound construction, the keel, like most of the ship was made from timbers and planks and then heavily caulked. Standing astride the keel, almost as if he owned it, Bask pointed downward and then along the whole length of the keel. Jack cursed as he couldn't pick out a word that was being said whilst they were in this huddled group. All the time, men were drawing and making notes but mostly nodding gravely, as Jack would later recall. They then pointed above them to what was, the orlop deck, but still, Jack could not make sense of it. Alongside the foremast were several breaks in the decks, a way of getting from one to another. This too had them all entranced and Jack deduced that their interest wasn't in the route upwards but of some redesign. He assumed this as, again, they were continuously measuring, sketching and writing. As they returned, Jack heard one comment and one only. It was issued by Bask himself.

'There will have to be a clear channel, just above the keel, that runs the length of the ship without damaging her integrity. The ballast will be replaced after the improvements.'

At that very moment, Jack took this as an ominous sign and also decided that he did not like and did not trust Sir Anthony Bask but kept what he had heard to himself for some time.

Jack, Aelfraed, now on his fourth leg, and Marcus became labourers to the skilled craftsmen that invaded the ships at Deptford. Work began by making the smallest of arches between all the compartments in the lowest parts of the ships. No one questioned this as it was not their place to do so. They knew the carpenters, engineers and designers to be better than them and assumed, simply, that they also knew what they were doing. It was another six months before all the hardware arrived. Apparently, there was to be an attempt to increase armaments aboard the Mary Rose but it was the arrival of the most curious and miscellaneous casts of bronze that had the crewmen scratching their heads. Cart after cart arrived carrying these anomalies which became stacked, seemingly in no particular order, at the port side of each ship. It was whilst this was taking place that Jack chose to speak out. The three of them were still very close comrades but, there was, as you'd expect, a hierarchy amongst them. Jack was in charge. An experienced gunner, he was respected by the regular crew of the Mary Rose and, truth be told, he could do almost anything on a ship apart from cook. Aelfraed had been in both the Commander and King's favour and, was senior in any other respect to Marcus.

'There something afoot. I can see it in my stools?' murmured Jack.

'You see secrets in your shit?' asked Aelfraed, rather intrigued.

'That I do. And there's something aboard that stinks worse.'

Alarmed, they waited for him to elaborate.

'Look yonder. What is all that? That's no weapon or ballast or sail I've ever seen!'

'Well' said Aelfraed, it's all new, isn't it? We're not meant to know. It's not for the likes of us but, if it helps us beat the French, then I'm all for it!'

On this occasion, Jack didn't take kindly to being corrected. He was convinced that something was awry and his suspicions were now somewhat ingrained and irrevocably permanent. Now, to put this into perspective, when portraying the three bucketeers, I am not talking about the founders and originators of modern espionage. A more fitting description, in relative terms, would be three saltwater idiots. Aelfraed was widely considered to be thick and, to be fair to him, he knew it. Jack was also a complete idiot but no one had told him yet. And, Marcus, at this point in his development, only had these two to look up to so no one was expecting anything better from him. Nevertheless, their hearts and their loyalties were completely sound and for those reasons alone, if nothing else, we can all be grateful that they were on hand.

'Look at that yonder' said Jack.

He was hoping for an instant and enthusiastic response but they did just that, look.

'Well?...what do you make of it?'

'I think it is called a gear' answered Marcus in a, very matter of fact, manner.

'Yes!...yes and, the rest. None of you know what they are, do you?'

Gormless, they conceded.

'I've seen things like that in drawings. From overseas...' added Jack.

Now engaged, they asked him about the drawings as grandchildren would, simultaneously massaging Jack's ego.

'I've seen pictures of the most wonderful and outlandish contraptions. Copies, mind you, but I know of their creator.'

He said this as if it was the greatest secret ever known to man and they were now willing victims to his, somewhat dodgy, storytelling.

'Leon Hard and Itchy!' He said in a confident and professorial manner with no doubt whatsoever that they would be impressed. So confident he was that he elaborated,

'There lived a man in Florence and he was called Leon Hard and Itchy.'

Not being able to suppress it any longer, Aelfraed blustered out a laugh with Marcus very quickly following suit,

'What was?' asked Aelfraed.

'What was what?'

'What was hard and itchy?'

The two of them were now spluttering with laughter and out of control but Jack was left unimpressed by their response.

'No. No! Now you're being daft. Not hard and itchy, Hard and Itchy!'

Perhaps it was Jack's Italian dialect that was causing the problem but, alas, his story was now in ruins. He so wanted to tell them of the strange mechanical inventions that he had seen evidence of on his travels but realised that his delivery needed some work. He waited until they had calmed down.

'I tell you there's something wrong and I will be proven right.'

Both Marcus and Aelfraed respected Jack. It would even be fair to say that they would have given their lives for him. However, although he wasn't aware of it, he did talk a lot of crap. He was given to fantasy, particularly when it involved his exploits and that, to be fair, was a given right of mariners. As the other two were that much younger he would, as all people do when they age, embellish his experiences and these were to become increasingly dramatic during his advancing years. It is also true to add, that the other two bucketeers saw no harm at all in the changes, as ships had been upgraded and developed ever since they had first added guns. This slight difference, however, would drive an almighty wedge between them.

Before the year was out, Jack had turned spy with the other two willingly supporting the restructuring that was gradually introduced by Sir Anthony Bask. In remembering this, Marcus realised that he had been somewhat naïve and, in his ignorance, let many an uncomfortable situation pass when perhaps he should have sought the counsel of his elders. Marcus was soon noticed by Bask as he was incredibly nimble and hard working. On the same day, he overheard one of the gaffers let slip that neither King nor Cromwell knew that Bask was now overseeing the work at Deptford which, if nothing else, created an atmosphere of conspiracy. As Marcus was employed as a fitter along the bowels of all ships, he took note of the new and most irregular design and the contraptions that were implemented. Still, he said nothing. Then, one day, Aelfraed, Jack and Marcus stood in spitting distance of Bask and Jack decided to make his stand.

'I don't believe that what you do here is in the King's name' he bravely declared.

A cold chill permeated the skin of every man present.

Jack looked to his two closest allies to back him up but they turned away. Out of everything, every detail, Marcus was to remember this very hour, no, that very minute, every day of his life afterwards. He knew Jack to be right but lacked the courage to stand up to Bask and all those, including armed men, who supported him.

Bask took Jack to task.

'Well, well. All this time in our midst we have had ourselves a chief engineer! An architect of naval vessels and, yet, he is dressed like a vagrant and talks like the village idiot.'

The laughter was instantaneous, if not sincere, and Bask took care to look at every man present as a way of ensuring that no one believed this fool. Again, Marcus and Aelfraed looked away.

'I give you life, man. You are paid well with, what is almost permanent employment and, yet, you have a complaint. Well, let's hear it. What is it you accuse me of?'

'I do not believe that the work carried out here is for the betterment of His Majesty's navy.'

Again, laughter as Bask walked right up to Jack. Many were cringing. They knew him to be right but he was now sadly, completely alone in his rebellion.

'This is possibly more nonsense than I've heard for a while. Anyone else think the same?' and Bask looked around.

Nothing.

Bask placed his left hand on Jack's right shoulder. Jack stood his ground but it soon became clear that he was now increasingly anxious, particularly as there was no other man there to support him.

'I have a solution' said Bask smiling 'I think that you are not wanted here so, forthwith, I terminate your employment!'

Almost everyone in the dock knew that there was a

sinister element rooted in Bask's nature and they also expected that Jack would either have his wages docked, be punished or even dismissed but not one of them could have accounted for what was to happen next. As Bask, very slightly, eased his grasp on Jack's shoulder, his gloved hand crept up from inside his gown and in it, was a dagger. His smile gave way to a grimace as he, yet again, tightened his grip with his left hand and, with his other, slowly thrust a dagger under Jack's ribcage. Dear Jack immediately slumped to the ground and, although he tried to speak, it was to no avail. He was dead within the passing of five minutes. Bask looked around to check that everyone present was suitably disciplined and, all were, many just standing with their eyes surveying their toes.

He beckoned to Aelfraed and Marcus to dispose of the body. They obeyed without question but, as Bask moved away, concluding business as if nothing had happened, Marcus wept like he never had before.

'Now lad, keep it in. You don't want to be a target. Save it until later if you can' said Aelfraed. Aelfraed, in turn, made an effort from that day on to protect his younger companion but nothing was said between them regarding this sinister event. Marcus would never know the depth of Aelfraed's conscience and he certainly wasn't one for giving much away. Deep inside, Marcus could not reconcile what he had done by not doing anything and, of course, day by day his suspicions also grew. It was also becoming clearer to the greater population of the work gang that all was not well and Marcus took it upon himself to get to the bottom of this intrigue.

His opinion would change almost daily. Yes, Bask was a rogue. Yes, he was cruel and yes, it seemed that, for whatever reason, King Henry had lost control of the upgrades on his ships. Unfortunately, this left Marcus in two minds depending on which day of the week it was. He once went a whole month both convinced and impressed that new cannons were being adequately installed with more functional gun-ports and doors. The keel was being strengthened with state-of-the-art ballast and the hull more watertight. What on earth am I worried about? He would ask himself. But, then, he would stand back, regard the work in its entirety and conclude that he had never seen the like before. All his prevarication came to an end when, routinely, one day he was invited into Bask's quarters to relay some diagrams to William Mewe. As he waited, he observed for the first time, an assortment of pieces of cast metal. They were set out in rows of three, no two pieces the same and every piece was kept separately in brown leather purses. Bask presumed that this illiterate seaman in his midst was completely ignorant. Ignorant of engineering and of the written word. So, as he glanced about, no one took much notice but as Marcus perused, he heard someone refer to the objects as keys. There wasn't any way, even by a considerable stretch of the imagination that there was any correlation whatsoever between the neatly cast lumps on the desk and a key, but it did make him immediately more suspicious. Then, he noticed that there was a detailed outline of each ship drawn, its name at the top and underneath, coding that linked that ship to three distinct lumps of metal. Everyone left, except Bask who made idle talk with Marcus. He wasn't, on this occasion, unpleasant but had chosen to reference the weather and the state of the dock. Marcus didn't hear a word. Uncannily, Bask left the room asking Marcus to wait as he had one more document for him to take back to Master Mewe.

In those first moments, when he had found himself alone, there was a torrent of thoughts, ideas and information racing around his head. At the fore was his guilt. How he had done nothing to support his friend. He thought of St Peter. I am like him, he deduced. We were as brothers or even father and son and I denied him. His eyes darted back and forth between the papers, the desk, the lumps of metal and the door. His breathing increased as did his heartbeat and this led to him muttering to himself. Do it now lad! Then he heard the same words but in Jack's voice. Do it now lad! As he looked down, his feet were over the threshold and beyond the office, three ugly lumps of metal, inside their purses, stuffed inside his jerkin. In later years, he would claim that he had no recollection whatsoever of picking them up. He soon found Aelfraed and, without thinking, kicked him.

'What the hell…what's?...'

'We have to go now, I have discovered something that proves Jack right. I am in true and real danger. We must leave now!'

'I don't know what you've done lad but I'm going nowhere.'

Marcus desperately and hurriedly tried to change his mind but he was not to budge.

'I will cover for you. That's the best I can do. Now be off with you before we are both dead.'

Marcus hesitated, not once but twice and eventually realised that he was alone. He was fast. Very fast and no one saw him slip beyond the dock and onto semi-dry land where there were bulrushes aplenty that hid him. There was, immediately, an almighty fuss with Aelfraed being the first to be threatened. Marcus's only friend was to wear fifty-five long and deep scars on his back for the rest of his life because of Marcus's actions but, by the day's end, all had settled and Aelfraed never bore a grudge. Even Bask presumed that the boy had stolen the metal as he thought it to be precious and initially thought no more about it. That was until he thought of how easy it was to make the key out of the three pieces and so had his men give pursuit.

Marcus then stirred from his thoughts, realising that he had drifted off and once again admired Oxford. That moment of sudden awakening was always the same for him. Guilt. He was ultimately to find confirmation that Bask was up to no good and that his mentor and friend, Jack had been right. He played, over and over again, that scene where Jack looked to his comrades for support but received none.

'I am Peter' Marcus muttered to himself allowing no forgiveness for what he had done to Jack.

The warm sun did, eventually, somewhat soothe the spectres and he thought to look back, just once, at the house belonging to Lady Bask. She was receiving another visitor but Marcus, politely, turned away presuming it to be someone else collecting debts. It may, however, been worth his while to look a little longer as her visitor was none other than Eirik.

17 york ransacked
February 1543

Robert had funded the mission to find and support Marcus and also whatever came after. The deployment of the Agents had been done speedily and without question. Their greatest conundrum was that the Agents now had a baby. Well, two of them did. You may think that Wynnfrith was to stay home whilst Silas took on the mission but, sadly, his unusual condition seemed to be worsening. Mrs Hall suggested that she looked after Mary but was increasingly anxious about the dangers that both parents would face. Silas and Wynnfrith mulled this over for a whole evening before deciding that Silas needed to snap out of his current disposition and also that Elspeth had tasked her sister, alone, with this task. Baby Mary was carried, sleeping, into the Hall's new residence but her parents were both shocked and surprised to see Eirik returned and in conference with Robert who was looking very pleased with what he was being told by his son. They greeted one other as family and Wynnfrith began to tell Eirik the whole tale. Robert informed her that he had already imparted the whole story of the keys to Eirik who, by now, was interested only in the baby. He picked her up and she blew bubbles at him contentedly.

1543 The Disfiguration

'He will be joining you' said Robert and little else was said. As Mary was put back into the arms of her mother for the last time before leaving, Meg came in to reassure Wynnfrith that she would support Mrs Hall tirelessly in tending to the child. Wynnfrith happily allowed Meg to make altogether silly noises to the baby and, in return, Mary chuckled. Meg then turned, intending to return to the kitchen only to find herself face to face with Eirik. Nothing was said although both were frozen in their tracks and stared at each another nervously.

'You know of each other?' asked Robert rather innocently.

They then began talking over one another, although little was intelligible. The words 'yes and no' could be heard amongst the confused ramblings.

Much more directly, Wynnfrith intervened.

'You know my brother?'

'Brother?...why...yes. Yes, my Lady.'

'No need for graces, Meg, we are friends. Is this a cause of embarrassment for you?'

'Oh no. Oh no. Not at all my Lady'

Within just a few of her words and the deafening silence coming from Eirik's corner, the Halls and Wynnfrith knew that all was not well. Wynnfrith's razor-sharp intuition came to the fore as she could draw only one conclusion.

'Scarborough fair?'

Meg nodded and Eirik, having arrived back in York looking like he would easily be mistaken for one of Henry's courtiers, now looked like a child about to shit himself.

'Are you saying that my brother is the father of your child?'

Eirik immediately came to life and was most vocal and sincere in his rejection of the idea. Of course he was the father of Meg's child but he knew nothing of it, until now. On the verge of being completely undone, Meg came to his rescue.

'Could we please just have a few minutes alone together?

1543 The Disfiguration

I promise you that this news will be a complete shock to Fletcher as, seeing him, is to me.'

Everyone reeled back, immediately concerned that she had either mistaken him for someone else or that Eirik had been using multiple names.

Out of courtesy for the trembling maid, they conceded and the two of them went into the kitchen and closed the door. Meg broke down in tears. She sobbed uncontrollably and, as much as Eirik wished to console her, he just did not know what was the most appropriate thing to do.

'Is it true?'

'He's dead!' she shouted. 'He's gone' and then she started to calm a little. 'You weren't to know, you were long gone but I waited. Two years I returned to the fair just to find you.'

At this point, Eirik felt brave enough to hold her hand and she reciprocated.

'I had only ever been with you. You have to believe me' she continued 'Oh, how stupid I was!' she added.

'Oh, Meg. Truthfully, it pains me that you suffered so. I did not know. That year, as I left you, things became so much more difficult. Please let me explain, I will tell you all.'

So taken with her plight and stewing in guilt, he chose to tell this girl, a practical stranger, everything, including the lies that he was now living with. Shocked at his kidnap by the mercenaries, she was already seeing him in a new light. They were in that kitchen for almost an hour. So long, I should say, that Mrs Hall was getting the most unbearable cramp in her legs from squeezing her body up against the door. This was to no avail as they were talking very quietly and the door may well have been made of stone.

'So they still think you are James?'

'Yes, yes. I swear none of this was premeditated. It started as a misunderstanding and then, well, I suppose, became something of a convenience. And, believe me or not they really are now my family.'

They talked about this for some time more, Eirik in no

doubt whatsoever that this girl now held a proverbial sword in her hand and that his head was on a block.

'Right!' she said in conclusion 'I have no intention of exposing you this day but you must be honourable and recognise our child. Although he is now with the Lord, he is thine and mine and that's an end to it.'

Eirik nodded in agreement.

'But, you must tell them one day about how you have masqueraded as James, simply because they will find out anyway. Lies always find their way into daylight. Your story only just holds water and the consequences will be worse if they find out first.'

For a few moments, he looked at her, clearly weighing up what had been said.

'Dear Meg, I have no wish to deceive you, believe me, so please listen to what I have to say. We embark soon on a most dangerous mission and, possibly, I may die. I will happily give my life for this family.'

He paused for a moment, careful not to use the word, Agents.

'If I survive then, once all is well, I will make a full confession' and he knelt as he said it.

She gently put her hand on his cheek, then his chin, raising his eyes so that they met hers.

'Agreed, and I shall pray for your safe return.'

There was little doubt that, in this moment, Eirik had been given a reprieve but that was not the top and bottom of what he was feeling. How could he have left this sweet girl so, hardly giving her another thought as he picked up his life again? He asked himself. She was still very beautiful and her eyes drew him directly into her soul which, at that very moment, was putting his troubles before hers. Without another thought, he kissed her hand and stood, directing her back into the hallway. Mrs Hall leapt backwards as the door creaked open and then ran toward the front door to give the impression that she had been there all along.

They all looked to Eirik but it was Meg that spoke first.

'Please forgive us. It has been so long since we have seen each other. Eirik has nobly accepted his place as the father of my child, although he knew nothing of my pregnancy or the birth.'

Already Mrs Hall was huffing and blowing with indignation. She wanted to say 'I have never heard the like!' But, of course she had and so had everyone else. Meg, cleverly, chose not to lie or create a cover story for Eirik but, at the same time, was not about to expose him. She told them that they had known one another at the fair. The word, known, meaning something completely different in the sixteenth century. She had not seen him after that.

'I was captured by mercenaries!' He reminded everyone which did, at least, explain why he never returned to Scarborough.

'Fletcher?' Asked Wynnfrith incisively.

'As well as baking, I used to help a friend on a bow and arrow stall. It was a, somewhat, sarcastic pseudonym.'

Meg neither nodded nor protested.

'Right!' said Robert authoritatively that's an end to it until the Ag...until everyone returns. Do you claim a betrothal to my son?'

He had said this in such an unfeeling and matter of fact way that the girl felt a little threatened. It was the first time that she had felt unworthy, common and almost as if it were completely her fault. Eirik intervened.

'What my father means to say is, because of your good name is it your wish that we marry?'

Apart from Robert, everyone in the room was impressed by this gentlemanly stance which certainly sang sincerity.

'No. No, but I thank you, sir. I do not wish anyone to marry me who does not love me.'

Robert made an 'harumph' sound which indicated that such a sentiment was complete nonsense only to receive terminal death stares form his wife. It would be unrealistic to estimate how much this young woman was impressing Eirik at this moment and there was no doubt that, when he left her this time, she would be in his thoughts whether he liked it or not.

Later that morning, Bayard set forth with Wynn sitting beside him and Peter and myself in the back. Dramaticus, Bayard's very strange actor friend, chose to walk. This didn't last long, I should add. William Fawkes had flatly refused to let his son Edward be a part of this unknown adventure. Silas, already much more at home astride Annie, rode side by side with Eirik. Oxford bound, I believed that this bunch of odds and sods was a force to be reckoned with, their previous successes walking a good five miles before them. Old habits were hard to conquer as Bayard wished to perform in every village and hamlet but, on this occasion, he was reminded hourly that we had no time whatsoever to spare.

All seemed to go quiet in York as this happy band disappeared over the horizon.

Later that same day, Father Matthew, probably very glad of the peace, prepared for a funeral that was to take place just after one o clock. As he knelt by the altar, the door flew open and a man entered at such a pace that he was in front of the priest in a moment.

'What on....'

'Father! Father! Come quickly! The old washhouse! It's on fire...'

It was Scorge. Horrified, the priest took flight immediately heading north along Goodramgate and begging the Minster constable to let him run through the yard as a short cut to Petergate and Bootham Bar. Already neighbours were using water from the Ouse to douse the fire. Unbeknownst to Father Matthew, Robert Hall was dashing out of his new house in Stonegate but heading in a different direction. It was times like these when the population of York were as one, regardless of class, gender, spiritual belief or occupation. The wash house, although roofless and almost gutted, was eventually saved from the fire thanks, mostly to the good citizens of York. Father Matthew was, of course, bewildered as to why anyone would wish the old building damaged so, presumed it to be an accident.

'Thank you, my good friend and ally, Scorge. I believe we have saved it although I have no idea what for' he said in an attempt to lighten the situation. As they left, the priest also thanked and blessed all those that had helped put it out, each one grateful that no other property was damaged.

'You may go now. I will see if there is anything worth salvaging.'

All went quiet as he was left alone to rummage amongst the scorched items. He completely ignored the creaks and cracks around him as all was now in array and disorder.

He, unconsciously, started to sigh at what he beheld but could not breath out again. A gloved hand, coming seemingly out of nowhere, had covered his mouth from behind and he was now also being restrained.

'If you make any noise, even prayer, priest it will be your last one. Be assured, I do not trifle. Your life is as nothing to me.'

Father Matthew tried to raise his arms in compliance and turned to find two armed, but plainly dressed men. Both almost twice his size.

'There is no reason for us to hurt you, we have seen your church and acknowledge that you are of the true faith.'

By 1543 Father Matthew hardly had any idea what that meant anymore.

'Tell us where it is and you will be left untouched as if nothing had happened.'

Of course, Father Matthew genuinely had no idea what this was about and implored them to believe him. He tried reason, prayer and even offered hospitality but it gained nought besides infuriating them. So inhuman had they become that they now only thought of how to move on and seek the next clue. As one, almost graciously engaged the priest in idle conversation, the other strode behind him and swiftly and without mercy cut his throat from one ear to the other. Father Matthew's innocent blood gave colour again to the charred possessions of Elspeth scattered about the straw floor. They left as quickly as they had arrived, completely unnoticed.

At that very moment, Robert and the sheriff stood in the living quarters of Silas and Wynnfrith's new home. There was hardly an item in it that had been left untouched. The seats had been shattered, doors broken, their marital bed turned up and smashed, windows were destroyed and Silas's title, that certified him as a Lord, was torn in two. Moreover, all the boards in the bedroom had been taken up including the one where Wynnfrith, in her frustration, had hidden the metal blocks. As Robert went back upstairs he looked into that chasm between the bedroom floor and the ceiling below only to see two gold coins. Clueless, he pondered why anyone would break in only to leave gold in the house. It was only three hours later when the body of Father Matthew had been found, that he was sure that the day's dire events must have been connected with Marcus and the secrets of Elspeth.

A watch was employed for the next three days both day and night but there were no reoccurrences, leaving Robert presuming that the culprits had either found what they had come for or, left empty-handed and, the latter, if true, would invite grave consequences.

Yet again, Robert's first thought was to employ Viscera. There would be no funeral for this beloved priest until everyone was back in York. Viscera was tasked with keeping his body 'as it t'were, hours before his demise' as Robert was to instruct. Immediately, Robert informed the Bishop who said that he would appoint a new priest to Holy Trinity Church before the day was out. Shattered and upset at the events of the day, he turned to Mrs Hall, babe in hand, to ask if there was anything that he had overlooked. She simply replied,

'The monk.'

'God's bowels!' He shouted already out the door and realising that he had completely forgotten about Brother Bede. As he arrived at the church, the door was already ajar with a cart and body waiting outside as a funeral service was expected. Somewhat irreverently, Robert barged in and rushed to the quarters that normally housed Bede but, to his dismay, found them vacated. There was no sign of a struggle but the monk had gone. Insensitively, he asked the funeral party if they had seen a stooped, overweight, scruffy and balding monk with a crater in his cranium but, quite disgusted, they told him that they hadn't and where he could go. Not that he was bothered but, as he left, he noticed a priest hurrying to the church to take over Father Matthew's duties. He appeared so young that he may have well still been in school, he mused.

Alarmingly, Robert was to encounter the young priest again sooner than he thought. Father Luke found himself, only days later, at Barley Hall panicking and wondering why the Mayor wasn't there. Of course, the Mayor was there but it was a different one, the Halls having left some time before. Fortunately, he was directed to his new abode and hammered on that door as if the building were on fire.

'For goodness sake!' shouted Meg but then corrected herself 'oh, sorry Father. Whatever is the matter?'

He insisted on telling Robert only, and in private. Although both Meg and Mrs Hall we're again adopting their best eavesdropping skills, the priest and Robert had bolted out of the living quarters and the building itself within less than a minute. They quickly arrived at Holy Trinity church and Father Luke pointed nervously at a blanket laid on the ground, a recently dug grave next to it. Already broken but trying to hold back tears, Robert peeled back the sheet to reveal an open coffin. Elspeth had been irreverently and roughly exhumed, the lid in complete tatters. Then he cried.

It probably wasn't as much the crime that set him off but what he beheld. There before him was Elspeth looking as if she was asleep. Viscera had done such a good job that she was no different from when she had just passed and it moved him deeply. On top of her hands, clasped in prayer, was a letter. It had been handled and thrown back again and it was evident that her body had been lifted and turned over. The letter was damp but the writing upon it was still eligible.

'What were these people looking for?' asked the priest.

'Oh, I wish I knew' whispered Robert without taking his eyes off her. Bravely, he decided to have a look around the coffin in case the culprits had left anything else. He took one last look at her and then kissed her forehead.

'Do you have a suitable prayer for this Father?'

Of course he didn't, this was almost unheard of but Father Luke rose to the occasion.

'Oh Heavenly Father, let us not dwell on the wickedness that has taken place here but grant us solace in the knowledge that these are but this young woman's remains. We remain assured that she now dwells with our Lord, Jesus, and smiles down upon us. We pray for her eternal salvation and peace.'

Robert's opinion of this young man had changed in an instant and he put his arm around him as he could see that he also needed consoling.

A crowd was gathering and the sheriff had arrived. Holy Trinity church was almost hidden from Goodramgate with only a narrow passage to reach it and so, fortunately, no one could yet see this macabre spectacle. Robert spoke to the sheriff with haste who then cleared the streets. Promising the sheriff that he would share all he knew about these crimes, and that being very little, he had him agree as to what should happen next. Within the hour, she was buried again with a brief, formal mass. No one was to speak of this. He urged the priest to do the same as he presumed, quite rightly, that it would be dangerous for all of them.

Later that day, Robert slumped into his favourite chair

wondering what the hell had just happened and realised that he was tightly clutching the discovered document in his right hand. He shooed his wife away and she did so without comment as she recognised that something very serious had taken place. It was to be another two hours before he could bring himself to read that letter, never expecting that it would make him laugh. This started as a chuckle, a light acknowledgement of what he had seen but it soon developed into such a deep guffaw, but punctuated with sobs, that all the household came running. However, he wasn't for sharing. Alone again, he threw it on the fire, the manically erratic flames immediately embracing it. One last time he looked at the words as they disappeared.

"What kept you? You will find nought here. You will find nought anywhere. I am the King's good servant but God's first. God loves you and is good. God does all things for good. Repent this day, deposit your sins in this earth for you have been already been saved. Please close the door when you leave as the lady cannot stand draughts."

'Oh, dearest Elspeth' he sobbed 'you were, and still are, a saint amongst saints. I swear that we will get to the bottom of all this and bring these people to justice. Please be patient with me as I have no forgiveness in my heart whatsoever at this moment but will do all I can to bring peace to this madness.'

Having been awake all night, Robert was in a mood to answer the door himself early the next morning.

'Why young Edward! What can I do for you? Is…'

'I am alone sir but my father knows that I am here'

Robert looked at the boy's face as he asked him inside,

'You know don't you?'

'Yes' said Edward 'but I swear none of it will ever pass my lips. I beg you, sir, in my spare time, let me take part in the reparations or I would be the only Agent left idle throughout this crisis.'

Bowled over by his candour and double-checking that

William Fawkes was aware of this visit, he agreed.

'When did you last visit Silas?' asked Robert.

'Why the day before they both left. I went to see the baby and take a gift from my parents.'

'And you have been regularly since the marriage?'

'Yes sir'

'Then you are familiar with the layout?'

Edward understood where Robert was going with this so offered his assurances.'

'I can tell you exactly how all should be! I'm your man!'

'Then you will be very useful indeed young man. Consider yourself employed!'

Edward sped off along Stonegate a happy boy.

Particularly now that Moonlight was involved, messages between Agents in the field and York were quite efficient and regular but Robert ordered that none of what had taken place since their departure was to be shared with any of the Agents excepting that they were to be told that they were now uncovered and in serious and immediate danger. Robert's time and funds would be spent trying to restore Silas's home and the abandoned wash house. However, only two days later he was to receive a message directly from the King. Astonished at what he read, he decided to personally write back to Henry and also contact the Agents, this being somewhat challenging as he had no forwarding address for them. Day and night he wrestled with this until he came up with the only possible solution.

18 agents assemble

Richard Shakespeare was laughing. He hadn't laughed so much in a while and he would ascertain repeatedly on this journey that there hadn't been much to laugh about those past two years. His eyes were set on the horse in front, the rider possibly being the least content in their journey as any he had ever witnessed.

'Stop laughing farmer!' Said Maud 'you're making it worse, see, it is his intent to floor me!'

Maud and horse didn't go well together. That wasn't to say that she didn't love horses and Maud did have her very own nag for drawing her ageing cart but she had never ridden one and she had never had any intention of riding one. Thomas Farrier had furnished her with the most comfortable saddle he had available but, for some reason, her backside was as an alien object to this leather masterpiece. That same backside was thrown up and down with every movement and, in tandem, Maud would squeak, howl, blaspheme and curse every time it did. This was altogether the best day out that Shakespeare had ever had.

'Doesn't help that you're there, behind me, looking at my arse! I knows it to be like the lid of a carrot pie but it does nought to cushion me!'

She hadn't intended this to be funny either but it now had both Shakespeare and Thomas Farrier giggling.

'Dear Maud' said Farrier 'you practically threatened to take my life if we didn't take you along! We can hardly engage in battle on a two-wheel cart!'

The words passed over and through her as every bit of her being was straining to get to grips with this new art form. And, although he was exaggerating, talk of battle did little to help.

Following Marcus's hurried exit from Worcester, Farrier was left concerned. More than that, he suspected that something serious was afoot. As he no longer had access to Hope, the pigeon who was used so successfully in thwarting the Cataclysm, he felt compelled to write to York but knew not who to write to as he was sure that Marcus was keeping a secret. Truthfully, he prevaricated and, one morning almost set out on horseback all the way to York but realising that Marcus could have been anywhere, and also that he would be no use to him in the north, he tried to put it out of his mind for some time. Months later, he saddled up intending to do just that, no matter how unwise it seemed, only to find, on returning to the stable, that someone was holding the reins of his horse. There he was. The outfit had been transformed but, unquestionably, that person was Moonlight.

'Agents must gather in Oxford to rally around Marcus. There is no time to wait.'

Although he had a hundred questions, Thomas Farrier said nothing as he knew he would get no answers.

So, without further hesitation, the next morning Farrier called at the farm in Snitterton declaring that all was not well with the Agents, although, he knew not what. He told them that he would have to go away for an indeterminable length of time. Instantly, Shakespeare was like a greyhound readying for a race. Thomas Farrier insisted that he had not gone there to recruit his friend but there was no holding him back.

'I owe them all my life and the lives of my family, twice

over, I will not linger here whilst I am needed' he had said and would not let Farrier leave until he was ready. Now in his mid-fifties, he was cautioned by his family and Farrier too, but he would have none of it. And, before the two of them had called in one last time to Wolverdington, Maud also passionately joined the ranks. Within days they were well away from their homes in a somewhat comical looking convoy.

Slowing the pace somewhat and changing the subject, Shakespeare started to quiz the blacksmith.

'How do you know that Marcus is in Oxford?' asked Richard.

'I had word. Marcus left hurriedly, without any idea as to what to do next but then the messenger appeared.'

'Aha the messenger!' said Shakespeare, Maud grateful that his attention was now diverted. Thomas Farrier was at the front but now uncomfortably craning his neck backwards to speak to Shakespeare.

'Yes. Strange man, so very strange but almost like our guardian angel. Now in dark blues and crimsons. At least he must visit the tailor now and again!' quipped Farrier 'certainly looks sharp!'

'Like that?' said the farmer and, as Farrier turned his head to look straight ahead, Moonlight was there, once more looking quite magnificent in the daylight. Immediately, Maud stopped her moaning and puffing and, awkwardly, tried to straighten her hair which, simultaneously, almost removed her from her saddle and gave the impression of her being drunk. Not that Moonlight was watching anyway. She carried on this bizarre performance throughout the few minutes that Moonlight was with them.

'I have diverged the contingent from York to Wodestock, north of Oxford. You are to meet there before approaching Marcus. God speed.' And off he went.

'Oooh!' said Maud leaving the other two wondering why she had.

'Good news!' said Shakespeare 'we are to be full strength.'

'I do hope so' added Farrier 'Moonlight has me thinking that this is a very serious business indeed. I pray that the mouse is back, we sorely need his counsel.'

Well, I was, and Moonlight had successfully secured an abandoned barn on the outskirts of Wodestock where we were to meet. As I entered, Peter carrying me in what was perhaps the most low rent-box that I had had so far, I was delighted to see Farrier, although his two companions were a surprise. Of course, everyone was excited to see one another and congratulations were bestowed on the new parents only to take a slightly sour turn when people started to harangue Wynnfrith, suggesting that she should have stayed home with the baby. I have decided, in good faith, to censor her reply for those of you who may be of a sensitive nature. Maud was to get much of the same but, when the gathered Agents became aware of the fire in her belly, all went quiet. Maud's attention went swiftly to Silas as she had become almost like a mother to him and was probably kidding herself that she had also become a grandmother for the first time. Silas and his new wife embraced her as if she was.

Democratically, I was chosen to take a lead. At least, that was in terms of intellectualising what we had before us. I implored everyone present to be completely honest with me as we had little enough information to start with anyway.

For our newcomer's benefit, Wynnfrith told again, but in some more detail, her tale first, omitting only the information regarding multiple Moonlights which she would share with me sometime later. Eirik confessed to hiding keys and documents on Elspeth's behalf. It was then that Wynn showed us the key, explaining that it had made itself so beautiful, having previously been only three lumps of nonsense. Having been perched on a beam close to the entrance, all eyes were now on me to make some sense out of all of this. I was struggling to, yet again, adapt to my alter ego and was battling with some of the more obscure elements of this mystery.

'My brave, fellow Agents. As always, I promise I will shed as much light as possible on this conundrum with which we are now faced. Seemingly, this is a tale of two keys and, possibly more. Although it is likely to be a coincidence, I thought only of one thing when I heard the phrase, two keys.'

'The Pope' shouted Richard Shakespeare.

'Exactly, the keys of St Peter.'

'Shall we make way for Rome!' suggested Peter and, although a somewhat ridiculous suggestion, did amply reflect his enthusiasm and energy with which few of us could keep up.

As I politely told Peter that going to Rome would not be necessary and, just as I was getting into my stride, Dramaticus leapt up and provided us with an impromptu impression of the Pope. Not that he'd ever met him, he just did a rather silly Italian voice, presumably unrehearsed. Annoyingly, Bayard applauded and Richard Shakespeare, ever obsessed with all things dramatic, started to talk to him about it.

'Finished?' I said in an undisguised haughty tone.

'Oh yes, sorry mouse' said Dramaticus and sat again.

'A Catholic plot against the realm no less, confirmed by Moonlight who had implicated the Poles, most likely Reginald Pole. However, that is the very bare bones of it. Marcus, during his last conversation with his beloved, Elspeth, entrusted his key, previously in three parts, to her. Although somewhat macabre, I believe that he wished to make confession to Elspeth although I know not what and, I do believe that the key was to be buried with her. Always several steps ahead of anyone else on God's earth, Elspeth asked Eirik to hide those pieces of the key and, post mortem shared this information with Wynnfrith. Wynnfrith and Silas found out how to construct the key out of the metal pieces and here it is at my feet. This, surely, has links to the King's navy, reflected in the complex, maritime, design on it.

1543 The Disfiguration

Marcus, therefore, holds a secret. Knowledge of something diabolical that will involve the King, his soldiers or even the ships themselves. Marcus had, in my opinion, very stupidly chosen to take this matter into his own hands as, in Master Farrier's words, he believes himself to blame.'

There was muttering and objection all around the barn as no one could envisage Marcus being guilty of anything.

'Add to that a further complication. Elspeth gave Marcus a key which we believe is still with him although we do not know what this betokens. My plan, our plan, is to find Marcus, insist that he engages our support and, together, we will get to the bottom of it all!'

'What's the key for?'

'Silas, I just don't know, we simply don't have enough information yet.'

I so wanted to reprimand him for not listening but, for once, bit my tongue.

Even though I was sure that I had everything covered, I told myself to be patient as this was going to be difficult for us all. With further maps and directions that had been gifted by Moonlight, we chose to eat and rest the night in that barn. The following morning, as soon as the sun was up, Eirik and Silas followed Moonlight's instructions that were to take them to a house on the outskirts of Oxford. Our numbers were a liability at this stage so it was essential that we moved separately and with caution.

A day later, Silas and Eirik had arrived at their destination.

'Look' said Eirik 'it is right up against the castle wall, it could well be York!'

'Tis incredibly familiar, brother.'

'That is the house…see. Just as in this drawing I have? It has two front doors.'

'Why on earth would it have two front doors?' quizzed Silas 'do you think one was for going in and another for coming out?'

For a moment, Eirik considered that this was, possibly,

one of the dumbest things Silas had ever said but chose not to react at all. Eirik was somewhat distracted himself, as he was thinking back to when he had so recently been at the home of Lady Bask nearby. He told himself to concentrate and remain on task.

'You must go' asserted Eirik.

'Me? Why? What do you mean…'

'Silas, I do believe that he will be genuinely pleased to see you. If I appear on his doorstep, he will be sure that half of York will be behind me.'

Giving up any further thoughts of protesting, Silas dismounted and began to crawl across the grass on his belly.

'What the hell are you doing?!' said Eirik in his loudest whisper.

'I thought….'

'Stop bloody thinking! Just call on him as you would anyone.'

'Oh right, I see' he said dusting off forty shades of shit and ignoring the expression of exasperation on Annie's face.

Silas could barely cope with knocking on a door. Not that there was anything the least extraordinary about this door, but all doors, and the waiting of course, frightened the flaming life out of him.

Marcus casually answered but then stood, agape, as he beheld his friend wondering why he would adorn himself with weeds and dog poo before calling.

'Why, Silas! How did you find me? What….how did….'

'If I could please come inside brother, I will tell you all.'

Stunned, Marcus did just that. At this point, Eirik's heart had stopped. He of little faith, wondering if Lord Silas was able to pull this off. Suspiciously, he kept his eye on both doors and the one to the rear as well, thinking that Marcus may bolt. He need not have worried. Silas, very politely told Marcus that the game was up. Elspeth herself had, from beyond, insisted that he was to go no further alone. Whether it was just good luck or, for the first time, good management,

Silas cleverly mixed good news, like the new baby, with the intrigue and there was no doubt that it did help to settle Marcus. He told him too, that the Agents lay in wait for him beyond the city and that he was to accompany Silas immediately for his own good. Marcus then began to anxiously pace the boards and, as he did, Silas realised that he was surrounded by documents. Many, many, pieces of paper and parchment that Marcus had annotated and there was a model that took up almost half of the room. Silas supposed that it resembled a puzzle from one angle and a ship from another.

'Can't do it Silas' said Marcus.

Having done so well, Silas didn't have a response for this so fell over his words and also the puzzle pieces that were on the floor. Sensitively, Marcus took a hold of his friend by the shoulders and sat him down again.

'I'm not refusing your help…in fact, I do confess that I can go no further without enlisting the Agents. But, they have to come here, at least to start with.'

'What, all of them?!'

'Yes. Wait until dark. You can bypass the road here' he said pointing to a path that followed the contour of the castle wall 'this will take you directly to the rear entrance. Come by the same route, where Eirik is yonder.'

'What? you knew he was there all….'

'I just knew you wouldn't be alone. I want you to relay this information to Eirik and return immediately. I have use for you again, straight away.'

Daunted by the incredibly brief mission before him, Silas knew already that he had the better deal as Marcus's home was warm and cake was on offer. As Eirik saw him returning alone he believed all hope to be lost and could barely take in the message that Silas had returned with.

'Marcus has drawn this.'

They looked at it together. It was a secret destination halfway between the barn and Marcus's current abode 'the horses and Bayard's cart are to be kept there but everyone is to return here tonight. Eirik initially protested but eventually conceded knowing that they had no choice and that Marcus, very likely, had good reason.

Once settled with cake and ale, Silas soon found out why he had asked him to stay. Marcus talked, and he talked. At times he wept, sometimes on his feet and other times, slumped in the chair but rarely in the history of espionage has a fugitive needed to unburden himself so desperately and Silas, of course, was exactly the right man to spill to. He was at times possibly even more engaged than Marcus as they also talked endlessly about Wynnfrith and Elspeth.

At nightfall, there was a pregnant hush around the house as they awaited the arrival of their fellow Agents. However, as a group, they were rapidly discovering that stealth was not their greatest strength. Cracks and crashes and thumps and squelches were accompanied by angry, but whispered: "it's not me!" And "hush" and more "it's not me."

With just one meagre candle lit in the whole downstairs of his property, Marcus opened the back door in the hope that he could get this anonymous travelling band inside without any further ruckus.

They streamed in, one after the other, placing blame, one after the other, only to be reminded, once again, by myself that soon the constables of Oxford would apprehend us. Eventually, as we settled into a relatively small living space, we all saw for the first time our lost friend. However, it was Wynnfrith who pushed to the front as I presumed that she wanted to be the first one to greet him.

'Why the bloody hell did you bugger off?! Have you any idea….?!'

And, as he started to defend himself, even she realised that this wasn't the right time. Silas stood between the two of them and she broke down. Hardly surprising as, physically, this mission was already becoming a challenge for her. She turned back to face Marcus, walked toward him and tenderly placed her arms about his neck and rested her head in his chest.

'Oh, dear brother, the things we have been through and I have not shown you any respect.'

She then faced him and thanked him for the wedding present and told him that they would not know what to do with it.

'We will make a fresh start here and now' said Wynnfrith and then she kissed his cheek.

As the rest of us also made an effort to make him feel more comfortable, I suggested that we all sat and updated our information.

Marcus now told his whole story from when he had been a child, how he had ventured northward in France and secured employment. About Jack and Aelfraed and, eventually, Jack's murder.

'And you say that was Bask?' asked Farrier.

Acknowledging this, he then told us about his escape.

'What became of you after you ran away?' asked Bayard as Dramaticus looked on, mentally taking note of this most exciting adventure.

'I did the same all over again. I sought work, settling on a farm in Oxfordshire. I slept in an outhouse and was fed well, I presumed that my life at sea was over and was grateful for this renewed existence. After only seven months I was disturbed one night by sounds outside the farmhouse…'

Dramaticus leant forward, noting how engaged Richard Shakespeare was as well. Peter was a child again revelling in Gilly's tall tales of the seas.

'I could see nought. It was dark inside and out but, before I knew it, a man was atop me trying to strangle the life out of me. However, I was armed and got better of him but the owner insisted on calling out the sheriff as I had taken that man's life. They took me inside the farmer's house to report what had happened. No one, including myself, recognised this man and it was only when the sheriff accepted my story and gave me leave that I stood and saw blood pouring from my own belly. Minutes later I was unconscious.'

'The farmer saved your life?'

'In a way, yes but…you'll never guess where I ended up?' he said looking directly at Farrier.

'No!...never. The monastery?'

'Not only that, but tended to by the most remarkable Bede. My tale is so very much like your own, Thomas. As I recovered, I helped out with the gardens, in fact, any way I could to repay the good monks. One morning, the sun almost burning the grass, I saw Bede amble out into the light by the cloisters so I went to greet him. However, as I neared, I realised that one of the buttresses was hiding a second figure, almost in the shadows. It was Bask.'

On cue, everyone gasped. Bede. Their Bede involved in intrigue? Without any question coming forth, he continued.

'I will tell all later but, suffice it to say, I had discovered that Bede was in league with Sir Anthony Bask.'

I decided it wise to interrupt and address everyone.

'This does make sense. Think about it my friends, both Brother Bernard and Brother Bede were a part of the Pilgrimage of Grace. They were ardent Catholics and completely against the King's marriage to Boleyn and his self-appointment as head of the church. If Bede could speak now he would tell you that he wished the King dead.'

There was quite a lot of head-scratching so I suggested that we let Marcus continue with his tale.

He told us that he had found employment at the infirmary in Worcester as a way of giving back to others that were sick and dying, particularly proud that one of his elderly patients recovered having been saved from the clutches of death. That same man, Titus Tull, had asked Marcus to continue administering one-to-one care in his home. When Marcus arrived at Titus's house, it was nothing less than a mansion. Although Marcus ended up being employed in a variety of tasks around the estate, he was paid well and counted his

1543 The Disfiguration

blessings, presuming, once again that he was settled for life. What he hadn't accounted for was Tull suddenly dying within the following few months. Following the funeral and Marcus then readying himself to move on once again, he was stopped by Tull's lawyer only to discover that Tull had left Marcus a small fortune.

'So how did you end up in York?' asked Eirik.

'I knew by then that I was, and still am, a target. Again, I chose to give my time tending to the poor and needy in York and was immeasurably content with that. I had no idea that both Aelfraed and Bask had connections in the north.'

He then quizzed Wynnfrith.

'I'm supposing that you have secured the lumps of metal?'

Wynnfrith, now contrite, told him, calmly, the tale of Elspeth's letters and what came after.

'However' she said ' all those years, I think you overlooked something.'

She turned to Silas who opened up a large bundle and, inside, was that glorious key.

'I don't understand' said Marcus.

'Almost by chance, we put the three together and out came this butterfly.'

'So it is a key! I had seen it labelled as such but never understood it!'

'So what does it open?' asked Wynnfrith.

'I am still in the process of working that out and I'm hoping, starting this very hour, that the mouse may help me.'

Throughout this discourse, most of them remained silent. Maud gawped at Marcus as if he was a statue and Bayard, surprisingly, listened with great intent. So, at this point, I suggested that everyone let Marcus and myself have some time together, reminding them that it was imperative that they kept quiet.

There was stuff everywhere. I say, stuff, because I could not recognise all of it. In the corner was a huge model of a ship which looked either half assembled or half dissembled

1543 The Disfiguration

and, everywhere else, paper and parchment documents, most of them scattered on his large desk.

I asked him to place me on the desk. Even though it was awkward for me having to scramble around, if I sat up, I could read what was under my arse much to the amusement of the audience.

'There is so much and in many languages. It's hard to know where to start' I said.

'I have some thoughts about most of these but this one, I cannot fathom' said Marcus.

'I believe it to be Portuguese although I'm not sure that I will be able to translate' I said.

From over Marcus's shoulder loomed Bayard's head.

'Perhaps I can help'

Now, to be clear, in my mind, the chances of Bayard knowing any language was slim, but, not wishing to exclude him or to seem rude, I invited him over.

'Bayard always seems to show up when you do mouse!' said Marcus almost without thinking. Strange, I thought, that's the second time I've heard that but could not make head or tail of whether it meant anything.

'Ah' said Bayard almost as if he had just had a personality transplant 'this is, indeed, Portuguese. It is from a man called Santos…mmm…yes, this is a contract, yet only a few years old.'

'Contract for what?' I said quite curtly, astonished at the change in Bayard.

'Well…it's a little delicate' he said nodding toward Marcus.

Marcus made it clear that anything, absolutely anything, uncovered would be helpful to him and the Agents.

'Well, you understand that for some time, slavery was the province almost solely of the Portuguese?'

'Yes'

'This is a contract that would systematically involve England in the gathering and sale of slave labour. A pact between the two countries if you like.'

I was shocked. Firstly as Bayard had used the word, systematically, but then that such a thing was possible. Although historically, England's slate wasn't completely clean regarding the slave trade, little would happen for some time. I stopped to run over events in my mind but found nothing that would suggest such an agreement happening in the 1540s. My thoughts turned to the despicable Henry the Navigator of Portugal who, as early as the mid-1400s had sent expeditions into Africa to measure the power of the Moors only to return with slaves which he believed to be compensation for his trouble. Unbelievably, by 1455, Pope Nicholas V supported Portugal's right to continue this diabolical enterprise. By the sixteenth century, ten per cent of the Portuguese population was made up of slaves working anywhere from homes to the mines. They had also spread their wings. Girls from Japan were exploited for sexual purposes and slaves were also captured in Korea and China.

From where I was, in 1543, it would be some time before the English picked up on this with the Godfather of English slave trading, Sir John Hawkins, choosing to pilfer slaves from Portuguese ships and then selling them on again, only pausing when he lost seven ships to the Spanish in 1568. Things would then be relatively quiet until the 1640s, booming again in the eighteenth century.

'You alright mouse?' asked Marcus kindly.

'Yes. Yes, my friend, just shocked.'

'My farmer parents in France. They were right, weren't they? I needed to keep going north for my own safety. In fact, I seem to keep moving further and further north!'

'At this very time' I said 'you are absolutely correct. Well, in general terms I should add'

'Bask has signed this agreement so I don't know what it now entails.'

'He has a brother' added Marcus.

'What?' I said.

'That's all I know so I do not know whether he is involved or not.'

'Yes he is' said Bayard pointing to the sixth signature on the list. Joshua Bask. He was up to his eyeballs in it. It was then that my tiny brain went into gear. Of course, this was the document shown to me at the institute and why I was sent here in the first place but that was a word-processed translation. King Henry would have had absolutely no knowledge of this agreement meaning that if successful, illicit and private trading would be taking place without the Crown knowing.

The stash that Marcus had acquired was a dark and shameful catalogue of wrongdoings. We moved our attention to an untidy pile of copied of letters that had been sent to Robert Hall in recent years, proof of his accusations of blackmail. Also, dozens of letters from lovers some of which he subsequently had tried to blackmail.

'Most of it I ignore' said Marcus 'as it is largely a distraction from my search.'

Almost holding all of this together, was a weighty document almost half the size of the desk but it was underneath everything else. I urged both Bayard and Marcus to free it and bring it to the top. We all gasped. This was a plan agreed between Pole and Bask that involved those at the highest level in Europe's Catholic states. The seal alone was over six inches across and the arrangement was precise in its aims.

There, before us was tangible evidence of a plot to place Princess Mary on the throne with detail of how it was to be achieved including the downfall of Henry and Prince Edward. Marcus and Bayard both asked questions simultaneously.

'Is the Princess involved?' asked Marcus.

'Why would he not hide all this? Asked Bayard.

'Firstly' I said ' it would be hard to read Mary's thoughts. She truly has been mistreated since the divorce of her mother with attempts, particularly after Boleyn's death, to bring her back into the fold. At this very moment, the King is courting Katherine Parr who, even though very much a reformer and of the new faith, will probably want the family together. But, no matter how much Mary complies, her Catholic conscience will never still.'

'Perhaps she will come to know the new faith before this plot has time to fester' said Marcus.

I said nothing in reply as, already, I was giving to much away. I knew that when, eventually, she would rule England it would be ruthlessly and with the intent of purging Protestantism completely. Strangely, as I looked at Bayard, it was almost as if he had acknowledged this too.

'In answer to your question, he probably thought that these documents were either secure or he had plans for them. After all, he didn't expect to be killed on the road from Knapton to York. It has also just occurred to me that it is likely that Lady Bask does not read.'

Then it went quiet. Except, that was, for Wynnfrith's snoring and Silas's heavy-footed attempt to dart from one door to the other and then from one window to another in his guise as a lookout with his strange, but new, potbelly wobbling as he leapt.

Another glance at the papers revealed that he had been in the habit of spying on people of influence in order to blackmail them later.'

'This man is as wicked and scurrilous as any could be' noted Marcus.

The large document had told us a little more about Henry's navy and there were still gaps, particularly in informing us as to what may happen next, bearing in mind that Bask was now gone. There was still a mound of papers to get through including printed leaflets but I wanted to know more of the huge and peculiar puzzle so Marcus led us to the model of the ship.

'I believe this to be a key in itself. I am sure it can tell us so much more but I've tried taking it apart and even putting it back together again. I am clueless!' he whispered.

'May I?' said Bayard.

Astonished, we let him play with the oversized toy. In seconds he was taking it apart, reassembling it, scribbling notes and then repeating it all over again.

Only thirty minutes later, he produced a document in which he had written copious notes and codes. Arrows and symbols I had never seen before. For a moment I wondered if he was having a joke. His entertainer's nature taking over events in the hope that it would lighten the atmosphere somewhat. He turned to us.

'That's it. I know what we have to do next. Tomorrow, when all is well, we plan and rehearse and then we can travel, heading toward the docks at Deptford.'

We were both so tired that we simply thanked him and, within minutes, Marcus had left us and was asleep. Bayard wished me goodnight but I was not having any of it.

'Goodnight my arse! You and I need to chat first!'

He laughed and then sat at the desk placing me in front of him.

'You need to tell me what's going on' I said.

'Well, Mouse, I suppose you could say that I've blown my cover? However, I have done this in good faith as I could not see how you would not have got any further without help. I should add, I am not allowed to do such a thing so, I'm hoping you will keep my secret.'

Secret? I thought. What bloody secret? This is Bayard, the bastard that stuck pins in my rear end when I first saw him, can't even spell his own name. Truth be told, I was struggling to work out how someone living in the sixteenth century was better at code-breaking than I was. Then the penny dropped and I was horrified at what I now suspected. He continued to smile, giving nothing away.

'I'm guessing you can work this out by yourself' he said calmly.

'I'm scared to even go there if I'm honest.'

'Imagine how hard it is for me' said Bayard 'Nick, you are the stuff of legend. In the same league as Newton, Picasso, Cernan, Roznek. To be honest, I'm struggling to come to terms with our friendship.'

Friendship? I thought. Not the word that springs to mind at this moment. My suspicions were now becoming reality and it worried me, particularly as I had completely submerged myself in the identity of Micklegate Mouse, once again.

Still, he said nothing.

'Ok! You are like me aren't you?'

He nodded.

'A pilot? But, in many ways, not the same because you have a, credible, human form.'

'Correct.'

'So you are from my future?'

'Correct again, Nick.'

'So what the bloody hell are you doing here, creeping around me?!'

He laughed again.

'I'm studying you.'

I went cold.

'Nick, you were the one great pioneer of our research and, I know from records, that this was so difficult for you. As you assume, long after your time the science developed and, what you see before you is a projection of the real me.'

I looked him up and down, not really impressed. The future of the common male physique in big trouble if you were to ask me.

'Haha, there are, of course, creative embellishments as you would expect but there are no longer any problems with the mix. I am completely in control. It is, at this point, as you would expect that I have to tell you that I cannot reveal all. Take heart in the news that your work will be a great success.'

'So I'm not imagining all of this?'

'If you are then I am an illusion too.'

'Now listen here dickhead!..'

Then he laughed so much that the others stirred.

'Oh, how I love that. You really do lose control don't you?'

Embarrassed, I questioned him again.

'Early missions were well documented but so were many suspicions about whether pilot's experiences were real or not. I'm looking into those early missions.'

'So…' I said 'until a short while before the start of my most recent mission, there was no documented record of a slave trade agreement in England in the 1540s? I'm here to see if there is any substance to that notion? And there is. I ask you, then, are we just discovering more evidence or are we influencing it?'

He laughed again. My mind rushed back to the day when he stuck a pin in my arse and suddenly, I wanted to punch him. I didn't get an answer and I was left further confused about what he was telling me and anxious that I might well be dreaming him up as well. If what he had said was true, I would spend the rest of the mission feeling like a teacher on teaching practice as long as he was around.

He told me to rest and then he did the same but not before we woke Eirik and asked him to keep watch as we were certain that he would be much quieter than Silas if nothing else.

Very soon, I felt myself dozing with a thousand conflicting thoughts spinning around in my mind.

19 food and weapons

The following morning reality struck home. My friends were already suffering from all sorts of aches and pains from the journey and the inhospitable sleeping conditions. Even the seasoned warriors like Eirik and Farrier could have used a refresher course but, as always, I knew we had to plan using what we had. It didn't help that, after a night's sleep, I couldn't work out whether Bayard was Bayard or a mirage. Play to our strengths, I told myself.

'Off we go to snare these scoundrels!' announced Thomas Farrier.

'We aren't going anywhere' I said 'we need time to fully prepare. You must trust me.'

I took Marcus to one side hoping that he had sufficient contacts in Oxford to supply us with what we needed. The bare-bones would be food as it was likely that we would be on the road for days so we needed plenty of non-perishable goods. I sat on the desk and my army stood in a semi-circle around me. What a bunch! I thought and then reminded myself of the steel and courage that flowed through the veins of this ragged crew. Perhaps that would be an advantage, I thought as most of them seemed harmless. The list that I dictated to Marcus was long and I knew that he would struggle to get everything. Included in that itinerary was space for our blacksmith, Farrier, to work. I asked them all, particularly keeping an eye on Bayard that if they had any hidden skills they should tell me emphasising that it didn't matter how embarrassing or irrelevant they may have seemed.

I noticed Eirik, hesitantly, open and shut his mouth as if he were mimicking a cod.

'Yes, Eirik? Anything will help.'

'I…err…I am good at making arrows.'

Good at making arrows! Thought I. He can make bloody arrows and he's never bothered to tell us. Calm yourself Mouse.

Wynnfrith glared at him.

'Ah, that trick you picked up At Scarborough Fair?'

'Mmm…yes' he said sheepishly.

'Then, once Marcus has a foundry secured you will work there alongside him'

'I can be a distraction' said Dramaticus.

Several, quite rude, responses came to mind but I thanked him, indicating that I had already considered this. Then Maud stepped forward.

'I could seduce any would-be attackers…'

I was speechless. So much so, that I couldn't bear to look at anyone but her, in case they made me laugh.

'That is a bold suggestion, dear Maud, but I do not think we would have you take such risks.'

'I'm a Lord!' announced Silas and silence followed.

Eventually, I took him to task.

'And?..'

'Well….just that…they may bow at my feet.'

'Oh God.' I said as quietly as I could.

Peter, having been both patient and quiet throughout,

enthusiastically threw in his tuppeny's worth,

'I can run fast...really fast and I can swim, like a fish. And...climb and chase and cover long distances without any help. Oh...and row. I can row well and tell directions from the stars!'

Not bad for a lad in his teens. I thanked him and assured him that most, if not all, of his skills, were likely to be put to good use.

'Let's leave it at that for I now and park any thoughts you may have that we may be leaving soon, we have much to do.

20 hampton court
One week earlier

Fifty-six miles away at Hampton Court, King Henry the eighth of that name was not in good spirits. Having said that, he was rarely in good spirits during this twilight of his days. However, he was confident about the imminent marriage to the formidable Katherine Parr, unsurprisingly twenty-two years younger and, he hoped to once again revisit his youth. However, his youth was as remote a possibility as a Papist running his finances. Nevertheless, he would have his way, always.

Thomas Heneage was still getting the brunt of Henry's moodiness, often alone in his privy chamber and witness to his deepest and often, most childish, thoughts.

'God's teeth! Heneage. How can it be lost?!'

'It is beyond my wit and understanding, Your Grace. I only know what your parliament and advisors tell you.'

'Parliament! A contingent of grave robbers, animal molesters! They even steal my shoes!'

Shoes? Thought Heneage, certain that something was amiss in what the King was trying to say.

1543 The Disfiguration

Thomas had learned long ago that, often, it was wise just to let his boss rant. Sometimes things were made worse by responding. However, on this morning, he was not getting away with it.

'Well?!!'

'Oh yes, Your Majesty, animals…'

'It is, beyond doubt, the most important thing in all of Christendom! That's why I have it. How the bloody hell can it be lost?!'

Heneage was also used to going around in circles in this fashion and would try to divert the King's attention by offering him anything from food and drink to poultices and enemas.

'Send for Sadler. T'will be him! Always been a thief…and he keeps animals too!'

Hoping for some relief, particularly from accusations involving animals, Thomas Heneage sent word immediately to Lord Ralph Sadler who, so recently, had acquired a new feather in his cap for his role in helping to unravel the murder plots against the King. The door opened, he bowed and doffed his hat waiting to be told to rise.

'We!...You! Need to get to the bottom of this!'

'Of course, Your Grace' which came out quite muted as his head was still in his codpiece.

'Well?!'

'I'm sorry Your Grace. If you could only tell me of the issue at hand.'

'Issue! Issue!! I'll bloody issue you!' For God's sake man, stand upright!...what have you done with it?'

'Ah!' said Sadler, both as a sign of relief and also an acknowledgement of what the bluster was about.

'I must indulge His Grace's patience. It was never in my keep.'

Henry stood, the pain from his bones and particularly his ulcered leg, amply reflected on his grimaced face. If he was angry before then it was as nothing compared to what was to come.

'Not in my keep! Well, let me tell you, my boy! It wasn't in *my* bloody keep!! And well you know it!!'

Struggling to stand unaided, he glanced down at the desk, calming a little for a moment or two. He thought of the skinny idiot from York that had given him the quill now resting on his seal and then the supernatural mouse that accompanied him. At that moment he had a mind to call on them again as all his advisors were interested only in their own skin and, after that, their bank accounts. Bravely, Sadler tried to appease him.

'Your Grace, the vault is impenetrable. It is forged from the densest steel in Europe.'

He paused and looked at Heneage, not sure if he was party to this knowledge but, as nothing was said, Sadler decided to continue.

'There is but a small door and it is impossible to get into it.'

Hoping that there was now some calm in the storm, Sadler took a step forward only to receive a further reprimand.

'Idiot! Haven't you considered! Had it not occurred to you?!…' he paused 'what if *I* want to get in it?!'

Sadler so wanted to say, well you can't, but, at this juncture, it just wouldn't have been wise. With nothing else to contribute, Sadler remained silent. Then, almost as if changing the subject completely, the King said,

'Oh, how I miss him! How I miss Linacre! There would be none of this mess if he were here!'

'But Your Grace' said Thomas Heneage ' he would now be in his mid-eighties and possibly with no wits remaining.'

'That would still be three times what my advisors have in total!' retorted the grumpy Tudor.

Maybe this was nothing more than nostalgia but there had been no doubt that Henry, like most people of his time, had been plagued with health problems. Add to that, his often sickly children and the numerous miscarriages, he would have given anything for a miracle worker. Only once since we met had he sat and considered that there was something about northerners that made problems a little more straightforward to navigate. If nothing else, he understood them to be open. However, mid-rant, Harry had possibly forgotten that Thomas Linacre, although Dean of Wigan was not originally from the north. But, he had been a most loyal and worthwhile Royal Physician since Henry had taken the throne. This was one wish that no one could fulfil. Thomas Linacre was long dead and that was the end of it. Determined to gather half the Court around him to share his dismay, he was now dispensing names by the second.

'Get me the Scottish bog!' he bellowed. Immediately calls were out for Edward Seymour, the Duke of Somerset who had recently been bequeathed the title of 'Warden of the Scottish Marshes' hence the rather unflattering shortened version. When Henry offered a very rare reprieve as he had done with Seymour following his role in the doomed Cataclysm of 1541, he knew that it would have also tightened his grip on their rein.

'What have you to say about this?!'

Seymour knew what was eating away at the King but the issue at hand was way beyond his province or responsibility and so just mumbled for a few minutes until the King changed his mind again. And, it worked.

'Send for Cranmer!'

It seemed as though, on this day, no one was to be free from his wrath. Arguably, however, the Archbishop was one of the few people at Court that had the gift of being able to soothe the beast but no one knew if it was going to be enough on this occasion.

'What do you say about all this Thomas? Whose fault is it?'

Surprisingly, Henry let him speak.

'As I see it Your Grace…' he paused presuming that,

already he may get shouted down 'I can only fathom that it must have been stolen and that it is unlikely that it is anyone at Court who is responsible.'

'How so? He grunted.

'Well, Your Grace, your enemies…'

'Enemies! Enemies!! I've got bloody enemies everywhere. Here, Wales, Scotland, Ireland, absolutely everywhere in pissing Europe. Even women. My women! Protestants and Catholics alike! What do they all want of me?!'

Henry slumped forward, still sitting on his bed, with his head supported by both hands. All eyes were darting back and forth to Cranmer as if to say, 'well, go on, sort this and quickly.'

Thomas Cranmer knelt before the King and spoke quietly.

'Beside the people in this room, there are but a few others who understand the contents of the coffer and all are of the new persuasion and understand its necessity. If I may speak freely…'

Henry nodded.

'There are those that, even threatened with treason will still speak of your demise…'

The King looked up and stared at Seymour who, immediately, became unsteady.

'And also have interest in the longevity of our dear sainted Prince, Edward. I have to conclude that anyone who has taken this may well be a Papist.'

Henry mumbled into his hands, seemingly somewhat calmer. Slowly, he looked up.

'You do grasp the importance of this Cranmer?'

'Of course, Your Grace. The importance of both. The contents of the coffer must be kept secure but, God forbid, the contents may be required anytime, so we do need to access it.'

'And the key?'

Cranmer now addressed all present.

'On pain of death. On pain of all our deaths, this key must be retrieved. As well as needing it to access the Royal chest, it is the Holiest object to ever grace our isles.'

Somewhat sceptical, Sadler cautiously pushed the issue.

'So, is it true?'

Henry stood again now waving his fist in the air.

'True?! True!! What would you know, you pig's arsehole? That key hath been touched by Our Lord, Jesus Christ Himself! The Blood that has saved us all from our sins has flowed gently over that very metal which now masquerades as a key.' He calmed a little but only because he was now becoming exhausted.

'Why…the knights Templar had this nail as a handle to a flagon. The very one that they used for initiations into their order. It has been with my family for over two hundred years and now….gone.'

It became very clear that Henry believed the object to have spiritual properties, possibly the gift of healing and, God knows, how much he was in need of that. He sent Seymour out and then addressed the others.

'I expect you to investigate this further, we may be in need of that key sooner than I would have hoped. And, much against my better judgement, I will have to engage with that ridiculous mouse once again…you may pull trapped wind faces all you will, he has a better brain than all of you put together! Heneage…write to that imbecile in York…what his name?'

'You mean the Mayor, Your Grace.'

'Yes, him. Tell him I'm in need of that mouse and his jesters.'

'Of course, Your Grace.'

'And…when you've done that, I'm in need of a good shit, so get to it, man.'

'Yes, Your Grace.'

Truthfully, no one at Court had a clue why the key had disappeared but the one person that could have helped them was now six feet under and in two pieces. The key had disappeared around the time that Catherine Howard was arrested although few suspected her specifically. However, the following morning, Seymour began to question anyone who was within her retinue or her family, and still breathing, causing further panic and upset at Court.

21 The argument

Marcus had rented the property in which we all, supposedly secretly, lodged whilst we prepared for the conflict to come. I found it heart-warming that the street was called Nun's Walk and that this choice had been influenced by his love for Elspeth. In later years it would become known as Oxpens road. A few days after our arrival, he had managed to acquire somewhere for Thomas Farrier and Eirik to work where they were relatively secluded and where no one would ask questions. He had also employed clothiers and seamstresses under the strict understanding that all the work had to be secret, this, in itself, pushing up the cost. It seemed as though Marcus could access or provide almost anything I asked for which told me that he had almost endless resources. Although everyone was getting nervous and, at times ill-tempered, holed up in the same house for days, there was a sense of camaraderie and I could feel that they all were, slowly, pulling together. Nevertheless, we were all becoming frustrated with how long everything was taking. The only real argument that took place was during one morning as Eirik and Marcus returned from the leather merchants, a jaunt in which they almost blew their cover.

Sent with precise instructions and measurements, they decided to go together against my better judgement. As they waited for the goods to be wrapped, someone else walked into the somewhat modest shop and they then claimed that they acted most naturally, almost as if the two of them were not together. Skulking back into the shadows, they allowed the woman access to the merchant only to realise that this was Lady Bask. If Marcus had had any thoughts of passing himself off as someone else well, frankly, he would have been deluding himself. She turned and headed straight for him.

'Why, Marcus. I'd have thought you far away from Oxford by now.'

'Had work to do my Lady, took lodgings close by.'

Fortunately, at this point, Lady Bask wasn't the least suspicious. In fact, she relaxed instantly into familiar conversation and gestured toward the shop owner.

'This kind man is taking the last of my furniture. I found out just two days ago that I will lose the house too. I'm secure for a few weeks and, after that, I may well be homeless.'

She smiled benignly as though she had accepted her fate, now tired of the constant anxiety. Marcus sincerely shared his sadness at hearing this news but, beyond that, felt lost for words. He almost chose to introduce Eirik as it was clear that they were together but it was then that Lady Bask spotted him.

'You?!' she said looking at Eirik. Then she turned to Marcus.

'You know each other?'

Clearly, she was hurt. Her happy-go-lucky manner, no matter how well-meant, was now gone. Marcus was direct.

'Yes, my Lady. From York. Normally we both reside there.'

Her mood darkened.

'You came into my home under some deceit about finding documents when all along, you were in league with this demon?!' she said to Marcus.

Marcus tried hard to appease her but was, of course, also trying to work why she was so bitter toward Eirik. She then turned, left a small note on the desk, bade the man good day and stormed out in tears. Subsequently, Eirik and Marcus argued all the way back and this could be heard well before they entered the property. I was furious.

'What the hell has gotten into you both?! You will alert the whole city! Explain yourselves!' I demanded.

Like children, they continued to squabble. Now losing patience, I stopped them and asked them to tell me, step by step, what had happened. Interestingly, when they had finished, Wynnfrith was the first to respond.

'More secrets brother?'

Indeed, that was what everyone was thinking. It was time for Eirik to explain. Somewhat bewildered, he sat and took us all back to that day when he had delivered the body of Sir Anthony Bask to her front door. The same body that had been embalmed by Viscera and had in its belly a small fortune which had been sent to pay off Lady Bask, as Robert believed that she had started to blackmail him once Bask could no more.

'So what happened once you had knocked on that door?' I asked.

'I felt so stupid! I politely told her that the body was there ready for burial and that his internals had been consecrated in York. At first she was confused so invited me in to explain. Only thinking of being cautious, I repeated the same, telling her that all she had asked for was in there. She became very angry saying that she had never asked for his body, neither did she want it and then catalogued the misery he had bestowed on her in life. Well, this should make up for it, says I, and she became even angrier! She agreed to accept the body but told me that it would get a pauper's burial at best. Truth be told, I was glad to get away.'

'So that's why you were in there so long?' said Bayard.

'What? You were watching me?'

'Only keeping an eye out young un' lied Bayard.

'So' I said 'when you got back to York and eventually relayed this to Robert he said…'

'He went mad!' said Eirik 'he kept saying, it's bloody obvious! But it wasn't to me. Clearly, it wasn't her who had sent the blackmail letter and neither was she expecting the money. And! She didn't flaming know it was there. Made a right dick of myself!'

'And the ransom ended up six feet under' I added.

'Exactly!' said Eirik ' but six feet under where? I was asking myself!'

Furious, Robert had sent him on a second expedition to query Lady Bask as to where the body was which, to say the least, didn't go down too well either. Lady Bask told him where to go in both senses of the word. Alone, at night, Eirik dug up Sir Anthony Bask, along with the four other reprobates on top of him and retrieved the gold.

'It is by far the most unholy and disagreeable task I have ever taken on' said Eirik.

'Well,' I said ' I think it's fair to say that you now have our sympathy. Robert has really put you through it.'

I had never seen Silas look so relieved to be overlooked for a mission, his chin trembled even as the story was told.

'So who did write the note? It means someone else knows about Robert's dark secrets' asked Wynnfrith.

'As yet we do not know' said Eirik ' but it is another burden I carry.'

He slumped back further into his seat feeling sorry for himself.

'Ah but…you are still our Lancelot!' said Peter and Eirik smiled giving him a warm touch on his shoulder. Ah, the innocence of youth, I thought. We will need that.

'Poor, poor woman' said Marcus.

'No more than a man's property all her life and now she's worthless, not a penny to her name!' added Maud. No one was in a mood to argue, we genuinely feared for the welfare of this ill-used and abused woman from Oxford.

I impressed on Farrier, Marcus and Eirik the need to expedite affairs. Not, necessarily, that we were in a hurry, but the house was very obviously becoming overcrowded and the locals were surely suspicious. Added to that was the risk that my Agents were now starting to get on each other's nerves and, the neat privy in the ditch outside that had been engineered by Marcus for himself, meant that the Agents were now getting to know each other much more intimately than they would have liked. They promised me that, by morning, all my requests would be fulfilled. So, the day after, with the room so full of paraphernalia that we could hardly move, we started to think about how this sorry bunch could take on the army of the Pope. I do, of course, exaggerate, but at that time, we had no idea as to what we would face. Somewhat fired up, or more likely scared shitless, there were rampant threats from my troops each declaring what they would do to the enemy and swearing by the Bible, mothers and sons, a slightly related cousin on their father's side and even someone they didn't really know very well but lived in the same street.

Silas, wisely, said nowt.

Wynnfrith asked me if she could address everyone and I, of course, was happy for her to do so.

'We would not be here if it was not for my dear sister. However, I feel compelled in the sight of God this day, to remind you of why the Agents formed in the beginning. If there is one thing that Elspeth still reminds me of daily, it is that we, as Agents, are sworn to follow the teachings of our Lord, Jesus Christ. We should endeavour to overcome our enemies but with as little violence as possible. Ideally, none at all!' she said waving her finger at us all 'although they may be misguided, we can assume that the evil deeds carried out by these people, including Bask, were done so believing that they had good reason whether we agree with it or not.'

She then quoted Galatians, reminding us of the people we had become and that Elspeth, as well as the Lord, was watching over us

'But the fruit of the spirit is love, joy, peace, forbearance, kindness, goodness, faithfulness, gentleness and self-control. Against such things there is no law. Those who belong to Christ Jesus have crucified the flesh with its passions and desires. Since we live by the Spirit. Let us keep in step with the spirit. Let us not become conceited, provoking and envying one another.'

Wynnfrith knew that, potentially, a long debate, dissecting the virtues of maiming and killing the enemy was imminent but she had, very sensitively, smoothed away such thoughts. At least, I should say, for the time being. In reality, my plan would mean overcoming the enemy and, as yet, we had no idea as to how many this would be. Maud, now inspired, asked that we all spend some time in prayer with everyone, selflessly, contributing. I say selflessly because, as Christians often do, no one prayed for themselves. There was much concern for those left in York and Father Matthew was highlighted in Thomas Farrier's prayers. Interestingly, Eirik mentioned Meg and Marcus included the most unfortunate Lady Bask. Maud asked Eirik who Meg was and, without any hesitation, he told the truth. She pushed the issue, more as a way of reaching out to this lonely young man that, seemingly, nobody would trust ever again.

'You sweet on her then?'

Embarrassed, he thought for a moment.

'I really do not know. I do confess that I have thought of her so much more since we have recently met than I ever did before.'

If ever there was an opportunity to throw in a cruel quip it would have been then, but no one said a word.

'Do you see her face in the strangest of places. Almost everywhere?' asked Silas.

'Mmm...yes, I do. Is that normal brother?'

'I have been so, Eirik. It is the most toxic thing on God's earth. Why...my heart would sing its own songs about Wynnfrith, her dark flowing hair and her pretty face. All of a sudden, everyone seemed to walk like this sweet lady and her voice was in the wind. My every day and night became all about this formidable and beautiful woman. God had sent an angel that moved my every thought and deed. Under loves heavy burden did I, happily, sink.'

No one in the room moved a muscle. Silas's speech had been so surreal, but at the same time unexpectedly moving, that people couldn't believe their ears. This passion that he had felt had presumably been bottled up inside him for over a year and it was unlikely that Wynnfrith had ever heard it previously. I looked at Maud who was weeping and then to Wynnfrith, her tears dripping into her lap.

Of course, Silas then thought he had upset everyone and so stood to console his wife.

'Oh, dear husband, how blessed I am to have you. Few women can have witnessed such heartfelt poetry.'

Silas was still clueless but also relieved that he was in his wife's good books.

Richard Shakespeare was kicking himself for never learning to write. He told himself that this was gold. People in their droves would one day marvel at such performances and he promised himself that if he returned safely to the farm, he would regale these stories to his children, knowing already that they weren't the least bit interested. Surely not? I thought to myself. Did this passion for storytelling really begin with Will's grandad? And then I reminded myself that, sadly, Richard would be dead by the time he was born. However, there was no doubting that Silas's final sentiment would, one day, find itself in one of William's most loved plays.

Called to arms and all loved up, I thought it was time that I started to rehearse my troops. Some of them would have to don new attire. I wasn't five minutes into my speech when

Maud protested.

'I'm not wearing that! Not befitting for a lady?'

I held my breath desperately hoping that no one would laugh. I patiently explained that Wynn would be dressed the same and this did appease her somewhat. Thomas Farrier and Eirik had done a fine job of fashioning bows, arrows, swords and daggers amongst other, specialist implements. I promised Wynnfrith that weapons were necessary but, hopefully, the last resort. By and large, they listened attentively. That was until I started to describe my role and what I would be doing. To be clear, at this point, I had previously asked Farrier to supply me with a costume that would protect me, as I would be in close contact with the enemy. Truthfully, I was already suspicious when so many of them insisted that I tried it on there and then, but hoped that they would see the bigger picture.

Fully dressed I resumed,

'Now. Once I am positioned, thus…'

'Haha!! Ha ha!...'

Eirik had started them off and, within seconds, everyone was joining in.

'Ok. Right…see…if I could have your attention. This is a matter of….'

'Oooh!...Haha!' bellowed Maud 'where's yer 'orse!'

'No but…if I…Look! I'm bloody taking this off if you carry on!'

'You'll never get that off without going back to the foundry!' Guffawed Shakespeare.

I was like the world's worst teacher with the world's worst class.

I had thought, in my planning, to cover my back with leather, perhaps a hood as well, to keep my head safe but, no, master bloody craftsman Farrier decides to make me a full suit of armour, visor, gauntlets, the lot

And I would swear that he had deliberately set the hinge in the visor so that it would clang shut every time I tried to speak.

'Now that you are all settled at last' I said rather sarcastically 'before any confrontation commences, I will be placed so..' Clang!!

More laughter. I let the sad bastards have their childish moment and then asked Farrier to get me out of that overwhelming steel vault. However, as I calmed myself I realised that Farrier's work was quite magnificent and may well save my life. As I sat, hot and exhausted, I looked around the crowded room and reminded myself, once again, of how amazing these people were. I had become so fond of them and, as they chatted, it was clear that they were bonding. Even if it was at my expense.

That evening, I sat with Bayard and Marcus once again as we tried to draw up a plan of the buildings and docks at Deptford. I found that I had a moment alone with Bayard so used it to question him further.

'What was all that about?'

He chuckled, clearly understanding what I was referring to.

'What's that Mouse?'

'What's that?! During our romantic interlude, you couldn't take your eyes of Maud. I'm certain I saw you drool at one point!'

'Aha! Discovered!'

'What do you mean…discovered!…I thought you were like me. That being, you're not really here.'

'Complicated…' he muttered.

He really was infuriating me so I continued to press him.

'You have to admit…she's quite a woman…' he said.

I was left in no doubt, at this point, that Bayard was lusting after Maud. I wasn't going anywhere without an explanation.

'You remember that once, you tried to tell your friends, here, where you came from?' he said.

'Yes, it was a disaster.'

'Truthfully Nick, if I tried to explain to you how much our tech has evolved since your days, you simply would have no hope of grasping it. Best I can do is to describe this almost as having dual personalities or dual roles. Except...I chose to be Bayard from the start, a fully constructed avatar. As such, I have also taken on all the variables that go with his personality, his behaviours, beliefs and thoughts.

'His nob too, then?' I crudely retorted.

'Ha Ha! You could put it like that, yes.'

Marcus was now with us so, for now, I knew that I would have to settle with what he had given me.

Marcus explained that his somewhat impressive design was based on what the docks were like when he had run away, years ago. Bask had left us a diagram of how the key parts had been stored but did not mention where they were located. At the very least, we would have to retrieve those parts and destroy them all. Marcus was very gifted. Within an hour he had crafted small figures, ships, boats and warehouses. Rough, I will grant you, but they were sufficient for us to plan.

It was almost midnight. Some of the Agents were asleep, others wide awake. In the 1540s it was rare for people to have regimented sleep times. Often, they would just sleep when they were tired. It would be the rigours of the industrial revolution, over two hundred years later, that would attempt to turn the greater population into automatons. Now the room was full. Full of bodies and full of stock for our mission. Ropes, grapples, arrows, bows, swords, daggers, batons and bludgeons, plants various, outfits, food, ale, horse tack and on it went. Marcus joked that it put him in mind of the cargo for the field of cloth of gold. I had everyone gather around the table and explained my plan, cautioning all present that there were still many unknown variables. However, I assigned distinct roles to everyone and I told them, as a way of rehearsing, to suit-up. For Farrier, Marcus and Eirik, it was very much, come as you are, as they already looked magnificent, donning arms which they were already familiar with. What I didn't expect was the reaction to Wynnfrith and Maud. It had been my intention to have them dress as males to both confuse the enemy and for functionality and comfort but certainly did not wish to introduce a kinky element to proceedings. Bayard could hardly breathe and was whispering "my, my…" as he gawped relentlessly at Maud. Wynnfrith was not unnoticed by her husband and also every other male in the room excepting Thomas Farrier, myself and Bayard.

'Right!' I said 'may I continue?'

Reluctantly, eyes returned to where I was sitting and I had Eirik bring forward a bottle. I explained that its contents would be used to aid our success and had Eirik demonstrate how. I then issued very strict instructions as to what each individual Agent was allowed, and not allowed to do. Our numbers were modest and it was imperative that everyone played to their strengths at the same time as working as one organised unit. I could see that there was an overwhelming presence of fear and told them, once again, that no one was obliged to take part in this. You can imagine the response. Although it was desperately needed, no one slept until we left the next day.

Even the journey took careful thought and planning. There were too many of us to travel together as it would have caused suspicion. Silas and Wynnfrith travelled in Bayard's cart under the pretence of being Maud and Bayard's son and daughter in law. As you would imagine, this was Bayard's idea as a means, no doubt, of getting close to the steamy flesh of Maud. Peter was in the cart too as the younger brother to Silas and he looked after me. Dramaticus and Shakespeare rode side by side a few miles ahead, presumably cataloguing the dramatic details of our conflict long before it had started. Marcus, Farrier and Eirik, the proper soldiers, were a full day ahead of us as they would task themselves with surveying the site and its inhabitants before the rest of us arrived. We all had makeshift tents to keep the rain off at night as bad weather and mud were as formidable an enemy as any of Bask's minions.

In turn, we all travelled through Windsor in an attempt to eventually approach the Thames from the south where the docks at Deptford were located. Bayard commented on the stark changes that had taken place over the past ten years. Once one of the most popular sites for pilgrims, it was now quiet beyond belief. The worship of saints and shrines was now frowned upon and many would be willing to report anyone doing so. Nevertheless, I was astonished by its simplistic beauty. Eventually we settled at Bermondsey known to me specifically for its connection with the Knights Templar. Here we would wait for word from Farrier. I had told those that were in camp with me that they could expect a long wait as I had tasked our three warriors with observing the site day and night for at least four nights to confirm who was there and in what strength. The rain had stopped and, seemingly in the middle of nowhere, we were left to our own devices, relatively relaxed but taking time to prepare for what was ahead. However, as a week passed we had to scavenge food as best we could, all the while sure that they would return.

The night after, whilst most of us were asleep, we heard rustling outside and Peter bravely rushed out to investigate. There they were. Filthy, hungry and desperate for some shelter. I decided there and then that we were to consider carefully the welfare of every individual in our band. The rest of us gave over our rations and provided them with the tent that had the least holes. I commanded them to sleep, despite their constant protestations. I also insisted that they would debrief once they had recuperated.

Another day passed.

Gathered around a fire, Marcus was appointed to relay what they had discovered.

'It is vast, much bigger than when I left. Some ships are

1543 The Disfiguration

stripped and in dry dock still, a few are actually in the Thames with mast and sail. There is no sign of William Mewe who was once in charge of all ordinary and repairs.'

I asked him to explain to everyone what, ordinary, meant in this context.

'By day it is very much a worksite and by night it has but a few watchmen. But...'

He looked at Eirik and Farrier, clearly concerned about what he had to impart next.

'Every other evening, everything changes.'

We waited for him to elaborate but then he turned to Thomas Farrier once more.

'Would you like me to continue' said Farrier. Marcus nodded seeming somewhat deflated.

'It is a most extraordinary occurrence. By night, every other evening that is, there is a contingent of approximately six watchmen still but one of the buildings is fully occupied. They have, in effect, built a church although it is unlike any other I have ever witnessed.'

A Catholic Church, I presume?' said I.

'Oh yes...well...' continued Farrier.

'But...' he looked at Eirik and Marcus as if to confirm that he wasn't delusional.

'It is the strangest of ceremonies. There are between ten and fifteen attendees including the priest. All are armed with swords but wear tabards.'

'Tabards?' said Wynnfrith.

'Like old fashioned Knights?' said Peter.

'Exactly so, young Peter. They wear full chain mail covered by a tabard with crossed keys emblazoned upon them. Mostly white and yellow.'

'The insignia of the Bishop of Rome, the Pope' added Bayard.

'They are called The Knights of the Rock.'

'How on earth do you know this?' asked Wynnfrith.

'They chant it! Bloody loud and in Latin too!' said Eirik.

'Of course' I said 'Jesus called Peter the rock. The rock on which you will build my church.'

'If the Pope is descended from my namesake, St Peter himself, he has to be the head of the church' said Peter.

Although no one could fault his innocent interpretation, he was immediately hushed as this was not to be spoken of now that Henry had denied the Pope.

'My...you very brave soldiers you have done so well. We must attack on a night when mass takes place and retrieve the key pieces at the same time.'

Instantly, I received all sorts of objections, not least that sentiment dictating that you couldn't attack someone at prayer. I assured them that this wouldn't be the case and that it would be the only way of thwarting this Papist infraction.

'I would not wish any harm to those who are merely maintaining the ships' said Marcus.

'Noted! And that is why we must resolve this at night. It will be my intention to remove the keys unnoticed but, if we are discovered, we must defeat this well-organised and dangerous enemy of our King.'

Listen to me, I thought. Defender of Henry the eighth I am, I am, and not even sure why. I stopped to think of April. It had been weeks, which meant that I had now been consumed completely, once more by this character that enveloped me. For completely different reasons I thought of Wynnfrith's speech and understood that we needed to avoid deaths on both sides if possible, as it wasn't at all unreasonable that these people were challenging the King's supremacy.

'Anything else?' I asked.

'It is difficult to say whether there are men aboard the ships at night so it's hard to give you exact numbers and...' said Marcus 'the office from which I stole the key has now gone, replaced by that which now appears to be a church but I would guess that what we want is in there.'

'Thank you, Marcus. The three of you have served us, and

the King, well. Bayard, magnificently, managed to get to the bottom of the puzzle that was disguised as a ship. It almost certainly has a counterpart, a facsimile, in that building. Seemingly, each piece of a key, or possibly each set of three, is given a unique code and that code assigns a key to a ship…this also means that, if there are several keys, no two are the same.'

'Why would you need a key in a ship, excepting to open a locker?' asked Maud.

'As yet we don't know. Close examination of Bask's remaining documents in addition to Marcus's testimony leads us to believe that the reparations on their ships were connected to the keys but, beyond that, and presuming that these devices were fashioned for wrong-doing, I can tell you no more. It is essential that we find absolutely every piece and, if possible, the facsimile puzzle and, if this can be done without being noticed then, I believe, we will have helped the King.'

'But they need stopping Mouse!' cried Silas.

'That too my friend, be prepared for anything.'

'Can you explain why they are dressing up?' asked Dramaticus.

'They are consolidating into a cult that will ultimately welcome and reinforce Catholic invaders as they arrive on our shores. Surely fanatics, they have replicated rituals and adornment of the long-lost Templar Knights.' I said.

'Thought the Pope banned the Templar Knights long ago?' added Farrier.

'Absolutely my dear blacksmith. As they chose to worship so overtly and extravagantly we can only presume them to be extremists and, therefore, dangerous' I turned to Eirik 'which would be the next night that they gather?'

'Why, that would be tomorrow Mouse.'

'Then tomorrow we will make our stand. Take rest, eat, keep dry and if you need to ask me anything further, even in private, do not hesitate.'

Having indicated my permission to do so, Thomas Farrier picked me up.

'Mouse, I have never understood what you are or where you are from. A talking mouse! I say it as though it were normal!' Everybody laughed 'But you have saved our skin, and that of the King, and so many others and we owe you our loyalty and a great debt.'

I looked upon everyone gathered as they cheered and I felt it deeply. At times, I had been like a child at play, consumed by this ridiculous frame. He was right. A mouse of all things! How bloody ridiculous. In that moment I hoped and prayed that, whatever Bayard had tapped into, was discovered in my lifetime. My real one that is. They smiled benevolently as though I was special. For a moment, just a brief moment, I was certain that no one cared whether we lived or died as long as we did the right thing. Then Wynnfrith started to pray again.

'God is good. All good things happen through him and we must submit to his will. As Agents we do not talk of whose side the Lord is on, only that His will be done. I am the vine and you are the branches. If you remain in me, and I in you, you will bear much fruit. For, apart from me, you can do nothing.'

There was a chorus of "Amen" accompanied by a few tears.

22 we attack

The land was largely flat on either side of the Thames but the Agents had found a small hill on which we could all rest, belly down, and observe the movements below. On this final leg of our journey, Shakespeare took ill. Many took this as a dark omen and, from the outset, had us rewriting our plans. Despite his protests, we told him that he would have to stay in a tent, inland, until it was all over. None of us, even Bayard, knew what was wrong with him. He was taken to safety, left with food and water to look after himself. Bayard told him that he did not think he would die but that may well have been to raise our spirits.

Over the period of about two hours, workmen packed up, sentries took their posts and what I could best describe as gentlemen, arrived individually on horseback. The atmosphere was cold and formal and there was hardly any greeting or conversation between the newcomers. A candle was lit inside the makeshift church but the door appeared to be slightly ajar. The building had an upper floor but no one was up there and it seemed as though that floor could only be accessed by exterior stairs. I had deduced that there may well have had a cellar too. Guards were posted about every hundred yards or so along the bank and some were around the building that we were observing. Some ships of the fleet appeared as though they were complete, others in pieces but it was altogether an awesome sight. Those still bearing cannons were fearsome even as they stood unmanned and dead in the water on this dark night. I noticed that almost everyone with me was spellbound. Besides Marcus, they had never, even in their most adventurous dreams, seen such a sight and perhaps it dawned on them how important this navy was, not just to Henry, but to England. Lying there on the damp earth you would never have thought for a moment that it was possible to do any harm to these juggernauts but that, sadly, was the reason why we were there. Marcus silently pointed. We all knew instantly that he was, proudly, showing off the Mary Rose. She was afloat, beyond the dry dock and in the Thames. I could tell that everyone just wanted to get on board and explore, not realising the irony that they may well have ended up doing just that at some point during the evening. The light was failing but the sky was clear and we could make out silhouettes quite well thanks to the stars.

'Are you ready to take positions?' I asked but Bayard hesitated.

'Are you sure you wish to do it this way, Mouse? At such personal risk to yourself?'

I appreciated the gesture and yes, like so many other things I had been involved in since arriving, our initial manoeuvre would be nothing short of audacious and silly. Nevertheless, I believed it would work, so thanked him and checked that everyone was ready. I addressed Dramaticus directly,

'Make sure you make no sound whatsoever until we are all in place?'

He nodded.

There was a small settlement approximately quarter of a mile east of where we stood. There can have been no more than forty occupants and it was likely that many worked at the docks. This is where we would start. I checked that

1543 The Disfiguration

Wynnfrith was fine.

'I'm as ready as I ever will be, Micklegate. I promise I'll try my best with my movements.'

Silas, bless him, was nervous for everyone, but bravely watched on as I took his beloved away and into danger. Wynnfrith, Bayard, Dramaticus and myself managed to navigate the bank until we were beyond the dock and east of the hamlet. The rest stayed where they were watching over us as we wandered into the small settlement.

'Now!' I shouted and Dramaticus, in complete and ridiculous jester costume, alongside Bayard and Wynnfrith began ringing bells and banging drums. As soon as this cacophony started, we danced our way into the village. Wynnfrith was dressed as a boy and fit in well with this makeshift entertainment troop. Within seconds they were making an unearthly din. On her upper body, Wynn wore a woollen jerkin with long sleeves. I was placed, or should I say strapped, to her right hand with my now, modified, suit of armour. Much lighter and camouflaged with colours of dirt and grass, I was blessing Thomas Farrier with every breath. As I peeped out, I was mightily impressed by their performance and even felt a little guilty at how I had often dismissed Bayard and his, slightly weird, friend. They hopped, danced and swung about flags, pennants and bells and then Wynnfrith started to sing. And, she was really good.

"All good children must go to bed
But not before a song
A sip of beer and a crumb of bread
Come outside and sing along!"

Children bolted out of the shacks and houses, whooping and cheering and, for the most part, their parents came out and smiled. Only one, incurably grumpy dad, asked what it was all about and, as Wynnfrith continued to serenade him, Bayard explained they were travelling entertainers heading toward the city. Dramaticus excelled as the fool, gurning and standing on his hands in the dirt. Remarkably, he pulled sugared almonds out from behind children's ears much to their delight. When it was clear that they did not want any money, they were very well received by this small population and the children didn't want them to leave at all. Kids being kids, they kept peeping up Wynnfrith's sleeve but, seemingly, I got away with it as she would swing her hand above her head and dance around in a circle. Neither did anyone object, well, except for the children, when the band had to leave moving toward the dock.

Of course, some of the guards, further along, had noticed the hullabaloo in the distance, and the nearest two had got together to discuss what it was. I stirred the band up once again, praising them for this magnificent start. The guards stopped them. Very politely, Bayard explained once again that they were heading toward the city for a morning performance but, unsurprisingly, was getting a very different reception.

'Can't come through this way' they were told.

'Ah you see, kind sir' said Bayard 'if we were to circumnavigate your docks it will add another hour or two to our journey. As you can see we are harmless and happy to quieten down as we pass the ships.'

Initially, they weren't giving any ground but Bayard became astonishingly persuasive and, possibly through simply being worn down by these wandering idiots, they conceded but with several caveats, the most important one being that they had to detour inland when they reached the lit building. My formidable trio then made their way much more quietly until we met the next guard who was rapidly being joined by the one a hundred yards further away. Very much, they had the same conversation again but, at this point, we had decided that we would not be rerouting inland. Again, Bayard tried persuasion but they were having none of it and were starting to turn ugly or should I say, uglier? I pinched Wynnfrith's hand and, immediately she moved to the fore.

'It's a lady!' one of them grunted and the other one made an indistinguishable noise too. Wynn's presence definitely disarmed them immediately but I had promised Wynnfrith that we would not be meandering down that lane where she would be used to seduce these morons. The shock of her appearance alone took them off balance, as even the entertainment profession was deemed to be unsuitable for a woman. And, whether I liked it or not, her natural beauty put these two morons on pause. I then pinched her hand again. She smiled and then leant in to touch the cheek of the nearest guard and then did the same to the other. For the first time, I could detect the panic in Dramaticus, Bayard and little Wynn as nothing happened. They stood, with nowhere to go, these two idiots grimacing at them, pleased but slightly bewildered as to why this pretty girl had taken an interest in them. Then, the first one coughed. Then he sneezed and, as he did, he hit the deck. His mate looked down upon him only to find himself swoon and fall on top of him.

'Brilliant, Mouse!' said Wynnfrith.

'Brilliant you three' said I 'you were magnificent.'

Hiding the two bodies behind us as we progressed even further, these bold jesters repeated the same performance yet again further along. Dramaticus presents: twice nightly at Deptford docks.

As they dropped I deduced that, seemingly, all the guards were equally stupid and that would work in our favour.

The two remaining guards ran over and these were the ones that we had persuaded to let us pass. Naively, we thought them too far away to follow our movements but they had done just that. There was no way that we could handle them so were relieved to see Marcus, Eirik and Silas running down from the nearby hillock now almost directly behind us. As Bayard, yet again, put his case to the remaining night watchmen, Eirik crept behind and bludgeoned the first one so hard that he slumped to the ground like a corn sack. The one that remained, turned to engage with Eirik who immediately drew his sword as Wynnfrith pulled her husband to safety by her side. Eirik's movements were so bold and so swift that, armed with only a dagger, the man fled home to be with his children. This was somewhat ironic as they were probably the same ones that we had entertained only minutes earlier.

'Mouse, it worked!' said Eirik.

'Yes, it worked. And, surprisingly well and… I still have some left.'

'What do you call it, Micklegate?'

'It's not what I call it but what you call it, or at least some of your quacks. It is dwale. Dwale is a mixture of bile, lettuce, bryony root, hemlock, opium, vinegar and henbane. The first three are useless, I should add, but I'm sure that many a man maimed in battle would have been glad of some. That is, of course, if it didn't kill them first.'

'Will they die' asked Wynn.

'No that's very unlikely but they may wake up anytime feeling very drunk and with blinding headaches. Hopefully, they have been given enough to disable them.

'With only a scratch?'

'Well, if I'm honest with you Wynn, I wasn't sure that it would work at all but a small amount on my claw pressed directly into the vein, seemingly makes it very potent, very quickly. It's unlikely that we can use it on those died-hard Knights in the church as we need both elements of surprise and proximity to succeed.

'But it has all worked out really well so far' added Dramaticus.

I was about to thank them all for their bold contributions when I detected some movement. Bayard, too, whipped around and I asked him if he had seen the same as me.

'Yes, mouse. The ship?'

'Yes, the ship' I said.

The Mary Rose had rocked slightly from larboard to starboard and yet, her sails were up, and there was no wind, leaving us with only one possible conclusion.

We squinted as visibility at that distance wasn't great but there, barely detectable, were the silhouettes of men dressed in black and they seemed to come out of nowhere, reminiscent of when you lift up a damp rock. Out they came running in all directions.

'It is over' said Bayard.

'We have no option but to hide.' I said.

We were now very near to the church and if we had not moved, there would have been no doubt of us being seen.

I told Eirik to signal to the others: Farrier and Marcus to stay with us and Maud and Peter to stay on the grassy hillock overlooking events.

I suggested that we headed for a warehouse that lay between us and the hill. So dense, overstocked and untidy was this building that it was easy for us to hide. I insisted that everyone stayed put, Eirik having practically buried the whole team under ropes and all sorts of other rigging parts whilst he remained as lookout. Again, this ridiculous embodiment that I had inherited, became an advantage. I was able to roam around the warehouse and the dock unseen taking care to avoid rats. I realised that, in a panic, I had possibly exaggerated the threat. There were six men dressed in black. Two were tending to the intoxicated and barely conscious guards, two returned to the ship whilst the remaining two were checking the church, where it seemed as though all was well and its attendees ignorant of the chaos beyond. Much to our dismay, this carried on for over an hour and during that time they had been in and out of the warehouse three times. To this day I cannot account for why we were not discovered. At one point we could hear angry words. I gathered that these black guards had assumed that the bargain-basement guards, that they had employed, were now all drunk. Perhaps it would have been wise of them to examine them more thoroughly, I mused but was thankful that they hadn't. I watched alone as they threw each of them

1543 The Disfiguration

into the water. Three never surfaced again but the ones that did survive were still barely conscious and tried, in vain, to run as the black soldiers chased them off wielding swords.

Four of those silhouettes then returned to the ship with two taking up the absented sentry positions outside the church. I returned to tell the others.

'We can't bloody well stay in here forever!' said Wynnfrith.

'If there are only two left, you must let me and Eirik take them out' offered Farrier.

I had no doubt that they could do this even though they were both already soaked and that Thomas Farrier was admirably hiding his ancient leg wound, but I could think of no alternative besides retreating which was what I suggested.

'No, absolutely not…we have come this far…' came a chorus 'the King….Spaniards!…threat to the nation!… Royal Secret Agents of the Word…' and on it went almost as if we had had dozens of successful options before us.

Eirik turned to Wynn.

'You have my word, sister, if I can do this without taking life I will' and Farrier nodded in agreement.

She placed her hand on his and said,

'Keep yourself safe, brother' and then kissed him.

'Then we will try my method first. I believe it will work but, pray, keep your distance.'

They both nodded.

I followed them to the warehouse door which was less than thirty yards from the church entrance. Maud and Peter watched on from afar. It was a wonder to watch how Thomas Farrier and Eirik moved in tandem and without sound. They crept, no further than about eight of those yards and Eirik stood, Farrier directly behind him but some good few inches taller. Farrier held his sword high in front of him and then froze, ready to surprise, charge and engage with both men if necessary. Eirik filled his lungs with air, drew back the longbow, lining it up with his right eye until he was looking

1543 The Disfiguration

along the shank of the arrow. True to his word, his chosen aim was to be the shoulder of the guard furthest away to injure rather than kill. As Eirik began to slowly breathe out, all that could be heard above the gentle lapping of the river was a smooth "swish." Both guards looked up, rather than to their right, and the target then reeled backwards as the arrow sunk into his flesh. He cried out as it cracked his shoulder bone. His companion thought first to assist him but immediately swung around not sure whether to run, duck or find the assailant. In the meagre light that was shed from inside the church, Farrier was certain that the target was now unconscious thanks again to the remarkable dwale, applied to Eirik's arrow tip. Feeling confident, Eirik let flight a second arrow almost instantaneously, realising that his aim wasn't quite as good. Now confident of the success of this part of the mission, they spoke.

'Did that….am I right in think…'

'Yes. In his eye lad. Serves him bloody right. At least we needn't worry about him coming round.'

Somewhat disappointed that he hadn't, fully, kept his promise to Wynnfrith, Eirik relished this support from his experienced companion.

Remarkably, they now had access to the church from which there was loud singing. It was unlike any Christian music they had ever heard before, so dark was this dirge that it carried its way all the way across the river. Knowing that, this too, gave us an advantage, Eirik and Farrier returned to consult me and to dig the others out from under ropes, rigging and broken pieces of mizzenmast. Complaints, groans and profanity were in abundance as my, very odd-looking, team were freed from their hiding place.

At this point, I so wanted to sound both confident and clever but things had definitely not gone to plan leaving me wondering as to how we would proceed. So, I waffled a while about what the current situation was.

'There are four black guards on the ship. Eirik has

counted twelve Knights in the church. We are hoping that what we are looking for is in the church cellar or, possibly, the room above. I favour the cellar as, unlike the upper floor, it is secure from both fire and theft. I would be happy if we could retrieve all the key pieces and scarper but I do worry that more of them will be made if we do not put an end to these strange rituals and alliances with foreign nations. Added to that is the very real risk that the black guards may be greater in number and will return.'

Nothing. It was as if we were at a dead end and, although I desperately wanted someone to contribute, nothing was forthcoming.

'I think it's worth having a closer look at that room. It's unlikely that they will see us through the glass for the reflected candlelight, especially if it's just a mouse' suggested Marcus.

I agreed immediately although to much opposition, as the majority of my little army was speedily becoming completely pissed off with being stranded in a damp and stinky warehouse and, I had no doubt that Peter and Maud would be anxious having been left on the hillock not knowing of our situation.

'You have my word that we will expedite this investigation and return.' I arrogantly announced.

And, before anybody else could whinge again, we quickly buggered off.

Marcus too was impressively athletic. It was almost as if he had glided the distance from the warehouse to the church. He squatted by a window that was near the entrance. The door was still slightly open and we could see that there were three steps going down into the room.

Curiously, he popped me on his head.

'They are now in a circle' I said 'They drone! I believe they are making an oath but they are stood, weapons in hand, pointing toward a circle in the centre of the floor. It is wooden and the cross keys are elaborately carved into it.'

'Is it hinged?' asked Marcus.

'Yes…yes! And it has a ring handle. There is a cellar!'

So excited was I that I was overheard by two of them and they turned around. I took a nose dive into the mud except that I bounced and landed right inside the mouth of the guard that Eirik had poisoned, my stupid suit of armour jamming in what remained of his teeth. My tail sticking out, Marcus could only hear muffled pleas as he felt around trying to find me. Once unplugged, he asked if he could look through the window. Risky as it was, I agreed that it would be wise to have a second opinion.

'Did you notice the man in the cloak, Mouse?'

'Yes, …he's not dressed as the others…standing next to the priest.'

'That's him. No doubt about it.'

'Who?!' I said somewhat impatiently.

'Bask's brother. Has to be, looks just like him.'

Having only ever seen Sir Anthony Bask with his head beaten in, I wasn't in a position to comment but this was good news. He was most likely the spearhead of this revolution although I still had no idea as to how we would take them all out.

'And the seated figure?'

'Yes,' I said 'I noticed that one of the Knights was seated.'

'It's Bede. Brother Bede. Looks as though he hasn't got a clue what's going on, mind you, but it's him.'

'Bede?!' I exclaimed, astounded 'what the hell is Bede doing here…oh no!...they must have been to York!'

For the first time, I felt fear. Real fear and, instinctively, I told Marcus to keep this detail from the others as long as he could. Realising that the door was still ajar, I was now so frightened that I was sure that it kept opening further. Sadly, this wasn't paranoia, as it then opened very quickly and a chain mail gauntlet grabbed Marcus off balance and dragged him inside. He stumbled down the step with me riding roughshod on his shoe, as yet unseen. Despite the dark overtones of the ritual and costumes, the Knights appeared aghast leaving Bask to return some order to their strange performance.

'You! Has to be. The thief! The boy who grew up on the Mary Rose then ran away! And, I'm guessing also the man that killed my brother.'

Marcus protested but was silenced immediately. The same gauntlet struck him about the face and he fell to the ground. As he did, I tumbled along the floor landing right in the centre of that ornate, wooden cellar door. Marcus lay there dazed as everyone else regrouped in a circle around him and me. Bask picked me up.

'It's a mouse dressed in plate armour!'

Allowing for a pause whilst some translations were made, there was the most chilling laughter. They sat me, next to Marcus, on the cellar door but, sensibly, I remained silent reviewing my brilliant plan which was now inexorably heading for failure. One of the Knights, seemingly very angry, started to rant in Portuguese but I could understand every word. It had no clue as to why I was able to instantaneously translate this but was too preoccupied to be concerned. He demanded to know why slave stock was dressed like a gentleman if England was committed to trading with European slave nations. I so wanted to butt in when Bask suggested that Marcus was a runaway from a travelling show. This did little to appease the Knight with the seriously silly accent. With some degree of argy-bargy, it was agreed that Marcus was "spoiled stock" and he was immediately sentenced to death.

'No!' I cried 'Hypocrites! Xenophobes! you must listen to reason!'

Amidst the apparent shock caused by my reaction, the tallest man in the room stepped back to where there was a somewhat throne-like chair and concealed behind it was a black robe. Ceremoniously, he wrapped this over his chain mail and everyone looked at him in awe.

1543 The Disfiguration

'Too many layers mate. You won't feel the benefit when you go out…'

No laughs just gasps as he alone took on the demon rodent. It was only when he spoke, in Spanish, that I felt as if they were now taking this role play too far. He either was, or was pretending to be, a Spanish inquisitor condemning me for being a witches familiar and a heretic, amongst other things. In less than a minute, I had been sentenced to burn to the growing chants of hatred from this incredibly odd congregation and it was getting louder by the second. I caught the eye of Bede who was following me. Yes, I thought, he recognises me but, beyond that, I don't think anyone could guess what was going on in his head. The wooden doors in the floor opened and I fell, heart in my head, ungracefully down into the vast cellar. At least that's what I had thought it to be but soon realised that it was a chasm, an underground warren, man-made vaulted corridors and rooms. Although hurt, the armour protected me somewhat but Marcus was not to have that concession. He tumbled down after me and I heard his leg crack as he hit the stone floor.

'Make a run, Micklegate' he groaned 'tis my fault we are discovered.'

'I will get you out of this Marcus. Although you are injured I will find a way of saving us both' I said without any bloody idea of what to do. For a few moments we were left there and he was writhing with pain. Although it was hardly my intent to sight-see, I was overwhelmed by what was before me. Somewhat curious as to why their Catholic chapel above was conspicuous by its absence of adornments and trinkets, I had now found the high altar below. There was gold everywhere, crucifixes, candelabras, medallions, statues and paintings. Portraits neatly lined up with Christ and Mary at the top, all the saints below and, yes, that included modern martyrs like More. Then, the Pope and past Popes. A large picture of Catherine of Aragon adorned the adjacent wall and there, beside her, was a painting of Princess Mary. Whether or not she was party to what was going in Deptford and beyond, I do not know, but these morons had chosen to put her on a pedestal. Then Sir Anthony Bask's portrait and his brother, Joshua. Chapuys and other Catholic ambassadors and, in pride of place, Reginald Pole. This place hadn't been built overnight and, in those few seconds, I presumed that the underground excavations must have been going on whilst Marcus, Jack and Aelfraed were still there although they were not aware of it. On the altar were rare relics ranging from swords to caskets and crucifixes to chalices and there was an astounding libation vessel. I had no doubt that these were authentic and that this cult had its roots in the legend of the Knights Templar themselves.

A rope was thrown down and two of the Knights clumsily negotiated it leaving me wondering how the hell they would get back up again carrying all that weight. One picked me up between his finger and thumb and he laughed.

'Do not laugh, Garsea, as you will be complicit in the devil's works' said his colleague. Garsea stopped immediately but as he picked me up I stuck my dwale-laden claw into his neck. He reeled back and threw me down. This time it hurt me, everywhere, and much to my disappointment, he remained upright. I was then carried high and away from his face as if I were a turd, as off we went into this labyrinth.

We passed through another shrine-like room and there it was. The same ship that Marcus had as a puzzle except this one was made of gold. Next to it were plan-chests concealing diagrams and documents and adjacent, a huge, incredibly ornate, oaken cupboard. I was sure that the metal pieces would have been in there.

Everything was lit, albeit dimly and we then went to another spacious room which, at first, could have been like any other. That was until we saw the instruments of torture. What was left of Marcus was put into manacles. He was moving, constantly, in and out of consciousness moaning as he did. For me, it was unbearable as was the burden of guilt that I carried. As I was taken away, I could hear his cries no matter how great the distance became. The Knight that had manacled Marcus then, uncannily, negotiated his way back up and into the church.

Eventually, I was alone with the Knight named Garsea and we entered a room in which the ceiling was much higher. Here, he had to light candles to see and it was at that point that I saw the pyre. This was a clandestine space designed solely for the purpose of burning people and there was evidence to suggest that it was used regularly. Surely he's not going to put me on top of that lot, I thought, as it was scaled for humans. I couldn't have been more wrong. Choosing the more convenient cook in the tin option, he popped me on top, tied me to the huge stake sticking out of the pyre, lit it and then collapsed in front of me as the dwale finally took effect. The irony wasn't lost on me. Instantly, there was smoke everywhere and I was coughing. A fire indoors, especially underground, didn't really make a lot of sense to me so I looked up and, there, through the smoke, I could see the smallest of holes in the ceiling and stars shone through. Perfect for burning after all, then, as everything else in this cave was made of stone. It became hot very quickly, I could barely breathe and sparks from the timbers were starting to damage my armour. I had but one idea and that idea relied almost entirely on hope. So, I did what everyone else did in 1543. I prayed. I prayed for one certainty. I stared and stared into that space above in the hope that my prayers would be answered even though I was becoming increasingly light-headed and starting to singe. Keep looking, I told myself, it will happen. And then, miraculously, his pointy nose and long strand of auburn hair peeped through that hole.

'Oh mouse…that's very bad…why!...you're on fire…' observed Silas keenly.

Of course I'm on bloody fire. Are you going to rescue me or not?!'

'Ah….oh…yes…of course…just…'
And then he started to dangle a leg through the hole.
'Silas!!'
'What Mouse?'
'Water! You need some water first!'
'Water. Aha! Of course…where…'
'You're next to a bloody river!'

Even that left some room for ingenuity which worried me. Obviously, Wynnfrith wasn't with him or she'd have worked that out. Pathetic as his attempts were, he did, slowly, manage to douse the flames one boot full of water at a time. It didn't help that it took him several minutes to get his aim right.

'I'm coming down'
'No Silas. That wouldn't be wise. There is no way out!'
'Listen to the mouse' said another voice.

It didn't help that he was still sporting his new look. The phantom pregnancy or whatever it was.

'Nearly…just the other…aaagghhh!'

As he slipped I saw Maud trying to help him back up but this had resulted in him pulling on her leg leaving her jammed completely in the hole with just her legs sticking through and little hope of getting out either way.

'Oh my God!' I said 'Silas…whatever you do, don't look up. Just do…not…look up!'

As he plummeted, he had managed to remove both of Maud's boots and her woollen hose, gifting me with a moon and star of her own. It was a sight from which Silas would never have recovered.

He landed awkwardly on the soggy straw leaving me lurching over to my left. Covering his eyes as best I could, I had him untie me. He suggested that we may be able to exit through the ceiling but I told him, again, not to glance upward and that it was no longer available as an exit, at least not in the traditional sense.

We stepped over the snoring Garsea and soon found

ourselves in a shadowy cavern trying to find our way back to Marcus. I could see Silas trembling and took a moment to admire his tenacity in the face of danger and also to reassure him. We could hear the echoes of chants from above but they were suddenly broken which stopped us in our tracks. Then there was uproar, the clear sound of swords being drawn and the clatter of metal. Unbeknownst to us at that time, our comrades had neared the church entrance, Eirik and Farrier advising caution until they had a plan. However Peter, dear Peter, having waited now for hours and in a frenzy, burst forth into the church with a dagger drawn. Before Eirik and Farrier could hold him back he was in the doorway and down the steps threatening the nearest Knight. He raised a dagger high above his head as he screamed and cursed but he was felled with one expert stroke of a sword blade. Thrown back onto the steps, he had been cut diagonally from waist to chest, so deeply that it split one of his ribs which was now blatantly exposed. The wound was mortal and he was losing blood rapidly. With no time to help Peter, Thomas Farrier lunged forward, jumped down the steps and cut the face of the assailant who staggered backwards and then thrust his sword deep into the unprotected armpit. Purposefully, Farrier squatted as, behind him was Eirik ready with bow, atop the steps. In under three seconds, he had debilitated two Knights, certain now that an arrow in the eye socket would do the trick. Whether he liked it or not, his promise to Wynnfrith was now becoming somewhat irrelevant.

Meanwhile, Peter had disappeared from the entrance completely as had the two guards that had so recently been outside the door. Eirik demanded that Thomas Farrier retreat leaving him to rapid-fire his arrows. Magnificent he was, alone, and issuing deathly shots at an uncanny speed. He had managed to kill or maim four of the Knights and he reached for his quiver one more time. Empty. There were no arrows. Not on him at least. Wynnfrith was carrying a replacement set but she was nowhere to be seen. Eirik felt a hand on his collar and he was lifted from his feet, up the steps and out into the mud by Thomas Farrier.

His head whipped around,

'Where is young Peter?' He asked of Farrier.

'Do not know. Gone. Need to regroup.'

Meanwhile, one hundred yards back in the direction in which they had first started, Maud, now fully dressed, was dragging Peter by his arms as far as she could from the threat. That was until she backed right into someone else. With all hope draining from her, she dropped Peter and raised her arms in surrender. Then she turned.

'You!' she cried 'how?....why are you?!...'

The stranger lifted up Peter's torso and dragged him into an open storage facility where there were blankets laid out. She could see water, dressings and his bag. He had brought his bag with him. Maud was astounded.

'You are him aren't you? The man who made Wynnfrith's sister so beautiful?'

'It is I!' said Viscera quite dramatically and, true to his nature, began to revel in saving the life of the young fisherman. Maud's mood, however, had shifted from initial awe and delight to confusion.

'Hang on. You do dead people don't you?'

'Yes I do missus, but I tend the sick to'

'He's beyond hope?' said Maud.

'Possibly but let…me…yes, this will do it.'

He giggled as he accessed a huge, and admittedly, not very clean needle and threaded it with gut. With glee, he moped, stitched, bathed, oiled and stitched it again until it looked like he may have stemmed the blood flow but Peter was, by now, blue and Maud was much more accepting of his fate than the crazy embalmer. Wynnfrith joined her and asked if she could do anything.

'I don't think so' said Maud 'did you clear the way?'

Wynn explained how amid the melee she had managed to remove any bodies that may hamper the movements of the

Agents. They then discussed what to do next and left Peter with Viscera.

Now outside the church again and with the intent of retreat, Farrier and Eirik became aware of the black guards that were now animated and leaving the ship.

To their left, tumbling out of the church, were the remainder of the Knights and to their right were the black guards. As his head swung back and forth trying to make a decision, Eirik caught the silhouette of Wynnfrith running back toward him.

'Here!' she shouted and threw another set of arrows to him. He caught it in his left hand and threw it onto his shoulder.

'The ship!' cried Farrier and they both headed toward the Mary Rose.

On one side of the church entrance and practically unseen, stood Maud and Bayard and Dramaticus and Wynnfrith on the other, passionately bludgeoning the Knights as they egressed. So animated and efficient were they, that the first two received as many as five blows each and collapsed like heaps of scrap, the third one falling over them. As the bells attached to their outfits, rang louder and louder, the angrier they became. The champion of loving all enemies, Wynnfrith, was so embittered at losing sight of her husband that she zealously laid into each one of them with only Maud convincing her that she needed to store some energy. The remaining Knights soon got wise to this and so began to exit blade first. That is when Maud shouted the retreat.

Below, Silas and I were lost for some time and both anxious and concerned for our friends as we heard the battle above. Eventually, we found our way back to Marcus. He could barely open his eyes as he had been beaten by the guard that had accompanied him. Everything he said was an apology. I calmly reminded him that he would never have succeeded alone.

'Mind you' said Silas in a very shaky voice 'we're all going to die anyway.'

When I'd finished bollocking him, I asked him to show me all his weapons. Silas, like his wife, would have gone to any lengths to avoid confrontation but did, always, carry a variety of knives and daggers. He found one, so small, that it was good for the manacles.

Perhaps one of the most astounding events throughout this messy adventure was how Silas, possibly being half the weight of Marcus, managed to carry him back to where we started. I urged caution although it was apparent that, above, the Knights were giving chase and leaving the church.

'I can get up that rope' said Silas looking at the rope that the two Knights had used to get from the church down into the cellar.

For all his shortcomings, I was sure, too, that he could scale it but, I told him to be careful as there may still have been enemies above us. Scared as he was, he took no notice of me and shimmied up that rope like a rat. As he landed on the floor above, he knelt, looking at Bede still sitting and confused and at the backs of the few remaining Knights running out. Behind them, but facing away from Silas, was Joshua Bask panicking and seeking a way out. As Bask turned to find the rope, Silas threw it around his neck, pulled it tight and, as he stumbled, he fell down into the chasm, the rope pulling tightly about his neck which would have surely killed him.

'Shall I free him Mouse?'

'Let him drop my friend!'

Bask, choking, slumped to the floor and, astonishingly, Silas slid back down the rope. Within minutes Bask was tied up and we took away from him over seven keys.

'You will not succeed you devilish rascals!' threatened Bask.

'Rascals?' I said 'who on earth says rascals?'

'Oh it is a wicked curse' said Silas and he told Bask to

watch his tongue.

Bask was hurt but he was possibly even more debilitated by being confronted by a talking mouse and held a cross to my face to dispossess me.

'Only just getting used to it myself mate' I quipped.

He then chose to dial up the threats somewhat.

'You Protestant pigs! Heretics! We will bring England back to the true church!'

His words, uncannily, rang in my ears. For one split second, I turned to the wall and, clear as day, there was Guy Fawkes looking at me.

'All your fault….' he said calmly and with a wry smile on his face. Then, he disappeared as quickly again. It startled me and snapped me out of my swashbuckling adventure momentarily. Yes, of course. England will be Catholic again and then it won't. What am I doing? I'm behaving as if I'm part of all this and I'm not. I'm only here because there was a document that hinted at some of these events. Why am I involved in this battle at all?!

'And him..' continued Bask 'that…that poor excuse for a man. I've had beards stronger and heavier than him.'

'You will show respect' someone said quite forcefully, and I realised that they were behind us.

'He is Lord Silas of Dead alley in York city and I am Lady Wynnfrith of the same and you, sir, are undone and will pay for your misdemeanours.'

Silas shook his head as he hadn't got a clue how she had got there. She was out of breath, full of all sorts of shite and her clothes were torn.

'I threw myself through that hole onto the doused pyre'

I saw that Silas was starting to blubber so I poked him.

'Wynn' I said 'in practical terms, I am of little use. I need you two to gag this idiot and then secure what we came for.'

Silas then took us back to the room where the golden ship was. We had temporarily left Marcus in the corridor.

Above, Dramaticus and Bayard had stood their ground

once Maud and Wynn left. This was, to say the least, foolhardy and Dramaticus was immediately struck down. His throat had been penetrated so deep by a sword that his head was half severed. He lay gurgling, desperately trying to communicate something to his beloved boss. Bayard stayed, leant over him and comforted him in his last moments. As Bayard's head hung low, the same sword swung across and severed it completely.

Eirik, running for the ship, stalled to pull tight a strap on his quiver and Farrier did the same with his weapons. As the black guards headed for the gangplank, they both plummeted into the water leaving the Knights and the black guards at a loss. In fact, they all, more or less, stalled in their tracks. They all stared at the dark river before them, the Knights having no chance of surviving in the water due to the weight of their chainmail. The wait seemed endless and they presumed that if these two had not managed to surface again that the battle must be at an end, bar one or two poorly skilled waifs and strays. After some ten minutes, the black guards visibly relaxed but still with an eye on the water. One hung his head over the larboard side to check one more time only to feel an almighty thump in the back of his neck. It was an arrow and this sent him reeling overboard with everyone else scurrying to trace the location of the bowman. Swish, thud! A second guard collapsed on the deck whilst a third engaged unsuccessfully in sword fight with Farrier who had occupied the forecastle knowing that his back was almost certainly protected. However, no one could detect his accomplice who was now settled above Farrier on the foremast between the fore-topsail and the crow's nest. Intermittently, Eirik was seeing the face of Meg, wondering whether this was spurring him on or whether it was there to hinder him. He looked down, exhilarated and certain of success as, soon, the remaining Knights of the Rock would be in shooting distance as well. He looked directly below to check on Farrier who was easily holding his own but then found himself glancing again and, to his astonishment, more and more black guards were emerging from the upper gun deck, the officer's cabins, the great hatch, and also from the other ships. He instructed Farrier to start climbing. Trapped they may become, but it was their only option. Eirik continued to fire, continuously until he was, yet again, bereft of arrows. Pulling him up into the crow's nest as he was pursued, Eirik suggested to Farrier that they would have to yet again, head for the water but, as yet, had no ideas as to how they would save the others.

'All may well be lost my good friend but you have fought valiantly. If we die, we die together this day!' said Thomas Farrier.

In the labyrinth, we were both anxious and astonished at the variety of blood-curdling sounds from above, even though it was clear that the Knights had left the building, there seemed to be constant and fierce conflict further away. Wynnfrith was unable to tell us anything about the others so we turned our attention to the huge oak cupboard that looked down upon the mysterious golden ship. This, so far, was the easiest part of the mission and the only one that had gone to plan. One of the keys opened the cupboard and another opened a chest within it and there, inside were many sets of metal pieces catalogued in threes and every one coded.

'Whatever this evil is...' said Wynnfrith 'there must be a set for every ship in the King's fleet.'

This was incredibly astute of her but she was wrong. There were nineteen sets leading me to believe that they were specifically made for hand-picked vessels. Although it made no sense to me, I was happy that we had them all leaving the chest completely empty.

'We will have to put them back in the chest.'

'You mad?' said Silas.

'We won't get them all out otherwise. We will have to leave them here for now until the battle is over and then we will return.' This, possibly being the dumbest and most naïve plan I had had to date.

Above, one Knight remained in the doorway. It was the one that had killed Dramaticus but now he stood and stared down at the body of Dramaticus and that of Bayard. Every time he seemingly removed Bayard's chubby head, Bayard just faded away and, then, moments later, simply appeared again smiling back at the Knight. After three attempts the Knight was trying to ascertain whether it was himself or Bayard that was bewitched. Bayard dragged his friend away from the church entrance and Maud then helped to drag him indoors where Viscera could, at least, make his body look half decent again.

If I'm honest I had run out of ideas. Stuck below and not knowing what else was going on it seemed as though we should make an effort to fight alongside the other Agents. But then I looked at the chest and I knew that it was a priority. It had to be secured.

'What next Micklegate?' said a desperate Wynnfrith.

I was about to make up an answer when I heard clanking. I feared that more Knights had found their way into the cellar and then realised that it was coming from above. Something was trying to negotiate the hole in the ceiling in the heretic burning quarters. We ran toward it. At first, it was indistinguishable and we presumed it to be a threat. We made sure that we were all armed and ready.

'Stand clear!' came the cry and, as we looked upward it became apparent that someone was trying to get a small anchor through the hole. Clank! Clung! Clang! It landed on the floor, a heavy rope attached.

'Secure the chest to the rope and anchor!'

'Look' said Wynnfrith pointing above. 'It is Moonlight!'

And so it was. A lithe and slender Moonlight unlike I had seen before. Did I say him?

We hurriedly attached the chest ensuring it was closed and locked and up it went disappearing amongst the stars. Then a remarkably firm bit of rigging was cast down and Silas, with me in his pocket and Wynnfrith just ahead, scaled it in seconds. Single-handedly, Moonlight returned to find Marcus and hauled him back up using ropes and counterweights. Genius. It was good to be in the fresh night air again but the sounds from the dockside were fearsome. Moonlight guided us around to the water's edge where we were yet unseen and now also wishing that we couldn't see either. Scores of black guards were joining the remaining Knights and were converging on the ship. We had to watch as, unquestionably, Eirik and Farrier were to meet their end. There was a further commotion to the west as even more were congregating, except these seemed to be different yet again. They marched in unison, with vigour and they were chanting.

'I think they are shouting, death to the King' said Wynnfrith

My heart sank, what a complete disaster and, at that point, I was sure that the chaos had been caused by my intervention. The latest soldiers to join were heavily armed as I could see the silhouettes of pikes, halberds and axes and there was even a horse-drawn cart at the rear. I looked up as Eirik and Farrier were about to plunge and glanced at the enemy they faced but it was then, and then only, that I was sure that I saw red and, I told the others.

'What does it mean, Mouse?'

'Look!' I cried.

'The King's own!' shouted a Wynnfrith.

There was no doubting it, these were Henry's guards wearing those distinctive and distinguished red uniforms with the letters H and R emblazoned upon them and they were also arriving on the opposite bank.

'He has an arquebus!' said Silas.

The King had sent enough men and firepower to sink his own ships if necessary. Eirik and Farrier stood their ground and cheered as the black guards headed for the water. The remaining Knights also tried to run but it was in vain and they were cut down where they stood. At the fore were both

Somerset and Ralph Sadler, two men who had rocketed instantaneously in my estimation. On the other bank, there was a man who Silas said looked like the King but I had recognised him immediately. It was Robert. Somehow he and Henry must have collaborated but it was beyond me how this plan had evolved. Standing next to Robert, exhausted, was Shakespeare who, despite his fever, had dragged himself to the battlefield to assist. He had his arm around a boy. Puzzled as to how he would have got his son to come such a distance, I then noticed that the boy was Edward. Robert had brought him along and he was, thankfully, at a safe distance.

Interestingly, the black guards chose to flee but, admirably, the few Knights of the Rock had decided to fight to the end. Both Sadler and Somerset fearlessly occupied the vanguard and, between them overcame the three remaining Knights. The King's troops closed in on them all with a whole brigade disrobing and plummeting into the Thames to apprehend those left.

In less than half an hour after the King's people arrived, we heard the cry,

'It is the King's day and the King's field!'

'Hurrah!!' They all shouted in unison and, somewhat carried away, we all joined in.

23 after the storm

Although there was an appalling amount of death and injury there was a point, soon after, when there was a welcome lull after the storm. Those of the enemy that had survived were taken prisoner and rounded up in the warehouse where so many of us had so recently hidden. Silas walked over to Bayard to check his wounds and was astonished to find him untouched. With little else to say, Silas decided to share with him the events of the last hour. Suddenly Bayard stopped him,

'Say that again young Silas'

'Of course. According to Micklegate, it was a most unfortunate accident that had befallen Maud, having lost all of her lower garments.'

Silas became aware of a sudden change in Bayard as his breathing became laboured and his eyes were gradually exiting their sockets. Thankfully, Silas did not detect this or suspect that this was Bayard aroused, a sight that no other man, or woman for that matter, should ever witness. And, to add to his joy, Maud came running over to greet him.

'Why! I was sure you were cut down big boy! I'm so glad

to see you in one piece!'

Thankfully, all this went over Silas's head and it was probably for the best.

Once all the Agents were back together, we found ourselves looking down upon the bodies of Dramaticus and Peter. Viscera insisted that there was some life left in Peter but few of us had any hope left for him.

'He will have to recover' I said naively 'his family are expecting him by Christmas and that's an end of it.'

Viscera was thanked by almost everyone as he had taken care of the disfigurements that they had both endured. He was asked to stay with, and tend to, Peter as long as there was even a breath left in the lad. Lord Sadler appeared and asked us to congregate in the church and began by asking about the old and senseless Knight that remained.

'Do not harm him!' Wynnfrith cried 'he is one of us, he had been kidnapped from York.'

Once identified, Sadler seemed happy with this excuse and Bede seemed pleased to see Wynnfrith but there was no other communication from him.

'What a bloody unearthly mess!' said Sir Ralph Sadler 'we had nothing but a few rumblings of these extremist Knights so the King will be very pleased with your efforts once again.'

Once we were all gathered, I decided, for once, to remain quiet as Sadler was flanked by two very large and hairy, King's guards.

'Yonder, out back, lies the chest with the key pieces in' said Silas.

'Yes, Robert Hall had communicated the same to us. Am I right in thinking that they would have been used to either steal or damage the fleet?' said Sadler.

'We think so' came a pathetic reply from the doorway. Marcus had been rescued and was now in splints being carried by two of the King's guards. Sadler motioned to sit him down.

'you will need the model of the ship as it carries a series

of codes that unlock the designation and purpose of each key' said Marcus.

'No need, my man. All will be destroyed in order to remove any chance of further danger' Sadler then addressed the most sinister element of the plot,

'And you. You say they treat you as an inferior?'

'That is true sir. It is like a pox spreading from Portugal. I fear that my kind will be, for all time, used as slaves.'

'Bloody Papists!' shouted Sadler. 'Well, I will tell you now, you will be a free man in England!'

The guards cheered, the Agents along with them but my heart was heavy. What a curse my knowledge of the future was.

'You will find further oddments and treasure below. I think there is little doubt, my Lord, that this was their headquarters.'

'I thank you' said Sadler 'for, even if it is not, we will chase down any more accomplices that remain on King's land.'

Sadler then nodded toward Robert, who stood with his arm around Edward. Edward still ignorant of his friend's fate seemed to be content under Robert's wing.

'I am sorry my friends. I am the bearer of even more sad news. If I could choose to keep it to myself, I would, but it is very much your business too' said Robert.

He then told us all about Father Matthew's death. Of the wash house break-in and the new priest. He said nothing of the devastation at Silas and Wynnfrith's home or the deplorable exhumation of Elspeth's body. Thomas Farrier, already slumped on the floor, tried hard to hide his grief at the loss of the priest but we all saw it. Robert told us that baby Mary was fine which did bring out a few smiles. Eirik then asked about Meg's welfare and seemed visibly relieved to find out that she too was unharmed. Robert looked to Sadler who now had a burning issue that he needed to address.

'This may not seem the appropriate time, but it is the only

time' he looked at Marcus 'am I right in thinking that you were wed to the chamberer that recently died?'

Marcus was confused. Of course, I thought, anyone associated with Queen Catherine Howard, or her retinue, knew Elspeth as a chamberer. Marcus looked at me and I gave a nod.

'Elspeth?' he said.

'Yes'

'Yes, that is the case. She was, and is, my beloved even in death.'

'Then I shall spell this out plainly. We believe that the misguided and treacherous, Thomas Culpeper shared with her a key. A key of such great import that you could not imagine.'

'I believe it to be made from a nail from the Holy Cross itself' said Marcus.

'Then why in God's name do you still have it, man?!'

'I was told to keep it safe by someone I trusted. Here, my Lord. Reach into my battered, purse and you will find it there.'

Sadler signalled to one of the guards and he retrieved it. He then produced an impeccably ornate casket and it was placed, ceremoniously, inside. A priest, part of the King's contingent, prayed over the casket.

'My men are building a camp a mile inland, although much of this mess must be cleared before dawn. The cult house yonder will be cordoned off whilst we make a full inspection and we carry out a proper and fitting investigation.'

'Will the innocent workmen lose their work?' asked Marcus.

'If their innocence is apparent then they will still be needed. We have to return this to a functioning shipyard as soon as we can. You will all be taken to the camp. Wounds attended to, and fed well and, tomorrow, you will be escorted back to York.'

1543 The Disfiguration

Transport arrived very soon and Sadler agreed that Bede could travel back with us. Robert asked me if I could speak to Edward about Peter which I, of course, agreed to. It was difficult and, at first, he broke down and just kept asking if Peter was still alive.

'Yes, but barely Edward. Sadly, we have little hope.'

'I want to see him!'

'Edward, I wouldn't…'

'He's my best friend and I want to see him!!'

How could I refuse? Selfishly, the last thing I needed was to watch young Edward break down over his friend's body. We crept towards Viscera, the body of Dramaticus was now covered and Peter, too, looked like a corpse but he swiftly covered his torso as we approached.

'There's a little light left in him' said Viscera 'but it is fading fast.'

To my surprise, Edward didn't break down. He lay down beside Peter, took his hand and talked to him, telling the story of how, together, they had scaled the walls of York and placed a statue on Micklegate Bar. When that was exhausted, he told him everything that he had been doing in Peter's absence. I turned to Viscera.

'Whatever happens, keep them together. If he is to die then I think he would like his buddy with him.'

As, eventually, we mobilised to move out, the last thing I saw of Deptford docks was the two of them lying side by side on a cart.

Farrier was far away in the shadows and was speaking to someone. The conversation seemed quite intense. Once finished, he marched over to us asking if he could speak to Silas, Wynnfrith and me only. Somewhat anxious about what he was doing, he then chose to speak directly to Wynn.

'I know' he said 'I know about them.'

Silas and Wynnfrith nodded.

'I am to be Moonlight' he added without any emotion whatsoever. I had no clue what this meant and looked to the

1543 The Disfiguration

other two for an explanation. They both embraced him.

'My good friend and heroic warrior, you will be perfect and it will give the whole of England peace to know that you are in their ranks.'

'But you cannot tell anyone' said Farrier 'I will explain to Shakespeare and Maud.'

Ranks? I was thinking. What in Heaven's name is he talking about? It would be sometime later when Wynnfrith would explain to me about the multi-faceted Moonlight league and, I too, agreed that Farrier would fit in perfectly.

He then took Silas to one side and took hold of his hand 'you…my good friend.. you understood. Nobody understands but I have told them…Moonlight that is…of my, well…unusual disposition. Moonlight, she said, reflects all human beings of good heart. Can you imagine that being said of me?'

Tears flowed from his tired and blackened eyes and Silas followed suit. They embraced.

'You are mightily loved my heroic blacksmith, not least by God himself' said Silas.

'I will settle all my affairs in Wolverdington and then I will be contacted by them.'

'Our love and good fortune goes with you and…you may need this' said Wynnfrith.

She handed him a soggy and battered prosthesis that he had used to replace his injured lower leg. He laughed and told us that he would make a much more comfortable and reliable one at his workshop.

Ready to leave, soldiers walked a bedraggled Joshua Bask past us, still cursing.

'Wait a minute' said Wynnfrith 'can I take a closer look at him please?'

They brought him nearer and one of the King's guards held a torch for her to see.

'You?!' she said 'Mouse…don't you recognise him?'

Admittedly, at first, I was clueless until she said,

'The beef thief! Remember? The very first time that you and Edward came to the wash house? The sheriff was chasing a beef thief except he seemed not to have any beef!'

'Good God!' I exclaimed 'truth be told, I would have struggled.'

'And again, he turned up at Barley Hall when the great window was being fitted and then collapsed. Robert!'

Robert Hall heard her call and came over. She pointed to Bask.

'Wasn't he a labourer when we were fitting the window?' Wynnfrith nodded.

Without another word nor query, Robert strode over and gave Bask such a kick in the shin that he collapsed howling so, Robert did it again.

'That's for your bastard brother, the devil's accomplice!' He turned back to us,

'These people have been spying on us for years?! A pox on them all!'

'Calm yourself Robert' I said 'it is all at an end, at last.'

As I said it. Wynn was leaving us and, bizarrely, visiting the dead and injured. I saw her in the dim starlight kneeling next to a cart with three dead bodies upon it, encouraging their souls to a better destination. She moved to another cart where one of its occupants was squealing in pain and prayed there. He cursed her, resenting her heretic petitions, but it had no effect on her whatsoever. We waited until she was completely done before departing together.

For a few moments, I was alone with so much to contemplate. I thought about home, April, the Institute of Historical Analytics. What was it all about? What have I gained except finding out some facts that were otherwise hidden? And the consequences. I felt as though my guts had been ripped out although, in my case, that was completely metaphorical. Life for these people was, at times, horrendous. Beyond compare with many of their twenty-first and twenty-second century descendants. Will they ever be free from fear? I thought and then deduced that, odd as my band was, it was made up of people whose core was good and with an indestructible faith and, as long as that faith maintained the consideration of, and belief in, others, then I construed that they could face anything. We were never to see Thomas Farrier in the same light again. On those very rare occasions when Moonlight appeared, we would all be taking a much closer look to see if it was our friend. Shakespeare, convinced that he had played a part in the greatest battle of the year, returned with a war wound, well, man-flu, with endless stories to tell and yes, it was his son John, who revelled in them the most so, who knows…

Viscera was, undoubtedly, the most unusual of creatures but he had won immeasurable respect on this day, not least from Sadler who had heard about his work on Elspeth and Bask and was commissioned with querying him about the "very necessary and desired permanence of his Majesty's body once his soul hath found itself in Heaven. God willing, that will never befall us." This was an extraordinary request given that no one was to ever mention the King's death and it was a sign that Henry himself suspected that his days were numbered. To my left, I saw Maud making such an awful fuss of Bayard. He was lapping it up although he wasn't injured at all. I heard second hand about his disappearance and reappearance and then thought that this would also happen to me but it had never occurred so far. I'm an avatar, for God's sake! Why would I die? It did leave me with a thousand questions, though. Whoever he is, does he now have a permanent life here as well as his alter ego at home? Does he control his personality and looks and, more importantly, why did he stick a pin in my arse? However, I was certain that, even if I grilled him, he wouldn't give any more away.

Following further questioning, Sadler's men released Marcus and he told us that he had to tidy up affairs in Oxford and Worcester but then would return, permanently, to York.

I had no doubt, that one way in which the King would

show his gratitude would be by ensuring that Peter got the best medical attention although I was convinced that it wouldn't be enough. The rest of us prepared to make camp and, later, head home. Maud, slightly embarrassed, apologised to Wynnfrith as she had all but adopted Silas. Wynnfrith hugged her and told her that, following the trauma they had all just endured, she would always be considered as family from that moment on.

'Oh well in that case..' she added, quite cheekily 'I'm of a mind to settle in York if it…err…it is acceptable to you good people.'

For the first time, we all laughed as we could see Bayard in the distance, pacing back and forth, awaiting an answer.

'But what means do you have Maud?' asked Silas 'how will you manage?'

'Well, handing the inn over is no trouble and…you see…' she took a very deep breath and proudly said 'Thomas Farrier has the biggest heart on God's earth, he has. A kinder man you will never meet. He's looked after me, the Shakespeares and even hid that daft pair, Farrimond and Ham, after they had rescued me. Truth be told, he bought that shitty pub off me for a small fortune even though I protested. So, there you have it and…whilst you're gawping at that lump over there…'

More laughter

'I won't be taking anything off him just yet!'

This conversation alone began to raise spirits.

'However, my dear and sweet young Silas, I do have a gift for you which will be delivered to your home in York as soon as it can be arranged.'

Silas badgered Maud for a good fifteen minutes on this subject although nothing was forthcoming.

By the time the morning work gang had turned up at first light, all that remained were a few of the King's officials and some guards. Everyone was interviewed and decisions were made about whether they would be kept on, arrested or interrogated. Within a week it was as normal as you could imagine and within a month it looked as if nothing had ever happened.

24 the holy relic

The following week, the King had been informed of the whole conspiracy and also of the involvement of the Agents. He put into place a scheme by which they could further investigate those with any intent of overthrowing the regime long before it ever got to that stage again. As always, innocents would be caught in the crossfire which only helped to make the King more unpopular.

'To tell the truth, Somerset, I am astounded that the key has returned so quickly to where it belongs and…it does give me some peace to see it again.'

'Your Grace, if you would allow…' said Somerset

'Yes. Yes. Yes.' Replied Henry now back in default character.

'The casket….the chest…it was my understanding that it was to be locked for all time. I'm not sure why…'

Staring at a huge, round, beetroot red face, Somerset and Sadler, who was standing by him, were mightily relieved that Cranmer intervened.

'My Lords…with His Grace's permission. I will shed light on this for you but it is my understanding that no one, besides ourselves and Heneage, can be a party to this

1543 The Disfiguration

knowledge.'

They both bowed as a sign of respect and Cranmer looked at the King for a sign that he could continue. After all, this, for Henry, was a very sensitive subject.

'Our beloved Lord of this land has been plagued for want of a healthy son for his entire reign. God hath blessed him, and the peoples of England, with a glorious son. But….'

He looked to Henry again.

'But he ails. The Prince's health is a concern constantly for His Majesty and us all. Imagine now, the consequences of…'

The King nodded again.

'…if we were to lose him. The casket contains details of every sickness and ailment that our beloved Prince Edward has suffered since birth. He has been attended by the best doctors, even from Europe and all….I mean, all, gentleman, has been recorded. In the wrong hands, what you have witnessed this week would look like a mere scrap. The reason why there is some urgency to access this is…well… his most recent complaint. In short, we need to be able to get at those documents, but they are for us only.'

'I see' said Sadler calmly ' and the key also has healing properties from Our Lord Himself?'

'Absolutely' said Cranmer.

The King was now seated and seemingly benign. He spoke in a soft voice, possibly the first time he had in some time.

'I simply cannot lose him, gentlemen. I just cannot. I have lost everyone I have loved, in one way or another. He must succeed me and, between you and I, once he is well again I would gladly forfeit my life for him to be seated on the throne, except he is still so young.'

Everyone protested. Whether this was feigned or not, it was the right thing to do,

'I should add' said Cranmer 'that when the Prince is presented at Court or beyond, it is only when he is well and,

1543 The Disfiguration

official records deny the constant relapses, only admitting his debilitation with quartan fever.'

Then, as it tended to do, the temperature changed in an instant and Henry was stumbling upright and raising his voice.

'God's teeth! What a bloody mess! How the hell did it end up with Culpeper?!'

'We cannot say with certainty, your Grace' said Somerset 'but we believe that, unwisely, the Quee...err...mistress Howard was boasting of it as it was kept on her person during your visits to Lincoln. We cannot be sure why but, once she was separated from that rogue, Culpeper, his response was to have it buried or destroyed, naively thinking that was the correct thing to do.'

Somerset's theory was very close to the truth. There was no malice in Culpeper's actions but as Catherine had told him that it belonged to a box "that must never be opened" he rushed to get rid, somewhat sensibly trusting a nun.

Henry was not impressed. The rant that followed lasted a good ten minutes and Cranmer, particularly, was now becoming tired. The mood had changed and all three of them thought it much more sensible to give abridged answers for the rest of this stressful inquisition.

'So, what in God's name, is all this about my ships and lumps of metal and Papists!!'

'Seemingly part of a plot, the disfiguration of His Majesty's fleet but now thwarted as all are recovered and destroyed.'

'and' said a cautious Cranmer 'there was a sub conspiracy to enlist slaves on our isle.'

Now he was furious. He was bloody furious. Despite his many flaws, this was a road that Henry did not wish to go down and little did he understand it either as he had at least one black man in his employ.

'I will make those barbarians pay. God's teeth I will!!...and you're sure you have all the conspirators?'

1543 The Disfiguration

'Absolutely Your Grace. Perhaps public executions to set an example at this difficult time?' suggested Somerset.

'No! I'll have no more martyrs made! I want all evidence of this insurrection kept quiet except for those that it touches upon. Who was the architect of this diabolical scheme?'

They looked at one another pre-empting the King's reaction. Cranmer discreetly prodded Sadler as he was the one to make the arrests.

'Well…Your Grace…'

'Out with it man!'

'This was an alliance made between Papists in over three different European countries, Pole at its head, and I am of the opinion that they were planning an invasion to supplant an imposter on the English throne…'

'My darling daughter, no doubt?'

'As yet, Your Grace, we have no evidence that she was personally involved or complicit.'

It took very little to make Henry's blood boil and he was becoming increasingly angry that he wasn't getting a straight answer about the perpetrator so, in a rage, he asked once again.

Again Sadler looked at the others for support but they had both decided to contemplate their feet instead.

'Sir Anthony Bask' whispered Sadler.

'What?! Speak up, man!!'

'Sir Anthony Bask, Your Grace.'

There was silence as this ageing pig's bladder was pumped up to bursting point before venting forth.

'Bask! Bloody Bask! That donkey's dick!! I thought him dead!! I ordered him dead years ago!!'

They tried to interrupt and inform the King that Bask's brother had expedited the plot following his death but he was not for listening further.

'An oozing pustule on England's backside! He was forbidden to use his title a decade ago! Thief! Blackmailer! Whoremonger! There were never any redeeming features about that privy rat. I want his body. Get it from wherever he was put and stick him on a pike at the Tower. His brother you say? Nothing less than boiled in oil! Write that down Cranmer...immediately!! Add to their crimes the following... shagging livestock! They'll be guilty of that as well..'

His rant continued, always particularly fond of the sex and animals trope, and, whilst indulging in a monologue, no matter how loud, it gave the other three a chance to relax a little as they were now, slightly, off the hook.

It took another fifteen minutes before the King was calmed again and he asked about how the Papist schemes had been undone. He listened carefully as Cranmer pushed the other two to be more honest about the involvement of the Agents of the Word.

'A bunch of northern inbreds got the better of my best advisors and spies?'

He went quiet and then he laughed and the laughter was, quite manic. Henry walked to the window, seemingly very happy, and waved without looking at them, giving them leave. If only he could have seen them trying to get their breath back on the other side of the door, congratulating each other for getting through it.

A day later, that most revered casket was brought forth and the Prince's physicians pored over previous medical notes and set about, as best they could, tending to the sickly boy. They recorded everything that they had witnessed and what they had done, put the key in the lock, locked it and then invited the Archbishop to pray over the Holy Key and for the Prince's health and well-being. Then it was hidden again for the period during which he enjoyed good health. Everyone involved in the conspiracy was interrogated, tortured and put to death. Henry, mindful of the limitations of his own physicians ordered the organs from their bodies to be saved for medical examination. Ultimately, Joshua Bask was hung, drawn and quartered and his body thrown in a pauper's grave. Sir Anthony Bask's corpse stayed where it was. What was left of their kin were told that Joshua had been murdered by his enemies. Foreign ambassadors petitioned for the release of their captured nationals but they were told that they had all died in shame, in an attack against the King's troops.

For some time, tales would abound about this affair and, if the details weren't already complicated enough for the Agents and for the King himself, it was nothing compared to how it developed as complete fantasy and folklore. One of the most popular being that the Pope himself had sailed a fleet up the Thames with an army of thousands to put himself on the English throne and lay claim to the whole cross of Christ as it was now kept in the Tower.

For most of his life and certainly for the rest of his days, Henry would struggle to count real friends and allies on one finger and it was mostly for this reason that he would often sit alone and yearn to be an everyday citizen of the land with the Agents of York having a particular appeal. He dreamt of riding alongside them, talking of everyday things, gossiping about neighbours, politics and foreigners with no more big decisions to make. As Henry aged, the grass was forever greener, particularly in York.

25 healing wounds

Marcus was so thankful that his injuries had been tended to as, in his mind, he still had much to do. Battered, cut and bruised, the only thing that was a semi-permanent injury was his leg which had been broken in the fall down into the cellar. Perfectly strapped and with a splint thanks to the King's physician, he could manage to ride and he could also walk with a stick. Despite their objections, he insisted that he had unfinished business but would see everyone in York as soon as he could. Neither did he take the shortest route as his business in Oxford was somewhat urgent.

He arrived back at the house in Nun's Walk that he had been renting, unable to avoid reminiscing about when the room was full of his friends. How quiet it was now. He made a swift decision about the mess and, despite his condition, chose to tidy the place himself and he personally burned the model ship along with all of Bask's remaining documents at the back of the property. When he had finished, he crossed the road and knocked on the door.

'You!' said the man who opened the door 'I thought you'd scarpered without paying rent.'

'Not at all sir' said Marcus 'apologies for my absence, you will find here your rent in full as well as some recompense for your inconvenience.'

He looked into the purse.

'Mmm…oh…I see. Right, well…that will do nicely young man. What happened, to your face?'

'I was attacked on the road, on the mend now…I have burned some waste at the back but all debris has just been taken away on a cart.'

Using his stick, he could move although his movement was slow. He had a thought to visit to the long-suffering Mrs Bask but kept changing his mind. Marcus was also sure that, if he got as far as the door, he would then walk away again.

However, as he turned the corner he saw men carrying out what remained of the Bask's possessions. There was also a constable and a guard and they were ugly in every respect. Certain to walk away, he spotted a forlorn creature sitting on the pavement outside. Lady Bask was unmoved and motionless, simply staring ahead. Neither was she crying or protesting despite the reality that even passers-by were commenting and pointing.

Somewhat comically, Marcus hobbled as fast as he could toward her. She looked up.

'Oh…hello' she said, trance-like 'didn't expect to see you again.' Her expression didn't change. At the same time, Marcus was aware that the constable was looking at him with some disdain. If there was one thing that recent events had brought to the fore it was that seemingly, he would always be singled out for his colour perhaps, except, if he stayed permanently in York.

'May I speak with you, Sir? asked Marcus.

'Depends. This any of your business?'

'Please hear me out, constable. I am as much an opponent of this poor woman's husband as any man on earth. I only have an enquiry to make.'

The constable nodded and then the guard moved forward to threaten Marcus.

'I believe there is much money owed by Bask?' he

1543 The Disfiguration

insisted.

'Well, you'd need to speak to the bailiff yonder but I can tell you that, even the sale of this fine house, won't repay what that rascal accrued in debts. Don't want to buy it do you?'

He said this so loudly, and sarcastically, that everyone, apart from Marcus and Lady Bask, laughed.

'Yes. Yes, I would like to do that if it is a fair price.'

Although the officials were dumbfounded, there was a spell where, unsurprisingly, Marcus wasn't taken seriously but when the bailiff told him the cost of the overall debt, he hobbled even nearer and said,

'I have in my means the ability to settle this very day. If you are agreeable, you can send a man around to this address, that is just beyond the university, and the occupant will account for my funds, here, in Oxford.'

The sheriff scratched his head and the bailiff scratched his arse but they ultimately agreed to humour him. Lady Bask looked on taking no notice whatsoever as she couldn't hear. She presumed that Marcus was making a complaint about Sir Anthony Bask and also enquiring as to how he would get his money back.

Within minutes the bailiff returned and, very loudly, pronounced,

'Put it all back. All of it! Return every item!'

Lady Bask jumped up. With no expectations of a reprieve, she was now anxious that the debt was once more falling on her shoulders. She immediately became animated. Now she was upset and she made it known. She had prepared herself for and would have accepted the worst but it seemed as though things were about to change once again.

Marcus approached her.

'Please, Lady Bask, do not fret so. We are allowed to go within. Please trust me.'

At this juncture, there were fortunately still two seats to sit upon inside the living quarters.

1543 The Disfiguration

'Please sit…I have the means. I am able to….I have paid off all of your debts.'

Her look was somewhere between disbelief and horror. What does this man want in return? She first asked herself, acknowledging that she had been a slave all her life and never wanted to be obliged to any man, ever again.

'Trust me' he said 'I have done this because I can. I have done this because you have been treated disgracefully throughout your life and I want you to know that not all men are like him. I want nothing in return. Nothing. This has cost me very little but I can return your home, your confidence and your status. Of course, you may refuse but it is nothing more than a gift.'

She leapt out of her chair and flung her arms around his neck.

'You are a saint, Sir and you leave me without words. If there is anything that I…"

'No.' He said firmly now holding her hands. 'Nothing in return, ever. I would be honoured to be your friend if that is acceptable but, if not, I promise that you will never hear from me again.'

Of course, Lady Bask had prayed endlessly for a miracle but, now that it was here, she could not take it in. It would be two weeks before she would fully absorb what had happened and she began to take pride in her home for the first time in years. Within a month, she was receiving visitors again and, as it had been agreed with her benefactor, she had taken writing lessons and had written her first letter to her friend in the far and dark north. Elspeth smiled down upon them both for it was a job well done.

With the pain in his leg beginning to ease somewhat, he headed for Wolverdington but, his friend and ally, the blacksmith was nowhere to be seen. Slightly dismayed and wondering if he had already joined the ranks of Moonlight, he decided to ask around. Eventually, he found someone who had been talking to him that very morning, Thomas

1543 The Disfiguration

Farrier was to be found at Maud's old pub, once called, ye dirtye pesant.

'Marcus! Friend! Is all well? The leg…is it?'

They embraced and chatted for a while and Marcus thanked him for his heroic efforts at Deptford. Embarrassed, Farrier swiftly changed the subject.

'I'll let this place out. Good little inn it will be when I've finished with it. Rather special, I think. It is…I suppose…where it all started, Marcus.'

Intrigued, Marcus asked him to elaborate.

'One day in the year of Our Lord, fifteen forty-one, our Silas marches in here and announces "I'm on a mission from God himself!" And he nearly got kicked out of the place!'

They both laughed.

'Where he very first met Maud, would you believe. I'm sure he hadn't a blue clue what his mission was but it was here that he persisted. My, there's been some water over the fall since then, I tell you.'

Marcus looked at the dilapidated building with some reverence, understanding why it had to be preserved.

'I am bound for Worcester, but will settle in York' he told Farrier and, after some small talk, which became somewhat protracted as they knew they would miss one another, they finally parted company.

Even though it was to be temporary, Marcus was insistent that there should be an infirmary for the sick and dying in Worcester and that it should be in the same building in which he had once worked, the same one in which he had also been abused on his most recent visit. He took some pleasure in seeing its occupants turfed out and he stayed another week to ensure that it was secure, staffed and funded. One morning, he stood inside, looking out and called over the new physician.

'That building down the street? There. Across the road. It has changed?'

'That is has' answered the physician as if everyone knew.

1543 The Disfiguration

Realising that the coin hadn't dropped with Marcus he added,
'Look about the street, sir. What do you notice?'
At first, Marcus noticed nothing. The streets were still quite filthy with rainwater and waste flowing persistently downhill. What more was there to observe? He asked himself. And then, suddenly, his head swept from left to right and then he turned around again.
'There are no street vendors!'
Marcus was alarmed, presuming that even those who tried to trade on the streets were now banned by the city altogether.
'You won't believe me when I tell you sir' said the physician 'one of those very street dwellers now owns that building yonder and, he will give bed and warmth to anyone who hasn't got a home or a hope whoever they are. Look! Can you see what it says across the beam?'
Marcus wiped condensation from the window but could see no clearer so then went out into the street. He stood staring up at the sign unable to believe what he was seeing.
"There is neither Jew nor Greek, there is neither slave nor free, there is no male and female, for you are all one in Jesus Christ"
'Galatians 3:28…Thaddeus….' He whispered to himself. Not knowing how, the kindness that he had shown to a stranger had spread like an infectious laugh. He did not walk inside, neither did he make enquiries, but remained in awe of this message of inclusion for days to come. Eventually, he settled his affairs and left the city with a smile on his face.
From Worcester, he travelled south to Bristol. Particularly in his current condition, this was to make his journey much greater. He considered heading north instantly but reminded himself why Bristol was so important. He had never been there previously and it was much bigger than he had imagined. What was familiar to him were the ships. The bustle of merchants and haulage being moved on and off the docks. Bristol had just been made a city by the King and had

its fair share of hostelries so he chose one in which he would stay for three nights and where he ate and drank consecutively for almost two hours on arrival.

A whole day of his time was spent trying to track down a woman. He soon gave up asking for her by name thinking that more people may have remembered her husband. Sensibly, he spent the second day making enquiries along the harbour. He found that some there were willing to help, whilst others were just downright rude. Almost at the point where he was content to give up, he finally connected. An old sailor had been so interested in his search, and personable in his manner, that Marcus accepted his offer of taking him all the way to a humble, but dilapidated, abode in the back streets of Bristol. This man was curiously called Storm and, so interesting was this assignation that Marcus asked him to explain but, as soon as his tale started they were at the door, so he never found out. Marcus could not think of another word to describe that door although, in reality, it was a lump of discarded planking leaning against the entrance.

'Good day, Lady! 'Tis just Storm a knocking?'

'What on earth do you want man? Haven't heard from you in an age..'

Storm explained that she had a visitor.

'Well, you'd better take that wood out of the hole then, gettin too heavy for me!'

Despite his injuries, Marcus was still best suited to this task as Storm could barely breathe or walk and the occupant was showing no interest in doing it herself.

When it was removed, Marcus stared at the woman and she stared back. He considered that she was possibly middle-aged but looked ancient. A cripple, with hardly any teeth and, truth be told, hardly any hair either. She was a pathetic sight. Added to that, was the interior spectacle that drew his eye away from her and inward. So poverty-stricken was this woman that it would have melted the heart of anyone who saw it.

'Well! I knows who you is' she said 'you're the little dark boy from the Mary Rose.'

'That I am, except I haven't been aboard the Mary Rose for some time' he said, images from the battle still flashing before him as he spoke.

'You must know he's dead?' she said.

'Why of course, madam, I was there when it happened but Jack died instantly and without pain.'

'Well, in that case, you might do me the courtesy of telling me what really happened. You'd better come in.'

Storm happily bid them both farewell and Marcus entered into the dark and dismal enclosure in which she lived.

'I'm guessing it was no accident? Accident I was told! All his fault they said!' waving her fist furiously as she spoke.

Once Marcus began to answer, there was no shutting him up.

'…finest seaman that ever lived in my opinion, madam, he was my superior but we were close. He was murdered by a scoundrel…'

'Bask?' she asked.

'Yes! Yes. He is dead now. Someone killed him and I believe it was Aelfraed who was..'

'I know Who Aelfraed was. If you see him tell him I send my thanks. Even people around here know about Bask. Devil's spawn, a born crook.' she added.

He continued for some time, telling tales of the trio's amazing adventures and he could see that this hopeless woman was warming to them.

'So you've come all the way from York just to tell me this?'

'No, madam. I am on a quest to right some wrongs and I pray that you will indulge me.'

As he continued, she was so engaged that, at one point, he thought she had stopped breathing. When he concluded his tale and delivered the suggestion that he had come to make, she broke down completely, falling to the floor.

'Madam! It was not my intention to alarm you...'
She interrupted him,
'If only you knew. I have spent years on this floor praying. I have no issue with my abode, it sometimes keeps the rain out but, at best, I only eat one day in five. You dear boy...I reject your most generous offer but, if I may, have a counter-proposal.'

'Anything' he said, intrigued.

There was a local scheme where pensioner sailors and their families could access one of the new nests of cottages. They were humble but they weren't free. Only sailors with good pensions, or those lucky enough to have been awarded compensation, could have one. She asked him if he could facilitate a move from where she was to one of those instead of giving her money, as offered. Delighted that she would accept help and also that he had managed to trace her in the first place, he set about legal proceedings the same day, ensuring that provision was made so that she would regularly access food. He spoke to her just once more and, on that occasion, she invited him to visit when she was settled but he told her that he thought that very unlikely. He then went to church, realising how long it had been since he had been inside one. He prayed incessantly. He prayed for practically everyone he had ever known and that included Jack and his widow, promising God that his insatiable and incurable altruism was not an effort to buy out his guilt but an attempt to redress the imbalance of the past few years. Marcus would never, ever, forget that day that he could not stand up to Bask and promised himself, as well as God, that it would never happen again.

By the time that Marcus had once more entered Yorkshire, his leg was healing. He had observed a rigid practice of cleaning his wounds and had been smart enough to keep weight off his damaged leg.

However, he prevaricated about his intended last visit. His conscience would swing one way then another so he would stop and ask Elspeth. She had been the most consistent person he had ever met, particularly when it came to her faith, even in death. He could clearly hear the words "carry on" almost as if he were saying them himself. But, it was with some trepidation that he entered Knapton on a warm day in 1543. More so than anywhere else, he was studied and gawped at as he rode in. This was a very small market hamlet, people were scarce but the ones that did reside there made it clear that strangers weren't welcome. It was also likely that this was the first black person most inhabitants had ever seen.

As he had asked around for Aelfraed's wife, people immediately clammed up and would then walk away. He had expected this. Not only had Aelfraed been put to death on a charge of murder, but the whole connection with Sir Anthony Bask was also something that wasn't spoken off. Eventually, he managed to engage with a girl who, he presumed, was in her teens.

'You must know of Aelfraed?' He asked 'it is his wife I seek.'

Of course she did. Unwittingly, Aelfraed had passed on his lumpy grimace to his offspring and she, somewhat reluctantly, agreed to take Marcus home.

Aelfraed's family had a slightly better standard of living than that of Jack's wife although it was clear, by the time that Marcus had got there, that the family had been ostracised by everyone else in the community. Now, no one spoke to them and the woman told him that they also struggled to get work and provisions in Knapton. When Marcus asked why, he was told that it was because of the murder.

Had Marcus forgiven Aelfraed? It was hard to say. He certainly felt bitter that he chose not to leave with him when he had run away. It would be some time before anyone knew the truth about how Aelfraed suffered at Deptford, how he eventually got away and how it took him years to release himself from Bask's grip but Marcus knew, already, that it can't have been easy for his former gaffer. And, there were few people who weren't glad that Bask had been taken out. In fact, Marcus could not think of anyone.

She was very nervous. She expected another reckoning or, at the very least, a reprimand.

'I will speak my heart to you. It will be simpler' said Marcus 'I could never condone what your husband did, but Bask was a most evil creature and I believe that no one on this earth will miss him. Aelfraed was my friend and he was a good man and I also know that you suffer because of his actions.'

She thanked him and then told Marcus of how Aelfraed had carried painful and deep wounds all his life for helping Marcus escape. For the first time during his post-battle quest, there were tears in his eyes. What times we live in, he thought to himself. Death, illness, poverty and skulduggery wherever you turn. He looked at them and, although he had gone intending to assist this family too, he realised that they were in an almost impossible situation and it was likely that they would starve if they were to remain in Knapton.

'I have an idea' he said 'I will need a few days in York before I can send someone to confirm my proposal but I promise you, on the Holy Bible over yonder, that I will not abandon you.'

Aelfraed's wife sobbed and grabbed Marcus, he having no clue whatsoever as to how to react. The daughter approached him, still with the woman hanging about his neck, and spoke softly.

'You are our saviour, sir. I will repay you. If it takes my whole life I will make good this kindness.'

Almost off his feet, Marcus didn't know what to say so simply thanked her at the same time as breaking free of her over-emotional mother. Marcus's conscience had had him on a quest to help people who needed it but was becoming increasingly uncomfortable with being called a saint and a saviour and particularly with tactile women.

'What's your name?' he asked the girl.

'Rose, sir.'

As he left he was sure that he had met a remarkable young woman, acknowledging that he was somewhat disturbed at seeing his rugged friend's face atop a dress.

Without knowing it, he took the same route to York that Silas had when he had first encountered Bask. The same journey on which Aelfraed had caught up with Bask and bashed his head to a pulp. He was tired but excited to see his friends again. He promised himself that he would only ever leave York in an emergency and that he would never see battle again.

Within a day, he had spoken to Wynnfrith about her father's tannery, surprised at how much she knew of the trade. He purchased a similar, but modest, property similar to the one that Elspeth and Wynnfrith had grown up in. Living quarters upstairs, workshop below and he had the deeds delivered to Aelfraed's widow with instructions about who to contact regarding learning the trade. Within months, Marcus would often find himself waving to Aelfraed's doppelgänger on his way back and forth to the undercroft where he revelled once again in his daily responsibilities.

26 robin hood

There was no doubt that everyone was glad to get back to York and, on Robert's suggestion, they all returned to their homes with the proviso that they had a meeting on the third day to reflect on matters. For the greater part of that period, I was alone at the workshop along Micklegate wishing I wasn't. I hated being there without Peter and, Edward's father had prohibited him from visiting too. Yet again, my mind throbbed with the conundrums that came with my strange juxtaposition. Once, I awoke thinking to myself, who am I? This dark retrospection was the last thing I needed and the solitary confinement didn't help. If Bayard was, really, two people, am I the same? I had no answer except that I had had relationships, feelings, I was unquestionably sentient. Then I pondered about my return. If there had been any instruction or agreement when I left, it had gone, I was clueless as to what should come next. Previously, my point of return had been the workshop but there I was and nothing was happening. I was thankful, for that bloody leg of Aelfraed's had gone but, after all the action, I hated being alone. Yet again, I was certain that I wanted to stay there. I missed my wife but strangely convinced myself that there must have been a way in which I could get her to join me

1543 The Disfiguration

there in York in 1543. Bayard would know, I thought. And then the worst anxiety of all. I wondered whether the horrendous conflict that we had all been involved in, was actually caused by me. I couldn't live with that thought. Perturbed, I nestled into some straw by Godwin's bench. It took me back to that very first day, the shock and awe of the great city of York. Then I laughed as I remembered how I abhorred the smells. Unbearable! I couldn't stop complaining about the smells and, thinking of Godwin, I thought of the people we had lost and particularly of that night as we kept vigil by little Lizzy's bedside. So many changes in such a short time. I then supposed that this was an adequate reflection of the sixteenth century and, again, thought about how hard life was for ordinary folk. Would I have been happy in a position of privilege if I had been alive then? I asked myself. I concluded that I couldn't think of anything worse than residing at Court, never knowing if you were still in favour on this day, the next or ever. Amongst my peers, however, I had never known so much love. For those who had made that choice to seek the very core of the Christian faith, to put others first, to take time to understand others, even enemies, I believe it served them well. The people that had become my friends had certainly learned how to love and move on, amongst all the chaos. They understood hatred to be their enemy along with fear, greed, selfishness and, yes, the lack of love, respect and compassion.

It came like the end of a long prison sentence when Edward finally came for me.

'I really am so sorry, Micklegate, my father had forbidden…'

'It's fine Ed, although I can't tell you how pleased I am to see you and get out of here.'

I could tell he was morose and it was very hard to witness it. Throughout, he had been a light, one that I would follow anywhere. So sad was he, that he hardly made conversation. Despite that, I relished the journey along Micklegate and across the river in the very same box that had been made for me when I had arrived in 1541. York was beautiful on this summer's day. Trade was lively and the church and Minster bells rang. Already, it was as if Deptford had been an age ago and I was happy to forget as much of it as I possibly could.

We entered Mulberry Hall and, in much the same way as we had done many times previously at Barley Hall, I was placed at one end of the long table with everyone else gathering and sitting around, except there weren't as many people as I had expected and Edward had been asked to stay outside.

'Family business!' announced Robert and told me that he wished me to be included.

'Eirik, having distinguished himself has requested an hour with Meg, our servant, before entering the meeting if that is acceptable to all?' Said Robert.

I looked at Wynnfrith. Like myself, she felt that things were coming to a head. I told Robert that I was happy to wait all day as long as he didn't lock me in that bloody workshop again.

Mindful of his promise to Meg, and particularly considering that he was alive and well, it was only gentlemanly that he spoke to her before saying anything in front of the gathered Agents. When I say everyone, Silas, Wynnfrith and a very happy baby were there. Edward's father, William Fawkes, Mrs Hall and Robert. The others were to join us later.

Eventually, Eirik walked in with Meg beside him and Edward was allowed to join us too. There was an atmosphere so tense that you could have divided it equally amongst all those present with some left over.

He nervously began to speak. He asked for one thing only and that was to be heard. He told us that he would accept any outcome, as long as he could be heard, which told us all that this was serious. Although he took quite a detour, eventually, he simply had to say that he wasn't, after all,

Robert's son, the adopted son of Ryia or the brother of Elspeth and Wynnfrith. Long before he had even got to that point, Robert's head had gone down. I do believe that Eirik expected him to be angry, even become quite violent, but he could not have been further away from reality. Robert was close to tears, now finally completely broken. He had clung to this alternate reality for so long, and with every breath he gave, that he simply didn't want to give it up. Internally, he blamed himself yet again for his illicit affair all those years ago. He couldn't speak which left a long, deathly silence. Wynn was brave enough to respond.

'I don't suppose many of us are bowled off our seats young man. You must know that we have, almost in turn, held all sorts of suspicions about you?'

Eirik held her gaze, certain that her question was rhetorical.

'The irony is that you have probably been accused of much worse since you arrived. But, this is hard, Eirik. It is really hard. One can only imagine what Robert has been through since he apprehended the MacManus's murderer all those years ago, added to the events of recent months. Look at him. The man is crushed.'

Baby Mary's eyes, the size of hazelnuts, smiled at Eirik.

'What's going on?' asked Silas

'He's not who he says he is dear' said his extremely patient wife.

'Who is he then?!' said Silas shocked.

'He's still Eirik my love….I'll explain later.'

Then more quiet followed.

Robert straightened himself and turned to me.

'Well, dear Mouse, for once I am speechless, truthfully, I would be glad if he left, for good, this minute but I seek your counsel first.'

I looked at Robert. He couldn't face Eirik.

'I am content to advise but I must be clear that it is simply that, advice and you must hold it, or drop it, as you see fit.'

1543 The Disfiguration

He nodded

'Is there a person present who hasn't had, at some point, their suspicions about this miraculous return of the prodigal son?' I asked, grandstanding somewhat.

In truth, I had expected some innocent remark from Edward but neither did he respond.

'So, of sorts, you have happily embraced this imposter all this time? My biggest concern has been that, between us, we have thought him guilty of practically everything that has taken place, including murder. The reality is that we wouldn't be here today if Eirik, almost single-handedly hadn't saved us at Deptford.'

'Please, dear Micklegate. If I could...' said Eirik.

I nodded.

'Please do not create a defence for me. I have none. Even if this good man here decides to take legal proceedings against me, I will comply.'

'Actually, I will advise as I see fit, as Robert has asked that of me. So, if you will let me continue?'

He shrank back into his nervous state.

I then looked directly at Wynnfrith, and she knew why.

'Oh...alright. Yes. It was actually Elspeth who insisted that you were James but you did go along with it!' she said.

He said nothing.

'That he did' I said 'so there is his entire crime. In an instant, finding a family. Something he had never had before and, after that, when he didn't cling to that lie, neither could he unravel it. Would you like me to continue Robert or am I making things worse?'

He said nothing but then waved his hand for me to continue but before I could, Wynn interrupted.

'If you, or anyone else says, what would Elspeth do? I'm warning you, I'll bloody scream!'

I, then, even detected the birth of a smile on Eirik's face even as, yes, we all knew what Elspeth would do.

'Eirik, I think it best if you and Meg leave the room, you

have my word that you will be called back in.' I said.

Robert's head shot up, again.

'I assure you that he will not abscond' I added and they left.

'I am about to put something to you and I know it may be the wrong time but time is something I do not have. How many of you in this room have come to love this young man? Dare I say, as a brother, friend and even a son?'

I could tell that I had already touched a few hearts but William Fawkes, expectedly, was stone cold. I continued.

'I can speak on behalf of Bede, Brother Bernard and Father Matthew and I believe I speak on behalf of James too. That young man out there is the last friend he had when he died and he was there, with him. So, here are your choices. You can start proceedings with the good William Fawkes here who can interrogate him today. You can send him away for good. You can wait until you are properly enraged and give him a good beating or…you can keep him.'

I could feel the shock of my conclusion ripple through the room so I gave it time to soak in and then continued.

'He would be the happiest man in the world to be accepted as a member of this family and…he is a great asset.'

Robert huffed and grumbled, shifting in his chair and then indicated for them to be let in again.

'Before I say another word' said Robert to Eirik 'what's going on with you and my bloody servant?!'

'As you know, Sir, shamefully, I am guilty of leaving this woman with child although I knew not at the time.'

William Fawkes covered his son's ears which looked quite comical, given the circumstances.

'As we were parted once again, my love has grown for her, and her love for me and she has agreed to marry me whatever the outcome' said Eirik.

'Even if you go to the gallows!' barked Robert

'Yes, I have promised the same' said Meg 'and I will stand by it and, the reason is that he swore to make a confession to you if he returned alive and has done so. I could have no higher respect for a man.'

This went down particularly well with the ladies present but Robert was still chewing his tongue.

'Have you anything else to say for yourself?' said Robert.

'As God himself is my witness, I swear to you that I am wholeheartedly ashamed for what I have done to you personally, Sir. You have been as a father to me and have been so kind' Eirik started to crumble, a tremble in his voice 'whatever becomes of me I will return everything down to a button of what you have gifted me.'

'That it?' said Robert, sure that he had finished.

'Just one thing, sir….' Continued Eirik 'Elspeth knew. She knew everything. All along, but it was not I who told her.'

'And I suppose she forgave you!' returned Robert, sarcastically. Eirik didn't answer.

Robert asked if William could secure Eirik somewhere, whilst the gifts and money that he had given to Eirik were returned. He agreed and Eirik willingly left with him. No one said another word on this subject and they all respected that this was Robert's decision. Temporarily, Meg was sent back to work.

'Shall we turn to other business' I suggested and it was then that Bayard and Maud joined us.

Wynnfrith wanted to speak so I relaxed and handed over to her.

'I'd like to thank Robert for his kindness…'

He came back to life a little, somewhat surprised that she had said this.

'You have, as promised, been as a father to us. Protected us and gifted Silas, myself and the baby with many things and I do feel that we all have to recognise that, without you, we would all have died in that shipyard…'

Robert, already quite broken, was fighting back tears. Although Wynnfrith's comments were very welcome, Robert

1543 The Disfiguration

was not in a fit state to receive them.

'Added to that are the repairs on our beautiful home…'

He almost leapt up, devoid of any reason why she would know.

'I think that there was a much greater calamity whilst we were on the road than you have told us of Robert, and you had to face those terrors with little support.'

In his heart, he was desperately praying that no one had found out about the disgraceful exhumation of Elspeth's body.

'Who told you?' he asked.

'I'm a woman. I know when someone has been in my home. A cushion moved is as much as a confession. Thank you, I would not have been able to bear arriving back to a ransacked house.'

Silas's face was so switched off that it probably would have been a blessing to slap him. The poor bugger looked totally confused wondering what had changed at home. He, wisely, said nothing.

'I too would like to thank you. It is only right and fitting that we all attend the funeral of our heroic and beloved Father Matthew. I can't imagine how much money you have put in Viscera's purse this last twelve months!' I said.

At last, a little laughter and, for the first time, Robert joined in.

'He's the strangest creature on God's earth but he's bloody good at what he does. I prevaricated endlessly about taking him down to Deptford with me but I thank God I did and also that he travelled separately!' said Robert.

'So, Robert. I gather that you managed to retrieve your gold from the coffin of Sir Anthony Bask? Who then, was still blackmailing you after Anthony Bask's death if it wasn't his widow?' I asked.

'Why, of course, his brother although, at the time, I knew not of his existence' said Robert 'why, it wasn't for Eir….anyway all is resolved and better in my purse that the

1543 The Disfiguration

grave!' he grumbled.

The atmosphere was now lightened somewhat so I turned to Bayard and Maud and asked them of their intentions. She said that she wished to settle in York whilst Bayard shifted around on his feet looking slightly embarrassed. I caught his eye and he knew that he was not going to get away without further interrogation from me regarding his origins.

Silas, at last, opened his mouth to speak but hadn't even uttered a syllable when the door burst open. Robert, furious, leapt up.

'He stirs! He stirs!! And…he is making sounds' said Meg.

Almost as one, everyone in the room tried to get through that door all at once.

'You will all stay here!' he growled and turned to follow Meg.

'Please Sir….' said Edward

'would…'

'Of course' said Robert and the two of them flew upstairs.

'Ed….are you…the workshop….Ed?'

Peter was talking and Edward, his best friend was in tears. So was Robert, deciding to stand back in the hope that no one else would notice. There was a physician in the room that Edward had never seen before and he asked Ed to stand away from the patient. Peter was still, very much, a pathetic sight. Thinner than Silas even, his pallor was shocking and his ugly wound was so pronounced that it would horrify the most hardened warriors. But, his head was up slightly and he was making some sense.

'A long way to go yet' said the physician but Ed begged him to let him lie next to him.

'I stayed with him all the way back from the battle and even when he was first put in this bed!'

Robert conceded and there was no doubt that there was now a little smile gestating on Peter's pale face. However, he hadn't a clue where he was and had remembered little about the battle. Predictably, Wynn and Silas, with mouse in hand, peeped around the door.

'My friends…you are safe…hurr…'

It was the weakest hurrah any man or woman had ever uttered but, in chorus, they cheered back.

Time froze for a moment whilst I considered what we had achieved. I held fantasies about parades where people cheered the Agents of the Word whilst the spirits of Elspeth and Father Matthew smiled benignly from behind but then thought that a very silly notion. Yes, I thought, we are secret agents for a reason.

As it turned out, few people beyond Father Luke, the sheriff and Robert knew about what had happened in the graveyard but he kept Elspeth's letters so, once we had returned to the hall, I picked up on that theme.

'Robert has kindly handed to Wynnfrith those documents of Elspeth's that were left at Barley Hall. Are we sure now that all of her papers and letters have been retrieved and secured?'

'I bloody hope so!' said Wynnfrith 'wait til I get up there!'

We all laughed and, when we stopped, Silas spoke for the first time.

'We thought it wise to destroy all evidence about the keys and the conspiracy, keeping those more personal ones so that my dear wife can reference them when she is sad.'

'So, it is concluded?' I said.

'Err…not quite…' said Silas.

Everyone honed in on him.

'What do you mean?'

'I have but one here and wasn't sure whether or not to mention it in this meeting.'

Wynnfrith looked furious and was about to reprimand him when he read it out.

"When all is done, I have this final message although, who knows, for I am elevated and grotesque."

Wynn leapt up almost falling over.

'You must be jesting!'

1543 The Disfiguration

'Err...no dear..' he said nervously 'just didn't want to trouble you with this unnecessarily.'

'Please, dear Wynnfrith' I said 'do not become anxious. I cannot see this being of any great importance now that we have thwarted the invaders. Possibly, your sister is still having a bit of fun. We'll look into it when we feel like doing so.'

Everyone seemed happy with this. At least for the time being.

Tired and ready to call it a day, we heard a knock on the door of Mulberry Hall. In an instant, it was clear that we were all thinking the same thing and nobody, absolutely not one of us, wanted to see Moonlight again for a long time. Thankfully, that wasn't the case. Robert returned with a very large package. Nervously, he handed me a letter and, as soon as it landed at my feet, I recognised the King's seal.

"To my ragged, incomprehensible and sorry-looking band of Agents. I honour your efforts in the recent rebellion which must not be spoken of on pain of death. I acknowledge that you even outwitted my most senior counsel, although I have no understanding whatsoever of how you do what you do. I insist that nought is said on this subject or our arrangement or, that you are, indeed, Agents at all.

I have sent a gift to my merry band to be utilised immediately."

We were truly shocked. The King had actually made an effort to thank us and each one of us was proud of this concession.

'Bayard' I said 'you'll have to open this bundle for me.'

It was cloth. Cloth in all sorts of colours almost as if it were for a pageant or a parade. On top of it all was a smaller package with the word "mouse" written upon it.

Wynnfrith took the package out and held up its contents.

'Haha!...hahaha....! she started, and everyone else joined in.

It was a little Robin Hood outfit dyed in Lincoln green.

'It is just a jest from the King' said I 'I'm not meant to wear it.'

They were having none of it. I would even go as far as saying I was bullied by them and I asked if William Fawkes could be brought back in to represent my case.

Reluctantly, I conceded and, to be honest, I looked pretty good. I played about with the little bow and posed. Pleased that this was bringing some levity to our day I relaxed and asked that the rest of the cloth be brought out except, it wasn't cloth. It was more costumes. Wynn was all over it but the others were much more reluctant.

'Who's bloody laughing now?!' I declared and insisted that everyone put on their robes. What created more mirth than anything else was Robert and Bayard arguing about who the friar tuck outfit was for.

'I'm clearly the sheriff!' Blustered Robert and sounding like an infant. Wynnfrith even found a little medieval baby costume, complete with capuchon and hood. She then commented that that King had gone to great lengths to find out about us whereas I acknowledged that it was more likely that we were systematically being spied upon.

Even Silas was passable in a scarlet costume but, unsurprisingly, it didn't fit. In the whole history of outfit making, there had not yet been one seamstress that could make clothes that would fit our Silas and, if they did, he would find a way of making sure it didn't last. Edward ran in looking forlorn.

'It's ok Ed' I said 'there are plenty for you to choose from' and Wynnfrith showed him what we had.

'There are practically enough for half of York!' I said smiling at this comical bunch before me.

'Robert, I have an idea' I said.

All went quiet whilst I explained and, admittedly, my plan got a mixed reaction at first.

'I'll have to speak to young Father Luke first' said Robert 'but I think it's just what we need.'

1543 The Disfiguration

'What happened to Bede?' asked Edward out of the blue.

'In agreement with Marcus, who is returning to live in York' said Robert 'we will be funding a new infirmary to support the work of the undercroft. It is to be called, Gabriel's Wings. This will be for those who need care or who have a chance of cure or survival. Might well free up my flaming spare bedroom at the same time!'

As everyone left that bittersweet meeting, things returned to something that seemed a little more normal. Only four days later, we all attended the funeral for Father Matthew, except that it was a send-off like no other. We had all been introduced to the somewhat naïve, but competent, Father Luke who was happy, on this day to make some concessions. Holy Trinity Church was looking comparatively bare as it became clear that the wave of the new faith was now washing over York. Everyone accepted this for what it was and had no doubts that our beloved leader and priest, Matthew, was heaven-bound. I will never forget the smiles on people's faces as they looked upon a congregation dressed as Robin Hood and his merry clots. The costumes were bright and inspiring and everyone was in a mood to celebrate the life and good deeds of a good man rather than fall even further into sadness and depression. I was kept relatively hidden in Edward's pocket leaving the spare, and normal-sized Robin Hood costume for Robin and Marian who stood alongside Robert. Robert, after some considerable angst had decided, for once, to take the easier and more sensible route and, following a quite heavy discussion with Eirik, and with many promises made, he decided that Eirik could stay and that, given time, they might build a new relationship based on truth and trust. Proud he was, with Meg as his Maid Marian and envisioning himself and his bride at the altar in the not too distant future.

At the back of the church, in the shadows, stood a figure so tall, strong and muscular in outline, he could have served well as our Little John. Adorned in blues and scarlets, there was no mistaking the now, familiar, Moonlight brand. It was, without doubt, Thomas Farrier come to pay his last respects to the man he had loved from afar but we all knew the rules. He would linger and then disappear and that was to be the measure of things thereafter.

Following the wedding, Eirik had sworn to Robert that he would find James's makeshift grave and organise his exhumation and final return to York where arrangements would be made for a proper funeral for him.

It may well have been the silly costumes, but the number of attendees at Father Matthew's funeral just grew and grew and there can't have been a person present that would ever forget that extraordinary day in York.

27 the inescapable error

The day after the funeral, Silas, Wynn and Mary were happily relaxing back into normality again. That was, until there was a gentle knock at the door and she rushed to open it.

'Marcus! Maud! Please enter!' said Wynnfrith, pleased to see them.

Silas rushed down the stairs.

'Brother! You are…you are well and walking!'

'Ha Ha! Just my friend, I hobble somewhat!' said Marcus.

'Welcome to the family…we all hobble!' said Wynnfrith, and they all laughed.

'It is so good to see you returned and safe. What have you with you?'

'It is a gift!' said Marcus but not from myself, from Maud here.'

'How exciting' said Wynnfrith.

'It is actually for Silas' said Maud.

They all sat and Silas, hardly yet having said a word, smiled upon his wife, daughter and his guests counting his blessings. Fortunately, both the swelling and the phantom pregnancy had subsided, the dramatic events of previous months, he had decided, even more frightening than having

1543 The Disfiguration

a child if that were possible.

At first, he revealed the back of the gift leaving him presuming that it may have solely been a piece of wood but, for once, he held his tongue. Eventually, so heavy was the gift, that it fell to the floor, right side up.

He so wanted to laugh as Maud had expected him to, but he cried. He cried quiet tears as he picked it up because, as Thomas Farrier had said, this is where the journey had begun. That journey that had turned ordinary folk of York into heroes, where Silas had befriended a King and eventually found his love. One in which he had returned to his childhood home to be gifted with a child of his own. For so long, hopelessness had been his companion. Where there had been light, darkness prevailed and his good heart was little understood and often mocked. He had grown up in a world where his anxieties were as predictable as the sunrise and his low self-esteem as sure as the sunset.

"Ye dirtye pesant" it read, having reverted to its original name. He just glared at it, weeping.

Maud took his hand.

'Do you remember that day when you arrived, only to bang your head on this very sign?' said Maud.

Silas, still moved, nodded and smiled at her.

'I'm on a mission from God himself' she said quietly and he smiled even more.

'Seem...seems....well...so long ago, Maud. A lifetime..' he snivelled.

'Goodness knows where you'll put this! But it's a reminder, dear Silas' said Marcus 'a reminder of how you are loved. How, without you, England could well be in turmoil and the King dead. Dear Mary Smith looks down from the Heavens upon you and her heart is full of pride for her Lord Silas, his Lady and their beautiful child.

'How people have mocked and derided you..' said Maud 'you have stood tall in the face of persecution for a lifetime and look where it has brought you.'

1543 The Disfiguration

Wynnfrith wrapped her arm around him and kissed him gently on the cheek.

'Blessed are those who are persecuted for righteousness sake' quoted Wynnfrith 'for theirs is the Kingdom of Heaven.'

As Silas made to wipe away his tears, he was tenderly embraced by three people who loved him.

Maud then stood and asked Wynnfrith if she could visit regularly.

'You are our mother from the south and as a grandparent to Mary. Marcus, you are our brother and the door is open to you both, always.'

Now Maud began to cry as Marcus consoled her.

It was reasonable to assume that after all they had been through, these people were at least, half-broken. As Maud and Marcus walked away from Dead alley that day, they acknowledged that they had witnessed the epitome of married bliss.

Generally speaking, almost everything settled down for a while. Peter recovered but it took some time. I insisted that his promise of returning home to Bamburgh be kept although it was essential that he had some help. Eirik and Meg accompanied him, as well as being his bodyguard. Apparently, Peter got his ear chewed on arrival but there was no question at all that his family were delighted to see him once more and Eirik insisted on telling his tales of bravery to everyone in the village. Peter was left with his family over Christmas whilst Eirik and Meg travelled to Scarborough not to reminisce, but to track down the burial place of James. It was eventually found and, the following February, 1544, Robert sent Eirik with a team of men to retrieve his son's remains so that he could have a Christian funeral and burial in York close to his mother and his adopted mother. Robert also found some funds to help the poor and notorious Mrs Grindem. She had fallen victim to syphilis which had taken its ugly course. She had been seen down the Shambles wearing a false nose, rambling incoherently to herself, eventually even forgetting who she was. Robert paid for a private physician to do what he could until eventually, she died.

As for me, I had dug in my heels. I wasn't for going back. The sum total of my experiences plus the unrelenting wave of symptoms caused by the mix had me convinced that I could co-exist with my wife at the same time as being a celebrity mouse in the sixteenth century. I was, of course, wrong and any attempts to connect with Bayard's knowledge and experience failed. Unfalteringly, he just told me to return from where I had come from. I had agreed with everyone that, now, my speech should be limited to those who already knew. Spending a lot of time alone at the workshop only served to keep those moments when I saw Edward, blissfully happy. Come the late winter, Peter was well enough to return to the workshop and we became incredibly close.

Life as far as I was concerned was perfect for a while and although it was not, and never would be, free of conflict and anxiety, it was probably our most peaceful spell to date. Robert wished to celebrate his birthday with all his friends and fellow Agents at Mulberry Hall. It was a fine affair with his generosity amply displayed in the spread of fine food, ale and wine. We found ourselves readily reverting to type once a few drinks had been imbibed. Mary was distracting everyone with her entertaining babble and ability to crawl from mother to father, even attempting the odd excursion on two legs much to everyone's enjoyment.

'See, she wobbles too!' said Wynnfrith.

We then awaited an agenda or speech as we always had done.

I realised that I was not only very merry but was drifting in and out, my concentration very poor and, eventually I suffered a slight loss of consciousness. Robert was talking about some of the carvings on the fireplace and also his paintings. He rambled for a while about his recently commissioned portrait which was, of course, of himself. For the first time ever, I noticed something in the corner, almost completely in the shadows although there was no doubt that it was meant to be on display. Now, only half-sensible at best, I focused, realising what it was and, unintentionally and abruptly, interrupted him.

'Good God! What on earth! Robert…what were you thinking of!!'

All eyes moved and then squinted to see what had, possibly, been on display in his Great Hall for months.

'Aha! That. Why not Mouse? It is one of the finest carvings in York, is it not?'

Edward spoke first.

'That it is, uncle but it is somewhat macabre. I'm getting chills just looking at it.'

One by one, most of those present agreed.

'And it came off a dead man!' added Silas.

'Ah well there, you see, young Silas, that is a matter of debate as…'

'We know the story, thank you, Robert. I'm sure no one needs to be reminded' I said.

'Godwin did that' said Edward 'whatever else we may think of the man, he was brilliant at what he did. A true Master Carpenter.

This temporarily silenced Robert as now, his past misdemeanours loomed large in front of him. But then, possibly in an attempt to lighten the mood, he once again said,

'Strange though, when I took it from the workshop it seemed so much lighter than when I first handled it.'

I looked around. Not one of them reacted to this. It was seemingly so innocuous that it wasn't worthy of any additional comment. I wanted to comment. I urgently wanted to comment.

'When did you take it from the workshop?' I asked.

'Oh…err…let me see. Oh yes, of course, when we all

returned from Deptford.'

I screamed. I screamed so loud that I went dizzy. I wanted to tell him how stupid he had been. How could he not have put two and two together or, should I say, one and two together? Hoping that we had some time to spare, my intention was to stop the party and raise the alarm. However, the louder I became, the more distant the room and my friends seemed. The screaming almost immediately turned to a constant noise in my head. A noise that seemed to go on forever and one which disabled my voice and my movement. I stayed this way until I realised that I was back. I was home, in bed once again with April's sweet voice breaking through.

28 the Keel

Aelfraed had made an escape not dissimilar to Marcus's but it was to be some years later. Like Jack, he had finally got the measure of Bask and decided it was time to go but not without doing some damage. He took what he could with him, returning to farm work and eventually settling in the north. However, Sir Anthony Bask had the best of spies and it wasn't long before he had tracked Aelfraed down. Never one to miss an opportunity that would swell his purse, Aelfraed was the ideal agent to collect funds from the nervous and habitually blackmailed Robert Hall. Of course, Aelfraed wanted nothing to do with it but now he had a wife and child and Bask had no hesitation in threatening them as well.

It is little wonder that Aelfraed finally cracked and revelled in putting an end to the life of Sir Anthony Bask. Neither did he expect to get away with it but insisted that he would be executed and buried with his, incredibly ornate, wooden leg. For in that leg was the set of three pieces of metal that he had stolen from the office of Bask just as Marcus had done. In a secret pact with Godwin, he had had the leg hollowed out, the pieces placed inside, and it sealed vowing to go nowhere, including the grave, without it. However, ironically, it seems as though he just wouldn't hang with the bugger on. After all those years, it was removed only so that he would die more quickly.

When Silas's house, the washhouse and Elspeth's grave were ransacked, so was the workshop. So untidy was it that no one ever noticed that it had also been broken into. The leg was the first thing that they looked at. Four screws out and the top removed, the invaders had what they wanted in minutes and left. Seemingly, they left the leg as they found it, sans metal parts.

Both Marcus and Bayard's reckoning was correct, more or less. Presuming that all the keys had been found and subsequently destroyed by the King's men, there wasn't a man in the kingdom who would give it further thought, especially as all the culprits were apprehended at the same time in one place, Deptford. However, nobody seemed to account for the fact that it would have been highly unlikely that the people who had killed Father Matthew would have got back to Deptford docks in time for the battle. Having said that, it was in their interests, once the game was up, to both hide their tracks and try to return to a normal life. The man that killed Father Matthew was called Cerradura and he was also the man that had successfully made a key from the metal pieces in Aelfraed's leg. He remained zealous, biding his time whilst his conspirators were executed presuming, quite rightly, that the plot would fade away, even in the memory of the King.

History tells us that on the 18th July 1545, a proud and confident King Henry dined aboard the Great Harry alongside the Admiral, Viscount Lisle knowing that the French fleet was on its way. This was no futile effort, being the best that the French could muster but this conflict was to be so significant that Henry stayed. When the French arrived, the King watched from the castle at Southsea, at that point with every confidence in the English fleet and its commanders. However, as there was little wind, the enemy already had the advantage. The fleet had reached Sussex on

1543 The Disfiguration

the 18th July and, having thus far made little impact, it then entered the Solent a day later. In the morning, it looked like the French would win the day as their galleys with oars would outmatch the English sail ships without wind. Henry had prayed for success, and in particular, on this day, strong winds and, by the afternoon, his prayers were answered and Lisle mobilised his ships.

Cerradura was not only aboard the Mary Rose that day but had been there for several months helping to prepare her for battle. He had been appointed by the commander of the Mary Rose and Vice-Admiral of the fleet, Sir George Carew. The very same George Carew who had previously been questioned in the Tower for his attempts to serve the French, more than once. He was not only pardoned by the King but eventually given this prestigious command. The English fleet rolled about relentlessly but confronted the French with some gusto, the wind now in their favour. Few were mindful of those intricate and puzzling designs that had arrived at the shipyard, years ago, along with Bask. For those who had been there when the ships were in ordinary, they understood that reinforcements and upgrades had taken place and, by and large, they would have been right. Noticeably, most of the ships sat a little lower in the water but not so much that anyone ashore would see. However, those reinforcements included cast bronze plates that had been concealed in the keel of almost every vessel. As it was, they were harmless and, it could be argued that they did offer some extra stability but they also slowed progress somewhat. The Mary Rose did not shy from battle and there was a reason for this. Once engaged, she fired from the larboard side doing little or no damage to the enemy. Then with the ship already lunging back and forth, Carew blatantly touched his beard twice with his left forefinger. This had Cerradura scrambling from the mizzenmast where he was posted to the forecastle. Everyone aboard was amply employed and had no time to be checking on the actions of a single seaman. Even for Cerradura, it was some feat to get from stern to bow without being washed overboard.

Already the ship was lurching toward the water on her starboard side and Cerradura saw this as providence. Cannons still firing, the wind howling and crew shouting instructions, no one noticed him heading for the orlop deck. There he opened a door, so small, that you may not have said it was a door and as he squeezed through, he found himself in an enclosed space barely big enough to fit him in. He was thrown in all directions, made worse by the fact that he was now in the dark. He felt around for the cover, a small brass plate that turned like a screw, but clockwise and, stiff as it was, he managed to remove it and placed it on his lap, for there was nowhere else for it to go. He clenched it between his knee and his chest so that it would not be thrown around and then pushed his right hand down into his doublet. There, on a chain, was the most spectacular key. There was no glint or sparkle as Cerradura was now completely in the dark, but there was no mistaking its size and its nature. Aelfraed's attempts to take this key to the grave with him were for nothing as now, at last, it would fully serve its purpose. Cerradura struggled to find that key's mate for this was no conventional lock, rather a male and female coupling, the key being the latter in this case. There. He found the rod that was now protruding. He pushed the key into it and turned it. At first, it felt loose as if something was wrong. His stomach-turning and doing his best to ignore cries from all around him, he continued until he felt some resistance. It eventually moved and sounded like a ratchet. Clunk. Clunk. Clunk. At first, he could feel those turns all the way up his arm but soon he could feel it throughout the ship. Within seconds, a macabre and deafening sound that was beyond the blasts of the cannons could be heard by everyone. Those same metal plates that had lined the keel for years were now, awkwardly, starting to shift and they shifted to starboard. Each turn moved one large plate from the keel and upward into the starboard hull and even he was stunned by its efficiency. Enough. He stopped, sure that he had done enough and promptly escaped from his self-imposed cell, welcoming the fresh air as he did. It felt like hell had repositioned itself in the Solent that day but he knew what would come next. He looked to the other ships. Crestfallen that this device could not have been used to sink the whole fleet, he looked to Carew who, in turn, looked for a boat. Yes, he and Cerradura had expected a boat, promised by the French but it was nowhere to be seen. The Mary Rose was inexorably tumbling one way and, as all the gun ports were open, her fate was sealed as soon as water entered them. Without further hope, most of the crew jumped overboard as did Carew and his ally but they were not to find their rescue boat. In minutes, the Mary Rose was underwater and four hundred and sixty-five hands, out of its manifest of five hundred were lost. The ship had taken on its new role as a great coffin, as most became trapped amidst its watery hold.

The wind dropped and people, for centuries, would blame the wind and the weight of the cannons for the Mary Rose's demise. What had started as a potential firestorm, ended as a standoff. The French having the advantage of numbers but the English having easy access to supplies. Ingeniously, Admiral Lisle managed to use the tides themselves to organise the English Fleet into a defensive position and by the 22nd July, the French chose to retreat.

Carew had left the Mary Rose cursing and was declared dead although his body was never found. This for Henry was, indeed, a victory cementing his authority not only as English King but Supreme Head of the English Church but in a small way, also a victory for his enemies.

29 home again

My awakening had been very much a repeat of my previous return except there was no question that the brusque manner of Micklegate stayed with me for much longer. Again, I was told to rest before debriefing but the mantra from everyone was endlessly about my career. In short, I was told that this was it. There would be no more missions and, consequently, no more risks.

I was having none of it and I was aware that, at times, I would sulk which furthered irritated my colleagues at the same time as amusing April. Whist still at my bedside they would, albeit politely, dictate what I would or wouldn't do and what I could and couldn't do. I had concluded that not only the work of the institute was important, but that it was also essential in informing future generations on how we viewed and studied history. At that point, I wasn't saying anything about Bayard as I knew that I wouldn't be believed. If the rest of my report would be the stuff of fantasies, God knows how his tale would translate.

1543 The Disfiguration

As I recovered, the conversation became more intense and, sometimes, very heated. I rambled somewhat about my friends, how they had gone previously unnoticed amidst historical records and how I believed that not only would the technology that we were using improve and evolve, but also that it was possibly the only way of getting to the root of so many historical anomalies.

I was asked to give a brief statement to support my case for staying with service and continuing to serve as a pilot. I understood that I would be allowed but a sentence or two, all the while believing that they had already retired me. I still hadn't recovered, so this was to be done remotely. There on my screen were all those pompous bastards that sat in the comfort of their own homes whilst I had fallen down pits, been chased by rats, set on fire and had pins stuck in my arse. The rather convoluted and detailed explanation that I was to give was there, before me but I found myself sighing and deleting it as it seemed pointless. I wondered if, in fact, the whole exercise was pointless. I was introduced and, almost without thinking, blagged it, seemingly speaking from the heart.

'I have seen…experienced people and events that are possibly beyond your imagination. I could probably talk for hours on the virtues of accessing history as we now do and, yes, why your most experienced pilot should continue to serve but I shall only say this. Everyone talks about the Mary Rose don't they? It was a magnificent triumph of naval archaeology when, long ago, she was found and saved. But, it's all about the Mary Rose. What I would like to talk about is how we, yes, we! saved the rest of the fleet. We saved the whole of the King's bloody fleet, bar one ship and, do you know what that means? It means that we saved England from a French invasion and Henry VIII from being deposed. We avoided a Catholic insurrection. We fought hand to hand with die-hard rebels to do this and people got hurt and some even died. Who are the "we?" Well…mostly ordinary, everyday folk of which we have no record. Even Robert Hall who was a Mayor, successful merchant and a member of parliament! We know so little about him. Go on try! I challenge you! I bloody challenge you to do it the old way and, while you're at it, look up Lord Silas! He's not a figment of my imagination, he was a great man. But, no, you will find nothing. More important than all of this is....the love. The love those people had for one another and yes, sometimes, even, strangers. The love and faith that they had for their God. A moral compass that I'm convinced would take any person anywhere they wished to go. Yes I'm emotionally attached and, yes, that may well affect my ability to remain objective but I will be well soon. There is more to do and I am the one to do it. I defy all your presumptions, bias and ignorance! I am Micklegate Mouse and I will return!'

THE END

ABOUT THE AUTHOR

Rob holds a degree in both History and Art & Design and for his postgraduate studies, concentrated on British History. He has taught both subjects for many years and his students have ranged from early teens to undergraduates. Later in his career, he specialised in the application of new technologies in special and alternative education.

Rob started writing when he ran his own business, Jester Productions, in which he wrote scripts for plays and musicals that were used eclectically, but most often in theatre groups internationally and for major tour operators. He has completed commissions that have ranged from magazine work and book covers to church interiors.

More information can be found at:
www.rwjauthor.co.uk
Instagram: robjones4043

Printed in Great Britain
by Amazon